BLUE HOPE

THE FINAL ADVENTURE
IN THE **RED HOPE** *SERIES*

— Note: This is a standalone sequel —

JOHN DREESE

For Lee, Daniel, Caroline,
George & Martha

ACKNOWLEDGEMENTS

This book is the product of nearly three years of effort. Without the help of many wonderful people, it would not exist. I am forever grateful to them.

My wife Lee supported this project in too many ways to count. Plot development was enhanced by the inputs of story consultants Daniel and Caroline. Many thanks to Kurt Chankaya for a discussion that greatly impacted the direction of the story, and to the support from members of the Dallas Mars Society — it would be difficult to find a more enthusiastic group dedicated solely to the progress of manned space exploration.

Finally, thanks to the test readers who, through the generosity of their time and talent, provided incredibly helpful feedback.

PREFACE

RED HOPE: BOOK ONE was released just before midnight on December 20th, 2014. Earlier that day I'd finished the last edit on a long flight home to Texas.

My goal was for Red Hope to be a fun story with a mild cliffhanger – I soon found out that readers were much more engaged with the characters than I'd imagined. Many readers even sent supportive messages while I was writing this follow-on book, all of which were appreciated.

What you hold in your hands is the final half of the Red Hope adventure — a story that started long ago with a late night phone call to the White House and ends with what I hope you will find is a satisfying conclusion. Thanks for waiting.

John Dreese
October, 2017

A NOTE FOR READERS:

As the **SECOND BOOK** in the **RED HOPE** series, the prologue and first few chapters of **BLUE HOPE** contain elements of the last few chapters of **RED HOPE**. This information was woven into the story to provide a bridge for readers who may not have read the first book or read it long ago.

PROLOGUE

Previously, on Mars...

Two desperate astronauts stumbled out of an ancient stone building on the Red Planet. Adam, the more experienced of the two, gasped for air, his hands pointlessly gripping the visor on his helmet. He reached down for his air tank, gloves flailing against the empty spot where it used to be. Adam collapsed to his knees gasping – his lungs starving for oxygen. He pulled a Y-tube connector from the pocket on his space suit and held it up to his colleague, Keller. Adam gestured for his friend to hook him up so he could share some of his precious air.

"*No*," Keller said over the headset.

Adam looked at Keller in horror.

"What? Hook me up!" Adam demanded. "I'm dying!"

Keller looked at his own oxygen gauge.

"I know. But I've only got four minutes left. If I share this...," he gulped. "Neither one of us will make it back to the ship alive."

Adam's eyes filled with bloodshot rage.

Keller's face betrayed the guilt he felt for his decision. He chose to abandon the man who had led him and two others safely to Mars – the first manned mission.

"I'm sorry, Adam. Look, I'm really sorry. I'll... I'll tell everybody that you died a hero," Keller said. "We'll bury you here on Mars, okay?"

Adam gasped for air like a helpless fish out of its tank. Keller turned away. "I know you saved my life back there, Adam, but, I gotta go right now."

Adam's vision began to blur, the colors of Mars fading to black and white. All he could see out of his visor was the floodlight tripod.

Keller stumbled toward the rover transport, pausing a few feet away to catch his breath. He slumped over with hands on knees; resting for just a second, trying to calm down his racing heart, no doubt caused by the explosion of guilt he felt for his friend.

Adam reached out a trembling hand and grabbed the floodlight tripod. He pushed through all his pain and light-headedness to stand up, climbing the tripod like a crutch. He stumbled up behind Keller and with his last remaining strength, swung the tripod like a baseball bat right into Keller's helmet, shattering open the glass on his visor.

Keller fell to the ground and didn't move – his last breath now part of the billowing Mars breeze. A crackle of ice formed over his eyes, stuck wide open and opaque. Adam rolled Keller's body onto its side and unlatched the coveted oxygen tank.

"I'm sorry, Keller. I've got a family that depends on me. *You don't.*"

PART ONE

"Pride comes before the fall."

— *Ancient Proverb*

CHAPTER 1

Building 12
NASA Johnson Space Center
Houston, Texas

Good news travels fast. Bad news even faster. The administrative director of NASA shuffled down a crowded hallway in his wrinkled suit, his eyes focused on the cup of steaming coffee in his hand. His black hair laid unkempt and greasy — he hadn't slept in the three days since the first crew of humans landed on Mars. Now death was devouring his agenda.

He coasted to a stop in front of a set of double doors. His frown eased into a smile at the sight of the wooden placard next to the door jamb. It read *NASA Administrator, Chris Tankovitch*. With his free hand, he rubbed his fingers across the sign, consuming each letter.

A chorus of "Director Tankovitch!" and "Just a quick question!" erupted from a gaggle of reporters streaming down the hallway behind him. Chris turned to look and then lurched through the doors of his executive suite. Once inside, he slammed the doors shut and leaned back against them. This room had become his safe haven. It was his office at the NASA Johnson Space Center — a temporary arrangement while the astronauts were exploring the surface of Mars.

Chris faked a smile toward the secretary — she stared at him with bemusement. He marched through the large room, knocking on her desk as he passed by.

"Buenos dias, Dotty," Chris said in a poor attempt at friendliness.

"That's what they tell me, Mr. Tankovitch," she replied, attempting to lighten the mood. She went back to watching cat videos.

Chris jogged straight into his own sub-office and shut the door behind him. Still going full speed, he rounded the corner on his metal government desk and plopped down into the chair, spilling coffee all over his lap.

"Ah, just *great*," he blurted out.

Chris grabbed a napkin and dabbed at the stain, but it was no use – the reporters would just have to understand; no time to deal with this now.

NASA was roiling from a public relations nightmare only a few hours old. A spaceship with three astronauts and one cosmonaut landed on Mars three days ago. It placed humans on the Red Planet for the first time in history – it was the pinnacle of human achievement.

And now one of the explorers was dead.

In the middle of the night, Mission Control had received a short communication from Adam Alston, the mission leader on Mars. It stated, "*A terrible accident has happened. Keller Murch is dead.*"

Despite desperate attempts at further communication, Chris hadn't received any more details. He had to assume that the remaining astronauts were busy dealing with the situation that led to the accident.

Agency public relations staff were meeting at the Mission Control Center across the parking lot from Chris. Huddled together in a large room with coffee-stained carpet, they were trying to write a press release for the public, working in close concert with Chris. He only had two hours left to prepare the final statement for the media. Despite the lockdown on news, information still leaked to the press corps. They knew that something bad had happened with the Mars mission.

"Director Tankovitch, you have a telecon with President Jennings in forty-five minutes," blared the chunky old business phone on his desk.

Chris looked over his glasses at the phone interface, noticing several blinking buttons. He pushed one and said, "Thanks Dotty. Hold my calls and please, no visitors."

No response, so he pushed another one and repeated himself louder, "Thank you Dotty. Hold my calls and visitors."

No response. His nerves were at their limit.

Chris cupped his hands around his mouth and yelled toward the office door, "I GOT THE MESSAGE DOTTY, THANKS!"

"You're welcome," squeaked a voice from the phone in

the most sarcastic tone imaginable.

"God help me," he whispered under his breath.

Chris opened his laptop to get back to work on his public statement. He'd just typed in his password when a loud knock rattled his door.

Chris dropped his head in disappointment.

"Dotty, you're supposed to block visitors," Chris said.

He looked up as the door creaked open and a head popped through the gap. It was the lead video telemetry engineer, Jimmy.

"Hi, Director Tankovitch. Sorry to bother you – I know you're dealing with a mess right now," Jimmy gulped as he paused. "But we just processed the video download from mission leader Adam Alston's helmet camera on Mars."

"Thanks Jimmy, but I'm preparing for a meeting with the president. Can it wait?" Chris asked, hoping Jimmy would leave.

"That would be a bad idea. It's fresh from the incident when Adam Alston and Keller Murch were both trapped in that building on Mars. It *shows* what was hidden in the building," he paused. "And it shows Keller Murch's death — I think you should see this immediately."

Jimmy took a deep breath. "You know how Captain Alston said it was an accident?"

"Yes, I know," Chris answered.

"He lied."

CHAPTER 2

Temporary housing for Captain Alston's family
Houston, Texas

One million, four thousand and three dollars. *And twenty two cents.* That was the bank account balance shown on the screen of Connie Alston's laptop. With her brown hair pulled back in a ponytail, she sat at the kitchen table, drooped over the archaic computer — it still had a DVD drive. The situation seemed all the more unreal because this wasn't even her kitchen.

Normally she and her family lived five hours north in Fort Worth, Texas. This kitchen was the executive guest housing that NASA Johnson put her up in while her husband, Captain Adam Alston, was busy running around Mars. So far she didn't like Houston because it was too humid — walking outside was like opening up a dishwasher and getting hit with the steam. *Houston did have a problem,* she thought. *Humidity.*

Holy crap, she thought to herself after seeing the bank account balance. She turned on her smartphone and took a picture of the screen. For a brief moment, she considered posting it on Facebook with the caption, "Big risks bring big rewards. Feeling so blessed."

Her finger hovered over the Post button.

She reconsidered.

Oh, I hate those kind of posts, she thought.

Connie put the phone down. A smile overtook her face as a tear ran down her cheek, surprising even her. Connie and her husband had spent years worrying about every bill, questioning every trip to the doctor – especially the emergency room visits. Never in her wildest dreams did she ever think they would have that much money sitting in a bank account. Uncle Sam would take forty percent of it, but $600k was still a lot of money to Connie.

That's a lot of money to anybody, she thought.

The money wouldn't be in her account for long though. The bank manager had just called and invited her to come down to the office and split it among several bank accounts. It was something about the FDIC insurance only covering up to a quarter-million dollars per account.

"You know," he told her, "in the unlikely event that we have a banking disaster or the world blows up."

She'd laughed nervously. The bank manager's fear wouldn't be a problem for long. Connie had a plan for that money.

Off to the side of the kitchen was a cold beige living room with the TV turned on and tuned to the 24-hour news station. The TV itself was bolted to the table like some cheap motel. The scrolling banner on the TV news said, "NEWS

ALERT: Problem on the International Space Station." Connie only half-watched the news while staring, dumbfounded, at her family's new riches.

Keller Murch, the Silicon Valley entrepreneur who was part of the Mars exploration crew, had promised each of his three crewmates a million dollar bonus if they accepted the mission. The money was an incentive that NASA found necessary because the A-list and B-list astronauts balked at riding an experimental spacecraft designed and built in less than twelve months.

As soon as the astronauts had landed on Mars, Keller's company was to wire the million dollars to each crew members bank account. Adam was the only crew member with a family, so nobody was looking at the bank balances of the others. Keller was aware of this *detail* and instructed his accountants to delay depositing the bonus into the other accounts, just in case they didn't make it back.

Today was the day that Connie had been waiting for so long. She picked up the phone and called the spine surgery clinic she'd been going to for years – ever since she'd mangled her back in a car accident and had to use crutches to walk.

An overly happy secretary answered the phone.

"Hello! You've reached the Back & Spine Institute of Texas."

"Hi, this is Connie Alston. I'm calling to —"

"Oh my, Mrs. Alston! We are so excited to hear about what your husband is doing on Mars. I held my breath through the entire landing sequence. Oh-my-gosh that was so wonderful."

"Thank you, I appreciate it. I'm just glad they're safe. We're still very worried," Connie admitted.

"Oh, I can only imagine! He's an inspiration to my children. He's such a good man."

"That's very kind of you to say," Connie replied, pausing and then restarting. "I think I'm ready to schedule the back fusion surgery."

"Okay. With or without the stem cell injection?" asked the secretary in a more serious tone.

"With," Connie answered.

"Now, you know that's the experimental one, right? Insurance won't cover it and it's... very expensive."

"Yes, yes, I know. Dr. Sanders and I talked about it extensively when I was there last month. Half a million dollars and some change."

"Okay, but that needs to be, well..." the secretary said with strain. "The financial aspect of it must be taken care of ahead of time."

Connie sighed and smiled.

"I know, and I'm ready to get the ball rolling."

"Oh my, do you want me to forward you to the finance office so you can work out a payment plan?"

"No, I'm ready to pay," Connie declared. "In full."

There was silence on the other end.

"You mean, like, pay right now?"

"Yes, I can wire it to you from my bank."

There was even more silence on the phone. Connie heard the phone get covered by a hand, some mumbling, another pause, and then the phone was uncovered.

"Okay, well, they don't let me handle the money, well, except for petty cash, but especially not a half million dollars," the secretary laughed nervously. "So I still need to transfer you to the finance people, okay? It'll just take a second."

"Thanks."

Connie heard a click sound and some relaxing saxophone music to put her to sleep while she was on hold. It barely overcame the sound of the cackling birds just outside the kitchen windows.

She looked toward the living room again to see what was on the news. A computer generated image of spacecraft capsules dangling from parachutes displayed on the screen. The scrolling banner said, "International Space Station Evacuated During Mishap."

Connie tilted her head and yelled toward the bedrooms, "Hey Cody and Catie, what are you two up to?"

Silence.

"Are you two playing Minecraft again?"

A weak chorus of "Yes..." came back.

"Hey, I told you —"

The saxophone music stopped. The finance person picked up the phone.

After a few minutes, her amazing bank balance on the laptop screen shrank by approximately five hundred thousand dollars. It was a real kick to the gut, but Connie was excited — a future without crutches was inspiring. She hung up the phone, satisfied.

Reality swooped in. Connie remembered that her kids weren't doing their chores. "Hey, I told you no Minecraft until you finish your chores!"

Outside, the sound of the birds chirping faded until it was deadly silent.

CHAPTER 3

Building 12
NASA Johnson Space Center
Houston, Texas

Ding!
The elevator doors slid open and spit out the NASA director
and his video technician Jimmy.

The two of them marched into the video processing
room located on the second floor. All footage sent from Mars
ended up in this room, to be uncompressed and synced up
with the audio streams. After that they were broadcast to the
major networks for release, usually within 24 hours.

The room had several long tables covered in computer
workstations, each manned by an engineer. Chris pulled out
his wallet and removed a handful of dollar bills. He whistled
to get their attention. When they looked, he waved the dollar
bills in the air.

"Okay fellas, you want to earn a dollar from the director of NASA? I need you to go down to the vending machines and buy yourselves a coffee. Give me and Jimmy here a few minutes to discuss some important information in private."

The engineers filed past, each one snatching a volunteered dollar. The last engineer to walk out stopped in front of Chris and smiled. He grabbed the last two dollars and left.

You little punk, Chris thought.

Chris Tankovitch and Jimmy sat down in front of Jimmy's computer. It was covered in Post-it notes holding Linux shortcuts that he used often.

Jimmy was a young, but knowledgeable video processing engineer. He reached forward to push the Play button. Chris held up his hand to pause him.

"Hang on, Jimmy... lock the door."

Jimmy leaned his chair back on two legs, shut the solid door, and turned the toggle lock.

"Okay, let's see it," Chris said, nodding his head.

Jimmy held his own hand up this time.

"By the way, there's no audio with this video. Normally the audio is transferred first and the two streams synched up later, but we never got audio."

"All right," Chris nodded. "Understood."

Despite the twenty-four hour moratorium on news releases, information had leaked that morning about the death of beloved astronaut and Silicon Valley entrepreneur Keller Murch. Chris was relying on this video to shed some light on the incident. Captain Adam Alston had mentioned almost no details in his initial email description of the event. In a follow-on audio message they'd just received before heading upstairs, Adam stated, "*We were trapped in the stone building. We ran out of air just as we figured out how to open the door on the stone building. Keller gave me his air tank to save my life.*"

Jimmy pushed Play .

The black and white movie on the screen looked like a driving simulator rumbling through the Arizona desert. Chris and Jimmy watched as the Mars exploration cart drove the two astronauts toward a surreal setting. Chris furrowed his brow, paying rapt attention. The cart drove down a steep hill toward a sparkly boulder. Just beyond that, the image focused on a building made from stone slabs leaning together, like a pyramid with the top cut off.

"See there," Chris explained. "That's the boulder with the fossils in it." He tapped his finger on the screen. "That's what the Curiosity rover found – the *thing* that triggered this whole mission."

"Cool," Jimmy said as he tinkered with some settings on the processing software, brightening the image. "These helmet cameras are really jerky. I'm turning on the image stabilization."

Jimmy's mouse pointer flew through some on-screen menus that made the image become much less jumpy.

The movie continued. The two astronauts stepped out of the exploration cart and made their way over to a granite-colored circular door leaning against the building. It was opened just enough to allow them to slide through sideways.

Chris had already seen hundreds of high-resolution

images of the pyramid interior. Adam and the Russian cosmonaut Yeva Turoskova had explored half of it the day before. Detailed engravings covered every wall. These images had been crowd-sourced to every major university on Earth to help interpret them. A group of students at the University of Moscow broke the code and deciphered them.

As the video showed the astronauts exploring the interior, Chris leaned toward Jimmy and asked, "Have you heard what all those engravings mean?"

"Some kind of history lesson, I think."

"Sort of. It tells about how the ancient Martians invented *something* that led to their own destruction. They sent an emergency mission of their own astronauts to Earth to see about colonizing it or maybe using it to grow food. However," Chris sighed, "they eventually lost contact with their explorers."

"I heard the Martians called those explorers their 'lost children'?"

"Yeah, that's the interpretation. Definitely a term of endearment for their lost friends. They waited for them to come back, but they never did. This stone building was meant as a shrine to what happened to their entire society. They built it from very thick granite to withstand the erosion. We assume there used to be whole cities, but they've been sandblasted out of existence over the past two hundred thousand years."

Jimmy's ears perked up. "Two hundred thousand years? Isn't that when modern-looking humans developed here on Earth?"

"That's right," Chris said, looking impressed at Jimmy's knowledge.

"Interesting," Jimmy said, revealing a mischievous smile. "I didn't actually know that. One of the guys in the telemetry office told me that yesterday."

On the screen, they saw the two astronauts walking over to a smaller alternate chamber inside the stone building. The carvings were more geometric – more mathematical-looking.

Jimmy turned away from the monitor and asked, "So what was this thing that destroyed them?"

"Well, we don't know yet," Chris admitted. "That's one of the things our paleographers haven't been able to interpret yet."

"Don't paleographers study fossils?"

Chris laughed and shook his head.

"No, you're thinking of paleontologists. *Paleographers* study ancient written languages."

Chris pointed to the new math-like engravings on the wall of the smaller chamber.

"Can you stop the video here and take some screenshots?"

"Sure. Zoom in and enhance, right?" Jimmy joked.

"Hah, just regular screenshots will work."

Jimmy took a series of screenshots that showed all of the markings on the entire wall.

"Email them to me and I'll forward them to the paleographers and interpreters," Chris instructed. "I have a feeling these engravings are going to tell us a lot about their invention."

"Screenshots taken, let's continue to the good part," Jimmy said.

At that moment, the video focused on a small black cube, roughly five inches wide, floating above a small stone table.

"That's it," said a wide-eyed Chris.

"What?"

"Yeva told me that they found a very peculiar cube that seemed to disobey gravity."

Jimmy laughed. "A cube of anti-gravity?"

"Yes, that's exactly what he called it."

They both stared intently as the astronaut's arm reached into view and pushed the cube around, showing that it glided in whatever direction it was pushed, never stopping. Jimmy smirked when he saw the arm reach in – it reminded him of the thousands of hours of first-person-shooter video games he'd played in college.

Suddenly, the video showed a lot of dust falling and shadows rocking back and forth.

"This is probably one of the Marsquakes they told us about," Chris said. "The seismographs in the main living habitat also recorded them."

"You mean the Little Turtle?" Jimmy asked.

"No, the Little Turtle was the transport ship that took the astronauts to Mars. The Big Turtle was the permanent living quarters. It had all of the scientific instrumentation and–"

Chris was interrupted by the onscreen action.

The astronauts took off running back to the round door, but the stone slab had rolled shut, trapping them inside.

Chris's mouth dropped open. "Oh no..." he trailed off.

Jimmy paused the video and turned to Chris.

"The next ten minutes is just them sitting, standing, pacing... obviously talking about how the hell they're going to move that big stone door. You want to skip to the action part? It's pretty clever."

"Yes.... please."

Jimmy fast-forwarded until they saw the astronauts do something fascinating.

Adam removes his own air tank and hands it to Keller. Keller, in turn, holds it in place up against the door. Then Adam starts hitting the valve on the tank with various objects – hammers, cameras, and finally the anti-gravity cube. Air shoots out of the tank like a rocket and slowly pushes on the granite door, which eventually falls away from the stone building and slams down to the ground.

The image falls sideways.

"What happened?" Chris asked.

"As far as I can tell, Captain Adam Alston fell over. He's on the ground. He's probably suffocating and can't get up."

Chris and Jimmy instinctively tilted their heads sideways to figure out what was happening.

The image showed Adam reaching up toward Keller, but Keller shook his head. It looks like his lips say, "*No.*"

Jimmy mimicked the "No" movement with his own lips, having obviously watched this video sequence several times already.

Chris noticed Jimmy and asked, "How many times have you watched this already?"

Jimmy shrugged his shoulders.

"A couple times."

The video continued.

Keller walks away from Adam's camera. He's leaving Captain Alston there to die.

"Don't do it," Chris muttered, as if talking to a horror movie.

The sideways video corrects itself. Adam stands back up, using the light post tripod as a crutch. He stumbles up behind an unsuspecting Keller. Adam grips the tripod like a baseball bat, reaches back and swings it violently at Keller's helmet, smashing the glass in the visor of the unsuspecting astronaut – the one who'd just left him there to die.

Chris's hand rose up and covered his mouth.

"Oh my God," he whispered.

Adam rolls the dead body over and detaches the oxygen tank from Keller's suit. He attaches it to his own suit and then stumbles over to the exploration cart, climbs in, and races back into the sands of the Martian desert.

"What happens after this?" Chris asked, almost afraid of the answer.

"He just drives back to base at the Big Turtle spaceship habitat. Then the video stops."

"Okay, you can stop it, then."

Chris loosely gnawed on his index finger knuckle, thinking.

"We just witnessed a murder," Chris droned. "I mean, we were only on Mars for two days and somebody gets murdered?"

Jimmy nodded his head.

"Well, you did send a C-Team of astronauts," Jimmy explained. "Besides, just because you send humans to another planet doesn't mean they won't act human. Who do we contact? The space police? Judge Dredd?"

"Nobody yet," Chris said. "I'll set up a telecom with the remaining crew on Mars and ask for more details. This just got much more complicated."

Jimmy's phone rang. He picked it up, put it against his

ear and turned away from the NASA director. He said quietly, "Yes, he's right here next to me. We're reviewing a video. Really? You're kidding. Oh man, oh man. Okay, hang on."

Jimmy put his hand over the receiver and turned to Chris, "There's been an accident on the International Space Station. They say it launched missiles toward Russia or something crazy."

Chris's mind began racing.

That *something crazy* event was something the Pentagon *promised* Chris would absolutely one hundred percent never ever happen in his lifetime. He started to hyperventilate, but acted calm for Jimmy's benefit.

"They just had to abandon the entire station," continued Jimmy. "The crew's taken the emergency return vehicles. Sounds like something terrible is happening. They need you in the Mission Control Center immediately."

"This day just keeps getting worse and worse," Chris said as he stood up. "Look, Jimmy, promise me you won't tell a soul about this video until I get everything straightened out."

"Of course. Do you need me to come with you?" Jimmy asked, obviously curious about what was happening.

"No thanks, I need you to send out those screen shots. Email them to me and my secretary."

Chris unlocked the office door and raced down the hallway. He skipped the elevator and trotted down the stairwell. His destination, the Christopher Kraft Mission Control building, was just a quick jog across the big parking lot through a humid wall of Houston air.

How could this day get any worse, Chris thought to

18

himself.

The hallway suddenly lit up with flashing warning lights. A loud Klaxon-type siren spun up, piercing the air with a grinding squeal. Chris plugged his ears with his fingers as he reached the exit doors.

Memories of his elementary school days in the 1980's flooded back into his mind. The last time he'd heard this siren was when he had to practice hiding in the school's bomb shelter, teachers protecting his classmates from the fictional nuclear attack Russia was sending toward his rural Ohio town.

With his fingers still plugging his ears, Chris opened the bump latch on the exit doors with his hip. He stepped outside and saw other employees standing around and looking upward. He was pushed out even further as a wave of NASA employees poured outside behind him. They assumed the siren was trying to warn them about a tornado and they just wanted to see it with their own eyes. People are funny that way.

The sky was blue and cloudless. The sirens blared, like a soundtrack to oblivion. Chris scanned the horizon and there it was – an enormous missile leaving a sputtering smoke-filled trail, heading toward downtown Houston. Further away, he saw another missile, but the nose had broken up into a hundred little dots, all streaming apart.

His eyes opened wide as he saw all the people still outside. Nobody was heading for shelter.

"Everybody, get inside!" he yelled.

A woman stood next to him, clutching the hand of a little girl. Their name badges said *Visitor*, probably there for a tour. Both were terrified and couldn't move. Chris ran up and grabbed the arms of the woman and the girl. He spun them around and pushed them toward the doors.

"I said get back inside! For God sakes, *run!*"

CHAPTER 4

Temporary housing for the Alston family
Houston, Texas

In the distance, Connie heard a faint horn sound, like that of a train or an old truck. She turned away from the kitchen and back toward the TV screen — it showed more coverage of the disaster unfolding on the International Space Station. Her mind turned to her husband Adam who was currently exploring Mars. Connie knew that the main high-bandwidth data stream from Mars used the ISS as an information relay.

I better call Chris about this Space Station problem, she thought.

Suddenly, every window in the kitchen exploded inward, sending a horizontal rain of shattered glass streaking through the air and into the living room. The accompanying boom shook the house and knocked every cabinet door open, clearing the contents as fast as if the house had been spun upside down. The jolt released decades of dust, causing the entire house interior to resemble a smoke cloud. The unnerving sound of shattering glass kept going and going.

Connie fell to the floor, shards coating her hair and clothes. Her arms had cuts and scratches, the glass just missing her face because she had been looking away from the kitchen toward the TV in the living room.

Connie's ears rang. She was stunned.

The laptop sat on the ground next to the TV, the screen still on, but partially blacked out; a piece of glass pierced through it.

Connie reached up for the table, her fingers finding broken glass. She screamed in pain, pulling her hand back. A shard of glass had pierced through the web of skin between her thumb and index finger. Her good hand reached over to help. With both arms shaking from shock, she closed her good hand over the shard and yanked it out.

"Ouch, ouch, ouch!" Connie cried.

Blood streamed out of the hole and down her arm. She stuck her hand under her armpit to apply pressure and mask the pain.

Connie reached up again, this time being more careful, wiping the broken glass away and pulling. With all her effort, she stood up and started breathing again.

So much dust. So much glass, she thought.

The ringing in her ears wouldn't let up. She was dizzy and leaned on the table to keep from falling. The nausea hit like a freight train, her stomach erupting up and out as she vomited onto the table. The pile of dusty glass shards stopped it from flowing off the table edge. She felt instantly better, then vomited again.

The ringing in her ears was quickly replaced with the cacophony of every car alarm and house alarm going off within a 50 mile radius.

Wee-ow-wee-ow-wee-ow!

She heard screaming coming from the bedrooms.

"Catie! Cody!" she yelled. "Mommy's coming!"

She hobbled up the stairs without her crutches and stumbled into the first bedroom. Two legs stuck out from under a bookshelf that had fallen over and landed on the bed at an angle. The legs were moving. She knelt down to look.

"Cody, are you hurt?" Connie asked.

"No, but I'm really scared!"

"Okay, okay, hang on. I'm going to help you get out."

She gently pulled on his feet. He slid out like a pan from an oven. Once he was out from under the bookshelf, he burst into tears. Cody stood up, clutching his favorite stuffed dinosaur. Connie gave him a tight hug and kissed his forehead.

"Come with me," she said, grabbing his hand and hobbling along the wall toward Catie's room.

They found a similar mess, but she was on the bed, curled up under a blanket and whimpering. A tall lamp had fallen onto the bed. Connie hobbled over to the bed and ripped off the covers. Catie was still clutching her iPad with Minecraft on the screen, but she wasn't paying any attention to it.

"Are you hurt anywhere?" Connie asked.

"Just my ears, they're ringing."

"Okay, sweetheart, so are mine," Connie said in an effort to comfort Catie, hugging her tightly. "We're gonna be okay."

"I'm sorry, Mommy, I was playing Minecraft."

Connie put on a tough smile.

"It's okay, Honey. I'm not mad about that at all."

Connie noticed that the room had gotten considerably brighter, and kept getting brighter. She stepped over the broken glass to the window and pulled back the shredded curtains. In the distance, from the direction of downtown Houston, a mushroom cloud was slowly building up toward the heavens. The house began to rumble with a low-frequency tone. The wooden chair rattled across the floor.

Her cellphone rang. The caller ID said it was from Chris Tankovitch, the director of NASA and now a family friend.

She answered. "Hello?"

"Connie! You gotta get yourself and the kids to the bathroom. Get in the tub and put a mattress over them and..."

The voice of Chris Tankovitch faded out.

Signal lost.

The ringing in her ears was not going away. She moved her jaw to try to get rid of it.

"We have to get out of Houston quick," Connie said. "Go, go, go."

The kids shuffled down the stairs trying to avoid the broken glass. Connie clutched the railing, trailing far behind her kids.

"Mommy, I'm scared," Cody complained as he waited at the bottom of the stairs, afraid of the mountain of broken glass and debris.

"I know, Honey, just walk around the edges, okay? Try not to touch any of it."

She grabbed her purse and crutches and led the kids out

through the front door. On the front porch, she looked around, stunned. This neighborhood was usually quiet during the day, but now all the alarms were blaring.

Connie scanned around the neighborhood. All of the windows were broken out of every house. She noticed her minivan. Her heart sank.

Ohhhh of course, she whispered.

The carport had fallen over onto the family minivan. It wasn't going anywhere.

"Change of plans kids. Let's go visit Mrs. Janson."

Connie flexed her jaw again to try to get rid of the ringing in her ear. She moved with great effort down the three steps to the front yard. The fence separating her driveway from Mrs. Janson's was too tall for her to climb. She had to walk all the way to the street and then then back up the neighbor's driveway. The kids just climbed over it.

Mrs. Janson was the former wife of Captain Robert Janson, a test pilot who flew many of the experimental aircraft for the Air Force during the 1960's. He died ten years ago, but she'd managed to live by herself next to the corporate housing that Connie and her family were using.

The sound of distant sirens and ambulances came and went, echoing throughout this suburban enclave like noises through a canyon. Connie peered up and down the street, but couldn't see the actual vehicles – only the hint of their sirens.

Then it sank in. Nobody was coming to help.

Knock, knock, knock.

Mrs. Janson didn't answer.

Knock, knock, knock.

Connie reached in the mailbox and took out the spare key that Mrs. Janson always kept there. She opened the door

25

and let it glide full open.

"Mrs. Janson? Hello?"

Connie suspected what she might find.

"Cody, Catie, you stay here, okay?"

She crutched into the doorway. Out of instinct, she flipped the light switch on the wall a few times. No power.

Connie eased through the living room toward the kitchen. On the floor lay the woman who'd been so kind to them since they arrived in Houston.

Mrs. Janson wasn't moving.

With much difficulty, Connie knelt down on the ground next to her, moving away a swath of broken glass for her knees to rest. She pressed her fingers on Mrs. Janson's neck and couldn't find a pulse. The glass had done irreparable damage to the old woman, leaving cuts everywhere.

Connie put her hands together over the old woman's sternum and began to push down and release, doing her best to remember the CPR training she'd had as a teacher. Every push caused a crunching sound to emanate from Mrs. Janson's chest – the result of cartilage snapping and ribs breaking. Connie was told this would happen during CPR, but wasn't prepared for the awfulness of it. Every compression caused the dozens of cuts to bleed a little more. Connie leaned down and put her ear to Mrs. Janson's nose and mouth.

Still no breathing.

Still no pulse.

Oh Mrs. Janson, thought Connie, *you poor woman.*

Connie pulled out her phone and tried to dial 911. Still no signal. Connie started CPR again, but slowly gave up, knowing the outcome was grim without any emergency help available. Connie looked around, sniffling back her tears of worry, wondering what to do.

She took a shawl from the kitchen chair and lay it over Mrs. Janson. She leaned down, kissed her on the forehead and whispered, "Forgive me, Mrs. Janson."

Connie reached for her crutches and stood back up. She saw the big wooden key on the kitchen wall that held all of Mrs. Janson's keys. Each one had its own hook. Connie took the old Honda key and crutched back to the front door where the kids were waiting. She exited the house and locked the door, depositing the house key back into the mailbox.

"Is Mrs. Janson going to be okay?" Cody asked.

"Yes, she's going to be fine."

One day Connie would explain the truth to them. Not now.

"Mommy, the cloud is getting taller," Cody said.

The mushroom cloud continued to climb. It finally blocked out the Sun, sending a shadow over the street.

"Mrs. Janson said we could borrow her car – everybody get in."

The kids climbed into the back seat and buckled themselves into the child safety seats. These seats often held Mrs. Janson's grandchildren when they visited from their condo in downtown Houston.

Connie climbed in. The one saving grace of her back injury was that she still had most of the control of her right foot, allowing her to legally maintain driving privileges. She could drive any car with an automatic transmission – like Mrs. Janson's blood-red Honda.

She eased the car out onto the street and drove to the main road, maintaining a low speed to avoid all of the debris in her way. Every traffic light was blinking red. She started to see more cars here and there, all heading for the outer belt known as Interstate 8, presumably to head north out of the city. She followed the hurricane evacuation signs meant to direct the massive outflow of cars during bad weather.

Connie got onto the freeway, heading north toward their home in Fort Worth, normally a five hour drive away. After only ten minutes, the traffic slowed to a crawl, high on a bridge above an infinite sea of oil refineries, some of which were on fire. Black smoke covered the entire area.

Traffic inched forward, taking over an hour just to reach the other side of the bridge. Connie found herself surrounded by scared and frightened drivers trying to escape northward from Houston. She exited the freeway and got onto the service roads which flanked the interstate. She saw several grown men yelling at each other and fighting in what must've been a fit of road rage. The service roads proved to be a godsend because they allowed her to advance at a steady rate. She made good progress in a situation that defied progress. Once Connie reached the suburbs in the far north part of town, she got back on the interstate and gunned the engine, ignoring speed limits.

"Kids, we're heading home."

"What about Daddy?"

"He'll be fine. He's not in Houston. He's on Mars. This doesn't affect him."

I hate lying to the kids, she thought.

CHAPTER 5

Blame this whole mess on Dmitri Stalov. He's the reason why Earth lost all power and communication during the attack. He's also the reason why so many people *lived*.

Dmitri grew up in a large house on the outskirts of Moscow during the 1960's and 1970's. His father, Fyodor, was an upper level member of the Communist Party. His job was to set yearly quotas for how much industrial farm equipment would be produced. Regardless of input from farmers, Dmitri's father would dictate how many tractors and hay balers would be made. Little Dmitri loved touring the factories with his father. He was too young to understand the closed-door meetings that involved a lot of shouting, loud boom sounds followed by screams, and his father leaving quickly while wiping blood from his hands.

Despite his naïve factory visits, Dmitri developed a keen

interest in all things mechanical and electrical. At the age of twelve, he built a doll house for his sister that had a working electric elevator.

With the help of his father, Dmitri entered the University of Moscow at the age of 17 to pursue his interest in electronics. The prodigy loved making gadgets to play tricks on his friends. His most successful device was a small battery-powered box that could scramble the signal of any radio within a thirty foot radius – all at the push of a button. His magnum opus came during the finals of the 1980 Winter Olympics hockey championship – that's when America played against the Soviets and won the so-called *Miracle On Ice*. Just when it looked like the Soviets were going to lose, Dmitri mashed his finger on the button of his radio scrambler and didn't let go. His family lost their minds with rage. They jumped up and down. They looked behind the radio. They bent the antenna. Occasionally when a family member would reach a ridiculous pose holding the antenna, Dmitri would release the scrambler's button, making the unsuspecting uncle think that holding the antenna while in a pirouette pose fixed the broadcast. Tears of laughter ran down Dmitri's face as he tried not to let on about his trick. With only seconds left in the game, he mashed the button down for good.

College didn't go well for Dmitri because he often knew more than his professors. When the days of university ended, Dmitri was sent to a missile design bureau to do the grunt work of a 21-year old engineer. That included getting coffee for the engineers who had earned their seniority in the bureau. Unlike his other compatriots, he stayed late to read the technical manuals written by his predecessors. He became an expert in the design of automatic guidance systems. When the USA launched the GPS satellite system in the mid 1980's, Dmitri was part of a secret team chosen to decode the purposely scrambled signal – with the goal being for the Russian military to use it. Combined with their own GLONASS GPS system, the Russian military had access to nearly double the number of positioning satellites, making accurate placement of military vehicles very reliable.

With such position information available, Dmitri developed small guidance systems that could steer micro-bomblets precisely to a target – all for the benefit of Mother Russia. His bosses took notice of his work and in his spare time Dmitri put together a plan that he thought would save all of humanity – he was young and idealistic.

He proposed the idea of taking existing intercontinental ballistic missiles (ICBM's) and replacing the large warhead cluster with 144 small GPS-guided micro-nukes. Instead of vaporizing all of humanity, his missiles would precisely strike communication hubs and power plants.

The bosses didn't like this friendly attack method because they thought the Americans were bloodthirsty animals whose only desire was to kill as many Russians as possible. Eventually, Dmitri convinced his overseers that the single act of destroying the enemy's communication and power supply networks would actually be *more disabling* than a single 10 kiloton nuke dropped on Washington DC. Several tests were carried out in real Russian towns on the Eastern Steppes. Only thirty six unsuspecting citizens were evaporated. By Soviet standards, it was a stunning success. Dmitri became the apple of the politburo's eye. His father was proud. With that said, Russia would still drop several 10 kiloton nukes on the major cities of their enemies for completeness sake.

Throughout the 1980's, a large portion of Russia's ICBM fleet was secretly re-warheaded with the load of bomblets destined to take out every major communication hub and power plant in America, Europe and China. Dmitri became celebrated and the young engineering prodigy settled into a comfy university teaching job in Leningrad. Every year he taught from the same notes. Every year he gave the same tests. Every year his students cheated from his old notes and old tests. This efficiency freed him up to pursue his hobbies and outside interests.

As a rocket enthusiast and a proud Russian, Dmitri's new hobby became proving that the Soviets' attempts at a Moon Landing in the 1960's could have succeeded. Not many people realize it, but the Russians desperately tried to beat the Americans to the Moon. They designed a rocket called the N1 which produced nearly ten million pounds of thrust, making it the most powerful rocket ever built. The Russians built four test vehicles and all four crashed, the second one producing one of the loudest non-nuclear explosions in human history.

Dmitri spent many years building detailed computerized mission models and sub-assembly models to see how each rocket dealt with common problems such as failed steerable rocket nozzles and guidance. Without realizing it, Dmitri became obsessed with the American Saturn V rocket, the rocket that eventually did take mankind to the Moon – just not for the Soviets.

After studying the most minute details, he realized that the Soviet N1 rocket was simply inferior in every way. In hindsight, it was inevitable that the Saturn V would make it to the Moon before the N1 did. In fact, he felt it would be difficult to develop any technology under the troubled environment that hounded then-modern Russia. Dmitri grew depressed.

On a particularly warm August evening years before the fall of the Soviet Union, Dmitri left his apartment to get dinner and never came back. Two weeks later, he showed up in an American submarine in New London, Connecticut, having defected to the United States via an old-school network of spies. Until his handlers could figure out what best to do with him, he stayed in a red brick house just up the hill from the Naval Submarine Museum, which he toured on a daily basis. His new name would be John Smith – although he didn't sound like a John Smith when he spoke.

John (Dmitri) was presented to the CIA as an intercontinental ballistic nuclear missile expert. And he *was* for the most part. In fact, he told his new handlers about an idea he had that would defeat the Russians even faster than a direct attack with mega-explosions. He explained how to use small GPS-guided bomblets to destroy the Soviet communication networks and power distribution centers. His classic line became, "Disabling their ability to communicate will prevent their ability for massive retaliation."

The CIA hated Dmitri's idea. That all changed on another warm August evening. While testing a microphone before a radio news conference, President Ronald Reagan jokingly said, "My fellow Americans, I am pleased to tell you today that I've signed legislation that will outlaw Russia forever. We begin bombing in five minutes."

It was a great joke, enjoyed by the nearby press. Unfortunately, it leaked and the Soviets put their entire Far East Army on high alert status. Reagan was surprised that Russia would ever consider that the USA would provoke a nuclear war. It was an almost inconceivable thought to him, forcing him to realize that they were just as scared of us as we were of them. In a timely meeting with the CIA, Dmitri's more humane missile warhead conversion idea was revisited and tentatively approved.

A test missile was created and dropped on a fake town in the New Mexico desert. Aside from a few vaporized jackrabbits, nobody was killed. It was a stunning success. A portion of the American warhead fleet was changed over to these so-called "CommKnock" warheads – the name had multiple meanings. Dmitri told people it meant Communication Knockout, but when Dmitri left the room, the generals said it stood for *Commie Knockout.*

Dmitri single-handedly caused both sides of the Cold War to re-envision themselves as the nicer and more humane of aggressors. His idea would lead to the saving of millions of lives not only in America and Russia, but in Europe and China and wherever else the thousands of ICBM's were aimed. Dmitri was happy and after three years in Connecticut, he vanished without a trace. His last note was an email to a colleague saying, "I'd like to visit the southwest. Oh, and I ate all your prunes."

Years later, these friendly missiles were *not* the type that secretly piggybacked their way onto the International Space Station (ISS) during preparation for the first manned mission to Mars.

A new ISS module was launched up and attached to the massive orbiting station for the sole purpose of temporarily storing all the equipment and materials needed for the impending Mars mission – the astronauts would disembark toward Mars from the space station. This stationary unit, dubbed the *Storage Wart*, didn't look much different from the existing modules on the ISS, but it was much larger. And on the outside was a large cabinet. It was specifically requested by the Pentagon as a tradeoff for temporarily giving up their budget to the Mars expedition.

During the bumpy ride up to the ISS, some of the wires were chafed and eventually began shorting out. This was most unfortunate because they were part of the ejection system attached to the eight top-secret thermonuclear B-61 bombs secretly stored in the outside cabinet. The bombs had been modified with rocket engines and new nosecones to withstand the atmospheric re-entry – all to help them reach distant targets quickly from space.

Having those weapons in space violated international treaties, of course, but the Pentagon thought it would be a great political trump card to bring out in the event of a tense international disagreement. And it *was* a great idea until the electrical shorts accidentally ejected the missiles – missiles that had been sent to space with some of the launch-code safeties *disabled* to make sure somebody on the ISS could trigger them in an absolute emergency, a so-called "last-man standing" scenario.

The sparking on the ejector mechanism eventually caused the eight thermonuclear missiles to eject from the ISS so violently that the resulting jolt broke the connections between several Space Station modules, causing a chain reaction of failures. As the missiles started launching toward their predetermined targets in Russia, the inhabitants of the ISS had to abandon their orbiting home, escaping in the Soyuz return capsules for a trip back to Earth. Below them, they could see mushroom clouds popping up near population centers in Russia.

Power was lost to the high-bandwidth antennas on the ISS which were the main communication channels with the crew on Mars. Their only hope now were the three deep-space antennas spread around the Earth.

Even before the ISS nuclear missiles struck Russia, the former Soviets launched a large retaliatory strike first against America and then Europe. As planned by Dmitri, many of these first wave missiles were the CommKnock type of missiles, destroying communication hubs and wiping out power distribution stations.

America went dark and silent, but not before sending their own CommKnock missiles to take out some of the same types of locations in Russia (and China for good measure). Russia retaliated with a second wave to take out satellite communication networks which included sending one missile to each of the three deep-space antenna sites around the world. The Goldstone facility near Barstow, California, the secondary facility in Madrid, Spain and the third facility in Canberra, Australia. Poof. All gone. Our team of astronauts on Mars was completely cut off.

Of particular concern to Chris Tankovitch and Connie Alston was the large 10-kiloton nuke that just wiped out downtown Houston, blasting out beyond the city core and damaging buildings as far away as Clear Lake where the NASA Johnson Manned Spacecraft Center was located.

Chris Tankovitch was huddled in a bomb shelter with dozens of coworkers. He stared at his phone. The screen said "Call terminated" and the top now showed *No signal.*

Connie and her two children were stuck in a sea of traffic trying to escape Houston back to their home in Fort Worth, hoping it was still there. She kept checking her cellphone. *No signal.*

On Mars, Captain Adam Alston and the only other surviving crew member, Yeva Turoskova, slept fitfully in the Big Turtle habitat spacecraft. They had just suffered the deaths of *two* beloved crewmembers and a series of unfortunate setbacks. Soon they would lose all communication with Earth. They would never know what happened. Twenty minutes after the last deep-space antenna on Earth was destroyed, the first sign of what was to come showed up as a blinking warning message on a laptop screen, the computer that monitored data transfers between Earth and Mars. *No signal.*

CHAPTER 6

The Alston family getaway car
Somewhere between Houston and Dallas/Fort Worth

The Honda was running on fumes, occasionally lurching as the engine gasped for more fuel. Connie guided the car off the freeway near the tiny town of Alma. The gas stations there were out of everything, including fuel and bullets. Using directions from a local resident, she continued on the small road away from the freeway, looking for the tiny town of Eugene.

Connie reached Eugene after a few minutes of driving and pulled into the small two-pump gas station. The engine gave its last gasp of life and died. She was trying to get out of her car when the attendant came out, wiping his hands with an old greasy towel.

"Howdy ma'am, need some gas?"

Why else would anybody stop in this hell-forsaken town, she thought.

"Yes, I was going to do it myself, if that's okay."

"No, it's not okay," he said with hillbilly authority. "Since all the stuff hit Houston, we've had a lot of people pump their gas and then drive away without paying."

Connie could feel the attendant's anger.

"Okay, can you pump it for me then? Please?"

The attendant leaned down to inspect the inside of the car.

"You coming from Houston?" he asked as he carefully pulled an oily rag out of his pocket.

"Sort of," Connie said. "We were just visiting, but we escaped from the southeast part of town. Have you heard any news?"

"No ma'am. All communication's dead. No TV signals either. It's bad whatever it is. We got our guns ready though," he said while patting his pocket. "Ain't nobody gonna cause trouble round here, unless they plan on stealing gasoline."

The attendant grabbed the gas pump nozzle and walked to the back of the car. He knocked on the car for Connie to open the hatch.

"Please open the gas cap cover, ma'am."

Uh oh, 'rental car' syndrome, she thought. It wasn't her car, so she frantically searched around the footwell to find the gas cap release, first pulling on a lever that opened the hood.

"Dammit," Connie muttered.

A chorus of "Mommy said a bad word!" came from the back seat.

The attendant scowled and knocked on the gas cap

again. Connie pulled on a different lever and the gas cap popped open.

The attendant rolled his eyes and then stuck the nozzle into the car and squeezed the handle. The slosh and gurgling of gas was heard by everybody. She contemplated gunning the engine and tearing out of here when it was full.

The attendant walked back up to Connie.

"Ma'am, you look familiar. Are you on TV or something?"

Connie looked straight ahead and moved her head side to side. "Nope...." she trailed off.

"She's Misses Adam Alston!" came a voice from the back seat. "Our Daddy is an astronaut on Mars right now. He's famous!"

Connie squeezed her eyes shut in anger.

"Please be quiet, Cody!" she shouted.

The attendant laughed out loud.

"From the ears of babies, right?" he said, mangling the phrase. The attendant stood up and turned his head toward the building and yelled, "Hey Bill! We've got ourselves a *very important person* here in our tiny town. This is Adam Alston's family! You know, one of them NASA guys on Mars right now."

A very rotund man waddled out of the small station office and across the blacktop. His belly reached the car first, the sheer weight of which closed the hood tight again. He was still licking his fingers from the meal he had just given no mercy.

"Howdy Ma'am. Well imagine you coming to our sleepy little town of Eugene," he said while trying to catch his breath from the walk. "I suppose the gas stations on I-45 are all emptied out, eh?"

"Yeah, that seems to be the case. Everywhere. The northbound traffic from Houston is pretty heavy."

At that moment, the pump clunked. All done.

Here's my chance to take off, thought Connie. The fat guy was standing in front of the car, blocking them in. She couldn't do it.

The attendant removed the nozzle and hung it back on the pump. Connie got out her wallet and handed her credit card to the attendant.

"What do you want me to do with this?" he asked.

"Charge the fillup, I hope."

"I done told you communication is all broke to hell. I can't process no credit card. You got cash? Maybe something else worth tradin'?" he suggested in his creepiest voice.

"Yes, I have some cash. How much is the total?"

The attendant stopped chewing his gum and turned to smile at Bill.

The attendant leaned into the window, breathing at Connie. He smelled like coffee, cigarettes and tooth rot.

"Seein' as you're famous and all... How much do you have on you today? MAYAM," he said, stressing the last word.

Connie opened her wallet and took out all her cash, totaling $90. She reluctantly handed it to him.

The attendant counted each bill slowly, pulling each one tight to straighten it out.

"I tell you what. We'll call it even," he said with his flawed logic. "Good luck on your trip north. And give our regards to your husband up on Mars. The town of Eugene is rootin' for him, ya hear? We love our Texans!"

The attendant and Bill walked back toward the garage, occasionally pointing back toward Connie and laughing.

She started the car and peeled out in the direction back toward the freeway. Once on I-45, their next stop would be home in Fort Worth.

I hope it's still there, she thought.

CHAPTER 7

Bomb Shelter, Building 12
NASA Johnson Space Center
Houston, Texas

"Thank God for cellphones," Chris Tankovitch said.

He and nine other people were using the *flashlight* apps on their phones to illuminate the room. They'd been in the bomb shelter for hours with very little information. The explosion had sent a shock wave across the facility and damaged a lot of buildings, including knocking a wall out of the mission control center building. The flag pole on the roof had fallen down and speared a parked Volkswagen Beetle.

"Anybody getting any signal? Any updates?"

A chorus of sad No's filled the room.

Chris stood up and walked over to the door.

"Okay everybody, I'm going to go take a peek outside."

Chris slowly opened the door and walked out. Ceiling

tiles dangled from the roof. All of the outside windows were shattered and glass lay strewn across the floor. The acrid smell of burnt electrical wires filled the air. Some of the non-load-bearing office walls had fallen down, but the building itself looked structurally sound. Chris continued toward the outside door and pushed it open. To the northwest he could see a glow coming from the downtown Houston area, no doubt caused by enormous fires. He saw a huge hole in the side of the Mission Control Center complex, papers blowing in the wind.

On occasion Chris could see emergency vehicles through the smoke, rushing up and down the main road. Chris wasn't far from the on-base medical clinic, which still had lights on.

Their backup generators must be working, he thought.

Chris walked back to the bomb shelter room and opened the door further. The glow from the flashlights pointed at him. He held his hand up to block the blinding lights.

"Come with me. The clinic has power and some of you need help."

One by one, they exited the room, some walking, some limping.

"Watch the broken glass," he warned them.

The group walked across the parking lot toward the new medical clinic. Chris was flanked by his two deputy directors. He barked orders to each of them.

"Get a list of all NASA facilities still functioning and see if there's any communication routes open. We may have to walkie-talkie and CB radio our way around the country. Execute the emergency protocols at all of them."

"Got it, chief," a deputy said as he jotted down notes.

Chris turned to the other deputy.

"The Space Station is crippled. We may have lost the deep-space wideband antenna to Mars. Find out if Goldstone or the other two deep-space antenna complexes in Madrid and Canberra are working. We can't leave our crew stranded without any communication."

The group continued walking toward the medical clinic. Chris made sure to drift over towards Jimmy, the technician who had shown him the shocking video from Mars right before the accident.

"Hey Jimmy."

Jimmy acknowledged with a head nod, but kept walking without looking at Chris. Jimmy had a new limp.

Too much silence followed.

"Yes?" Jimmy said to Chris.

"You know the video you showed me?"

"Of course," Jimmy confirmed, nodding his head.

"Is your computer okay?"

"No, it was crushed by a wall. I barely got out. There was a small fire, too."

"Damn," Chris said in despair. "But you have backups, right?"

"Of course we do. We have an offsite backup, you know, for safety reasons."

Chris was overjoyed to hear that.

"If we can get power back on and get you a new computer, how soon before we can get to your backups?" Chris asked.

"That might be a bit tricky," Jimmy said as he stopped walking.

Chris stopped walking, too.

"Why is that? Where are they?" Chris asked.

Jimmy frowned.

"Downtown Houston."

CHAPTER 8

The Alston family getaway car
Nearing Dallas

The Honda approached the southern outskirts of Dallas on its way to neighboring Fort Worth, having driven nearly seven hours.

Approaching any large city brings the same universal sights. The exit ramps become more frequent. More fast food restaurants. More hotels. The oddly placed adult megabookstore.

Off in the distance, Connie could see the familiar Reunion Tower with its big spherical top.

We're so close, Connie thought. Both kids were asleep in the back seat.

Tonight was very different from the other times they'd

driven in at dusk. At the bottom of the exit ramps and on the distant side streets, Connie could see the blinking stop lights. Everything was running on emergency backup power. None of the skyscrapers downtown were lit up. Just dark obelisks stabbing up at the sky. The sight of the buildings brought joy to Connie though because it meant no bombs had struck Dallas.

Fort Worth is probably okay too, she thought.

She barely noticed the tiny figures ahead on the freeway. As her headlights got closer, she saw a dozen thugs standing across the freeway, each one holding a weapon of some sort. A mix of baseball bats and two-by-fours. Connie saw a car that had stopped – the driver was being beaten senseless.

Not today.

She gunned it and aimed for the biggest gap in the line. Instead of moving apart to avoid the automotive death-machine approaching them, the thugs started moving together. Connie didn't slow down. She passed right through the line at full speed. A loud BANG hit the drivers' side mirror. It flung back for a brief second, but bounced right back into place. The mirror itself was shattered. She looked in the rear-view mirror just in time to see a body rolling along the pavement.

"Mommy? What was that sound?" Catie asked, freshly awoken from a back seat nap.

"It was nothing. We... we hit a bird. You two go back to sleep."

"Okay. Are we home yet?"

"Almost. We're in Dallas. We'll head west for a while

and then we'll be home.

Maybe Houston was a terrorist attack, she thought, even though the car radio still couldn't pick up any stations.

Once she reached the outer belt, Connie headed west toward her hometown of Fort Worth. The two giant cities had grown together into one massive city often called the *DFW Metroplex*. This urban blob even had its own airport.

One more hour to go... hopefully.

Connie looked in the mirror at her sleeping children. They had survived unscathed.

Thank God for small victories.

The Honda drove down the long sweeping exit ramp leading right into the main intersection entrance to Wanigas. She had to stop quickly due to the backup of cars. This intersection, the only entrance to the city, was blocked by a police blockade. The officers were turning many people away. After what seemed like forever, Connie reached the front of the line. A policeman knocked on her window and she rolled it down.

"Hi, Officer, I need to get to my house. I live here."

"Ma'am, can I see your driver's license?" he said without emotion.

"Sure," Connie said quietly while digging through her purse. She handed him her driver's license.

The policeman wondered why she was whispering. With his left hand on the hood, he leaned over and stared into the open driver's window. He saw the two sleeping children – the officer understood. He leaned back up and had a huge blood stain on his shirt where it had rubbed on the side-view mirror. It was at that moment that Connie realized just how hard she'd struck those freeway thugs back in Dallas. She stared in horror, but the policeman didn't see it. Her eyes quickly moved up to his face.

"Ma'am, where are you coming from?"

"We were in Houston, but we were able to get out."

"What happened there? What did you see?" the curious policeman asked.

"I think it was a huge bomb or something. Probably a terrorist attack," Connie said pensively.

The policeman shook his head and said, "Could be. We think it was more than Houston though, but we don't know what's going on."

The policeman inspected the driver's license carefully and raised his eyebrows, realizing who she was.

"Are you the wife of Adam Alston?"

"Yes I am. We were down there in some temporary housing, but we got up here as fast as we could."

"Well, okay. Your husband is our hometown hero," he said happily, almost ignoring the total hell that today had brought. "Okay, as I said, we don't know exactly what's going on."

The policeman handed back her license and continued.

"All we know so far is a nuke struck Houston and hundreds of smaller bombs hit our power plants and communication centers up here. So, the power's out and phone lines are dead."

"What about the cellphones?"

"Hah, check your signal. Those are dead, too. The cell tower backup generators ran out of juice a few hours ago."

"Is it nationwide?"

"Um, we think it's *planetwide*."

"Oh no..." she trailed off.

"Obviously you live here, so I'm going to let you pass. Drive carefully. We've got police all around keeping the peace."

"I'm glad to hear that," Connie said.

"Ma'am, do you own a weapon?"

She briefly looked at his bloodstained shirt and then back at his face.

"Yes, of course. This is Texas, right?" she laughed. "We have a shotgun that we keep locked up."

Then she added the detail, "Mossberg brand. I think it's an antique."

"Do you know how to operate it?"

"Yes, we've taken it to my mom's farm a few times to shoot clay pigeons. She lives north of here."

"Okay, well make sure it is readily accessible by you," he looked toward the back seat before continuing, "and *not accessible* by the little ones. Remember, 911 isn't working right now. Drive safe. If you need help, you'll have to drive yourself."

Connie eased away from the police stop and drove down the empty streets of Wanigas. The roads themselves looked normal, but residents were outside sitting in their yards cooling off, realizing that the invention of air conditioning is the only thing that made Texas habitable.

Kids were spraying each other with water – thankfully water towers work on gravity so at least the town still had water pressure for the time being, until the tower tank emptied.

After a few lazy turns, she pulled into her neighborhood and realized that she'd never seen it cast in total darkness before. Not a single streetlight was lit. The only illumination was from the occasional flashlight beam from fellow resident's yards. After two stop signs, she turned onto her street and eased into the driveway of their aging ranch house.

Instinctively she pushed the button on the garage door opener. Nothing happened. Connie laughed. She got out of her car, looked around and sighed.

"What a mess we're in," she whispered.

Normally at this time of evening, the air was filled with the cacophony of home air conditioners kicking on, but it was utterly silent tonight. Each of her footsteps clopped loudly. Her keys were as loud as a bell.

Connie walked up to the front door of the house and unlocked it. After opening the door, she once again instinctively tried to turn on the light. Nothing. Again, she laughed at how ingrained the expectation was.

She walked back to the car and saw that Cody was awake. She picked up Catie and directed Cody into the house.

Connie paused to hear the wind blowing through the magnolia trees and the occasional searing caw of the Grackle birds.

A simple smile overtook her. One word was on Connie's mind:

Home.

CHAPTER 9

Astronaut landing site near Mount Sharp
Mars

Every morning the shadow of Mount Sharp retreats from the plains of Mars, pooling in the ancient riverbeds and hiding beneath the exposed bedrock cliffs. Ironically named for the Roman god of war, this red dusty ball was defenseless against the ravages of time and solar radiation.

As the Sun rose, the vanishing shadows uncovered many new things that were invasive to the Red Planet – all of which were sent here by mankind.

The Curiosity Rover had been brought back to life when the visiting astronauts refreshed the radioactive power source that drove the vehicle. However, it fell dead again several days ago when it stopped receiving commands from NASA. Dusty whirlwinds flowed in and around the stone pyramid structure built as a memorial by the ancient Martian society before they perished. This was the same building that had seen the struggle of two astronauts and the death of Keller Murch.

The most important site on Mars was a flat region just a few kilometers away near Mount Sharp where two roundish spacecraft sat huddled together. The largest one, endearingly called the *Big Turtle*, was a permanent craft that acted as the long-term living quarters for the first crew to ever set foot on the Red Planet. It was roughly 30 feet in diameter, painted a mixture of black and white colors. It was filled with simple things like beds and a kitchen. It also had the complex things — scientific equipment that had only been partially used so far.

Outside the Big Turtle was a ground transportation craft light-heartedly nicknamed *The Golf Cart* – the astronauts used it to drive back and forth to the pyramid structure. At the moment it was broken and unusable. Just a few feet away on the ground was a makeshift grave, dug for the bodies of Keller Murch and another crewmember, Molly Hemphill, who had died recently from asphyxiation. Things were not going well on Mars.

Only two crewmembers were left: Captain Adam Alston and the paleontologist cosmonaut named Yeva Turoskova.

An elevated hallway connected the Big Turtle to the smaller craft, dubbed the *Little Turtle*, that was used to bring the crew to Mars. During their six-week long journey, all four of them were cooped up in this smaller ship. It was also meant to be their lifeboat home to Earth.

The Turtle moniker for both ships came from the geodesic-domed roofs covered with faceted solar panels.

Days ago all communications to and from NASA suddenly stopped. Professional and frightened, the remaining crew carried out their task lists including an early attempt at terraforming – ultimately leading to the formation of elevated air pressure, clouds, and brief rain showers. However, reality was setting in. Temporary losses of communication happened from time to time, but one this long could only mean something more serious had happened on Earth.

After much deliberation, the crew decided to return home immediately.

Captain Adam Alston's last external journey would be a final walk-around examination of the Little Turtle. He exited the ship and walked down the ramp, stomping into the dusty ground cover before ducking under the elevated tunnel which connected the two ships together.

Laying on the ground were the flattened parachutes used during their descent to the surface of Mars. Their original planned use was for the return re-entry to Earth. However, during the Mars approach, the Little Turtle wasn't slowing down enough, so Adam made the executive decision to use them here instead – hoping they could be repacked. He studied their condition and they weren't too bad, mainly just dirty. He walked along each chute, knocking the built-up muck from them. After cleaning them off, he thought to himself, *I think they'll work fine.*

Adam straightened up the parachutes and refolded them, much like one folds up a tent after camping. First he folded them into halves, then half again until he had long folded mounds of material. Finally, he rolled each one up and wrapped the cables around the outside like strings around a sleeping bag.

Adam grabbed hold of the external ladder on the side of Little Turtle and climbed up to the roof, stepping on the rigid structure to avoid the fragile solar panels that covered the roof. One by one, he pulled the wrapped bundles up to the roof. He stuffed the first parachute into one of the roof containers, shutting the hatch cover to seal it in. Adam moved over to the other containers, holding on to the tall long-range antenna for more support.

When he was done, Adam looked around, surveying the area and all they had accomplished during their short stay. He looked at the last page of the checklist, but didn't see the single bullet-point that had been page-breaked to the back of the next page.

The wind was something new – a result of their experiment with short-term terraforming. Up until a few days ago, the thin Martian breeze was too light to feel. Now, after the terraforming experiment, a stronger wind blew by. It caused the checklist Adam had clipped to his suit to come loose, the last page flying away in the breeze.

Only Adam didn't notice. He clambered down the ladder and breathed a sigh of relief at being done. He scanned the sun-drenched red horizon – a view he could never forget. Adam turned, walked up the ramp and back into the airlock in the Big Turtle.

For the next hour, Yeva and Adam moved the remaining food, water and other supplies from the Big Turtle over to the Little Turtle. All that was left when they were done was the final checklist for interior preparation.

The *other supplies* comprised several hundred pounds of Martian rocks — the return trip to Earth would not be empty handed. In addition to those rocks, traveling with them back to Earth in the Little Turtle were many priceless items such as core samples and a black cube, the latter being a gift of sorts from the ancient Martians themselves.

Despite the fact that the cube was strapped to a bulkhead for the trip home, it may have been the most important find on this mission, maybe even in human history. It was a small black metallic cube roughly five inches on all sides and it didn't seem to be affected by gravity. Lift it into the air and it would maintain its position. Push it slightly and it would glide sideways (or up) forever. Curiously, it was always warm. The possible technological breakthroughs were endless.

Soon, both the rocks and the crew would be leaving Mars for the long journey back to Earth.

The return process was very straight forward – in theory. The Little Turtle would ignite its main engines for 45 seconds, pushing the capsule up and out of the Martian atmosphere until it reached sufficient speed to orbit the Red Planet.

The Little Turtle sat silently with the crew strapped into their seats. The billowing wind sent swirls of dust from the edges of the Turtle spaceships. With a "pop" heard by the crew, the connector hallway fell off the Little Turtle and retracted, dragging it's sad end along the Martian ground.

The countdown started. Eventually it reached the exciting end:

Three...

Two...

One...

Instantly, four rocket flames exploded from the bottom of the Little Turtle. Being very lightweight, it started lifting immediately and rose two meters from the ground. The vehicle stopped abruptly and swayed from side to side. The harsh thrusting rocket fire seared the ground beneath.

"The grounding cable!" Adam yelled. He'd forgot to remove the grounding cable that the Little Turtle had shot into the bedrock to keep static electricity from building up on the ship. Now the cable that protected them from getting shocked was preventing them from leaving Mars.

In his excitement to leave Mars, the grounding cable was the one bullet-point on the checklist that Adam failed to see.

Mars would not let go of the astronauts – it was hungry for two more bodies. Adam unbuckled himself and hopped onto the controls of the small remote-controlled rover that was still down on the surface.

He manipulated the control sticks on the remote control transmitter.

Near the edge of the landing site, a small rover vehicle came barreling toward the Little Turtle. It hopped and swayed as it gained speed, heading straight for the underside of the Little Turtle – obviously being steered by Adam. The rover slammed into and through the grounding cable, releasing the bucking beast from its Martian doom. Like a cheetah unleashed, the Little Turtle rocketed upward at blinding speed. Adam was immediately thrown against the floor of the ship.

The violent lurching toppled the long-range antenna which used to tower above the geodesic roof of the Little

Turtle. As it fell, it ripped away some of the solar panels and careened past the porthole windows, striking even more fear into the astronauts. Even if the problems on Earth were fixed, the astronauts' long-range communications options were just eliminated. They would be flying in silence all the way home.

The ascent continued at breakneck speed. With the antenna and some of the solar panels gone, Little Turtle was experiencing uneven aerodynamic forces. The Martian atmosphere was thin for sure, but at their speed, it caused the ship to start vibrating. And shaking. And shimmying. The anti-gravity cube broke loose from its straps and began bouncing around the cabin, seemingly unaware of the extreme acceleration the ship was undergoing. It slammed into a small cabinet painted with warning stripes, knocking the door open. Inside the cabinet were little bottles of poison, to be used by the crew if they found themselves in a situation where all was lost. As the anti-gravity cube knocked open the cabinet door, it also smashed open two of those bottles. The contents sprayed everywhere, filling the cabin with a red fog.

The shaking continued. Yeva saw the escape hatch door starting to buckle. To her horror, with a loud screech, the door launched off into the void of space.

All of the air rushed out of the cabin. With the sudden loss of air pressure, the water bags exploded, creating a cascade of ice crystals streaming out of the open hatch.

The engines stopped. The ship was in orbit – a temporary status until the booster rocket pushed them for a while, followed by the MM10 motors kicking in to slowly push them back to Earth. Checklist pages and ice crystals floated effortlessly out the escape hatch hole. Inside the ship were a stunned astronaut named Adam and a stunned cosmonaut named Yeva.

She was bleeding from her nose inside her pressure suit helmet.

"Yeva, can you hear me?" Adam yelled.

She nodded her head. The blood blobs floated around inside her helmet, getting stuck in her hair. Adam had to get the ship's environment restored before her blood fouled the breathing apparatus inside her pressure suit.

Their main problem was the gaping hole where the escape hatch door used to be. It was ominously large, roughly two feet in diameter. Adam looked around inside the ship frantically. He didn't see anything that would make a good strong cover.

"Yeva, I've gotta find something to cover the opening. Try not to move, okay?"

She gave him the thumbs up signal. A glob of blood floated right in front of her forehead.

Adam looked frantically for anything large enough to cover the hatch door opening. *The locker doors?* He floated over and quickly studied how they folded open like an accordion. The doors hung from roller tracks that appeared to be relatively weak. Adam wondered if they could be pulled from the track if he worked hard enough. He wedged his boot behind the cabinet and yanked.

Nothing happened.

He wedged both boots this time and pulled with all his strength.

The doors ripped from the roller rails and wobbled back and forth like spindly sheet metal.

"Finally!" Adam cheered. "Some good luck."

He repeated this action on the other two cabinets, harvesting twelve long slender doors. Adam stacked four of them together side by side and wrapped a blanket around them. He floated over to the escape hatch door.

"Think! Think! Think!" he said out loud.

Adam put another blanket over the opening as best he could, then stacked four of the cabinet doors over it. The moment he turned away, the contraption started to float apart.

"Yeva, I know I said don't move, but I have to hold these in place while you try to pressurize the ship. Can you float *slowly* over to the environmental control panel and crank up the pressure?"

"Yes," she said sparingly.

Yeva manipulated her pressure suit over to the environmental control panel while Adam re-assembled the door stack.

"Slowly now, just enough air to hold this in place," Adam explained.

Yeva turned the valves to allow pressure from the storage tanks into the spaceship interior. They heard a creaking sound and saw the panels over the escape hatch starting to bow outward.

Hold, baby, hold, Adam thought to himself.

Crunch!

The single layer of door panels buckled and blew out the door opening. Adam grabbed onto a wall bulkhead just in time to not get sucked out himself.

"Damn, that was close. I'll try two layers of panels. That's all we got left."

Adam floated back to the sleeping bay, picked up

another blanket and went back to the hatch opening. He put the blanket over it and then stacked two layers of the sheet metal doors over it, interlocking their edges to make it stronger.

"Okay, let's try that again," Adam said. He circled his hand in the air to signal Yeva to crank up the pressure again.

Yeva slowly turned the valve this time. The panels barely creaked. She halted the valve to examine the situation.

Adam gave her a thumbs-up.

Yeva started increasing the pressure valve again. "We're at 8 psi right now. Almost ready to breathe."

She continued increasing pressure. The doors bowed out even more with a severe creaking sound.

"Something is wrong, Adam. I keep opening the pressure valve, but the cabin isn't maintaining pressure. The blankets must be a terrible seal. We may be done for."

"Not yet," Adam declared. "We'll figure some way to make it airtight."

Adam had to seal where the blankets were getting smashed against the door frame opening. He floated over to the kitchen and searched through the food box for something that could work as a sealant. He saw the bags of liquid steak and pulled two out. They were frozen hard as rock.

Adam put them in the microwave.

"Can you believe our survival relies on a TV dinner?" Adam quipped to help Yeva's mood.

As he waited, Adam saw Yeva grabbing at her helmet and panicking. Her blood had finally clogged the air valve and she couldn't breathe.

Adam stared at the microwave and yelled, "Come on!"

Before it finished, he opened the microwave door and

grabbed the mostly thawed bags of liquid steak and pushed over to the panel-covered hatch.

"Crank up the pressure just a little bit for now," Adam commanded. Yeva tried to comply while fighting her own emergency.

He tore open the bag and some liquid steak floated away. He caulked a very uneven bead along where the blankets were squeezed between the panel and door frame. The liquid, pressurized from the air inside the spaceship, soaked into the blanket material and partially out the hatch where it froze instantly, creating a near perfect gasket between door edge and the panel cover. Adam quickly put another blanket over the door stack and applied even more of the food-based sealant along the seams between the metal doors.

Yeva was still struggling for air.

Adam let go of the empty steak bags and spun around. He jettisoned himself over to the environmental panel and cranked the pressure all the way up. No time to wait.

"Yeva, it's almost there!"

The dial moved just barely into the green "safe" zone. Adam grabbed Yeva's helmet and unlatched it. It popped off and floated away as she gasped for air. Deep, starving breaths.

Adam removed his own helmet and looked around for towels to wipe the blood from Yeva's face.

"Yeva, you gave me quite a scare there."

The panels on the door gave off a loud creaking sound.

Both astronauts stared at the door cover assembly.

"Do you think it will hold?" Yeva asked.

"I hope so," Adam confessed. "Those panels are the only

thing between us and Jesus."

The first order of business was to determine which systems were damaged and which systems were working. To minimize the air pressure on the makeshift door cover, Yeva kept the ship at around three quarters of typical cabin pressure. Unfortunately that meant upping the oxygen levels which was not the safest thing to do. A similar oxygen-rich atmosphere contributed to the deaths of all three Apollo 1 astronauts in 1967. Until Yeva and Adam could rely on the door cover, that's what they felt safest doing.

Adam inventoried the food and water supply. They started off this return mission with enough food and water for four people. During the violent escape and the sudden decompression, they lost half of their water supply. Since there was only half of the crew, this was a bit of luck. If they began to use more water than necessary, they could rely on the water vapor recovery system which kept the humidity at reasonable levels while at the same time extracting it into liquid drinkable form.

The water vapor recovery system was dead. Yeva saw this during her examination of the ship's systems. She noticed the walls had condensation on them. Since they were in zero gravity, the condensation didn't drip from the walls. Instead, it just grew like a thick layer of goo along any metal parts.

Adam tried to get the radio system working, but he knew it was pointless. The long-range antenna was gone, having fallen off during the turbulent ascent into orbit. They would be without communication until within about 300,000 miles from Earth. At that distance, the short-range antenna could start working for two-way communication.

Their real worry was the propulsion system. Even with their luck on the food inventory, it would mean nothing if they couldn't get the high-tech MM10 motors up and working. These brand new magneto-plasma dynamic rocket motors were the whole secret to this mission, giving them a constant push for the next 60 million miles. If all went well, they would be home in two months' time. The return voyage was not as simple as the arrival voyage, leading to the extended timeline.

Before kick-starting the return trip, the Little Turtle's flight controls ran a series of system tests. The news was not promising.

First, the small booster rocket that would accelerate them out of Mars orbit and into a home-bound trajectory was reporting that it only had enough fuel for seventy five percent the required burn time.

Lastly, half of the miraculous MM10 rocket motors were not responding to the system tests at all. If the remaining half could be relied upon, that meant a voyage home that would take five to six months. These engines had not been tested to run continuously for that long. Adam and Yeva would be that test.

Adam realized that they faced, at minimum, a four month trip in very uncomfortable conditions. Systems would begin failing due to condensation among other things.

During a quiet moment, Adam realized that his hands were shaking.

"Yeva, my hands and feet are going numb. I'm shaking uncontrollably."

Yeva stopped checking the environmental controls panel and floated over to Adam.

"The air temperature is normal. You should be fine," she assured him.

"We have a four-month trip ahead of us and I'm not sure if we'll make it."

Yeva wiped the sweat from her forehead.

"Adam, I think what you are experiencing is an anxiety attack."

"No way," he laughed with a rigid smile. "I've never had one."

Yeva smiled.

"Well, you've never been trapped in a tin can sixty million miles from home facing an inevitable series of system failures and certain death."

Adam stared at Yeva as if he'd just been hit with a frying pan.

"Good point," he said.

Yeva pushed herself over to the personal storage bin of their former fellow astronaut, Keller Murch. She dug around in there and pulled out a pill bottle. She moved her head back so she could read the small print.

"How much do you weigh?" Yeva asked.

"What?"

"Forget it, I'll just guess."

Yeva dug her fingers into the bottle, took a pill from it and floated over to Adam along with a bag of water.

"Here, we will test my theory. Take this pill. Here's some water," Yeva explained like a nurse.

"What is it?" Adam asked.

"It's from Doctor Feelgood," Yeva laughed. "That is the American song, right?"

Adam nodded his head.

"How much of a supply did Keller have?" Adam asked.

"That's up to you. If you take it continuously, maybe two weeks. However, much longer if you just take it on an as-needed basis," Yeva said. "For both of our sakes, I recommend taking it sparingly."

Within a few minutes, Adam stopped shaking.

The astronauts had postponed the MM10 ignition phase until they could ascertain the damage to their systems. With that complete, it was time to leave Mars orbit.

Adam started up the navigation program to return home. It went through the bit checks on all of the propulsion systems. The screen blinked, awaiting confirmation from the navigation engineer. In this case, that was Adam.

He initiated the Mars-to-Earth trajectory injection process. What fuel remained in the traditional rockets was fed to the engines to get the Little Turtle up to the escape velocity.

The acceleration was palpable. A shower of rain fell from every metal beam and raced through the floor grates, pooling in one main area. During the trip, Yeva would find herself scooping the water up and putting it into reservoir bags. It would be a tedious process, but would be necessary to keep some modicum of control on the humidity.

After a tumultuous visit to the Red Planet, the Little Turtle finally left the orbit of Mars. The remaining Murch rocket motors powered on. With their gentle push activated, both crew members slowly floated down to the wall that would now be designated as the floor.

Adam looked over at Yeva.

"With any luck, the next stop is Earth."

"And a nice gentle stop, I hope," Yeva said. "I am glad we are going home."

Adam looked away to glance at the navigation computer. Yeva winced and grabbed the right side of her abdomen.

CHAPTER 10

Alston family home
Fort Worth, Texas

"When is Daddy coming home?" Catie asked. She followed her mom who paced back and forth in the kitchen.

"Please, sweetheart, stop following me like that. You're making me nervous," Connie said sternly.

A muffled ringing sound emanated from the living room. It was the first time she'd heard her cellphone ring since arriving home from Houston the previous month. Connie ran into the room screaming, "We've got signal! We've got signal!"

She rummaged through her purse and pulled out the cellphone. The call was from Chris Tankovitch. Connie pushed the Answer button.

"Hello!" she screamed into the telephone.

"Connie? This is Chris."

She breathed a sigh of relief.

"Chris, please, tell me you've heard from my husband."

Chris paused a little too long.

"Not yet, Connie, but we're trying to get our systems back online."

"Same here, we haven't had power in a month," she lamented. "My neighbor has a generator that we're using to charge up the cellphone, but the towers have been dead until, I guess, right now!"

Connie suddenly noticed that both of her children were standing next to her, looking up, forlornly, hoping the phone call was about their daddy.

"Hold on, Chris."

Connie wandered out through the back door and into the yard to get some privacy. The kids tried to follow her, but she shooed them back in and closed the door.

"Look Connie, the International Space Station is dead. We can't use the high-bandwidth antenna on it anymore. In fact, the damn thing is probably going to re-enter the atmosphere sometime in the next month or so."

Connie wandered off the patio and into the grass, the phone plastered to her head.

"Okay, but there must be another way to talk to them, right?"

"Connie, we're working on it. The infrastructure here at NASA Johnson has been devastated. We don't know how long it will take to fix everything. For the sake of the Mars crew, we're considering moving all of our remaining resources north immediately — closer to you in fact."

"Just tell me I'll hear from my husband again. Tell me that my kids will see their Daddy again."

Silence.

"Connie. I am your friend and I won't lie to you. If they followed protocol, they likely left Mars and are heading home

70

right now. When we get a line of communication up and working, we'll try to contact them. As of right now, there's no reason to believe they are in harm's way. If we can't re-establish communication, well, that's a bridge we'll cross when we get to it. We're doing everything we can."

"Okay, Chris, I trust you. But I need you to keep me informed."

"I'll call you every week, okay? Now how are the kids holding up."

"Well, they want to see their dad badly. We miss him so much right now. We're not getting much news. It's just, well, scary. Some radio stations are back up. One of the guys at church is a ham radio operator and he's getting some scary information about Europe and China."

"I know, Connie. Call me if you want to talk, okay? It's a terrible time right now – let me be a shoulder for you to lean on."

After his last words, Connie heard him cover the phone and mumble something to somebody nearby. Then he got back on the phone.

"I was just reminded, I'm driving up to DC next week to get grilled by Congress. They're meeting at some temporary facility west of DC from now on until they clean up the damage there. Mind if I stop by your house on the way?"

"Sure, Chris. It'd be good to see a familiar face from NASA."

"Okay, see you then. Hang in there, kiddo."

Connie turned off her phone to save power. She sat down on one of the kids swings and swung back and forth using one foot, all the while crying quietly to herself.

The next week arrived with Chris driving into Fort Worth in his black Ford land-yacht. He stopped by the Alston house, but Connie wasn't there. He left a note on the door to let her know that she wasn't all alone – she had a friend.

Chris left her house and drove to the west side of town to inspect a dormant fighter aircraft factory. NASA was considering it for the new Manned Spaceflight Center while Houston was rebuilding. The facility was huge with a lot of manufacturing space and a lot of cube farms for engineers.

After finishing the tour, Chris stood under the American flag outside the front lobby and shook the facility manager's hand. "Expect a call from my Houston counterpart tomorrow. We'd like to start moving people and equipment up here as soon as possible."

"Sure thing, Mr. Tankovitch," the manager said, clearly happy to finally have a tenant.

Chris's next planned stop was Washington, DC. He eased his giant sedan out of the parking lot.

What really caught his eye was the oddly placed mesa just west of town. Perched on top was a gated community with some of the largest homes he'd ever seen – the grand structures on the mesa-like hill reminded him of Mount Olympus. These homes were meant to be seen, the *polar opposite* of inconspicuous.

As Chris began his long drive to Washington DC, he got one final glimpse at the mesa in his rear-view mirror.

Some day, he thought to himself. *Some day.*

CHAPTER 11

Interstate 81
Rural Virginia

In his youth, Chris always dreamed of a rag-tag driving adventure across America. This wasn't it, but he was trying to make it memorable by taking the scenic route – that meant avoiding all the cities that had been bombed. It'd been two days since he left Texas and so far he'd made it to the rural parts of western Virginia. He was scheduled to testify in front of Congress tomorrow. His large Ford sedan cruised along the nearly empty roads.

The cellphone reception was very spotty, with substations just recently coming back online in the big cities. The constant roaming kept killing his battery, so he kept it plugged into the charger during the entire drive. However, here in the middle of nowhere, a call made its way through.

The familiar old-time phone ringtone screamed out. He looked down, hoping to see a call from Connie. He didn't recognize the number.

Chris picked up the phone.

"Hello?"

"Yes, is this Mr. Tankovitch?" asked the friendly woman at the other end of the line.

"Well... that depends," Chris said with a grimace.

"This is the switchboard operator at the new White House. I have a call from President Jennings."

"Oh, then yes, this is Chris Tankovitch."

"Please hold."

Chris heard saxophone music playing. It was intermittently hit with static. His phone was losing bars. As he made it around a particularly tall mountain, his bars rose again.

"Chris?" a gruff voice asked.

"Yes, Mr. President, this is Chris."

"Great. Long time no talk."

"It's only been two days, sir."

"Whatever. Look, we need to talk before you get in front of Congress tomorrow."

"I'm all ears, DJ."

Silence followed as the president showed his disdain for the nickname they used when both attended college together in the late 1980's.

"We've talked about using that nickname..."

Chris cut him off.

"Look, we're far beyond niceties now, DJ. What are you calling about?"

"I've decided to fire you. I know we're old college friends, so it's nothing personal. The surviving media is on a witch hunt and I need to throw them a bone and," he paused.

"Chris, you are the bone."

"I don't underst...," Chris trailed off.

"Anyway, I wanted you to know about it before you got here to DC. Where are you anyways?"

"I'm in western Virginia," Chris said, his mind entering a state of numbness.

The president covered the phone and mumbled something to somebody nearby. Then he uncovered it.

"Okay, whatever. There is one more thing. You've been a good public servant. I don't want you to lose your federal employee benefits."

He took a deep breath and continued, "I've talked with your replacement..."

"Wait, what? Who's my replacement?" Chris asked with an angry tone.

"Forget about that, you'll find out when the press release goes out this afternoon." The president sounded irritated now, "Like I was saying, I spoke with your replacement and he has a job for you lined up in Fort Worth at the new Manned Spaceflight Center – that's a go, by the way, we've just approved funding for the new center there."

Chris saw his dignity flushing down the toilet. However, he was somewhat relieved that he'd still be working in the astronautics division.

"Full benefits?" Chris asked.

"Retirement, vacation and most importantly health insurance. We'll take care of you, you know, *if you take care of us* during the Congressional testimony."

"You want me to lie?"

"No, I want you to tell the truth. You know... *my* truth."

Chris rolled his eyes.

"Full benefits?" Chris asked again.

"Yes. *Full*," the president confirmed.

Chris thought about his options.

"I'll see what I can do."

Chris ended the call and exited at the nearest off-ramp. He pulled into the gravel parking lot of a roadside diner, bypassing the boarded-up McDonalds. The large food chains hadn't recovered yet due to the total loss of communications which upset their logistics. Chris pulled into the gravel parking lot and walked into a dark diner.

"Be right with ya!" a woman's voice yelled from the kitchen.

"You got power?" Chris asked, standing just inside.

"Sure do, hon. We got the lights off to save the generator."

Chris walked to the first booth and sat down slowly. His knees creaked and popped. Clanking dishes and gushing water sounds emanated from the kitchen. An older woman came through the spring-loaded door. Her hair was pulled back in a bun. She pulled out her order pad, pen, and then formed an on-demand smile.

"Whatcha drinking, darlin'?" she asked.

"I'll have a Coke," he said too quickly. "Wait, make that a beer. I just got fired and I want to celebrate."

"Just got fired?" she said with a chuckle. "Well, that is something special, now, ain't it? Honey, this one's on me."

CHAPTER 12

January of 1967 turned out to be an eventful month for America. Ronald Reagan became governor of California. The Doors released their debut album. And three weeks later, tragedy struck America's space program, killing three beloved astronauts during a launchpad test for the new Apollo program.

On the same day as the launchpad tragedy, the United States, the United Kingdom, and the Soviet Union entered into an international agreement called the Outer Space Treaty. It outlawed the placement of nuclear weapons in space. Today, nobody remembers or cares about the treaty, but that's what America was worried about in 1967.

Some five decades later when the Mars mission was being rammed through Congress, President Daggett Jennings grabbed thirty billion dollars from the Department of Defense to fund the rushed mission. And he completely violated the Outer Space Treaty.

In return for giving up some of their budget, the Air Force asked for a favor. They wanted a top-secret container box to be added on the outside of the module they would attach permanently to the International Space Station for Mars mission support. The president, always looking for a political edge, suggested that the Air Force put modified B-61 nuclear bombs in the box, converted to become guided rockets. It was a good theory and would only be revealed in a dire political standoff between America and some foe. It was the ultimate Ace up our political sleeve that would probably never be used.

But then it was used.

All of these facts came to light eight weeks after the truncated nuclear war, dubbed by the media as "World War 2.5". Much to the chagrin of anybody who understood Roman numerals, it was often written as "WWII.V".

Somebody was going to answer for this worldwide disaster. Congress decided they should take the upper hand and start throwing blame around. A large concert hall in Reston, Virginia, just west of Washington D.C., had been commandeered as the impromptu Capitol Hill building replacement. Sitting at the big oak desk in front of key senators was the freshly *former* head of NASA, Chris Tankovitch.

He was ready for his close-up.

"Mr. Tankovitch, it is my understanding that you played a key role in the *foolishly* quick development of the Mars space craft, the so called," the Senator looked down at his paperwork and read slowly, "Big Turtle and Little Turtle as well as the Storage Wart? Is that true?"

"Yes, senator," Chris answered dryly.

Chris knew the mission was too quick and dangerous and he'd likely be thrown under the bus if anything happened. Today he was firmly wedged under the bus tires. These senators were going to back the bus up and run over him again.

"Can you explain to me why we placed nuclear missiles on a Space Station co-developed by our Russian friends?"

Chris looked down to gather his thoughts. *Be careful*, he told himself, *they want you to hang yourself.*

"Well, that's a good question. Let me explain some misconceptions. We sent two spacecraft to Mars. The first was the main science and living quarters – we called it the Big Turtle."

"Yes, we know all about that," the senator admonished.

"Now, you asked me a question and I will be complete," Chris shot back. "The second spacecraft was for taking the astronauts *from* the International Space Station, or ISS, all the way to Mars and back. Okay? We couldn't launch those two vehicles up to the ISS fully loaded. It was too much weight. So ahead of time, we sent up what y'all are calling the *Storage Wart*."

"Yes, again, I think we've already established this fact."

"That so-called Storage Wart was a large module that was permanently attached to the end of the International Space Station. Think of it as the extra freezer that you all have in your garage. Using several supply flights, we packed it with food and water and fuel — you name it. Once the Turtles were in Earth orbit, we transferred all of those items from the Storage Wart to the Turtles and then sent the astronauts on their merry way to Mars. The Storage Wart was a vital part of this mission."

Chris paused and drank some water. His hand shook from nerves. He could hear and see the senators mumbling to each other.

"Nobody is questioning how vital the Storage Wart was to the mission—," the senator said with fake concern.

Chris cut him off to answer. "What you need to know is that a short time before the Storage Wart was to be launched up to the ISS atop a Whittenberg Space Launch System rocket, the president notified me that the *Air Force* was adding an additional storage container to the outside of it. I personally was not aware of the contents of that container. He said it contained some type of military hardware which I assumed was a radar or surveillance equipment."

"And that was not the case?"

"No sir," Chris answered.

The senators' shock looked real. Almost.

"Mr. Tankovitch, did the president know what was inside that container?"

Chris paused to think.

About his retirement.

About his job.

About his life.

"I *doubt* that President Jennings knew what was inside the container," Chris said with utmost care.

The senators looked at each other, covering the microphones to talk privately with their neighbors. They spun back around.

The lead senator uncovered his microphone.

"Mr. Tankovitch, can you tell us what was in that storage box?"

Chris turned to see the other senators staring at him with laser beam focus. Many of them were personally involved in these clandestine design contract changes, but none would own up to it now.

They're making sure I hang alone, Chris thought.

"Well, the box contained eight modified nuclear missiles. Through an unfortunate hardware failure of some kind, they launched prematurely."

"Hardware failure?" the senator asked incredulously.

"Look, designing the Mars space craft in less than a year required some shortcuts, okay? After reviewing the error logs and talking with the surviving ISS crew, we believe that there was probably some wire chaffing on the missile launch hardware. Probably some electrical shorts that ultimately triggered the launch mechanisms on the missile ejectors. They were all pushed out of the box and their hardwired targeting systems were engaged. They all headed to targets in Russia."

"But don't nuclear missiles have safety locks to prevent accidental detonations?" the senator asked with maximum smug.

"Normally, yes," Chris confirmed. "These were sent up with some of those safeties disabled."

A mumbling roar came from the senators.

"And why would you ever do that?"

Chris looked offended.

"Well, *I did not do that*, Senator. I suspect that the Air Force did that to prepare for a 'last-man-standing scenario'. That's to prepare for the situation where launch communications from ground-based facilities are cut off and an astronaut would have to give the final launch command."

"That seems, well, just stupid if you ask me."

"Well that wasn't up to me," Chris answered quickly. "And perhaps, given the situation, it wasn't so stupid."

Chris looked down at the desk to avoid the stares.

"Mr. Tankovitch, when the Russians launched retaliatory missiles, they devastated sixteen of our cities, Washington DC, New York and Houston being the worst hit. Their CommKno..." the Senator quickly halted himself, realizing that the name *CommKnock* was top-secret. "Their *missiles* took out every communications and power grid on this continent. My office hasn't had air conditioning for eight weeks!"

"That is a tragedy... no human should be without AC," Chris said while the visitors in the audience laughed.

"Your little hardware glitch caused the death of over fifty thousand American lives!" the senator yelled, pounding his fist on the table.

Chris looked up from the table and calmly added, "And one hundred thousand Russian souls. Our retaliatory missiles caused the same devastation to Russia and most of Asia. I haven't forgotten any of that."

"What did you say?" the angered senator asked.

"In the end, a hundred thousand Russians died as well as fifty thousand Americans. Cancer rates have also spiked, which can only be due to the fallout. President Jennings was able to call the Russian president in time to let him know it was a mistake. But not before hundreds of their missiles had landed and thousands of bomblets had taken out our main communication hubs and most of our power plants."

"Thank you for that history lesson," the senator quipped as the room full of elected officials laughed.

"My pleasure, Senator," the recently fired NASA director answered.

"I do have one more question for you, Mr. Tankovitch. It's come to our attention that we may not have sent our very best astronauts to Mars. Why is that?"

Chris rolled his eyes in contempt.

"I assure you that the astronauts we sent were qualified and went through a vetting process," Chris explained. "What you are referring to is the fact that the first two teams we offered the mission decided against it. They had safety concerns."

"Because of the atomic bombs on the outside of the International Space Station?"

Chris sighed.

"No, didn't we already establish that nobody outside of the Air Force knew about the missiles?" Chris asked sarcastically. "Their safety concerns had to do with the fact that the spacecraft were being built so quickly. I assure you that the spacecraft themselves were safe. However, the astronauts had to make a personal safety decision."

"Fair enough. Can you tell us the status of our 'C-Team' crew on Mars?"

"No, sir, I cannot. As I'm sure you know, we still have not re-established communication with them. If all went well, though, they should be on their way home right now."

The senators leaned toward each other and whispered for a good long minute.

"Thank you, Mr. Tankovitch. I pass control to the senator from Oklahoma. He will be the last one speaking with you today."

"Hello, Mr. Tankovitch. Thank you for coming up here.

Um, my understanding is that you are no longer the NASA administrator?" the senator asked , just to dig it in publicly.

"That is correct, as of yesterday. The president felt that NASA would be better served right now with some fresh talent."

The Senator looked down over his glasses to read his paperwork.

"Yes, well we appreciate all that you did, sending us to Mars in less than a year," the Senator said. "I see your replacement is Mr. Howard Kelty? Have you worked with him before ?"

Chris leaned into the microphone.

"No comment."

Hours later, during his walk of shame out of the auditorium, Chris's phone dinged to indicate a text message. It was from the president: "Good job today Chris. You followed orders well. I'm still president and you've still got your retirement fund. Go back to Fort Worth."

CHAPTER 13

Whenever disaster strikes around the world, America is one of the first nations to offer up people and other resources to help. It sends canine search teams to earthquake stricken nations. It sends medical ships to the shores of areas hit by plagues. But when a disaster strikes America, it becomes fiercely independent from the world, effectively giving the middle finger to any nation that wants to send help to the former colonies. Like a toddler, *America wants to fix itself despite the worlds offer of assistance.* That may not be the right thing to do, but that's what America does.

In the case of World War II.V (sic), all of that went out the window. Every nation was laid flat regarding electricity and communication resources. In just the US alone, nearly two dozen downtown city centers were devastated by the few missiles that were traditional nukes and *not* the more humane CommKnock warheads. For expediency, the states called out the National Guard and those city centers were being covered by layers of fill dirt and rubble to keep down the radioactive dust and debris. Unfortunately, it was too late for most people. Within just weeks of the attack, doctors started reporting skyrocketing cases of patients with complicated bronchial problems — ultimately proven to be lung cancer.

In the Midwest, a hastily assembled conference of oncologists put their handwritten data together to show that lung cancer cases were up 2,600% in just the first four weeks following the attack.

The living conditions were improving thanks to the recovery efforts, but the prognosis was falling. With many hospital resource chains still in shambles, a black market developed for the existing chemo stockpiles.

For those outside of city centers, life was strange, but without the devastation. Electricity came from generators. Cell networks were off and on as regional networks were being repaired.

Construction workers were being sucked away from the suburbs to cover the downtowns with thick layers of dirt. A risky job that paid well, in cash. Certainly, there were more effective ways of handling the radioactive debris that had settled down, but "any port in a storm" was the current mantra.

The real test of recovery willpower hadn't arrived yet. Television was still out, but it was only days away. With a presidential election coming, politicians thought that would be just the thing to make people feel normal again. While downtowns were being covered with a layer of dirt icing, thousands of electrical workers were getting the power grid to a more reliable state and trying to get TV turned back on.

Houston seemed to be the city with the most damage. There were rumors that two missiles had actually hit the downtown area, but that had yet to be proven true. The Federal Emergency Management Administration had freed up the money and manpower to start the recovery planning. They estimated it would be two years before people could safely return to anywhere within a five-mile radius of downtown.

For the core of the downtown area, engineers felt that a thick layer of dirt wouldn't be enough for Houston. Instead, thick layers of concrete, rock debris and old asphalt were being considered. However, the area was still highly toxic with radioactivity and anybody visiting the area had to wear special suits. Even then, they would only visit for just an hour a day. After a month of those daily exposures, they couldn't come back. Ever.

Now back to the people helping people issue. The same chain of events follows every natural (and unnatural) disaster. Everybody offers help. Massive help. More help than a community can absorb. Mountains of donated teddy bears show up. Storage facilities bulge with bottled water and cans of food that nobody particularly likes. Old clothes with small, but unacceptable holes and tears come rolling in by the truckload. But then the help wanes. Even before recovery is complete, interest fizzles in fits and bursts. Eventually it isn't on the radio broadcasts every single night. In the end, the victims are left wondering what they're going to do with forty-five tons of canned beets and a thousand gallons of Red Bull.

The power came back on fulltime in most American

cities just before the presidential election – all cities were electrified again after just two more weeks. It took a gargantuan effort by the utility crews. As more and more regions came back online, those utility crews hooked up their trailers and hauled themselves to regions that needed help. It was truly a sight to see this particular sector of society come together to get it done.

President Daggett Jennings and his running mate, the likable Beatrice Bexar, did minimal campaigning, mostly via bus. They put out only radio advertising. The opposition candidate, Mike Riley, did almost no campaigning – running against a wartime recovery president has been historically pointless. Mud-slinging politics ceased as it would only look like he was attacking a sitting president while the man was working hard to recover the nation. In fact, the re-election of President Jennings was almost inevitable. At this point, he could have snorted cocaine while touring a daycare center *and still won the election.* Americans loved the guy.

Two days before the election, TV came back on like a clap of thunder. Prior to that moment, people walked around their neighborhoods at night talking and socializing with the folks in their front lawns. And like the flip of a switch, every living room window in America regained that flittering blue glow. The people disappeared from their yards. The relationships with their neighbors fizzled. They threw out their fifty pounds of canned beets and ten gallons of Red Bull. The best of life returned and so did the worst.

CHAPTER 14

Alston family home
Fort Worth, Texas

(Mid-November)

"Don't be a wimp, General. Just get me some nukes on the Space Station," a crackly voice on the television said.

Rewind.

"Don't be a wimp, General. Just get me some nukes on the Space Station," the voice repeated.

Connie leaned back into the couch, one hand holding the remote control and the other covering her mouth in disgust.

"Mommy, what does he mean?"

"Quiet, Cody!" she said automatically. "They're explaining it."

The TV screen showed a news reporter holding his earpiece tightly to his ear, receiving an update of some sort.

He looked up into the camera.

"Ladies and gentlemen," he said with a look of shock. "This is an incredible breaking news story. We've just learned that a whistleblower at the top of the US Air Force has released a secretly recorded message of a conversation he had with the president. Apparently, almost a year ago."

The reporter paused to hear more information. "Okay, we're just getting this in. The tape you just heard is that of the president demanding that the Air Force break the Outer Space Treaty of 1967 and put nuclear weapons on the International Space Station. We're switching to a remote reporter who wants to introduce us to somebody."

Connie wanted to scream.

Daggett Jennings, what have you done, she thought. *So many people died and my husband was abandoned on Mars, all because you made a damned fool decision to put nuclear bombs on the Space Station?*

Both hands were now pulling at her own hair while tears streamed down her cheeks.

For months the media had hounded the Air Force to find out who gave authorization to include the clandestine cabinet on the outside of the ISS Storage Wart. They'd focused in on two possible culprits. Neither of them were standing next to the reporter on the TV screen. It was a military person whom no reporter had ever heard of.

The mystery man wore an ironed military suit and stared calmly into the camera.

"General Richard Alan Fenton," the reporter stated with the authority of a mother calling out her child. "You are now being called a whistleblower. You're a 32-year veteran of the Air Force. You've been awarded several times for your secret

90

night-time flights over the Middle East during all of the US actions in the 1990's and early 2000's."

The general nodded in agreement with all of those statements. The reporter continued.

"General Fenton, the presidential election was not long ago. President Jennings won an overwhelming majority. He was even credited for his strong response as a so-called war-time president. Why are you *just now* releasing this damning evidence?"

The general stood next to the reporter, his hands dropped to his side. He looked up at the camera again.

"As a member of the US military, I have to support my commander in chief at all times. I didn't want this to seem politically motivated. However, the media was hounding my superiors for a scapegoat. My commander was about to take the blame for putting the missiles on the space station and tell the media that he was responsible. But he was not responsible. He was asked by the president to do it. I was there when it happened."

The reporter looked at his notes.

"How did this recorded conversation come to be?"

"About a year ago, I was called into a special meeting with my superiors. That meeting included the president. It was about shifting budget away from DOD projects," the general paused. "That's *Department of Defense.*"

"Yes, we know what DOD means. Go on," the reporter assured him.

"Anyhow, they needed to shift money away from the DOD projects and into the Mars Mission. The president suggested that we assuage the DOD's concerns by putting some tactical small-scale nukes on the outside of the ISS module that was being built. You know, *killing two birds with one stone*, so to speak. The module was almost done, so this was a last minute addition."

"Well what were the *other* options?" the reporter asked.

"Good question. We considered putting in some satellite relay packages or perhaps some information gathering hardware."

"Spy technology?"

"Yes, well, call it what you want."

"But instead you put," the reporter looked at his notes. "Eight B-61 thermonuclear bombs modified with rocket thrusters and guidance kits?"

"That's correct."

"You did this because the president wanted the nukes option?"

"No, the president *demanded* the nukes option. Later on in the recorded conversation, he threatens to cancel many of our black-budget programs if we don't give him nukes on the ISS."

"How did you happen to be recording this conversation? Is that normal protocol?"

"No, sir. This was actually the third meeting we'd had with the president. I felt his decision was so reckless that I'd obtained a recording device as a way to, well, protect myself and my superiors in case anything went wrong."

The reporter flipped through his notes, stopping at a page about Chris Tankovitch's witness appearance in Congress.

"In the hearings before Congress, the former NASA administrator Chris Tankovitch mentioned something about the arming mechanisms?"

"Yes, they were sent up to the ISS partially armed just in case."

"Just in case what?"

"Just in case there was a data communication failure. Somebody on the ISS would be able to trigger the last remaining launch protocols."

"But we had a total communication failure, not just data," the savvy reporter said.

"That's right."

"But they *still* launched," the reporter stated. "And tens of thousands of innocent Americans died because of our president?"

"Yes. Unfortunately, that is true. And more continue to get sick."

The TV image switched back to the news anchor sitting in the studio. He was on the phone and quickly put it down when he saw himself on the live-feed camera again.

"Hang on there, guys — General Fenton, pardon me. I've just found out that the president is about to have a press conference. General, will you stay with us?"

"Yes, of course," the general said.

Connie continued to watch the TV with unbreakable attention. Cody sat next to her on the couch. He didn't understand what was being said, but he knew it was serious.

The glowing image on her screen switched over to a hastily assembled press conference in the new White House media room. The president's press secretary was speaking, but the audio wasn't working. The press secretary stepped away. A few seconds later, the president of the United States of America walked up to the podium. He jumped right into his statement.

"My fellow Americans," he paused and leaned toward somebody to the side. "Is the audio working now, guys?"

"Yes, Mr. President," came a chorus of voices from the press corps.

"Okay, everybody just sit down. As many of you already know, our nation, and the world for that matter, experienced a terrible tragedy a few months ago that will take years to recover from. Some families never will. I want you to know that I made decisions that, well, some might call *reckless*," he said, using a word that the general had used. The president took a drink of water.

"But, reckless is the wrong word. I made these decisions to help plan for the long-term safety of our nation - to have an Ace up our sleeve in case our enemies ever tried to hold our feet to the fire."

The press corps erupted with questions.

"Hang on, folks, I'll get to your questions in a minute," he assured them. "Last week the American people re-elected myself and my Vice-President Beatrice Bexar. They voted with their feet by going to the polls. They liked what we were doing. They liked what we had done. Especially the recovery efforts from the nuclear attack. They wanted four more years. Well, this latest revelation throws a wrench into the works, I admit."

"But you knew the truth all along, Mr. President?" yelled reporters.

The president held his palms up to calm them down. He stared at the top of the lectern, deep in thought about his next words.

"I want you to know that Ms. Bexar will make a great President."

The room suddenly got quiet.

"She has worked tirelessly for this nation. As a middle-of-the-road populist, she has always fought for the middle class and she doesn't have a mean bone in her body. More importantly, she had no part in this whole bomb misunderstanding."

The sound of silence was overwhelming.

The TV viewers at home heard a muffled *I think he's resigning* from one of the on-air reporters.

The press room filled with whispered conversations.

"President Jennings! Are you resigning?" a reporter yelled from the front of the room.

"I'm getting to that," President Jennings said as he took a long drink of water, savoring it.

He had an uneasy smile. The room grew quiet.

"You may have noticed a familiar face sitting over on the side of the stage today. I'd like to introduce Robert Donaher, the United States Secretary of State," the president said, pointing to an older gentleman in a dark suit holding his arms crossed. "Mr. Donaher, could you please join me here at the lectern?"

Mr. Donaher eased out of the chair and walked over to the president. They shook hands like old friends and Mr. Donaher took his place, standing next to President Jennings.

"Thank you, Secretary Donaher," the president said with a smile before turning back to the crowd of journalists. "I have done everything I could to make this nation better and safer. A lot of accusations are going around today, but even if I *did* approve putting nuclear weapons in space, unknowingly endangering the crew, well, I did it to maintain our military advantage. The last thing I want is a fair fight.

As your president, I have done many good things — among them, I want you to remember that I sent humans to Mars and led this country through the aftermath of a small scale atomic war."

"Yes, but Mr. President, you caused the war!" a reporter yelled.

The president bit his tongue and pointed his finger at that reporter.

"You guys used to love me," the president said, his eyes welling up with fake tears. "Didn't you? You loved me. What fickle friends you all are. You people, this press corps, you're nothing but a viper's nest and I refuse to let you use me as a punching bag. I have done nothing wrong. Absolutely nothing."

"A nuclear war is *not* nothing!" a voice yelled from the back of the room.

The president leaned down to the microphone and squinted his eyes to see the back of the room.

"Who said that?" the president ask angrily. "I demand to know who said that!"

The rest of the press corps was silent. Only coughs and pen clicks could be heard.

"I guess there's not a single Spartacus among you all. I suppose my next step will satisfy your bloodlust."

The president closed his eyes and reached into the breast pocket of his suit. He reluctantly grabbed something that had the weight of his lifetime in it. He pulled out a letter and handed it to Secretary of State Donaher.

"With this letter, I hereby resign as president of the United States — effective immediately."

The press room erupted into chaos.

Among the noise, President Jennings shook Mr. Donaher's hand again and then walked over to his press secretary to shake his hand, too. The press secretary, looking shell-shocked and freshly unemployed, refused to shake the president's hand. The photographers went wild — a guaranteed front page photo opportunity.

The president looked bewildered as he turned toward the journalists in the room. He was blinded by all of the flashes.

"I have one last message to the press corps. This one is very sincere."

"Speak louder!" yelled the reporters, noting that the president was no longer near a microphone.

"I said," the president yelled, "I have one last message for the press corps."

He raised both hands high above his head, giving the middle finger to the reporters in the room. He continuously thrusted his hands in the air, making sure that every reporter saw it.

Back in Fort Worth, Connie leaped for the remote control and smashed down the power button. The TV turned off.

"Mommy, what was the president doing?"

"He was demonstrating a new way to say goodbye."

"Oh, can I do that, too?"

"No, no, no," Connie said. "That's only for presidents."

"Okay," Cody agreed.

"Let's go play outside," she said.

Television cameras followed the former president as he walked across the lawn from the press room toward a waiting helicopter. A marine saluted him as he boarded the aircraft. The former president went straight to the pilot.

"Get me the hell out of here."

"Sir, the control tower at Andrews Air Force Base told us they are seeing reports of wind shear — all incoming flights are being delayed thirty minutes."

"I can't wait that long," the president said. "Get us up in the air, pronto."

"Sir, it's not safe right now. We recommend you take the limo to Andrews."

"You want me to walk out of this helicopter in front of all those bloodthirsty reporters and do a perp walk across the lawn to the limo? The press would have a field day with that. I command you to fly me to Andrews Air Force Base."

The pilot shook his head.

"Frankly, you are no longer the president and, unless getting you to Andrews is a national emergency, I cannot risk the safety of this aircraft and its crew just because you want to fly."

The president leaned down to the pilot and his copilot.

"Young man, I'll beg if I have to... please give me the dignity of one last flight."

The pilot looked at the co-pilot. They exchanged a look that said they realized how dangerous it would be. They shouldn't go. It's not safe. However, former President Jennings was still their boss in spirit — at least until they dropped him off at Andrews Air Force Base.

"Please take a seat," the pilot said.

The president went back and sat down.

The pilot advanced the throttle on the engine and lifted up on the collective pitch handle. The aircraft slowly ascended into the sky.

"Andrews tower, this is Marine Two, we are inbound with golden cargo," the pilot said.

"Negative, Marine Two, do not approach. Still getting reports of micro-burst wind shears."

"Roger that, Tower, if there is no other traffic, we'd like to make approach."

"Marine Two, no other traffic in vicinity, but the shears are strong. Can you wait thirty minutes?"

"Negative, Andrews," the pilot said, looking at his copilot. "It's... an emergency."

The pilot turned around to look at the former president who stared back at the pilot and said, "Let's get this show on the road already. Come on!"

"Andrews tower, we are inbound with golden cargo."

Having shut off the TV, Connie and the kids played happily in the back yard. Had they been watching the news, they would've seen the chaos in the press room after the president resigned. They would've seen Vice President Bexar being whisked away from the National Library Association's yearly lunch to be sworn in as president. They would've seen the initial reports of a helicopter accident just inside the property line of Andrews Air Force Base. They would've heard the news of the two marines and their passenger that all perished in the accident.

But Connie and the kids didn't hear that news. Instead, they played happily on the swingset until the last rays of sunset shone on their smiling faces.

CHAPTER 15

The president's office
New White House
Reston, Virginia

(One week later)

"Let me know when he answers," President Bexar spoke into her phone. She set the receiver down and spun in her chair to face out the window, just barely able to see the Pentagon far to the east from the new White House.

Her phone rang. She reached back and grabbed it.

"Hi, is this Chris Tankovitch?" she asked.

"Yes, Madam President. How can I help you?" a tinny sounding voice asked, obviously from a cellphone.

"Chris, I want you to know that I always liked you and what you did for the NASA and the Mars mission."

"Thank you, President Bexar."

"I've just fired Howard Kelty, the NASA director who President Jennings picked to replace you."

"In all honesty, he's as boorish as they come."

The president laughed at the elitist language that Chris used.

"That leaves me with a problem," the president said. "I need somebody I can trust to run NASA right now."

Chris had a sudden infusion of hope.

She's going to ask me to run NASA again, he thought.

"Obviously, I can't pick you," she said, crushing his hopes. "But who would you recommend to run NASA now? I trust your opinion."

Chris thought for a long moment. Everybody who had followed him up the chain of command at NASA had ultimately stabbed him in the back. Except for one person – she'd kept her opinions silent. At first Chris couldn't believe he was going to say it. He couldn't. He wouldn't. But finally, her name fell from his lips.

"Alexis," he said. "Tankovitch."

"But isn't she your..."

"Ex-wife, yes," he said uncomfortably. "She is, but she's also the best project manager I've ever seen in action. And she's one of the most executive members of the remaining team at NASA. She'll do a good job."

"Are you sure? Her main office will be down near you in Fort Worth."

Wow, he thought. Chris once told himself that he would never speak to her again. He would never lay eyes on her again. And yet, he just recommended her to run NASA. Sometimes the heart and the brain of a man don't always get the same memo.

"Madam President, you won't regret hiring her to run NASA."

But I might, Chris thought as the smile left his face.

CHAPTER 16

Alston family home
Fort Worth, Texas

(One month later)

"Any word, yet?" Connie asked. She paced around the kitchen island while talking on the phone and hobbling on her crutches.

On the other end of the line was Chris Tankovitch.

"No, nothing yet," he sighed. "We were able to power up the deep-space antenna complexes and we've made contact with the Odyssey satellite orbiting Mars, but, still, no signal from the crew on Mars. Hopefully they are midway through the return trip."

Connie let out a sigh of frustration.

"Okay. So, now that power is relatively reliable, I'm

going through with the back surgery. It was all paid for before the bombs hit and I'm ready for something to take my mind off my worries about Adam. The surgery is scheduled for Monday."

"Hang on," Chris said. He covered the phone to ask somebody nearby a question.

"Sorry about that. So who's watching the kids?" Chris asked.

"A good family friend named Libby is watching them. My Mom is going to take me to the hospital and basically take care of me for a week."

"Well, best of luck. I know Adam wanted you to have that surgery for a long time. And, I'll make you a deal. I promise if I hear anything about Adam or the crew, I'll give you a call immediately. Okay?"

"Thank you, Chris. Bye bye."

"Wait, Connie, I do have some news. NASA has decided to build a temporary base right there in Fort Worth. It will be the replacement for the NASA Johnson Space Center in Houston. They are going to call it the NASA *Jennings* Manned Spacecraft Center."

"Nice," Connie laughed. "Doesn't that seem like a poor choice for a name?"

"It serves as a memorial *and* a warning. But honestly I think it's more of a warning. Don't screw things up like ex-President Jennings or something like that," Chris said.

Connie was growing to like the updates. Chris was the only tangible connection she had right now with NASA and her missing husband. Whenever she called him for the news, it was partially for the update, but mostly it was to have an adult to talk to. He was a caring man whom she knew she could trust with her worries.

Monday morning came fast. Connie and her mom walked into the hospital in downtown Fort Worth at 7:00am. To prepare for surgery, Connie hadn't eaten since dinner the night before. That morning, her electricity had gone out again, but she'd long since switched to an old mechanical alarm clock. Close call avoided.

Connie waited nervously in the lobby. Every channel on the TV news reported about the rebuilding of Houston as well as DC and countless other foreign cities.

"Are you sure Libby can watch the kids today?" Connie asked.

Her mom patted her arm.

"Look, she's watched them many times. She's a very trustworthy neighbor."

"It's just that, well, I'm their only parent left... and," Connie trailed off.

Her mom kissed her on the forehead.

"You're going to be just fine. Trust me," she assured her daughter. "Adam will return. I promise. Now remember the time when you got ear tubes? You were so scared then and it turned out great."

"I was three years old, Mom. I don't remember."

"Well, I do!" her mom laughed.

Connie's leg was fidgeting up and down looking for a place of calmness.

The office door opened and a nurse walked into the lobby.

"Mrs. Alston?"

Connie raised her hand and limped over to the nurse. Connie looked back one more time at her mom, who waved back at her and said, "Go on, you'll be fine."

Connie put on the cold paper gown and laid down on the table. The nurses took blood samples, urine samples, and a pregnancy test. Connie gave the nurse a funny look at the pregnancy test.

"We must be *completely* certain," the nurse explained.

The room was quiet except for an annoying beep every few seconds. After a few minutes, a boisterous man dressed in a surgical gown came into the room. He picked up Connie's hand to comfort her.

"Hi, Dr. Sanders," Connie said sheepishly.

"Relax, Connie! This is going to be great. You'll throw away those crutches in a matter of weeks."

The doctor picked up the clipboard at the end of the bed and read through her medical stats.

"Uh huh, yep, yep. Looks good. I should probably sign your back with a Sharpie so I know which one to remove, right? Hahaha," the surgeon laughed heartily at his own joke. Then he walked out the door.

The room got very quiet again.

At 9:05am, another nurse walked in and put an IV into the back of Connie's hand. Once the IV was taped up, the nurse injected a syringe into IV tube.

"That's just to relax you," the nurse said. She smiled.

Connie felt suddenly relaxed. And sleepy.

"Hahaaaaa, nice," Connie said, melting into happiness.

The nurse put her hand on Connie's shoulder and said, "I thought you'd appreciate that."

Several orderlies came in and wheeled the bed out the door and down the hallway. They went into an operating room where everybody was dressed in full surgical gowns and masks. The surgeon's forearms were pointing up to keep them from touching anything.

"Connie, the anesthesiologist is going to put a mask on you right now and," the surgeon paused.

Another person in a surgical gown pressed a clear plastic mask onto Connie's face.

"Okay, I want you to count backwards from ten right now, okay?"

Connie's eyes slowly panned over toward the surgeon.

"Sure thing, Doc. Here we go. Ten, nine —"

Silence.

CHAPTER 17

Las Cruces, New Mexico

All year long the wind tumbles warm and dry through the town of Las Cruces – slowly blowing the topsoil east toward Texas. Nightly walks through the desert scrub reveal the lives squeezing out an existence in this desolate area. The gray blurs are jackrabbits with their freakishly large ears — skittering through the cacti and kicking up clouds of red dust. It's the type of environment that makes you crave ice cream back in town.

"What can I get for you?" the cashier asked. He tapped his foot impatiently, standing behind the register at the Wendy's restaurant.

"Just a Frosty," the old man said, never breaking his stare at the menu.

"Large?"

"What? No, just a small."

"Chocolate or vanilla?"

The man crinkled his brow, looking confused.

"Since when did you make vanilla Frosty's?"

"Probably since before I was born, sir," the cashier replied coldly.

"It's been a while since I was here. Let's go with choco..."

WOOMP.

The man's dairy desert order was interrupted by a loud sound. It was more of a feeling than a sound. The building shook as if it were hit by a giant rubber ball. The hubbub of conversation in the dining room halted and the customers looked outward at bright flashes — like lightning, but nonstop. One by one, the diners headed for the windows. The cashier hopped over the counter and opened the door to the outside.

A long spark-filled streak filled the sky – complete with glowing branches breaking off from the main trunk. It was high up and quiet at first, except for a few resounding woomps. Suddenly a grinding roar came from every direction, rattling the skulls of everybody watching. Hands jumped up to cover ears. The sound echoed off of every wall, cliff and canyon. Car alarms shouted in a rising crescendo.

The residents of Las Cruces were witnessing the rarest light show in human history. The disabled International Space Station had slowly but steadily slid out of orbit for months. As it inched closer to Earth, the miniscule amount of atmosphere that it rubbed against slowed it down a little bit more every day. Just as a slow irritation causes a pearl to form over time, the ISS continued to slow down and eventually fell toward Earth.

Hitting the bulk of the atmosphere now at seventeen

thousand miles per hour created enormous friction. As the largest manmade object in space, it provided an equally huge light show for the residents of New Mexico and western Texas this evening.

The old man stepped into the parking lot, wishing he had that Frosty to enjoy with the light show. He stared up with the wonderment of a child. Colorful lights reflected off his trifocals.

Now isn't that a doozy, he thought. *I gotta get back to Arizona.*

For humanity, it meant the end of a three-decade project and many billions of dollars of investment — now just a long streak of smoke in the sky. The loss of the ISS marked the end of any near-term chances for a return mission to Mars.

For the jackrabbits running around the desert that night, the strange lightshow was just a brief distraction from another night of not being killed.

CHAPTER 18

NASA Jennings Manned Spacecraft Center
Fort Worth, Texas

The new NASA Jennings Manned Spacecraft Center was officially opened in mid-January. The expedited timeframe was helped due to the fact that it was built on an existing Air Force base and airplane factory. The loss of the International Space Station provided an extra bit of impetus. It also helped that Fort Worth hadn't been bombed.

The facility was temporarily the new manned spacecraft center, replacing NASA Johnson until Houston got cleaned up — a process expected to take many more years. As is often the case, however, there is nothing more permanent than a temporary solution.

Chris drove along the road leading to the new center. He had the roof down on his old black Ford convertible and eventually pulled up to the security gate.

"Hello, Mr. Tankovitch," said the armed guard reaching for Chris's identification badge.

"Is the power on today?" Chris asked.

"Yes, sir. It's been on for 16 hours. So far so good."

"Excellent," Chris laughed. "That's a new record."

"I hope it stays on for good this time. Go on through."

The guard pushed a button and the stanchion posts sank down into the ground. Chris drove over them. He continued on for a quarter mile and turned left into an enormous parking lot – mostly empty. He maneuvered his heavy car into his personal parking spot, located in the middle of the vast sea of emptiness. Chris stepped out of the car and slammed the door closed – so far from the nearest car that the pained creakiness of his door generated no echo.

He manhandled the convertible top up and over the cabin, carefully attaching the front two clips to the windshield. He grabbed his briefcase and began the long trek across the acres of blacktop toward the guard shack.

Chris reached the air conditioned lobby a few minutes later and showed his badge to the guard sitting behind a stamped metal desk. The guard waved him through with a polite "Good morning, sir" and a head nod.

Chris continued down the long hallway.

And walked.

And walked.

And walked.

He passed by some whirring machinery. Finally, he turned into a small room that was outlined with several offices. A workman was standing at Chris's new office, squeegeeing some new words onto the glass in the door:

CHRISTOPHER TANKOVITCH

DIRECTOR OF...

The workman's shoulder blocked the rest.

He moved.

...VENDING & FOOD SERVICES

Not quite the same ring as NASA Administrator, Chris thought to himself. *But it sure beats nothing. And it has full medical and retirement benefits.*

Go me, Chris thought with blank defeat. He walked up to the workman.

"Thanks for the new sign. Please excuse me," Chris said as he opened the door and walked through.

"What happened to Mr. Gregg?" the workman asked. "He used to be in charge of all the vending machines."

"Well, he's on medical leave," Chris said with realistic compassion. "Mr. Gregg was in Houston during the bombs and he's developed lung cancer. I'm his temporary fill-in while he recovers."

"Okay. Mr. Gregg was a nice man," the workman said. He collected his tools and walked away.

Chris sat down and logged into his computer. He checked his email. Fourteen trouble tickets about broken vending machines in Building 4 alone. These were emails that came in from engineers complaining that the machine ate their 75 cents without dispensing any crackers or coffee. From the wording of the emails, the loss of their money was the worst thing in the world. As several emails stated, *there would be hell to pay.*

Several months earlier, Chris was running the show on the first manned mission to Mars – a thirty billion dollar endeavor. Now he was chasing down six bits of fraud.

I'm only one week into this job. Crap. Time for coffee,

he thought.

Chris stood up and walked out of his office to the vending room just outside the office cluster. A group of engineers were standing there having a lively discussion. As Chris approached, they all shut up.

Thanks infamy, he thought to himself.

"Hey fellas. How's it going?" Chris asked. He dropped some coins into the coffee vending machine. A cup dropped out and a brownish goo filled it.

The engineers averted their eyes, not wanting to speak to the pariah known as Chris Tankovitch.

One young man decided to fix the awkward silence.

"We're doing fine, Director Tankovitch."

Chris laughed.

"Thanks, but I'm no longer the head of NASA."

Chris tasted his coffee and grimaced.

The young engineer, egged on by his friends, added, "That was a shame. You were very good at what you did."

"Well, that's how it goes. A new president gets elected and his appointed underlings all get axed," Chris said.

Silence.

"So..... Chris," said the young man.

"Hey, I'm still *Mister* Tankovitch to you young pups," Chris corrected him.

"I thought you had a PhD?"

"Yeah, okay, call me Dr. Tankovitch then. The 'doctor' just scares people away, so I usually say 'mister'."

The young engineer smiled. He was bursting to ask a question. "Do you think we'll ever see the Mars crew alive again?"

Chris thought for a moment.

"I'd like to say yes..." Chris trailed off.

He sensed a very morbid turn to the conversation and attempted to resurrect it.

"...but we didn't send them with any potatoes."

CHAPTER 19

Manfred Insurance Building
Fort Worth, Texas

Post-surgery recovery went quickly for Connie. Daily rehabilitation at a downtown facility generated huge improvements in her leg control and ultimately her ability to walk. These medical visits also generated huge bills and, as wonderful as her positive improvements were, her bank account shrank violently. After medical bills and income taxes, her million dollar bonus from the Murch Motor Corporation had dwindled to $51,000.

Connie had always heard anecdotal stories about how medical bills were the number one cause of personal bankruptcy in America. She was on a trajectory to prove the myth true.

It had been many months since NASA had last heard

from the Mars crew and it was time to pursue declaring her husband, Adam, legally dead. She didn't want to do it, but she was facing a financial disaster.

Connie called Adam's life insurance broker and arranged a meeting — a terribly somber meeting.

Without crutches, Connie walked confidently up the stairs to the second floor of the Manfred Insurance Building. Her mother, a short woman of 79 years of age, followed behind her. Connie stopped on the stairs and helped her mom climb the last few steps. They emerged into the lobby of the Life Insurance division.

Connie signed the appointment sheet on the desk and then sat down next to her mom.

"Mom, thanks for coming here with me."

"Sweetheart, you know I didn't want you to do this alone. I'm glad Libby could watch the kids."

"Again, right?" Connie joked. "I may have to start paying her babysitting fees."

"Hah, well I think she understands. Nobody wants their kids to see this stuff." She looked around as if searching for the evil insurance demon. "I'm sorry *you* have to deal with this stuff."

The door opened and a smartly dressed secretary walked out with a clipboard.

"Mrs. Alston? Can you please follow me?"

Connie and her mom stood up and followed the secretary down a long hallway.

"Are you related to Captain Adam Alston?" the secretary asked.

"Um, yes, he's my... *was* my husband."

"Oh, I'm sorry to hear that. It's a national tragedy."

The secretary opened a wood-paneled door and led both women into an office. The secretary began her introductions.

"Hi, Richard. I have Mrs. Alston here to see you."

A thirty-something bald man sat behind a desk with his back facing them. He spun around and smiled.

"Hi, Mrs. Ashton. Thank you for coming down here today."

"It's... Alston, actually."

"Yes, I'm so sorry."

He stood up and shook both of their hands. The secretary pulled the door closed until it made a quiet click sound.

Connie saw the man was confused at the presence of somebody else. She said, "Oh, this is my Mom, Roberta."

"Nice to meet you Roberta," the man said without caring, looking at his desk. "Um, I think we have everything to get started."

They sat down and the man pulled out a folder and opened it wide on his desk. He leaned on the desk, studying it for an uncomfortable thirty seconds. Then he clasped his hands and looked at them.

"Well, the paperwork is all complete. Are you familiar with how this works?"

Connie looked at her Mom and they shook their heads implying they had no idea.

"Well, okay, it normally takes a lot longer to declare somebody dead," he caught himself, "*deceased*."

He paused to look down and study his notes some more, then looked up.

"However, that process has been sped up quite a bit since your husband has experienced what we call 'imminent peril'."

Connie crinkled her forehead, confused.

"That just means he was in a situation where survival was assumed to be impossible. It's the same for violent airplane crashes, nuclear explosions, you know, that kind of thing," he explained nonchalantly.

Connie nodded her head up and down with a tear falling down her cheek. The man wanted to be compassionate, but he had a busy day ahead of him. He pulled out two sheets of paper and slid them toward Connie.

"Here is the distribution paperwork. If you could sign here and here," he said as he pointed to the document in front of Connie. She signed each location.

The man took the paperwork and dropped it on his desk a few times to square it up. He reached into his middle drawer and pulled out a check.

"This is the lump-sum payment for Captain Alston's life insurance policy. It is for twenty thousand dollars."

Connie looked scared.

"There must be a mistake. I mean, I'm sure it was for five hundred thousand dollars. He told me it would be enough to cover college costs for the kids."

The man smiled.

"Yes, but he went with the more affordable policy that didn't cover accidental death and dismemberment."

"But how do you know that's how he died?" Connie asked with a very upset shrill.

"Well, in extreme circumstances like this, we have to assume he had a violent death."

"You can't assume..."

"Ma'am, he died on Mars for Christ's sake. I assume *violent* is the *only* way you die on Mars."

"But you can't just assume!"

"Mrs. Alston, you are *not* going to win this argument."

Connie burst into tears. "No! This just can't be happening. We need that money."

"You are the wife of a national hero, so let me give you some advice. Please don't be greedy. I've seen this happen so many times, I was hoping you would be different. Think of it this way, you had *nothing* ten minutes ago and now you have twenty *thousand* dollars. People rob banks for less money than that."

He took the paperwork, put it in a manila envelope and threw it on a pile marked "DONE."

"Now, if you'll excuse me, I have a busy day ahead of me. The number of my clients dying from cancer has gone through the roof. And I'm way behind on their paperwork."

As he stood up, he added, "That reminds me... didn't Mr. Alston say that he was going to receive a one million dollar bonus?"

"Well, yes, that's true, but we've spent pretty much all of it on medical bills. And we owed a lot in taxes."

"That's a bummer," the man said, agreeing by shaking his head up and down. "You've got *one-percenter* problems. Must be nice..."

Connie's mom interjected, "Can you please recheck what's happening here? There must be a mistake."

"I'm sorry, ma'am. It's not me. *It's the policy.*"

Her mom, sensing defeat, continued, "Well can't you go talk to your bosses at the butt-head factory and see if there was a mistake?"

"All right, all right, it's time for you wonderful ladies to leave." He walked toward the door and opened it, summoning them with his other hand.

"Then there's nothing you can do to help us?" Connie cried.

The insurance man paused and looked over the top of his glasses at the two women. He gave a mischievous smile.

"I'll bet you wished you'd never come in here today. Look, I'm afraid that boat has sailed. Good day, ladies."

CHAPTER 20

Office of vending services
NASA Jennings Manned Spacecraft Center
Fort Worth, Texas

Chris stared at his computer screen, pondering how he'd fallen so far from his previous job. He read through the complaint emails that had come in just since 6:00am. His eyes were so heavy — just a little sleep would help.

Wow, my fellow engineers like to complain a lot, he thought. *Are we all like this?*

His desk phone was blinking. He pushed the voicemail button and a loud whining voice rang out – some man complaining that he'd lost 75 cents to a coffee vending machine. Chris noted the address.

"Let's see... Building 600, Column 73, Row 40."

He stood up, checked the warden's ring of keys on his

belt and walked out of the office. His trip went through the bowels of the building subsystems and, after twelve minutes, he popped out near a remote lunchroom. These were spread around the facility and sat empty most of the day, with only occasional workers arriving to get their caffeine fix.

Chris found the offending machine. There was a big sheet of paper taped to it with the following message written with a Sharpie: "THIS PIECE OF $#&@ STEALS MONEY!"

It actually had a handwritten dollar sign, hash tag, etc.

He removed the paper.

Chris jumped when a voice behind him announced, "Hey, you better leave that there, mister."

It was an old engineer, complete with pocket protector holding a Sharpie. Chris suspected it was the offending Sharpie that created the offending hashtag symbol.

"Oh, hey. How are you?" Chris asked. "Are you the one that called?"

"Yup, that was me. This machine has taken my 75 cents at least once a week for the past few months."

"Have you tried one of the other vending machines?"

"Why should I have to do that? I'm not the one at fault in this equation.."

"Yes, Mr.... Franklin, I understand," Chris said, squinting to see the engineer's badge. "I'll see what I can do, but please use another machine until we get this one fixed up. Our repair budget is a bit tight right now."

"I don't care about your repair budget. This machine robbed me of my hard-earned money."

Chris grew frustrated.

"Look, I get it, I'm going to try to get it fixed."

"Well, you better because if you don't I'm going to talk

to your boss and get your lazy butt fired."

Chris stopped fiddling with the machine's change box and turned toward Mr. Franklin again.

"What?"

"You heard me. This machine stole my money!"

"Sir, it took 75 cents," Chris said. He reached into the machine and removed three quarters and handed them to the engineer.

"Doesn't matter," the engineer said. "I'm still gonna call your boss."

Chris's foot fidgeted, his temper going beyond his control.

"My boss? MY BOSS? You mean the president of this damn country?"

"Not anymore, you loser."

"What? Look, buddy, I was in charge of all of NASA just a few months ago! How dare you threaten to get me fired over three freakin' quarters?"

"No need for that lang—"

"Shut up, asshole," Chris said, so mad that his veins were throbbing in his neck like ropes under his skin.

The engineer set the three quarters down on the nearby counter top and said, "Here, you take it. You need it more than I do."

The engineer disappeared into the depths of the concrete columns.

Chris was all alone again.

He put both hands on the front of the machine and took a deep breath. He let out a guttural yell as he pushed the machine backward until it fell over. The glass did not break.

How disappointing, he thought.

Chris took a long hike back to his office. It'd been many years since he'd lost his temper in public, especially at a coworker of some sort — it violated all of his Dale Carnegie training courses. He sat down and logged back in to his computer. The clunky vending-machine management software was on the screen. Chris set up a service repair call to diagnose what was wrong with the coffee machine. There was no menu option for "I wrecked it."

Chris sat quietly for an entire hour, ignoring his emails. He drew doodles portraying the arc of his career, starting with a cheering college graduate, a rocket to Mars, and then crashing into a paper cup of coffee. He ruminated on the tragically dull path his life had taken — he was now a curiosity around the facility. People whispered when he walked past. He appreciated the humming sound from his computer — it didn't gossip.

Chris jumped when his phone rang.

"Hello. Vending services. How can I help you," Chris said sarcastically, rolling his eyes.

"Hey Chris, this is Alexis, the new director of NASA."

"And my ex-wife," Chris added.

"Yes, that is true. *And your new boss.* Are you busy right now?" she asked.

"Let's see," Chris paused for effect. "I've got seven misbehaving vending machines and three microwave ovens that keep overcooking Hot Pockets."

Chris heard the new NASA director laugh on the phone. He missed that laugh so much.

"Well don't let me distract you from your busy day ahead of you," she chuckled.

"All joking aside, what's up?"

"Well, Chris, did you know that the Little Turtle spacecraft transmits a special signal when it gets near Earth?"

"Yes, of course, that's the short-range *beacon* signal," Chris explained.

Chris heard Alexis tapping on a keyboard and clicking a mouse.

"Well," she paused. "I'm looking at a computer screen that's lit up with the beacon signal from the Little Turtle."

"Are you serious?" Chris asked in a bewildered tone.

"Looks like our astronauts might be paying us a surprise visit after all this time."

Chris chimed in, "Where are you? Are you in New DC or here in Fort Worth?"

"I'm at the new mission control center, across the street from you."

"The microwaves can wait. I'll be right over."

CHAPTER 21

Little Turtle Spaceship
Two weeks away from Earth

"What are you scribbling?" Adam asked. His salt and pepper hair had gone stark white since leaving Mars.

Yeva sat on the floor, lightly. The MM10 motors pushed constantly, accelerating the rocket just enough so that one wall of the ship was definitely considered the floor. She stopped writing and looked up at Adam.

"It is likely that this ship will make it back, but we won't. Our luck is too bad. So I am writing a history of everything that happened to us."

"Everything?" Adam asked, wondering if she would include the details about how he betrayed her on Mars.

"Yes, *everything*," she said slowly for emphasis. "Even when you abandoned our agreement to first set foot on Mars together as a team."

She looked back down at her notepad and started writing again.

"Well, maybe I should start writing too?" Adam declared.

Without looking at him, Yeva answered, "Absolutely. Write your lies. It will be up to history and God to decide who to believe."

If the Little Turtle spaceship was a patient in a hospital, the condition would be listed as *critical, but stable.* Their low-power automated beacon signal seemed to be transmitting, but it didn't contain much information. With their long-range antenna gone, they had no hope of real communication with Earth until they were a few days away from arrival. At that point, their short-range antenna would normally provide all of their communication needs.

Except, of course, their transmitter was partially broken. The "Push-to-talk" button functioned, but the microphone wasn't working. Adam surmised that condensation was wreaking havoc with the electronics just as it had done with several of their sensors – shorting them out like a glass of water spilled on a toaster.

Adam sat down near Yeva and tried to look over her shoulder at what she was writing. She leaned away.

Adam cleared his throat with a cough and said, "We should talk about the whole 'stepping on Mars first' thing. I guess I lost my balance."

She looked at him incredulously.

"Oh yes, you mean how you leaped ahead of me to get all the glory?" she asked. Yeva started flipping back to the front of her notebook, then held up the notepad to face

Adam.

"See!" she screamed. "That is on page one!"

"Okay, okay, fair enough," Adam said. He stood up and climbed the short ladder to the pilot seat.

They'd left Mars many months ago and by their estimates, would arrive on Earth in two weeks or so — assuming that the guidance computer was working properly. They had dialed down the oxygen to make sure it would last them for the unexpectedly long return voyage. This resulted in them feeling lightheaded sometimes and occasionally euphoric.

"Hey Adam, do you know the difference between airplanes and spaceships?"

"Huh? Is this a joke?" Adam asked from the pilot's seat. He turned to face her.

"No, it is not a joke. I said, do you know the difference between airplane flight and spaceflight?"

Adam nodded. "Yes, of course, one is through air and one is through a vacuum of space."

"I mean with regard to the pilot."

"What are you getting at?" Adam asked.

"With airplanes, you are in total control of where the plane goes and what it does. It's usually very safe and quite fun," Yeva said, now smiling. "But spaceflight — the astronaut's only goal is to not die. That's it. You're along for the ride and all you can hope for is to not die and return back to the wonderful Earth."

Adam smirked.

"Yeva, that's an interesting way to look at it – but we still have control of the spaceship. Most people consider space flight to be very exciting. It has its moments of terror I guess," Adam said. "If we do get back, my space flying days are over. Hell, my flying days are over. I won't even get on an airplane."

"That's an excellent promise. I hope you keep it."

Yeva put her notebook in a small metal briefcase that had "Turoskova" stamped into the outside. She dragged her hand across the name label to wipe away the condensation that gathered on every metal surface in the ship. The briefcase had a three-number lock on it and she spun the dials. She looked up to see if Adam was watching.

He was, but he looked away instantly.

With a shove and hoof, she stood up and bounced across the floor toward the only porthole window that wasn't cracked. She stared out longingly for that blue dot in front of them, barely blinking. As the return trip wore on, Yeva spent a lot of time staring out that porthole. Her home planet couldn't come soon enough.

Nobody on Earth knew they were still alive. That would soon change.

CHAPTER 22

New Mission Control Center
NASA Jennings Manned Spacecraft Center
Fort Worth, Texas

Chris could pick Alexis out of any crowd. She was exceptionally short, the result of a childhood adrenal gland disorder. She would've been even shorter, but doctors caught the problem in her teenage years, accelerating her growth to the point where she eventually reached a height of four foot ten inches.

What she lacked in height, she made up for in ambition. As college graduates, Chris and Alexis both rose quickly through the ranks at NASA, unaware of each other's existence until they met at the Oshkosh International Airshow, held in Wisconsin every July. Separately they'd been invited to the semi-secret dinner held by the Laminar Flow Believers Club. They exchanged business cards and formed a relationship that ultimately had them married in the test section of a wind tunnel.

Their careers continued on a stratospheric trajectory within NASA. Chris eventually became the administrative director, thanks heavily to having been a college classmate of president Daggett Jennings. This began a competitive rift between the overachieving husband/wife team that eventually led to mutual contempt and then divorce. Chris still quietly adored her, even though he'd lost nearly everything but his car in the divorce. She even took half the penny jar.

Chris wound his way through the mission control desks until he reached her. She'd pulled her brown hair back into a ponytail and was knelt down on one knee as she typed on the computer and moved the mouse around the screen.

She glanced over when he arrived.

"Oh hey, glad you're here," she said. "Look at this."

Chris looked over his glasses at the computer screen. He saw a live plot updating left to right. It was a typical hilly radio wave signal that looked like a lulling ocean wave. However, the waves were jammed together in clumps.

"When did it start coming in?" Chris asked.

"Yesterday. It was faint at first," she said, tapping on the screen. "But today it's really strong. The funny thing is that it went off for a few hours this morning. Then on and off in random succession. It's been back on for hours now."

"You mean like Morse Code on and off?"

"No, we have some ham radio guys here and they said it's just random, no Morse Code patterns."

"Okay. Well, the beacon signal is supposed to contain data about the condition of the Little Turtle spaceship. Have you processed the signal?"

"Working on it right now," Alexis said. She stood up, searching for somebody.

She yelled out, "Hey, telemetry guy! Have you processed the beacon signal for me yet?"

A man with a buzz cut on the other side of the room nodded his head and began walking toward Alexis. He arrived with a sheet of paper.

"Hi, director," he said anxiously. "And hi, former director. The beacon signal is listing the condition of the various systems. There's a lot of damage onboard."

"Life support?"

"That is surprisingly still working, but barely. The oxygen levels are really low and the humidity is off the charts. Half the MM10 engines are not working either. That explains why it took so long to get back to Earth."

Alexis nodded her head up and down to show understanding. "Have you triangulated distance?"

"We estimate that at the current speed, the ship will be here in about ten days."

"Have you tried voice communications?" Chris asked.

Alexis rolled her eyes. "Yes, obviously we've tried that. All we're getting is static with occasional pop sounds."

The telemetry guy added, "Even if they made it on the ship, they're most likely dead by now."

Chris chuckled.

"What's wrong with you?" Alexis asked. "How could you possibly laugh right now?"

"I can tell you two things for sure," he stated. "The voice communication radio on their ship is broken. And the crew is still alive."

Alexis looked confused. "What makes you so sure? I think the beacon signal is an autopilot thing."

"That's true to a certain extent. Except the autopilot only turns it on when it's two days from Earth. However, this ship is still ten days out. Somebody flipped on the power switch. You said the voice signal has been going on and off in quick starts? Somebody is trying to fix the entire radio system and they're powering it on and off in the process."

Alexis laughed and put her hand on Chris's arm.

"I am so glad I kept you on the payroll after all."

CHAPTER 23

Conference room
NASA Jennings Manned Spacecraft Center
Fort Worth, Texas

(Two hours later)

Alexis Tankovitch walked over to the doorway and looked outside for stragglers. The hallway was empty – she closed the door and turned around to face the group of engineers and managers.

"Ladies and gentlemen, thank you for coming here on short notice."

The conference room was perfectly square with walls made from dry-erase boards floor to ceiling. In the middle was a U-shaped oak table and a TV screen hanging on the wall — messy cables ran over the floor under the desk. On the screen were four somewhat pixelated faces from remote sites. In the room were ten people all sitting around the horse-shoe shaped table. Some wore military uniforms. Some wore polo shirts.

Alexis walked into the open central portion of the table and proceeded to look at every person's badge, one by one. Midway, she found a man whose badge did not have the telltale red stripe on it.

"You don't have a Secret clearance, sir."

The man fidgeted, suddenly anxious.

"I know I don't, director Tankovitch. But I'm a telemetry engineer. Mr. Spinks asked me to attend this meeting in his place."

"You don't have the clearance," she said with derision. "Get out. Tell Mr. Spinks I made a mistake hiring him."

The man gathered his notepad and trudged out of the room. Alexis waited for him to close the door.

"Okay, folks, I have bad news and good news."

Alexis walked back around the table and sat down in the lead chair. She swiveled back and forth slightly as she spoke.

"As you know, early on in the Mars mission our paleographers deciphered most of the inscriptions from the Martian temple."

"Temple?" a red-headed engineer asked.

"We're calling it a temple for now. It's a stone building created to last eons. It contains a history of a long dead culture and it contains a gift to us. So, *temple* it is."

She stared into the red-headed engineer's eyes. She squinted. He looked away.

Chris, now the director of vending machine services, piped up with a softball question. "Can you give everybody a synopsis of what we know so far?"

She smiled at the simplicity of his question.

"Sure. The Martians had a thriving modern culture similar to our own. They invented *something* that lead to their destruction."

Chris added, "And do we know what that is now?"

"We do," confirmed Alexis Tankovitch.

The rest of the people in the room looked at each other in anticipation.

She continued. "On the screen is a man named James Stimple, the head of the NSA paleography group. They've finally deciphered that portion of the message."

One of the glitchy faces on the TV screen came to life. The man started to move his mouth, but it was quiet.

"James?" Alexis interupted. "I think you have mute on."

The man looked down away from his camera, smiled, then said, "Can you hear me now?"

Everybody in the room nodded.

"Okay," he continued. "It took us a long time to figure that part because it wasn't a language really, but it was a set of chemical equations."

"You mean chemical formulas," the red-headed engineer interrupted again, with an overwhelming arrogance.

The man on the screen was caught off guard, but then he smiled.

"The term *formulas* is what they use on late night infomercials. Chemical equations are what chemists use to write down stoichiometrically balanced chemical reactions. It's what we learned in high-school chemistry class."

"Mr. Stimple," said Alexis. "Please ignore our red-headed engineer. He keeps validating my poor opinion of him. Continue."

The man on the screen took a drink of water before continuing, holding his pointer finger up as a pause.

"What the Martians gave us was a chemical equation for the production of a medicine that controls cell-growth rates. We can create customized rates. Up or down. It's quite groundbreaking."

The head of aviation medicine spoke up, "Are we talking about controlling cancer cells?"

Mr. Stimple nodded his head. "Yes, indeed."

Everybody looked at each other to acknowledge the weight of this information.

"The timing couldn't be more perfect with cancer rates going through the roof," Alexis said.

Mr. Stimple added, "That's correct, but we must be careful. Keep in mind that this is what ultimately spelled their doom."

Alexis sat up in her chair and put her elbows on the table.

"How is that so?" she asked.

"Unintended consequences," Mr. Stimple replied. "Suddenly, their death rates plummeted. People started living much longer. Mars is much smaller than Earth and it couldn't keep up with the sudden demand on food production."

"Do you think that would happen here?" Alexis asked.

"Well, good question. I don't *think* so," Mr. Stimple answered with some doubt.

Chris leaned forward to speak.

"Logistically, are you manufacturing this by the ton right now? We need it immediately."

Mr. Stimple shook his head. "No, this chemical, what we're dubbing *Blue Hope*, can't be produced here on Earth. Not yet at least."

"Let me guess, it has to be made on Mars?" Chris asked.

"No sir, not even on Mars. It requires a low-gravity environment."

"Low gravity?"

"Yes, many of the experiments on the Space Station taught us that certain chemical mixtures, er, solutions, can react very differently in zero gravity situations. The Martian inscriptions describe this along with the actual chemical equations. It added to the complexity of deciphering their messages."

Chris was confused, "Why would gravity matter?"

"Well, there are certain chemicals with very different densities that will not mix properly in the presence of gravity. Just as helium likes to float, lighter liquids also like to float. The Blue Hope medicine requires a mostly homogenous mix, but the components don't mix at all in the presence of strong Earth-like gravity."

The head of aviation medicine chimed in, "Look, we can't just sit on this information. We need to launch a rocket into orbit to start making this so-called Blue Hope."

Alexis piped in, "Well, Mr. Stimple hasn't told you everything just yet."

"You're right, Alexis. It's more complicated. Blue Hope doesn't need *zero* gravity either. In fact, that's just as bad as mixing it here on the Earth's surface. Blue Hope needs to be produced in an environment that has between ten and twenty percent of Earth's gravity to get the buoyancy mix just right – it's such a fragile process. If done correctly, the chemical still separates, but into very subtle layers – think of it like how crude oil is separated into various useful components in a distillation tower with gasoline near the top and asphalt materials near the bottom. Not the same process, but you get the idea."

While Mr. Stimple spoke, some members of the crowd Googled crude oil and distillation towers.

"So we couldn't even use a rocket if we had it," Chris said with disappointment. "Or even the Space Station."

Alexis felt the room develop an all-is-lost feeling. She stood up and walked toward the dry-erase board wall.

"There are two options," she said, grabbing a dry-erase marker and writing 1 and 2 on the marker board.

"As you know, right before our crew left the Mars site, they discovered an anti-gravity cube inside the Martian temple. We believe that was a gift to any future explorers because it gives us an idea of how to manipulate, at least locally, gravitational fields. That's the technology that the Martians must've been using to produce the chemical. Think about it. They couldn't mix the Blue Hope on Mars either – they must've had laboratory facilities with customized local low-gravity fields."

She wrote "Anti-gravity cube" next to the number 1.

"What about sub-orbital flights?" Chris asked. "We can tailor those to any acceleration level we want. We could borrow the Vomit Comet or use the Burt Rutan ship."

Alexis pointed the marker at him, implying a good point.

"The problem with that, *mister* Tankovitch, is that sub-orbital flights can only provide that low level of gravity for a minute or so at most when they fly their parabolic arcs. Blue

Hope requires a slow steady cylindrical mixing for at least one hour."

"Do you have any good news for us?" asked the red-headed engineer.

"I'm getting to that," she assured him. "I have huge news to share with you. We now have evidence that the Little Turtle spacecraft is not far from Earth."

A murmur went up among all of the people in the room.

"It's true," she said. "We've acquired a beacon signal from it. We suspect that it's less than ten days away from rendezvous with Earth."

"Are they alive?" yelled somebody on the TV screen.

"We don't know. The communication channels are dead. Only the automated beacon signal remains. However, if our astronauts managed to get the anti-gravity cube on board, then they may have just saved mankind from the dubious actions of our," she paused for effect, "previous president."

"And what if they didn't get the anti-gravity cube on the ship?" the red-headed engineer asked.

"That brings me to option number two. There's only one place we could even conceive of going that would provide that constant low level of gravity."

Alexis uncapped the marker and wrote two more words on the dry-erase board: "The Moon."

CHAPTER 24

The president's office
New White House
Reston, Virginia

Chris and Alexis were the only two people in the room. They occupied opposite ends of the sofa. Chris nervously checked his watch wondering just how late the president would be. He stood up and walked over to the front of the grand wooden presidential desk. He'd heard rumors that the front contained a trap door – he nudged it with his foot.

Nothing.

"You know," Alexis said. "That's not the real desk. The White House was damaged in the attacks. I assume they got a replica."

Chris frowned and nodded his head.

"Alexis, I honestly don't think the president is going to go for it," Chris said.

Alexis gave a look of incredulousness.

"I don't agree. She's being handed the keys to the greatest cure in human history. She'll go for it," Alexis said with an assuring tone.

The door to the office burst open. Chris turned around. President Bexar and two of her assistants walked in. Alexis and Chris both stood up to shake her hand.

"Sorry for the delay," the president announced. "It's been crazy today. Would you like some coffee?"

"No thanks," they said.

"Well I certainly do," the president replied.

The president grabbed a cup of coffee and gulped it down. She motioned for her guests to sit back down. She followed and sat down across from both of them.

"Your note said you had exciting news," President Bexar said with anticipation. "I could use some good news for a change."

Alexis straightened up and cleared her throat.

"Yes, in the last forty eight hours we've learned of some significant developments and wanted to tell you in person."

"That's awfully brave with the current state of the airlines."

Alexis nodded her head, "Yes, it was difficult to get here, but it was worth it."

The president sighed, ready to be amazed.

"In short, our Mars crew is coming back."

The presidents jaw dropped open.

"Well," Chris corrected. "We *think* they are. We're receiving a communications broadcast from the Little Turtle spaceship. It's barely functioning, but we think they may still be alive."

The president smiled with hope. "This is fantastic news! Our country is in a rut and we really need something positive like this."

Alexis nodded.

"Agreed, but we also have more information. Our scientists have deciphered another part of the message from the Mars Temple. It's a chemical equation that describes how to make a medicinal compound that can effectively cure cancer."

"This just gets better and better!" the president said with excitement. "I've been getting reports, *secret reports*, that the cancer problem is much worse than the public knows about. And it's only going to accelerate. This new development couldn't come at a better time."

"There's a catch," Chris said.

"Oh, there's always a catch," the president laughed, rolling her eyes.

"The medicine requires a mixing environment with very low gravity. Fortunately, the Martians left a physical example of how to manipulate gravity. Inside the Temple, they left a cube that, from what the astronauts said, defied gravity. We can study this and figure out how to make local variations on gravitational fields, inside the laboratory. We hope the astronauts have that on board."

"What if they don't?" the president asked, suddenly very concerned.

"Then we'll have to think of something, or *somewhere*, else."

"Somewhere?"

"Realistically, if the returning ship doesn't have the anti-gravity cube, the only place we could mix the chemical would be on the Moon."

The president stared off, trying to run the numbers in her head. She looked them dead in the eyes.

"This is the greatest news I've ever heard, but right now there is no budget for any launches and the rocket industry is in shambles."

Alexis chimed in, "We know, but with proper budget incentives, we can get somebody like Whittenberg Space Launch Systems back in business."

The president nodded her head. She opened her mouth and paused, waiting to share some private information.

"Mr. Whittenberg is retired. He told me that he holds himself partially responsible for the Mars mission disaster and wants nothing to do with aerospace anymore."

Alexis and Chris both looked defeated.

"Is there anything else?" President Bexar asked.

"No," Alexis said. "That's everything."

"Don't look so sad," the president said. "Our crew is returning from Mars – this is incredible news. This requires a press conference immediately. I'll hold back on the announcement about the anti-cancer medicine until we find out about the anti-gravity cube."

The president stood up.

"Thank you for coming all this way. My assistant will show you out." Then she left the room.

Alexis and Chris looked at each other in silence. They stood up.

"Follow me," the presidential assistant ordered.

The two NASA personnel followed the assistant out of the room and through a series of hallways. They picked up their jackets and cellphones near the front lobby. As they walked down the stairs, Chris sighed, now having met with two Presidents in his lifetime to announce a surprise astronautical discovery.

A limo slid up to the stoop in front of them. The driver got out and opened the door for them, only saying, "Hello, ma'am." They climbed in and sat across from each other. Chris turned on the radio, searching for the local news. He put the volume on low. The limo accelerated away from the new White House.

Chris stared at Alexis who somehow looked completely rested and ready to go, even after a long day of travel. The low hum of the radio news mumbled into the limo cabin like white noise.

"Why'd you make me split the pennies?" Chris asked.

"What are you talking about?"

"In our divorce settlement, you required me to split the penny jar in half," Chris said solemnly. "It's a question I've wanted to ask for years."

"It's not like I made you count them. I told you to just divide it in half by weight."

Chris nodded.

"Yeah, I know. I still counted them. I wanted to be maliciously compliant."

Alexis shook her head.

"That was foolish, Chris. I wasn't being mean. We just... grew apart. It happens."

He obviously had a thought on his mind.

"Do you ever look back and think, perhaps, if we just started over, but with the right mindset...."

"No," Alexis interrupted him. "Never. Nada. You. Me. Never again in that respect. But I'm happy to be your boss."

Chris looked out the window as all expression melted from his face.

"My fellow Americans..." echoed from the radio speaker. The president was already giving her news address about some of the information from Alexis and Chris's visit. Still keeping it close to her vest, the president only released the news about the Little Turtle spaceship returning from Mars. They listened as the buildings of Reston, Virginia slid by outside the limo.

Alexis's phone rang. She answered it and put it on speakerphone.

"Hi, NASA folks, you're on speaker phone with Chris and I. What's going on back in Fort Worth?"

A tinny voice rang from the phone.

"We've finally completed all of the Martian temple deciphering. Are you ready for something crazy?"

"I'm always ready for crazy," Alexis laughed, rubbing her sore heel.

"Okay. It says they had a base here on Earth and they even gave the location."

Alexis looked stunned.

"They give you the location?" she asked.

"Yes," said the cellphone voice. "It's complicated. They gave us coordinates, but obviously they are a unique system, to say the least. The cartography team has spent the past twenty four hours trying to interpret them."

"And?" Alexis asked.

"I think we've got it figured out," he said with excitement. "There's only one detail left, but it's a pretty huge detail. Please come home ASAP so we can brainstorm this. I don't want to jump to conclusions, but this may be the greatest archaeological find in history."

CHAPTER 25

Rural road
Fort Worth, Texas

The flights back to NASA Fort Worth were perilous. The first one ran into engine problems over Tennessee and made an emergency landing in Nashville. After twelve hours and two airplane changes, Alexis and Chris made it to DFW airport just after breakfast. Unfortunately, their luggage didn't. Carrying nothing, they drove the long trek back to NASA Fort Worth.

Chris decided to tell Connie about all of the information before the media got their claws into it. He called her cellphone, but she didn't answer. He knew that Adam Alston's mother-in-law lived nearby. Chris looked up Adam's NASA personnel records and found her contact information.

He typed in her number and it rang and rang. Finally a friendly older woman's voice answered.

"Hello? Roberta speaking."

"Hi, Roberta. This is Chris Tankovitch calling from NASA. I'm trying to reach Connie, but she's not answering."

"Well hello Chris. You know, Connie thinks so highly of you."

"That's kind of you to say, but do you know where she is? I have some information for her."

"Oh yes, she took Cody to the park out by Eagle Mountain Lake to ride his bike. They've got nice wide bike paths out there. That might be why her cellphone isn't answering."

"Thank you. I'm going to take a drive out there. If she calls you, please have her contact me."

"All right. Will do, Mr. Tankovitch."

Fog rolled silently across the rural Texas road, oozing around the black sedan Chris drove. As the Sun rose on the right side of his car, the fog lifted, revealing rows and rows of old Mesquite trees. Suddenly, he saw several signs for the park up ahead. He slowed down and spun the steering wheel toward the gravel parking lot. There was only one other vehicle there — the Alstons' newish minivan. He pulled up next to it, got out and stretched his back.

Chris walked to the edge of the parking lot and looked down the incline at Connie chasing her son Cody on his bicycle. She turned around and saw Chris, waving at him. He was struck by just how beautiful she was. It was the first time he'd seen her walking around without crutches and she was filled with lively energy, chasing after Cody's bike.

"Hi, Connie! Hi, Cody!" he yelled to them.

Connie and her son walked up toward the parking lot.

"Long time, no see, Chris. Cody, you remember Mr.

Tankovitch, right?" Connie asked.

Chris leaned down and shook Cody's hand.

"Young man, I bet you're a bicycle expert by now. NASA may need you in the astronaut program when you grow up."

The little boy smiled politely as he shook his head side to side. He wanted nothing to do with space travel.

"Mommy, can I go play with my Rescue Bots?"

She leaned down to speak with Cody at eye level.

"Sure. Go ahead, and put your seat belt on, too."

She patted him on the head as he put the bike in the back of the minivan. Cody climbed in over the bike and crawled through the interior, finally flopping down into the back seat.

Connie crossed her arms and let out a comfortable sigh.

"So what brings you all the way out here today?"

Chris smiled and said, "A lot has happened since we lost contact with them last year."

"That's quite the understatement," Connie replied.

"From the way you were running with Cody, can I assume the experimental back surgery worked?" Chris asked.

"It's been like a miracle cure. It's all healed."

Connie did a slow pirouette on the gravel to demonstrate how her spine operation had succeeded. In some ways she reminded Chris of his ex-wife, but Connie was much friendlier.

Chris laughed. "That's fantastic, Connie. I'm glad it worked out so well. I know Adam really wanted that for you."

An uncomfortable silence rose up between them.

"Chris, I'm sorry that you aren't the head of NASA anymore. I know it meant the world to you."

Chris chuckled.

"That's just the way it works when you are in a job appointed by the president. Besides, there's a lot of people in the world right now that have it harder than me. I made out pretty easy, if I may say so."

Chris moved some gravel around with his foot to avoid what he had to say next.

"I wanted to share some new information with you before the news media gets it. The president spoke about it in her radio address yesterday, but she left out some very important details that pertain to you. This is strictly off the record, okay? It's serious stuff."

She answered in a worried tone, "Yes, of course."

"Okay. Some of the surviving engineers at NASA finally got the deep-space antennas at Goldstone back online last month. That's a remote antenna complex out west. They were able to re-establish partial communication with the Curiosity Rover, but without the long-range antenna on the space station, there was no way to communicate with the Little Turtle. NASA was in the process of building a duplicate of the long-range antenna here on Earth when, suddenly, the new Mission Control Center here in Fort Worth reported getting a beacon signal from the Little Turtle."

Connie looked confused.

"I don't know what a beacon signal is. Does that mean that the ship started working again? Is the signal coming all the way from Mars?"

Her expression turned to one of hopefulness.

"Not exactly. The beacon signal is a simple data stream that the ship sends out as it gets near Earth. It uses a short-range transmitter on the Little Turtle. The main purpose of the beacon signal is to help Mission Control get a better fix on its location."

Chris looked over at the minivan and then back at Connie. He continued, "Frankly, the beacon caught NASA by surprise."

"Okay, but what does it mean?" Connie asked.

Chris looked over the top of his glasses at Connie.

"It means the ship is still alive. The crew was able to at least launch off the surface of Mars and enable the communications equipment. It means the Little Turtle is coming home."

Connie's eyes welled up with tears. She said, "You mean, somebody on board is still steering it? Maybe? Possibly?"

Chris shook his head side to side. He didn't want to get her hopes up – even if the crew were still alive, they had a good chance of dying during re-entry. And NASA couldn't communicate with them, anyway.

"No," he said. "Well, there's a remote chance..."

He looked down to search for the right words.

"They likely made it off the planet and possibly most of the way. We don't know its condition or how it will handle re-entry. Besides, the beacon signal says that only one emergency life-support system was activated right after takeoff. Whatever happened wasn't good. I wanted to tell you firsthand before this hit the news. I don't want to give you any ideas that Adam is coming home alive. It's just not in the cards."

Connie rocked side to side, crying. Through the tears, she said, "But there is a chance? Some hope?"

Chris shook his head.

"I'm so sorry, Connie. I don't think so."

She brought her hand up to wipe away the tears that crowded on her cheeks and looked down, unable to make eye contact.

"Okay, I understand," Connie whimpered.

She looked up at Chris suddenly.

"Do you think he died a foolish death?"

Chris didn't expect a question like that.

"I'm..." he said before pausing again for several seconds. Connie could tell that he desperately wanted to tell her something.

"Let me answer you this way. I'm not supposed to tell anybody this yet – I'm not even supposed to know about this officially – but we finally figured out what the early Martian discovery was that ultimately brought down their society. The translation was very difficult because it used chemical equations that our chemists didn't understand until just recently."

Chris paused. His mind searched for the right words.

"You might think that an advanced culture like theirs would've touted interplanetary space travel or anti-gravity as their quintessential achievement, but most of the walls in that room were a presentation of a chemical equation and how to manufacture it. Our own chemists are trying to synthesize it here on Earth right now. The Martians invented a way, a medicine of some type, to control cell growth rates. They could slow it down, speed it up, or maybe even stop it."

Connie squinted her eyes in confusion.

"I don't get why that's important, Chris," Connie said as she wiped a hair from her face.

"Being able to control cell growth rates has far reaching consequences. In addition to slowing down the aging process, they effectively cured cancer and any other disease that has to do with runaway cell growth. To them, treating cancer was probably like we treat heartburn today. Take some medicine, and the cancer goes away. They didn't have to worry about exposure to carcinogens because, well, anybody who got cancer could be cured. They were smart enough to know that their greatest achievement was something that would save the lives of so many people. Not interplanetary flight. Not anti-gravity. Just a cure for something that has dogged us since the dawn of time."

Chris crossed his arms and continued explaining.

"Unfortunately, their society wasn't ready for the results of their discovery. Mars is smaller, so their food resources couldn't keep up with the exploding population. They destroyed their planet by trying to keep everybody fed. Our experts are sure that Earth is different. We can absorb that kind of population growth. That's what they say, anyway."

Chris rubbed his chin with his hand.

"We're not there yet, though. Part of the manufacturing process requires the use of anti-gravity and, unfortunately, that technology is either still on Mars or — if we're lucky — inside the Little Turtle, on its way home. That's the vital missing piece. With cancer rates skyrocketing from the bomb radiation fallout, I hope to God they put that cube on that spaceship."

Chris walked closer and put his hand on her shoulder.

"Connie, your family's sacrifice will ultimately save the human race from infinite misery. Rest assured: Adam did many great things."

Connie's eyes overflowed with tears.

"Yes, but I still miss him so much," she cried as she

hugged Chris. "It sounds like he went there for a good reason, then?"

"Yes," Chris answered. "He went there for the best reasons."

Connie nodded her head and wiped her eyes.

"Okay, Chris. Well, thank you for coming all the way out here. I won't tell the kids about the news; I don't want to give them false hope. They're having a hard enough time as it is."

Connie walked to the minivan and opened the door. Her head tilted up; she looked over at Chris who hadn't moved. She climbed into her seat and sat there silently. Cody played with his robot toys in the back seat. She started the engine, pulled onto the road and drove away.

Chris stood there reflecting on what had taken place: his journey all the way from visiting Keller Murch's beach house to getting a team of astronauts to Mars. He knew much more about what Adam had done on Mars, but he would never tell Connie about it.

Chris walked toward his car, but slowed down. He paused and changed direction, meandering down a dirt bike path that ran near a casting pond. There was no bench nearby. He sat down in the inviting grass to enjoy the quiet solitude. He had a peaceful view of the calm water right in front of him.

Birds flew overhead as Chris watched the puffy cumulus clouds consume the bright blue sky. The strong smell of freshly cut grass wafted past. It reminded him of the night spent observing Halley's Comet with his dad. Chris looked to his left and then to his right. Finally, he looked straight upward and said, "Show me a miracle, Adam. Make me a believer again."

He knew that the crew was unlikely to survive re-entry with so many failed systems.

"Please be dead already," he prayed. "If you know what's good for you, drink that Red Hope before you burn up during re-entry."

CHAPTER 26

Office of vending services
NASA Jennings Manned Spacecraft Center
Fort Worth, Texas

This job is the worst, Chris thought to himself. *Perhaps I should resign before I ask somebody to drop a vending machine on me.*

Chris looked forward to the meeting with the NASA engineers later today – they would divulge their big find regarding the Earth base left behind by the Martians. Chris wondered what the missing piece of information was.

His phone rang. The caller-ID said it was from Alexis.

"Chris, the Little Turtle is arriving early. I postponed the scheduled meeting. Come on over to the mission control center as quickly as possible," said the voice of his ex-wife.

Ten minutes later, Chris ran up the steps to the Mission Control Center, taking two at a time. At the top, he stopped and leaned over to catch his breath. With one last deep breath, he swiped his card, opening the secure door to the new mission control room. He walked into a sea of engineers, all looking up at the large screens surrounding the room.

A blurry and shaky image of the Little Turtle glowed from the biggest screen at the front of the room – the result of a video feed from the tracking telescope. The ship was due to enter the Earth's atmosphere in ten minutes.

Chris scanned the crowd, looking for Alexis. She was standing and talking with the mission director. Chris walked over to the group.

"Have you re-tried the emergency communication frequencies?" Chris asked.

The mission director nodded his head.

"We've got the 145.8 megahertz voice frequency channel open. Nothing yet. However, we are getting some random tapping sounds."

"Random tapping sounds?"

"Yes, sir," the mission control director answered. "It's coming over the broken voice comms, mixed in with the beacon signal."

"I've got an idea," Chris said. He reached down and picked up the microphone. "Quiet down, everybody!"

The room hushed.

He pushed the transmit button and thought for a moment.

"To the crew of the Little Turtle, this is NASA dir.... Um, Chris Tankovitch. If you can hear me, please acknowledge."

Waiting.

Waiting.

Nothing.

Chris leaned toward Alexis and the mission director. "If they can't transmit, does that also mean that they can't hear us?"

"Not necessarily. It's two separate circuit boards."

Chris looked down, tapping his fingers on the desk to think. "What about guidance? Has it changed course or attitude?"

"Yes, there were some last minute corrections, but we're not sure if they did it or the guidance computer did it."

Chris looked at the tracking map and saw it way off course.

"Where are they coming in?"

"They'll be arriving over North America, most likely the west coast. Very shallow angle I'm afraid."

"They're coming in over land?" Chris asked incredulously.

The mission director nodded his head with a frown, implying the danger of this approach.

"How many minutes before radio silence?"

"Two," the mission control director said.

Chris pushed the transmit button one more time.

"Little Turtle, this is NASA trying to reach you. If you can hear me, please push your transmit button three times."

Waiting.

Waiting.

Silence.

Chris looked at Alexis and asked, "What do you think they..."

Click, click, click.

The room went deadly silent, every conversation halted mid-verb. Only the hum of the computers could be heard. Some rhythmic static sounds came through the speakers.

"This is NASA again, just to confirm, push your

transmitter button *four* times if you are hearing me."

A few seconds passed.

Click, click, click, click.

Chris nearly dropped the microphone. His heart was beating a mile a minute

"Are you prepared for re-entry? Three clicks for yes or two clicks for no."

Waiting.

Silence.

Chris held his breath, afraid to make any movement or sound.

Click, click, click.

Chris decided to ask another question.

"Okay, you'll be hitting re-entry in less than thirty seconds. We'll be in radio silence. Do you understand?"

Click, click, click.

Chris let go of the transmit button and looked at the people around him.

"Only a few seconds left before radio silence," Chris announced to the people in the room.

He bit his knuckle to think about what to ask before the radio went dead. He pushed the transmit button one last time.

"How many are still alive on board?"

Waiting.

Waiting.

Click.

PART TWO

"Don't you know you can't go home again?"

— *Thomas Wolfe*

CHAPTER 27

Southwestern coast of the USA

A teenager in San Diego saw it first. Just like every morning, he pedaled up and down the street, delivering newspapers to the mansions in the upper-crust neighborhood of Del Mar — there was even a beach house on his route that was shaped like a castle. He set his earbud volume on max and hummed a tune while working his monotonous job.

A flash caught his eye. He looked upward. A streak dragged across the sky, starting in the southwest and spreading northeast. The Little Turtle was returning to Earth at twenty-five times the speed of sound. The teenager had heard that a ship from the Mars expedition was coming back to Earth, but he didn't care — he was a teenager.

The lone astronaut on board the Little Turtle, Captain Adam Alston, was having the worst day of his life. He just spent four months isolated in a spaceship with one other person —

then one week by himself. He'd done his best to position the ship so the heatshields on the bottom were aimed in the general direction of travel. However, due to a broken flight-control computer, he didn't have a lot of say in his actual trajectory or where he'd land. The original plan of the mission was to hit the Pacific Ocean, but Adam saw the California coast approaching and he knew it was time for Plan B because Plan A was going to hell.

"I hope I land somewhere soft. At this point, I just hope I land on Earth," Adam said out loud.

The ship began plowing into the upper atmosphere. Adam's stomach pushed into itself because of the deceleration. All the frictional energy from the air impacting the bottom turned into a fiery blaze that came up and past the windows. It looked like the ship was sitting in a huge bonfire with embers and sparks streaking past the windows like lasers.

Only the mechanical gauges were working at this long point of his voyage. They jumped around, but reported Mach 25, then Mach 24. The ship shook violently, putting airplane turbulence to shame. Adam tried to breathe regularly, but his fingers had a death grip on the seat handles. The G-forces of the slowdown were titanic. Adam looked around the ship's interior. Anything not tied down came flinging to the bottom of the ship. He flinched as heavy items slammed down next to him

Mach 22, Mach 21...

The ship oscillated left and right, sending a cascade of flames off the alternating downward side of the ship.

Mach 20, Mach 19...

The cabinet panels covering the inside of the escape

hatch fell off due to the extreme heat, breaking the seal. They came screaming to the front of the ship, their sharp edges hitting Adam's seat and slicing through one of his seatbelts. During one of the oscillations, he fell partially out of the chair.

"Whoaaaaa!" Adam yelled.

Mach 18, Mach 17...

Adam held on tight as the oscillations grew stronger, thrashing him around like a rider on a mechanical bull.

Mach 16, Mach 15...

The flames outside were subsiding. Adam could see an occasional blue/black horizon as the ship rocked. He could make out the Rocky Mountains — *now behind him.*

Mach 14, Mach 13...

The Little Turtle screamed over the Mississippi River at an altitude of 120,000 feet. The fiery ride continued.

Mach 10...

Sonic booms were just hitting the ground in the Midwest. People wondered if a car had just slammed into their houses. They made their way outside, surprised to see a smoky streak across the sky.

Mach 8....

Indiana gliding below. A minute later...

Mach 5...

Ohio...

Mach 2...

At an altitude of 10,000 feet, Adam clawed his way up to grab the parachute handle.

He pulled.

It didn't work.

All this way and I'm going to die because of a

parachute failure? Screw that!, he thought.

Adam grabbed the handle and jerked with all his weight, but he couldn't get maximum effort. Reaching down, he unbuckled the last part of the seatbelt that held him to the ship and lifted his feet up to the ceiling, powering against the amplified gravity from the deceleration. He put one foot on each side of the parachute handle and pulled with the loudest grunt of his life. The switch opened and Adam fell violently to the floor.

The parachutes rocketed out of the storage cabinets on the roof. This would be their second official use since being carefully repacked many months ago on Mars.

Both parachutes deployed perfectly. Unfortunately, there should've been *three*. The last parachute didn't come out. Adam found out immediately. The Little Turtle dangled awkwardly from the two and wasn't slowing down like it was supposed to.

The ship started to spin, causing all hell to break loose in the cabin where the debris and the pilot were free to roll around like dice in a squirrel cage. At long last, the third parachute came out and, when it reached full extension, it ripped a huge panel from the roof of the ship. The chute and the panel fell limply away far behind the breeze, destined to land somewhere over northern Ohio. With the deafening roar of high-speed wind alternating into and out of the hole in the roof, the ship's spinning became violent just as it headed for the Northern coast of Ohio near Sandusky.

If it weren't for his helmet, Adam would've been knocked unconscious many rotations ago. As it was, he was still being slammed and bruised on the inside of the cabin. Interior ship parts pelted him like dodgeballs before they bounded out of the huge gaping hole in the ceiling.

One of the two extra space suits which were fastened to the wall broke open and the anti-gravity cube casually sailed out of it, bouncing off the walls a few times and then, to Adams horror, it flew out of hole and into the great blue yonder, destined to land in Lake Erie somewhere.

"No! No! No!" Adam yelled out.

The ship still spun and shook violently. Another panel ripped from the side of the ship, resulting in a strong howling gust coming straight through the cabin. Adam grabbed on to the seat firmly to make sure he didn't get blown out.

Suddenly, Adam saw his worst nightmare.

Yeva had been fastened into her seat for re-entry. For the last two million miles, she had been inside her suit, trailing behind the ship at the end of a tether. Just hours ago, Adam had reeled her back in and buckled her into her seat. Under the current violent ship vibrations, she ripped free from the seatbelts.

Adam reached for her leg, but the bucking of the ship made his fingers slip away before getting a good grip. They would either both get thrown free of the ship or Adam would have to let her go.

He let go. He had to. He'd brought her all this way. And he let her go. *She may have been dead*, he thought, *but she didn't deserve an ending like this.*

Adam looked on with terror as the suit containing her frozen dead body departed the Little Turtle – a ship that both saved her life and saw her death. Adam sobbed openly, but didn't lose grip of the seat.

Just hang on, he thought. *Do not let go of the ship.*

Trust the ship.

In a few moments, the Little Turtle careened through the airspace above Lake Erie and over the tower-like Perry Monument. It slammed into the water, producing a transient crater of water and a rooster tail.

Throughout the previous half hour, news of Adam's return flight had spread quickly and most of America was outside to watch the spectacle. Hundreds of people stood on the shore of Lake Erie and watched the Little Turtle take its final dive.

Within a minute, a ski boat left the harbor toward the direction where the long parachutes were seen falling gently into the water.

When the boat arrived, all it found were the parachutes. No sign of a space capsule.

It had sunk.

Adam was barely conscious, but awake enough to pull the handle on the self-inflating raft. With a thunderous expansion, it inflated instantly and rocketed upward. Adam held onto the handle and ascended with it. They popped out of the water like fishing bobbers, about fifty feet from the ski boat. Adam clawed his way into the inflatable raft and fell down onto his back, removing his helmet when he landed. Suddenly, for the first time since the harrowing re-entry phase had begun, he heard nothing.

Such a beautiful blue sky, he thought, viewing it through tears of joy for having survived – for having outlasted the nightmare.

Months of anxiety melted away into immeasurable bliss. He was finally home, the only sound being the water lapping at the raft edge.

A growing engine-noise broke the silence. It got louder and louder, but then cut off just before reaching the raft.

A head appeared over the edge of the raft. It was an older man with scraggly hair poking out from under a baseball hat embroidered with "Boat hair, don't care."

The boat driver squinted his eyes to see Adam more clearly. He asked, "Are you the Mars guy?"

Adam nodded, but didn't say a word.

The boat driver laughed.

"Boy did you miss a real clusterf—"

"Please," Adam interrupted him. "Just one more minute of quiet. I've had a rough day."

CHAPTER 28

Quarantine
Wright Patterson Air Force Base
Dayton, Ohio

A Jet Ranger helicopter zoomed in through the morning fog and followed the landing pattern for the main runway. It hovered twenty feet above the ground, following the taxiways before settling down in front of a modern-looking steel-framed hangar. A man in a wrinkled suit stepped out, ducking as he walked out from under the spinning rotor and toward the hangar. He approached the main entrance and waved to the armed guards on either side of the door. They checked his badge and allowed him through.

The inside of the building was largely empty except for a long hermetically sealed tank, painted silver like a huge art deco medicine capsule — it was the quarantine tank. A dozen desks sat just outside the tank at one end, each manned with physicians and nurses — they were tasked with helping their new arrival recover from the long journey and to study his physical recovery now that he was back on Earth.

Along the side of the tank was a metal door and next to that was a very thick window. Just below the window was an old-fashioned phone used to talk with people inside the tank. Chris walked across the empty hangar to the big silver tank and knocked on the door. It echoed throughout the hangar.

After a few moments, a ghost of a man appeared at the glass inside the tank. Adam Alston's salt and pepper hair had gone stark white during his return trip to Earth. His skin was sickly pale and his hair matched the unkempt look of his beard. Chris looked on in shock as he picked up the communication phone. Adam did the same.

"Adam, you look like hell."

Adam shrugged his spindly shoulders.

"They won't let me clean up until they run some tests," Adam explained.

"Have you had a chance to speak with anybody about what happened to the world in your absence?" Chris asked.

"That's a good question, Director Tankovitch..."

"*Former* director," Chris corrected him. "Just call me Chris."

Adam tilted his head in confusion.

"Wow. I guess a lot *has* happened. Tim told me about the president," Adam explained.

"Yes, that was very sad, he... wait, who's Tim?"

"Oh, he's the boat driver that found me in Lake Erie."

Adam waved to Tim who was sitting just behind him, also inside the tank. Chris leaned to the right to see further into the quarantine tank. When Tim saw the visitor, he smiled and gave him the middle finger.

Adam continued.

"So, about that, Tim is upset about being stuck here in quarantine with me for twenty one days. He runs a boat charter on Lake Erie and, well, he's not making money in here."

"I understand," Chris agreed. "Look, Adam, as you can imagine, I have a lot of questions."

"I figured," Adam said. "How much of my helmet-camera video did you see?"

Silence.

Calculated silence.

Chris ran over the options in his head about what to say. Play dumb about Adam's murderous attack on Keller? Or spill the beans right away? The only other person with knowledge of that video, Chris's former telemetry expert, had joined a disaster recovery group and was currently somewhere in Eastern Europe.

"I didn't see any of it," Chris said. "It was garbled."

Adam looked into Chris's eyes to see if he could detect dishonesty. Nothing. But Adam was always a terrible judge of honesty and an even worse judge of a lie.

"Adam, please tell me what happened up there. Tell me what happened to the crew."

Adam closed his eyes and bit his lip to think.

"It's very upsetting and I'm not ready to talk about it."

Chris nodded to imply understanding.

"We're going to send in a counselor today to help you – we assume you are experiencing serious PTSD from your trip. Adam, we need you to talk about what happened on Mars."

Adam nodded. He understood.

"Can you talk about Yeva and Molly?" Chris asked.

"Molly died on the planet from asphyxiation, but I don't think it was a mistake. While I was there, I found out she had a serious medical condition."

"I knew," Chris interrupted. "We all knew. We saw it in her medical readings shortly after you left Earth orbit. We still haven't told the press about it, and we probably never will."

"I think that's a good idea," Adam said.

"And what about Yeva?" Chris asked carefully.

"Yeva escaped from Mars with me. She was alive for most of the trip."

"And?" Chris leaned toward the glass.

"She didn't make it. I was the last soul on board."

"Adam, what happened to Yeva?"

Adam's hands began to shake. Both of them noticed it.

"I'm sorry, but I just can't talk about that right now. Give me time."

"I'll be honest, the president and the press are going to want answers."

"I know, I know...."

Chris looked at a note scribbled on his palm, where he often wrote important questions. He looked back up.

"What happened to the anti-gravity cube?"

Adam looked away from his shaking hands and back at Chris.

"That made it back for the most part. Right to the last few minutes. It's here... on Earth. Somewhere in Indiana, or maybe Ohio."

"You lost the anti-gravity cube?" Chris asked with

extreme frustration.

"Well, it just sorta fell out during that rough re-entry," Adam said. "Did you guys ever figure out what it was good for?"

Chris smiled, trying to hide his anger.

"That cube was the key to a whole new class of medications that can cure cancer."

Adam looked dumbfounded.

"Cancer?" Adam said incredulously. "Really?"

"Yes. And you lost our only chance," he scolded Adam. "I'm afraid you're about to become the pariah of the century."

"Way to go, bucko!" said a voice from behind Adam. When Adam turned around, he saw Tim giving him the thumbs-up sign with extreme sarcasm. Adam looked back at Chris.

"That may be true," Adam said. "But not for three more weeks."

CHAPTER 29

Alston family home
Fort Worth, Texas

Running the family while she was under the constant threat of financial ruin took its toll on Connie. She climbed into bed every night, exhausted – to the point where she usually fell asleep in her day clothes and shoes.

Just after sunrise, an old-fashioned telephone ring echoed from the kitchen and into the bedroom. Connie's groggy eyelids ripped open as she tried to figure out where she was. The phone rang so rarely these days that she jumped out of bed and ran into the kitchen, slamming her little toe into the door. She jumped up and down, hooting and hollering as she lunged for her cellphone.

"Hello?" she cried, trying to mask the foot pain.

"Connie, this is Chris. I have news."

"Okaaaay," Connie said cautiously.

"I'm sure you heard the president announce that the Little Turtle returned earlier today."

"Yeah, sure, totally," Connie said, oblivious to that news, having just woken up. She had purposely avoided the news after Chris said the crew was most likely dead.

"Brace yourself, Connie," he said with anticipation. "Adam is alive. I just spoke with him. I have some people coming to pick you up."

"WHAT? Where is he? Is he okay?" she screamed with utter joy.

"He's in a quarantine tank in Dayton. The capsule crash-landed into Lake Erie and it was the closest facility."

"How is he?" she yelped.

"He's had a rough time," Chris admitted. "Gather your things for a long stay. He's in quarantine for three weeks. Our guys will be by to pick you up in a couple of hours."

"Thank you, Chris. Are you in Dayton or here?"

"I'm in Dayton right now, in between meetings, but I'll be down to meet you."

"Okay, I'll see you then."

Connie searched the house for Catie and Cody. They were in the front room playing multi-player Minecraft.

"Kids, I have some news for you."

"Yeah?" they said in unison, distracted by the video game.

"We're going to visit somebody very special."

"Who? Is it Gramma?" Cody asked.

She leaned toward them and spoke in a whispered tone.

"It's your Dad. He's in Ohio and we're going to visit him."

Both kids turned their heads toward their mom with their jaws dropped.

"He's *alive*?" they screamed.

Connie nodded vigorously, tears streaming down her face. The kids jumped up and ran to her.

"He's alive, kiddos. Your Daddy is alive."

She gave them both a big group hug.

"Okay, now go pack your bags," Connie instructed. "We're going to be in Ohio for a few weeks."

The kids hopped up and ran to their rooms. Connie dragged her biggest suitcase down from the attic and began filling it with clothing. She wheeled the stuffed bag to the front door.

"Kids, bring your suitcases here!" she yelled down the hallway. They came running, eager to travel.

The knock came quicker than expected. Connie opened the door. Two large men wearing mirrored sunglasses stood on the porch.

"Hello, Mrs. Alston. We're here to take you to the airport."

The taller of the two men showed her his government ID badge.

"Hi, fellas. These are our bags," she explained. "Hey kids, come on, time to go."

The men picked up the suitcases like picking up toys and transported them out to the black Cadillac Escalades lining the street. Connie and the kids got into the middle one. They drove out of Wanigas and to the Meacham Business Jet airport a few miles away.

The convoy of Escalades approached a large chainlink gate at the edge of the airport. The driver handed his badge to the security guard manning the gate. The guard looked over the ID and eyed the driver before finally signaling for him to go on through. The vehicles rumbled through the gate and out onto the tarmac, pulling up next to a large white business jet. The kids piled out after their Mom. They looked in awe at the jet.

"This is for us?" Connie asked.

"Yes, ma'am," the driver assured her.

She walked up the small flight of stairs and onto the airplane. Sitting in the back was Chris Tankovitch, typing on a laptop. He looked up to see Connie and her brilliant smile.

Chris looked confused.

"Is it just you?" he asked.

Just then, two loud children rambled up through the door, fighting about which of them would fly the airplane.

"Hi, Chris. It's the whole Alston clan today," she laughed.

"Great," Chris said. "Buckle up and we'll be off. It'll take us about two hours to get there. It's good to see you again, Connie."

"Oh, you're too sweet, it's good to see you too, Chris."

After everybody buckled in, Chris walked up to the cockpit to let the pilots know it was time to go. The kids watched out the windows as the Cadillac convoy drove away from the airplane. Excitement filled the cabin as the engines spun up and the airplane taxied out to the runway.

Connie leaned toward Cody and Catie.

"Next stop is your Daddy."

CHAPTER 30

Quarantine hangar
Wright Patterson Air Force Base
Dayton, Ohio

A long beam of sunlight illuminated the floor of the hangar like a laser – turned on briefly and then dimmed back to darkness, turned off with the closing of the main door. A woman and two children stood just inside the main entry door to the quarantine hangar. They hesitated for a moment, but then quickly walked and then ran toward the center of the large cavernous building.

The quarantine tank sat prominently in the room, slightly larger than the classic silver airstream trailers of the previous century. Adam had been laying down on the cot in the quarantine tank. He'd popped up when he heard the squeak of the door; the scientists and physicians never used that entrance – only the few visitors that had come. Adam walked over to the window. A smile took over his face. Walking toward him, yes *walking* toward him, was the love of his life and the two little children that caused him to fall in love all over again. Uncontrollably, tears of relief streamed down his face – for months he thought he'd never see them again and yet, here they were. He hadn't seen his wife walk without crutches in years. All his dreams were coming true at once.

Connie walked straight to the window, her smile outdoing even his. Her hand lifted up and pressed on the window. Adam lifted his hand and pressed it on the glass, matching hers.

"Daddy! Daddy!" yelled both kids at the same time. They jumped up and down and slapped at the glass. Adam knelt down and slapped the glass, too.

"Hey kiddos! I'd give you a big hug if I wasn't potentially carrying a deadly alien virus," he laughed.

Both kids suddenly backed away.

"Your hair, Daddy! It's all white!"

"I know, right? Who knew Mars would turn my hair white?"

They giggled with laughter.

Connie looked at the kids and then back at Adam.

"Well, I..." she trailed off.

"Yes?" Adam asked whimsically.

"What do I say to the man that I thought was dead, but has miraculously come back to life?"

Adam shrugged his shoulders. "Halleluiah?"

She laughed. "Nice. How long do you have to be in there?"

Adam stood back up.

"About twenty one days in total. It's not so bad. I have all the creature comforts."

"Aren't you bored?" Connie asked.

"After the trip I just took?" Adam laughed. "I crave boredom. Seriously, I want zero excitement."

Adam pointed his finger behind him to a guy sitting on a sofa. "Besides, I've got Tim here. He was the boat driver that pulled me out of Lake Erie. Now he's contaminated, too. He's pissed."

"Oh my," she said, snickering. Then she yelled, "Thank you Mr. Tim for saving my husband!" It echoed off the cavernous hangar walls.

Tim gave her a two-fingered peace sign before returning to his magazine.

Adam suddenly remembered his recent VIP visitor.

"Oh, and the former NASA director came to visit. Chris Tankovitch is still a top-notch guy."

"Chris has been our savior all these months. He kept us informed whenever anything happened."

She shook her head from side to side with a pitying look.

"You've had such a rough journey, honey," she said. "I want to know everything about it, but part of me doesn't care. I'm just glad you made it home."

"Me too," Adam said. He leaned closer to the glass. "To be honest, I'm having a hard time hearing you. Can you pick up the phone?"

He pointed down. Connie followed his direction. She picked up the phone and held it close.

"We thought," she paused as a tear ran down her cheek.

"We thought you were dead all this time."

"I know, sweetheart. I'm sorry I ever left."

She lifted her other hand up to the window. Adam mirrored her movement again.

"We even cashed-in your life insurance policy."

"Oh, really?" Adam said with a grin. "How much was I worth?"

Connie leaned her head to one side.

"Unfortunately, not much," she admitted with a frown. "But none of that matters now."

She caught herself smiling again, ear to ear. The kids tugged at her hand.

"Connie, I noticed you walking over here. I take it the surgery was a total success?"

"I had the surgery several months ago and the stem cells worked like a charm."

"That's awesome. I'm glad Keller Murch's million dollar bonus was put to good use."

Connie grimaced at the thought of that million dollar bonus. It was all gone, but now was not the time to tell Adam. She reached down and picked up Cody.

She furrowed her brow. "Has NASA provided you with some professional people to talk to about the trip?"

"You mean a psychiatrist?" Adam asked.

Connie nodded.

"Not quite that bad. They did send in a couple of psychologists to chat with me for a bit. They were friendly. I mean, I've only been back for what, 12 hours? But yeah, they've got some good people helping me. They say I have mild PTSD, you know, from being stranded on a foreign freakin' planet fifty million miles away."

He saw that she didn't like his humor or language.

"Sorry, sorry. Yes, I'm talking with a doctor here."

"I'm glad. Well, do you mind if we just have a seat here while you go about quarantining yourself?"

"For how long?" Adam asked.

"For as long as it takes," Connie answered.

Adam gave a chuckle.

"Sure, hey I have a few books here. How about I read to the kids?"

"Yeah, Daddy, read us a book. We'll sit right here," Catie said.

"Your hair is really scary," Cody added.

CHAPTER 31

Conference room
NASA Jennings Fort Worth Manned Spacecraft Center
Fort Worth, Texas

"Adam Alston lost the damned anti-gravity cube," Chris Tankovitch said to the crowd of engineers and managers sitting around the table. A palpable groan cascaded through the audience. "I've just returned from his quarantine hangar in Dayton."

"Why didn't Alexis go up there?" the red-headed engineer asked. He glanced from Chris to Alexis.

Alexis leaned toward her microphone.

"Because I wanted Adam to see a familiar face. He doesn't know me from Adam, no pun intended," she said with a chuckle.

"Tell me," Alexis said, "do you have any contingency plans?"

"Well, I'm just the vending-machine services director," Chris replied.

"No, you're my unofficial deputy now. You're my liaison to Adam," Alexis confirmed.

Chris looked around to see a few heads nodding approval.

"Okay, then," Chris said with authority. "Here's the situation. Cancer deaths are skyrocketing and the key to a potential cure was just lost. Plan A is to find the anti-gravity cube. It was last seen travelling down at an angle toward either Indiana or Ohio. Adam couldn't remember."

"He couldn't remember?" Alexis asked.

"I guess the Little Turtle was literally ripping apart during that stage and we're lucky Adam isn't somewhere in Indiana... *and Ohio*. But I have other news. Perhaps a Plan B."

Chris nodded toward a long-haired man named Nathan, known as *MapGuy* to his coworkers.

"Nathan Cannon is a cartographer here and he'd like to share the big news about what his team has discovered."

Chris sat down as MapGuy stood up and handed out a small packet of papers.

"Hi, I'm NateGuy," he said nervously. "I mean Nathan, but everybody just calls me MapGuy."

"Hi, MapGuy," Alexis said, leaning her head to one side to show she was paying attention.

"Well, okay. I'll just say it right up front. The translation of the Martian text states that they had a laboratory here on Earth and it even gives the coordinates. Given the news about Adam Alston losing the anti-gravity cube, we hope the laboratory may have a similar example of that technology that we can use instead."

A mumble of side conversations snowballed around the room.

"But it's not that easy," MapGuy interrupted everyone's excitement. "If you look at your packet, you'll see a set of coordinates. Exact longitude and latitude. But wacky huge numbers, right?"

The people in the room looked down and studied the stack of papers in front of them.

"Are you assuming that the Martians used a similar method to map their globe like we do?" Alexis asked skeptically.

"That's right. We tried several methods using various cartographical standards, but settled on our human method because the numbers made more sense. It turns out that history often picks a winner based on technical merit. Not always, but sometimes, what works best does indeed become the standard. We're *assuming*."

Alexis thumbed through the paperwork again and then looked back up at MapGuy.

"What's the importance of 660?" she asked.

"Ah, yes, you jumped right into the meat of things. Their circles are divided up into 660 degrees," MapGuy said.

"That seems silly," the redheaded engineer laughed, his shirt embroidered with the phrase *Flight Controls*.

"Well, maybe at first, but ask yourself why we divide our circles into 360 degrees," MapGuy asked. "That seems pretty silly, too, right?"

Everybody shrugged their shoulders at this seemingly trivial pursuit.

"Let's talk about *our* circle first. We think it may have

been originally based on the early Persian calendar which had 360 days — maybe even further back to Babylonian times. Each month had 30 days. For example, to go once around the Sun took 360 days, according to the ancient Persians."

Alexis chimed in, "Yes, but our years are 365 days — wouldn't their calendar have drifted off as the missing days piled up?"

"Yes, of course, but they fixed that by adding an extra month every six years."

"Oh, okay," Alexis laughed at the seemingly arbitrary solution.

"We guessed that the Martians may have followed the same logic. It takes about 668.6 days to go around the sun."

"I think you made a mistake," Chris retorted. "Mars takes 687 days to go around the Sun."

"No, that's how many *Earth* days it takes for Mars to go around the Sun. The Martians didn't know about Earth when they developed their early geometry. So they used their own definition of a day which is roughly 24.6 Earth hours. Obviously we don't know what units they used to divide each individual day into."

"Okay," Chris said, embarrassed at the correction.

MapGuy continued.

"So, as I was saying, if we assumed that the Martians followed a similar line of logic in their early days, then their circle would end up with somewhere between 660 and 670 degrees, depending on how much error they accepted."

The red-headed engineer laughed, saying, "They could've had 666 days in their year?"

"Yes, that's very possible... but unlikely. I think it was

660 because it's an even number, easily divisible."

"But so is 666," the engineer said.

"True, but we think it was likely to be 660 because it's sexagesimal"

"Sexa-what?" Chris asked.

"That just means a base-60 counting system, similar to early mathematics on Earth thousands of years ago. You know, just like the Babylonians? These ancient base-60 mathematics are pervasive throughout modern day society. After all, it's why we have sixty minutes in an hour and sixty seconds in a minute."

"Whoa, information overload," the redheaded engineer laughed nervously.

"Cut to the chase, please," Alexis said.

"Of course," MapGuy said. "If you convert what the Martian translation tells us — I mean convert it to our 360 degree circles, then you get a rough angle of 100 degrees East for longitude and 17 degrees South for latitude."

Alexis turned to the laptop on her desk and began furiously typing.

"Alexis?" Chris asked.

"I'm typing them into Google Earth," she said. "Okay, that puts us right in the middle of some ocean water west of Australia. Nowhere special."

MapGuy laughed.

"You're making a mistake."

"I am?" Alexis asked.

"Yes, and you've discovered our biggest problem," he said. "We have what is essentially a treasure map and it tells us how far the X is from the start, but the problem is we don't know *where* to start."

"What do you mean?" Alexis asked, squinting her eyes at the screen.

"You just typed into Google Earth a longitude of 100 degrees East and 17 degrees South. But our longitude is based on an arbitrary starting point of Greenwich, England. When the Martians were here, Greenwich was just a forest on the southern bank of what we now call the Thames River."

Alexis laughed at her assumption.

"So what did they use as the zero-degree location for longitude?" she asked. "The *so-called* starting point?"

"That is exactly what my entire team has been struggling with. The Martians left out that bit of information."

"And what do you think the answer is?" Chris asked.

"Well, if you were putting coordinates on a foreign planet, what would *you* use as a starting point for longitude?" MapGuy asked.

"Some prominent geographic landmark?" Chris asked.

"Bingo," MapGuy confirmed. "And we think we've figured it out. But I need to check one more thing to confirm that theory."

CHAPTER 32

New York City

"After you, Captain Alston," Connie said to her husband, now wearing his astronaut uniform (minus the helmet) and standing in the lobby of the Grand Morgan hotel in New York City. With the quarantine period over, it was time for Adam to celebrate.

"No way! After you, Mrs. Alston," Adam said. "And after my lovely children, too."

The concierge opened the door to a cheering crowd of thousands gathered in front of the hotel. Adam and his family walked out and climbed aboard a parade float made up to look like the Little Turtle spaceship. While in quarantine, Adam dyed his hair black to get rid of the pure white that had grown in during the return voyage. He and Chris agreed that the stark white would've been disturbing to the general public.

One of the largest ticker-tape parades in New York City

history took place on August 13, 1969 to celebrate the triumphant return of the first astronauts to walk on the Moon. Just as the Moon landing achievement had been overshadowed by Adam's achievement of being the first to walk on Mars, the current ticker-tape parade record was being smashed this day – celebrating the miraculous return of Captain Adam Alston, the apple of America's eye. Adam was the hero for a troubled time.

He sat proudly atop the parade float, waving to the mass of humanity lining the streets. His family sat in seats near the front. The float moved slowly down Broadway. A downpour of glitter and ticker tape filled the sky. The crowds cheered him on, maintaining a deafening roar. Catie and Cody smiled while covering their ears.

Adam finally felt the pride he'd searched for his entire life. Like a sponge, he soaked up every hoot and holler, every cheer and yell. He looked to his side to see if Yeva was enjoying her newfound fame, too. Just as if getting punched in the gut, it all rushed back. The terrible final weeks of their voyage. How could he forget. He must forget. The truth was too awful. She was still in her suit, in a lonely field somewhere in the Midwest. NASA search teams hadn't found her yet. A sudden wave of panic set over Adam. He breathed heavily.

Calm down. Breathe slow, he told himself. That's exactly what Yeva told him to do.

As the convoy of floats rounded the last corner near the end of the parade, Adam spied a Catholic church and signaled for the driver to stop. The crowd watched in confusion as Adam clambered down the side of the float, nearly falling off the final step. The crowd caught him.

"Thank you, kind people," he said to them.

Connie and the kids looked confused too, but they stayed in the float. She raised her hands, palms up, to tell the kids she had no idea what he was doing.

Adam wiped the ticker tape and glitter from his space suit. He was consumed by the crowd as he struggled up the limestone stairs toward the old wooden church doors. He pulled on them and they creaked open. The outside roar muffled itself as he closed the doors behind him.

A security guard followed him in. "Captain Alston," he said as quietly as possible.

"I'm fine," Adam said. He looked like a man on a mission.

Unable to stop Adam, the security guard spoke into the headset to let the other security detail know what was happening.

Adam walked right up to the back of a line of people who were waiting for the confessional. He tapped his fingers nervously on the wooden railing. Frustrated, he walked past the entire line and approached the woman standing at the front. He held up a $20 bill in front of her.

"I'm in a hurry, would it be okay if I cut in front of you?"

The woman looked at the money and then nodded to him without saying a word. She grabbed the money, then turned to the woman behind her and shrugged her shoulders. Adam opened the confessional door and stepped inside the tiny room. He sat down on the wooden seat.

I don't remember it being this claustrophobic, he thought.

The priest on the other side of the wall gave a cough that implied he was ready to begin.

"Hello," Adam said.

"Hello, my child," the priest said in a compassionate tone.

"So, would it be okay if I talked first?"

Silence.

"Young man, are you Catholic?" the priest asked.

"I was when I was a kid," Adam admitted. "I went to Catholic school for a few years."

"Okay, well, let's just say you're a bit rusty. That's okay. What's on your mind?"

"Well, I've sinned and I'm looking for any type of forgiveness I can get."

The priest contemplated a good answer.

"Well, what is the nature of your sins?"

Adam swallowed hard before speaking.

"I killed a man and, technically, a woman, too."

"Oh my," the priest said.

"On Mars," Adam added.

The priest gave a lopsided grin.

"I see. So you were on Mars and killed a Martian?"

"No, no, no. I was on Mars for a few days and I killed a man. The woman happened later on."

The priest let out a sigh.

"Well, my son, those are very serious sins against all that we stand for in Christianity. Have you considered turning yourself in to the authorities?"

Adam pondered the question.

"No, not really. In a way, one was self-defense and the other was mercy."

"Even mercy killing goes against..."

"I know," Adam cut him off. "Nobody seems to know

about it here on Earth. I'm just stewing in my own pot of guilt."

The priest rotated his wrist to look at his old Timex watch. *Another kook,* he thought. "Just because nobody knows you have committed these crimes — that doesn't make it all right to go unpunished. I think you know deep down what you have to do."

The security guard walked toward the confessional door, prompted by a group of new security guards who'd followed him into the church. The guard knocked on the door and explained, "Captain Alston, we have to return to the parade if we want to stay on schedule."

The priest was shocked back into reality. He jumped out of his confessional and opened the door to Adam.

"Wait a second, are you *the* Adam Alston?" asked the priest. "Hey, everybody, this is the first person to walk on Mars. And he's in our church!"

The priest shook Adam's hand as the security guard led him away and back to the parade. The priest smiled, pointed his finger at the front door and said, "Now there's a true American hero."

CHAPTER 33

Alston family home
Fort Worth, Texas

(Three days later)

"No man can step in the same river twice," Adam said as he walked into his living room for the first time in nearly half a year.

"What are you talking about, sweetheart?" Connie asked.

Adam looked around, soaking in the ambience and feel of the house. It was just like he'd remembered it, but with enough subtle differences to make him know that, from this point on, it was not the same house.

"It's an old saying that means time is constantly flowing by, so if you revisit someplace from your past," he paused. "It's in a different location in time. It can never be the same."

"Your adventure has made you introspective. Are you saying we're in your past, too?"

Adam laughed — snapping out of his nostalgic mood.

"You are my past, present and future," he smiled, giving her a kiss. "Hey kids, let's go out to the swingset. I assume you didn't throw that out?"

Connie gave him a friendly punch on the shoulder as the kids and Adam ran into the back yard. Connie joined him and they stayed outside until sunset.

On the following Sunday evening, Adam drove to Dallas to give an informal talk to the Mars Exploration Society. Even before the mission, they'd asked him to come speak, but he felt he had nothing productive to share yet — he hadn't earned the right to speak. Now, back from Mars, he was ready. He asked them to not make a public announcement about his visit. Adam just wanted to speak to a group of manned space-travel enthusiasts about his experiences on the Red Planet.

After a fine dinner at the Spaghetti Warehouse, Adam stood up at the front of the meeting room and gave a heartfelt talk about the nitty gritty details regarding everyday life during the trip. He went into the awe and wonder of what they found while exploring the Martian temple.

At the end of his talk, one member of the audience, a retired engineer, asked, "What really happened to the crew?"

Adam looked down at the lectern and thought quietly for ten awkward seconds.

"You know, that's a really good and fair question. We faced challenges that were life and death. Keller gave up his life to save mine and, well, I'm just not ready to go into the details about it. I'm sorry about that."

The club president stood up, saying, "That's okay Adam. Everybody, let's thank Captain Alston for coming here tonight. It's a long drive from Fort Worth."

"And a long flight from Mars!" another engineer yelled over the applause.

The sound of that clapping, which he heard a lot these days, felt awesome and strange in his memory during the drive home from Dallas that night.

Adam kept thinking about the lie he perpetuated about Keller's heroic behavior. Like all big lies, he hoped that if he told it enough, he'd soon remember it as the truth.

A message was waiting for him when he got home. Connie handed him a Post-it note telling him to call a man named Oliver Woolie.

"He said he has some paying jobs for you," Connie said.

"I'm not going to call him," Adam lamented. "He's just one of those leeches that got our phone number."

Connie looked panicked.

"Adam, sweetheart, please call him. He sounded legit. And we need the money."

Adam chuckled.

"We should have plenty left over from the Keller Murch bonus. Your surgery was only half a million."

"Not... exactly," she admitted. "There were extra expenses and taxes and physical therapy."

"How much is left?" Adam asked, now concerned.

"Nothing."

"Nothing?" Adam said incredulously, his voice rising.

"Actually, *less* than nothing. Not counting the mortgage, we're in the hole by eighty thousand dollars."

Adam's jaw fell open in astonishment.

"We've got debt collectors calling us," Connie grimaced. "They even called my mom to get to me. It's very embarrassing. I've been trying to hide all this from you, but we're all maxed out."

Adam slumped down in his seat.

"I'm sorry," Connie cried. "I thought you wanted me to get the operation."

"Yes, absolutely," Adam admitted. "You did the right thing. It's just that, when I left for Mars, we were struggling and when I got back, well, we're still struggling."

Adam sighed.

"But in between," he said with a grin. "You got your independence back and you kept our kids alive and happy."

Adam gave her a big hug.

"We'll get through this," he said.

"Call him," Connie said. "Please."

After breakfast the next morning, Adam dialed the number for this Oliver Woolie person. It rang and rang.

"Hey Adam!" a high-energy voice answered.

"Is it too early?" Adam asked.

"No, no. I'm on the east coast," Oliver replied. "I'm an hour ahead of you."

"I got your message. What's up?"

"Look, Adam. I want to help you," Oliver said, sounding like a used car salesman. "I work in the NASA public relations office — I'm actually handling all of the press releases regarding the Mars mission. But I've got a deal I'd like to talk with you about."

Here we go, Adam thought, rolling his eyes.

"Look here, Adam, I am willing to go rogue and be your manager. You know that speech you gave last night at the Mars Exploration Society?"

Adam could not figure out how he knew about that.

"Don't worry," Oliver laughed. "I don't have spies. Your wife told me."

Adam laughed in relief.

"Adam, how would you like to give that same speech over and over, but get paid fifty thousand dollars every time?"

Adam took a deep breath, nearly jumping out of his skin with excitement. "That would be nice," he said, trying to hide his true emotions.

"You're right, that would be nice. It would be damn nice. And I'll only take twenty percent as my commission."

Silence.

"Do we have a gentlemen's agreement?" Oliver asked.

Adam nodded his head.

"Are you nodding your head, Adam? Because I can't see through the phone."

"Yes, it's a deal," Adam said, laughing.

"Great! Let me get a schedule together so you can start making some serious money."

"And you'll make money too," Adam said sarcastically.

"Adam?" Oliver said softly. "Don't make this about me. This is about you. You're about to become a very rich man."

CHAPTER 34

Conference room
NASA Jennings Manned Spacecraft Center
Fort Worth, Texas

"I think we've confirmed the reference starting point for longitude," MapGuy said to the room full of engineers.

Chris looked around the table and stopped at Alexis. Her stare turned into a smile.

"Well? Go on," Alexis said, leaning back into her chair.

MapGuy was very animated. He hopped out of his seat and started pacing.

"We've been eliminating a lot of false starts and poor choices, but I think the Martians chose the one single point on the planet that could not be confused for any other. One point that would be here for a long time."

He nearly jumped up and down with excitement.

"Anybody want to take a guess?"

"No," Alexis said. "Just do your job and tell us."

MapGuy's balloon of excitement popped.

"It's Mount Everest!" he yelled. "We think the Martians would've chosen the highest point on the planet."

Chris shook his head. "But that's way too far north of the equator."

"Yes, but this isn't about the lines of latitude, Mr. Tankovitch. We're talking about the vertical lines of longitude. Draw a line from the top of the earth to the bottom of the earth, passing through the top of Mount Everest — *that* is the Martian line for zero longitude. It's almost too obvious, right?"

Alexis spun to her laptop and started to type, but then stopped. She shook her head.

"I can't just type the Martian coordinates into Google Earth as is, can I," she stated.

"Right. You'll need to shift them using Mount Everest as the starting point. Type in the following. Latitude is the same at 17 degrees South, but type in the shifted Longitude of 172 degrees West."

"You mean East?" she asked.

"No, it's *West*. Trust me, I did the math for you."

Alexis typed furiously.

"Well, look at that. The Tonga Trench. One of the deepest locations on Earth."

"Exactly," MapGuy said, nodding his head up and down. "The coordinates point to a hill near the bottom of the Tonga Trench. Perhaps that *was* the deepest part of the ocean back then — perhaps tectonic movement has changed things."

Chris shifted in his chair.

"I doubt tectonic movement could change things that

much over just two hundred thousand years," Chris said with a skeptical expression. "Besides, if I was going to build a laboratory on a foreign planet, why would I build it thousands of feet below the ocean? That seems like way too much work."

MapGuy shrugged his shoulders. "*Tens* of thousands of feet. And we don't know. Perhaps they did it to minimize their interaction with earthbound flora or fauna or bacteria."

"What do you recommend we do now?" Alexis asked.

"Well, let's see," he said arrogantly. "You get a research sub and a crew and you go down there. But here's the catch. I think you should do this carefully and quietly. At a minimum, *do not* release the coordinates. You'll have every treasure hunter and James Cameron wannabe trying to get there first. Take your time. Get a machine that can work at that depth. Then go exploring."

Alexis nodded in agreement.

"We must be careful with this," she said, staring at each person in the room. "No leaks, people. Got it?"

MapGuy sat down, his hand curled tightly into a fist, to celebrate having given a perfect presentation.

He tapped the table with this other hand.

"Do not," he paused for effect. "Release those coordinates."

CHAPTER 35

The large banquet room
Cleveland Energy Club
Cleveland, Ohio

Adam stood frozen in front of the microphone. He looked down at his notes on the lectern, but only managed a cough to clear his throat. Eight hundred people paid $500 to listen to Adam recite his Mars adventure. The sea of people sat in front of him, staring at him. They wanted their money's worth. This was the first in a marathon series of speeches scheduled every day for the next month. His take, after manager and facility fees would be just over $150,000 *per night*. This talk alone would eliminate all of his debt. The clock was ticking. He reached out his clammy hand and took a drink of water.

His manager, Oliver Woolie, sat offstage behind the curtain and gave Adam a look that said *start talking!* Unable to speak off the cuff, Adam simply started to read from his notes. It wasn't very professional, but it was better than being mute.

"Ladies and gentlemen, wonderful citizens of Cleveland, thank you for having me here tonight. Normally, I would ask who travelled the farthest to this talk, but I'm afraid that answer would be me."

A few people laughed.

Remember to remove that joke, Adam thought.

"Tonight I want to tell you a story. It contains excitement, drama, and sadly — tragedy. That last part is the tough part and, thankfully, it is at the end of the story. When NASA asked me to be the leader for the Mars mission, it was the proudest moment of my professional career. It wasn't easy. It meant being away from my family, training for the mission in California. It meant spending time away from my family."

Oh man, I just said the same thing twice, Adam thought.

"I mean, it meant taking a risk that I might never see my family ever again."

Adam gulped more water.

"Our crew of four astronauts launched up to the International Space Station, we called it the ISS, where we prepared for final departure on the Little Turtle spacecraft. Little Turtle had been launched up to the ISS previously and awaited our arrival. We transferred over to the Little Turtle and with a mild clunk, we left for Mars."

Oh crap, I'm saying Little Turtle too much, Adam thought.

"No big rocket boom or anything. The amazing Murch rocket motors gently pushed on the spacecraft and never stopped pushing. We accelerated almost all the way to Mars.

However, we turned around and ignited traditional rockets to slow us down. Our final descent into the Martian atmosphere was done with the emergency parachutes. I say emergency, but they weren't really. They were designed to slow us down in the Earth's atmosphere on the return voyage. However, we were going too fast and it was our only option. Without those parachutes, we would've all perished."

A mumble went through the crowd. After all, the rest of his crew *did eventually die* under his leadership.

"After putting down our grounding cables to make sure we didn't have any dangerous buildup of static electricity, we went about setting up both the Little Turtle and the larger ship that arrived previously — we called that one the Big Turtle. I love those names, don't you?"

The crowd gave a brief, forced chuckle.

"We lowered the ground transport vehicle, which I will call the Golf Cart here and we were ready to go. Myself and cosmonaut Yeva Turoskova, exited the Big Turtle and went to the edge of the ramp. As we had agreed, I took the first step."

Sweat dripped from Adam's forehead — this was the first time he'd told that lie in public.

"I can't lie to you good people — it was amazing to set foot on Mars. To be the first human to ever walk on a foreign planet."

Adam felt it — his character. His public character was forming before his eyes. *Be a confident explorer*, he thought. *They will eat it up.*

"The surface was such a strange substance. A mixture of dust, powder, gravel and large stones – we call it regolith. The red sand dunes were incredible. We drove to the alien structure and found a stone building with only one way in. It had a big round door. I've been told that the stone building is now being called the Mars Temple."

On the large projection screen behind Adam appeared a photograph of the Mars Temple. Adam turned around to see the image. In the corner of the photograph was Yeva. Adam stopped talking. His thoughts drifted for a moment as more sweat poured down his face. He slowly turned back around with a blank face. He felt Yeva looking at him from the picture. The brief pause grew into an uncomfortably long pause. Off stage, Oliver snapped his fingers to get Adam's attention. Adam came to and located where he left off in his notes.

"This round door you see behind me was quite the puzzle. Yeva and I dug the sandy soil out from underneath one side and the door eventually rolled open. So we went inside. It was a huge room with a smaller room off to the right side. Inside the large room was a temple to the Martian's history. Their lives, their language, their accomplishments, and a clue to what happened to them. These Martians had invented a cure for cancer and they gave us the instructions for it."

More water. Adam sweated profusely now. He was starting to skip details. He quickly figured that he'd already earned about forty thousand dollars.

"In the smaller room, written on the wall, were balanced chemical equations showing how to make this amazing cure-all medicine. The next day, Keller and I explored that room and that was when the first tragedy struck. During our process of photographing the walls, there was a small tremor, a *Mars-quake* for lack of a better term.

The round door rolled back and trapped us in the Temple. We tried to communicate back to the Big Turtle, but the signal couldn't get through the thick walls. We took one of our oxygen tanks and knocked the end off of it — that briefly turned it into a rocket and we used it to push the door open."

A murmur went through the crowd as people discussed this clever use of an oxygen tank.

"This left us with a problem. We didn't have enough air left for both of us. So Keller," Adam paused. "He gave me his remaining air and told me to go on. He made this amazing decision because I had a family and he did not. I can never apologize enough for such generosity and selflessness. Keller saved my life."

Apologize? Crap! I meant thank, Adam thought.

Adams collar was now soaking wet. The lies were piling up.

"When I got back to the Big Turtle, Yeva and Molly were clearly upset about the situation. After getting sufficient oxygen supplies, I returned to the Mars Temple and recovered Keller's body. We buried it next to the Big Turtle. Unfortunately, during this process, Molly exited the station with a flawed pressure-relief valve. She knelt down next to the grave to pray and slowly fell unconscious — before we knew it, she had passed away. Mars is more than *hostile* — it is *incompatible* with life. It was truly the worst day of my life, having lost two dear friends and coworkers, one because of an act of selflessness and one because of an accident."

Adam paused and put his hand in a salute position over his eyes to shield him from the bright stage lights. He scouted the front of the stage to find the stage manager. Adam pointed to his empty glass of water to signal that he needed some more. The stage manager ran off into the shadows to get him another drink.

One thing Adam couldn't get past was the sound of silverware clinking on the plates as his customers ate their chicken parmesan or tilapia.

"This was about the time that we lost communication with Earth."

Adam was forgetting details left and right, just wanting to finish.

"Yeva and I eventually completed most of our tests, I mean tasks, and prepared the ship for return. Unfortunately, during this phase, I somehow forgot to remove the grounding cables that we'd put down after first arriving. During our initial ascent, we were halted by the grounding cables. Fortunately we still had a remote-controlled helper vehicle on the ground and I was able to maneuver it to hit the cable at high speed. That broke us free from the grasp of Mars."

Adam received his new glass of water and drank it to prepare for final part of his talk.

"We had enough rocket power to leave the surface and enter orbit. Two things happened during the ascent that forever changed our chances of surviving the trip home. First, our long-range antenna broke off. Second, during the ascent our escape hatch blew away, leaving a huge gaping hole in the ship that was supposed to transport us back to Earth. I was very scared. So the first thing we did was put a pile of blankets and metal cabinet doors to cover the hole. The blankets acted as gaskets and the metal doors provided the structure. Then we pressurized the ship."

Adam paused to prepare.

"During the four-month journey home, we tried like hell not to die. This was very difficult as our systems were failing one by one. Humidity was collecting on every metal surface because we'd dropped the temperature to save energy. Only half of the Murch rocket motors were working. We were in bad shape. Finally, we reduced the oxygen in the cabin to conserve the surviving systems and resources. This was a tough decision because we knew it would make our thinking unreliable."

"Only a few weeks before returning, Yeva developed a bad pain in her lower abdomen. Using the emergency medical instructions, we determined that Yeva had appendicitis. Unfortunately, we'd lost most of our medical kit when the escape-hatch door blew off. I was hoping she could make it back in time for medical care here, but her pain became so severe that she was going in and out of consciousness. We had to try something."

Sweat poured into Adams eyes and he began to tear up.

"We used scissors, of all things, to make the incision. It was awful."

Adam paused and peered out at the crowd. The clinks of silverware on the plates halted as the audience sat transfixed.

"Keep in mind the only medicine we had was Tylenol and a few anti-anxiety medications. Yeva was a trooper, though. I was able to remove her appendix, but we couldn't stop the bleeding completely. She grew more and more faint and she was in so much pain. I was quietly hoping she would pass on during one of her bouts of unconsciousness. However, during one of her conscious moments, Yeva asked for one of our last two remaining Red Hope vials."

You could hear a pin drop. The only sound was the air

conditioning powering on.

"What I'm about to tell you was considered top-secret, but a lot has changed and I don't care about that classification anymore. I want to tell you. Our spacecraft was equipped with four small vials of poison, only to be used in a catastrophic situation when all hope was lost. The code name was Red Hope. I gave her one and she drank it and... she began foaming at the mouth, but it didn't work. She didn't die. She was shaking terribly. She asked for the second one, but was shaking too badly to take it. So I helped her. I held it as she drank it. I helped her pass on to Heaven."

Adam stopped and looked down.

"The woman that I trained with. The woman who trusted her life to me, in the end, had to rely on me to make her pain go away."

Waiters were flooding into the room to clear plates, making space for delivery of the desert dishes. Adam had to speak up over the noise of ceramic plates clinking.

"This mission had an enormous cost. America lost two great individuals. Russia lost a great scientist. Now, I don't know what ultimate good will come from this mission, but I hope that it won't be in vain. I hope that we will be able to find that cure for cancer – the gift that the Martians gave us. Thank you for listening and God bless you and your families on this beautiful evening."

The audience stood up and clapped loudly. Adam nodded to thank them, briefly forgetting that that he'd just made $150,000.

The banquet hall manager came up on stage, signaling for the lights to be brightened a little. He shook Adam's hand and lowered the microphone to his own short stature.

"Okay, ladies and gentlemen, I know I'm tearing up right now, but Captain Alston has agreed to have a few questions. First is you, over at the blue table."

The banquet manager pointed to a teenager standing at a blue-draped table. The kid was wearing a suit that was way too big, hanging off his shoulders. The teen spoke loudly.

"Hi, Captain Alston, I have a question and I don't mean to be disrespectful or anything, but why did you bury Mr. Murch and Ms. Hemphill on Mars instead of bringing them with you and, well, what happened to Yeva?"

The banquet hall manager covered the microphone and whispered to Adam, "Are you okay with answering that?"

"Yes, it's okay," he replied.

Adam cleared his throat and raised the microphone back up to his height.

"That's a fair question. We didn't have provisions on board for transporting their bodies on the ship. Our problem was very similar to what the early ocean explorers ran into when a crewmember died during a voyage. Because of the potential for disease, they would have a quick ceremony and dump the body overboard while they were at sea."

"And what about Yeva?" the teen asked again.

"Well, that was a special situation. We were so close to Earth and I didn't want to dump her overboard so to speak. I put her in her space suit and then I put on my own space suit and I essentially tethered her outside the ship. I opened the main door and used a nylon strap to keep her attached to the spacecraft. Her body would freeze in that situation and stay preserved so that she could have an honorable burial when we returned."

"She was just dangling behind the ship?"

"More or less, yes. I realize it's a terrible thing, but keep in mind that I couldn't keep her inside the ship."

The teenager sat down.

Adam added one more detail.

"Just prior to atmospheric re-entry, I brought her back in and belted her down using seatbelts. Unfortunately, the Little Turtle broke up during the final phase and most of the things inside the ship, including Yeva, were lost."

Adam was clearly becoming emotional and held his hand up.

"I realize I promised you a good question and answer session, but I think I have to stop. I'm sorry, folks."

The banquet manager patted him on the back and said, "Adam, I think we all understand." He turned to the crowd and said loudly, "Let's give him one more round of applause."

Adam received his second standing ovation of the night. He nodded his head in thanks and turned to Oliver who was still standing off-stage. Oliver gave him a thumbs-up sign. Adam walked toward the stage curtains and disappeared.

"Well, Adam, that's one down, thirty to go," Oliver said, shaking his hand. "The next one in Chicago pays even more."

"That was rough," Adam admitted. "I hope I can keep up the pace you've got scheduled."

Oliver laughed.

"This might make it easier."

He handed Adam a piece of paper. It was a stub from a check for $150,000. Adam stared at the impossible number.

"It's not a real check," Oliver said. "Just a stub. The payment has already been wired into your account. Congratulations, you're rich. *You're welcome.*"

"I can spend this?" Adam asked incredulously.

"Absolutely, buddy," Oliver said. "Go splurge. *Tomorrow*. Go splurge tomorrow. It's too late and you need to get some sleep."

Adam stared at the paper and then looked up at Oliver.

"I know exactly what I'm going to buy first thing tomorrow. And I want you to cancel all of my airline flights."

CHAPTER 36

Office of the administrative director
NASA Jennings Manned Spacecraft Center
Fort Worth, Texas

"That's a nice desk," Chris said. "It's oak, right?"

Alexis nodded her head, confirming Chris's suspicion.

"Must be nice. My desk in Houston was just a stamped metal government desk. Hadn't changed since the 1970's."

"Neither have you," Alexis joked, leaning her head slightly.

"Nice," he said sarcastically. "When's the president's press conference?"

"Right about now."

Alexis walked over to her conference table and turned on the office TV. The big three networks were already broadcasting from the new press room at the replacement White House. Chris and Alexis watched as the president entered the room quickly and adjusted the microphone.

President Beatrice Bexar began speaking.

"My fellow Americans. I have an announcement and I'll make it short. Our folks at NASA have been hard at work translating all of the findings from the Martian temple. Their latest discovery is that the Martians built a laboratory here on Earth roughly two-hundred thousand years ago. They even gave the coordinates, but of course, there was a catch. The Martians did not state clearly what their starting longitude line was — those are the vertical lines that slice the earth into 360 so-called orange slices. NASA's investigation found that Mount Everest was the starting point. We are assembling a team to go to this laboratory, but now, for their safety, we are not releasing the actual coordinates. Not yet."

The journalists in the press room went wild, hollering for attention to ask questions. The president would have none of it.

"Thank you for coming here today. I realize I haven't given you much to go on, but our people at NASA need some time to organize things before they release anything else. I will not be taking questions today."

The president left the room just as quickly as she entered it. The reporters all looked at each other with a sour smirk, as if they'd just be admonished by a teacher. There would be no coordinates for them today.

Back at NASA, Alexis breathed a sigh of relief. "Thank God," she said. "I'm so glad the president followed our recommendation and kept the coordinates secret."

"Well, it's only a matter of time before they get leaked," Chris saids. "Are you assembling a team?"

"Yes. We've contacted the team that runs the Deep

SEAK Explorer ship – that's the one that went down to the bottom of the Mariana Trench with a three-man sub. They are already booked, but I've asked them to reconsider. This is the US government after all. I told him it was their patriotic duty. Right?" Alexis said, laughing.

"Okay, well please keep me informed," Chris said. He stood up, straightened the pleats in his pants and walked out the door toward his new office.

No longer the vending machine manager, Chris was down the hall from Alexis, acting as her unofficial deputy director. His official task was overseeing the re-establishment of ground-based communications to all of NASA's satellites and deep-space exploration vehicles. It wasn't the same as being the director, but it sure beat fighting with engineers about broken coffee makers.

The job wasn't the only new development for Chris. As a man who'd always done the right thing and planned for the long term, he did something unexpected and irresponsible. Several weeks earlier, he cashed in a major portion of his retirement account to buy a house. Not just any house, but one of those modern houses perched up on the mesa overlooking Fort Worth. He called the neighborhood *Mount Olympus*.

It was a gated community with a guard during the day. The roof of his house had red ceramic tiles and the outside was covered in beige stucco. On his first trip to Fort Worth, he'd seen this mesa-top neighborhood from the freeway and was jealous of the people who lived there. He wondered how they paid for it. Now he knew. They paid through the teeth.

Every afternoon, Chris would sail past the guard and

wave at him, pretending that he himself was part of the idle rich that made up his neighborhood HOA meetings. Then Chris would cruise around the mesa top, going out of his way to view most of the streets. Finally, after arriving home, he would grab the mail before going inside his house — the smallest mansion on the hill.

As a new homeowner, his mail consisted mainly of junk. Three days after the president's press conference announcing Mount Everest as the reference longitude line, a plain white envelope showed up in Chris's mailbox. The return address simply read:

DMITRI STALOV
WINSLOW, AZ

Chris opened the envelope and found a single sheet of folded paper. The message was typed using an old mechanical typewriter that left subtle imprints in the paper. It read:

"Dear Director Tankovitch,

You will always be my favorite NASA administrator. I am writing to tell you that NASA has chosen the wrong reference line for longitude. They have the right idea, but the wrong starting point. They will be looking in the wrong place and delaying the cure for cancer, which is what I assume this treasure hunt is all about. Please come visit me for a chat next Tuesday at noon. If you don't know where, ask your American friends. I do love this country. Your discretion is appreciated.

Sincerely,

Dmitri Stalov

PS. I invented the CommKnock missile system."

Normally, Chris would've written this guy off as a crackpot except for one word — *CommKnock*. That name was top-secret, known only to the upper echelon of the military and the scientists that helped work on the rocket launch platforms. Chris fell into the latter group, having worked on rocket propulsion for his PhD dissertation three decades earlier.

Wow, this guy is willing to go out on a limb and put that term in a written letter, Chris thought.

Without anything other than a name, Chris was at a loss as to how to meet the so-called Mr. Stalov.

Chris wondered, *Why should I ask my American friends?*

CHAPTER 37

Porsche Dealership
Cleveland, Ohio

Adam stood in front of a Porsche, admiring the flawless candy-apple red finish. As he ran his fingers along the roofline, Adam saw in the reflection an image of a vehicle approaching the front gate to the dealership — he turned his head to look.

A man exited the car and opened the gate, occasionally staring suspiciously over at Adam. The man got back in his car and weaved his way through the car lot towards Adam. When he arrived, he rolled down his window.

"Did your car break down somewhere... far away?" the man asked with implied suspicion.

Adam chuckled. "No, I took a taxi here."

"Kind of early, dontcha think?"

"Yes it is," Adam agreed. "But I have to buy one of these quickly. I only have ten hours to get to Chicago."

"Well, I'm the manager," he said, reaching out to shake Adam's hand. "Let me go park and we can get started on the paperwork."

The manager drove to the main building. Adam followed him in through the front door.

"Please," the manager said, pointing to a chair. "Have a seat."

"Thanks," Adam said. He sat down in a black leather chair wrapped in fine wood.

"Is this one of those Eames lounge chairs?" Adam asked.

The manager paused for a moment.

"Yes, it is. I can see you recognize fine craftsmanship," the manager said, adding layers of flattery. Adam knew it and he liked it.

The manager logged in to his computer and asked Adam for his information. Adam handed him his driver's license. The manager paused for a second and looked up at Adam.

"Are you *the* Adam Alston?"

"Yes, I am," Adam said enthusiastically. "I was here in town to give a talk last night."

"Oh, yeah," the manager paused. "My boss went to that. He sent me a text — said it was great. I thought about going, but I couldn't aff..., well, I mean, I had other plans unfortunately. You know how it is."

"Just trying to share my story," Adam said.

The manager stood up and shook Adam's hand again.

"Thank you so much for gracing my dealership today. We get big sports stars in here all the time, but it's not very often that we get a real American hero. Can I get a picture?"

Adam approved with a head nod.

The manager walked around the desk and put his hand on Adam's shoulder. He held up his smartphone and took a selfie. The manager touched the screen a few times, posting the image to Facebook.

"Thanks, Captain Alston."

The manager walked back around and sat down.

"So, how would you like to pay for it today? Finance? We have some low-interest options."

"No thanks, I'd just like to wire the whole payment."

"Oh," the manager said with a smile. "Excellent. I'm glad to hear that you've reached the one percent club."

Adam handed his payment stub to the manager. It had his bank account information on it. The manager typed the information into the computer. He held his finger high up, pointed at the Enter key.

"Are you ready to pay?" the manager asked with a smile.

"You bet," Adam answered.

The manager plunked his finger down on the Enter key and looked at the screen over his glasses. He smiled again.

"All done, Captain Alston. Payment transferred. Let me go get the keys for you."

The manager left his desk and walked into a small room at the back of the lobby. He came back with the keys and a pouch.

"Inside the pouch is your paperwork and warranty information. And here are your keys."

"Thank you, sir," Adam said.

"Can I convince you to stay here for a while until the rest of my guys get here? I'm sure they'd like to meet you. And that would give us time to detail the car before you take off."

Adam shook his head.

"I'm afraid I really have to get going."

"All right then. Thank you for choosing Cleveland Porsche. Have a safe drive."

Adam walked through the doors with a head full of pride. He squeezed the key in his hand, the first real rich thing he'd ever bought in his life. It was a feeling of power and comfort. Most importantly, it was a feeling of financial stability — something he'd lacked for a long time.

So this is what the one-percenters feel like every day, he thought.

Adam unlocked the Porsche and climbed in, making himself comfortable. He peeled the price sheet from the window and threw it behind his seat. Adam pushed the start button on the dash and gunned the engine.

"Chicago, here I come."

CHAPTER 38

Chris Tankovitch sat at a break-room table just down the hallway from his office. A cup of coffee kept one hand warm. The letter from Dmitri Stalov sat in his other hand like a brick. He read through the simple wording from Dmitri, over and over, focusing on the key part:

"NASA has chosen the wrong reference line for longitude ... Please come visit me for a chat next Tuesday at noon."

Laughter interrupted his attention. Chris looked up to see several engineers in the room, all sitting at a table and looking at one of their smartphone screens. At another table an older guy read a newspaper while he drank his coffee —

he did not look up.

Out of the blue, Chris decided to quiz his fellow breakroom attendees about the surprise letter.

"Hey everybody, can I ask you a question?"

The lone engineer kept reading his newspaper. The gaggle of young engineers stopped laughing and turned around, giving some respect to the once-great former NASA director.

"See, I have a friend who is playing a treasure hunt game," Chris said.

"What kind of treasure hunt?" a young engineer with a crew cut asked.

"Well, he wants me to meet him for coffee, but all I know is the time and town," Chris replied. "Unfortunately, he didn't tell me the specific location."

The young engineers mumbled amongst themselves.

"What's the town?" the crew-cut engineer asked, now their spokesman.

"It's in Arizona. A town called Winslow."

The engineers looked around and then dove into their phones for Google searches.

"It's in Navajo County, Arizona, but that's all we can find."

The lone engineer laughed out loud and dropped his newspaper.

"Are you guys serious? You don't know this?" the loner asked.

"What?" Chris asked innocently.

"Come on Director Tankovitch, you're over forty years old, you should know this," the lone engineer complained.

Chris shrugged his shoulders.

"I guess I've had my head buried in research for too long," Chris admitted.

"Take it easy," the lone engineer said.

"I am," Chris replied. "I'm just trying to solve this riddle."

"No, Take It Easy — the song. You know, the song by the Eagles? It's a great American song," the lone engineer said.

"The song was written in Winslow, Arizona?" Chris asked.

"No...," the lone engineer groaned. "You know, the lyrics talk about standing on a corner in Winslow, Arizona? Surely you've heard it."

"Oh yeah, it's a fine sight or something?" Chris added.

The lone engineer nodded his head up and down with great exaggeration.

"Yes, yes, that's it. Your friend wants you to meet him at that corner. I think they even have a park or something there just because of that song."

"Thank you, kind sir," Chris said.

The lone engineer took this opportunity to admonish the culturally inexperienced group of young engineers.

"And as for you young kids, you need to stop listening to that modern crap and listen to good rock and roll."

They nodded their heads and then went back to laughing at the cat videos on their smartphones.

Chris speed-walked down the hallway to his office. He plopped into his seat and immediately Googled the Eagles song lyrics. Sure enough, there was a monument in Winslow dedicated to the song. Chris only had a few days to plan for this quick trip. It would be too long of a drive, so he decided to take his chances on the unpredictable airlines.

Chris stood up and pushed his black hair out of his face — he needed a haircut. He walked down the hallway and knocked on Alexis's door.

"Come on in," she said, putting down a manila folder she was reading from.

"So, I need to take an unscheduled vacation day on Tuesday."

"Okay, what's up?"

"I'm going to see an old friend for lunch."

"Who?" she asked. "We were married. I know all your old friends."

"You don't know him. It's just one day."

Chris turned to walk out.

"Here in town?" Alexis asked.

Chris paused.

"Actually, no. It's in Winslow, Arizona."

Alexis raised an eyebrow. She was curious now.

"Winslow. You mean like the Eagles song?"

Chris chuckled.

"Yes, same town. I'll be back Tuesday night."

"Wow, you're going all that way just to have lunch?"

"Good friends are hard to find," Chris said with a smirk. "Old friends are worth keeping in touch with. You understand how it is."

Alexis spun around in her chair, away from Chris and picked up her manila folder, starting to read again.

"I do," she said quietly.

CHAPTER 39

The large banquet hall
Science & Technology Museum
Chicago, Illinois

"With that last question, I thank you for having me here as the keynote speaker tonight," Adam said. "I hope you enjoyed the story as much as I enjoyed telling it."

He took a modest bow and walked off the stage and into the hallway.

Another 150 grand in the bank, he thought to himself, doing a modest fist-bump hidden from the audience.

Oliver, Adam's manager, was not at this venue. Instead he was at the next evening's location in St. Louis, taking care of some contractual issues that popped up. During their setup telecom with the banquet hall this morning, the St. Louis personnel did not mention the requirement that Adam have a bowl of green M&M's on his lectern. Adam didn't particularly like green M&M's, but this clause was hidden in the text of Oliver's standard contract to make sure that the event coordinator read every last detail. This trick was used by keynote speakers and rock stars alike. Oliver had just made sure that a bowl of green M&M's would be on the lectern. He looked at his watch. Adam's talk should've been over by now. Oliver pulled out his cellphone and dialed Adam.

Adam sat outside of the banquet hall at the museum, around the corner from the main door. He craved isolation after being the dancing monkey for one thousand paying customers. The cellphone in his pocket buzzed. It was a call coming from Oliver.

"Adam!" Oliver yelled excitedly. "Did you knock 'em dead tonight? Speech number two and you're twice as rich now."

Adam laughed. "You know, it went much better than the Cleveland speech. I added a few more jokes. Like the one about how 'I make this look harder than it really is'. They liked that."

"Great, man," Oliver said. "Hey, I need you to go down to the museum gift shop. Tell me when you're there."

"Okay," Adam said with suspicion. He walked down the large hallway toward the gift shop at the front of the museum. He stepped through the glass doors, not sure of what he was supposed to do.

"Oliver, I'm in the gift shop now."

"Good. Walk over to the magazine rack."

Adam stepped over to the modest magazine rack that

sold weekly news magazines and some niche monthlies.

"Okay, I'm here."

"Find Popular Mechanics. You can't miss the new issue, it's got a bright red cover. Store owners were supposed to put them out this morning."

Adam scanned the magazine rack up and down. Somebody had put a Time Magazine in front of the Popular Mechanics stack. He shifted the Time issue and then he gasped.

"Oh... my," Adam said.

Staring back at him was an image of himself and the headline, "To Mars And Back: The New American Hero."

"How about them apples, Adam?"

"Wow," Adam said. "Just wow."

"Do me a favor. Take a copy up to the cashier and buy it and see what he says. He's gonna go nuts. Get ready to sign your autograph."

Adam looked over at the cashier.

"It's a she," he reported.

"Even better. Go buy a copy. I'll wait."

Adam picked up five copies and took them to the cashier. She scanned them with a listless glare.

"You must really like this magazine," she said with zero emotion.

"I like this *particular* issue," he said, jamming his finger down onto the image of himself.

She tilted her head.

"Whatever floats your boat, dude. With sales tax, that comes to $27.52."

Adam paid and left the store with his loot. He walked to an empty meeting room off the main hallway, switched on the lights, and sat down to thumb through the article about himself.

Take the inherent instinct to find yourself in a group photo and multiply that by a thousand. Adam read the article voraciously, over and over.

The story told of his childhood, his experiences as an astronaut, and a brief summary of the Mars mission. Adam was stunned at the lack of specifics. It was a quickly done article that was light on details, but had lots of great color pictures.

His cellphone vibrated on the table. The caller ID said *Connie*. Adam picked up the phone and touched the answer button on the screen.

"Connie?" Adam asked.

"No, Daddy," a little boys voice said. "It's me, Cody. Mommy is sad."

Adam raised his eyebrows with worry.

"Cody, why is your Mommy sad?"

"She said she misses you. She said you just got back into our life and now you're gone again. When are you coming home?"

Adam let out a frustrated sigh.

"Cody, can you put your Mommy on the phone?"

"No, she doesn't know I'm using it. She's outside with Catie and Mr. Chris."

"Wait, you mean Mr. Tankovitch?"

"Yeah, he came over to give her an update and they're pushing Catie on the swing."

"Isn't it kind of late?"

"Yeah, but we have the lights on."

"Cody, do me a favor. Take the phone out to your

Mommy and tell her that I called."

Adam heard the sound of little feet walking on tile and then a door opening. After a few more footsteps, he heard the muffled sound of a child saying something. The phone made some scratchy sounds.

"Hello?" a confused Connie asked.

"Hi, honey. I just wanted to see how things are going."

"Well," she paused. "We really miss you. How did the dinner talk go?"

"It went well. Chicago is nice. I saw the Sears Tower building."

"I don't think they call it that anymore," she corrected Adam.

"Right, it's called the Willis Tower now. Go figure," Adam laughed.

An uncomfortable silence stilted the conversation.

"Connie, I miss you. I'm only going to be gone for a month. We're making between $100k and $200k every night. You can kiss our money problems goodbye."

"I know. That's a huge relief," she admitted. "Up until last week, we were getting scary calls from bill collectors."

"Never again," Adam said with confidence.

"Are you going to take a break anytime?"

"The last talk is in twenty six days. And it's in Dallas."

"Okay..." she said with disappointment.

"So what are you up to tonight? Adam asked.

"I'm just outside pushing Catie on the swing."

"Anything else?"

"Nope. Just enjoying the nice evening."

"Oh, well, okay," Adam said with a falsely upbeat sigh. "Goodnight and I'll call you from St. Louis tomorrow."

"All right. Goodnight, honey," Connie said.

Adam hung up the phone and stared at it for a long while. He set it on the table and rubbed his fingers on his chin to help him think. He looked over at the stack of Popular Mechanics magazines. His own smiling face stared back. Adam laughed out loud. To an engineer, this was one of the pinnacles of achievement. It meant he had reached the double whammy of career accomplishment and technical fame. Adam flipped open the magazine and read all about himself again.

CHAPTER 40

Winslow, Arizona

Tuesday arrived faster than Chris thought possible. He found himself walking down the hallway at DFW airport and stepping into a puddle-jumper sized airplane. It had turboprops instead of jet engines and the tedious flight to Winslow took nearly four hours. The destination airport was small. He had to exit the airplane and walk down a mobile stairway onto the broiling tarmac and then trek his way into the terminal. For such a short trip, he had no luggage. Just himself.

Chris grabbed a rental car and meandered through town to the corner of Kinsley and Second Avenue. There was a bronze statue of a guy leaning on a road sign holding a guitar. By all definitions, this was a tourist trap. "It's a trap!" he whispered to himself with a big laugh.

Some tourists hugged the bronze statue while other

tourists took their pictures. A couple of teenagers pretended like they had the guy in a headlock while their friends laughed hysterically. Then they pretended to steal his bronze guitar.

Chris was an hour early and decided to just sit in his car and wait.

And wait some more.

Noon came and went. Chris got out of his rental car and wandered around the bronze statue. He took a few pictures to prevent anybody from thinking he was some lurking creepy dude.

He checked his watch. It was 12:30.

So much for meeting me at noon, he thought. *I guess this guy was a crackpot after all.*

Chris walked back to his car despairingly and climbed in. After clicking his seatbelt and inserting the key, he was ready to hit the highway. Until now, he had always considered himself immune to trickery.

What a waste of time, he thought.

Without warning, Chris's door whipped open. An old homeless man with deep-set eyes and a long gray beard stared at him. The man said something, but Chris didn't understand because of either a speech impediment or a thick accent.

Leave here now!, Chris thought quickly.

The man looked frustrated. He reached into his pocket.

Chris flinched, accidentally put the car in neutral and gunned the engine. He went nowhere.

"Crap!" he cried.

Chris glanced at the old man and saw him remove two full rows of dentures from his pocket and insert them into his mouth. The old man laughed hysterically.

"I've always wanted to meet you, Director Tankovitch."

Chris was in that rare mode where the body tells a person to run like hell, but the brain is just curious enough to ignore the brain's signal.

"Hello?" Chris said reluctantly.

"It is me. Dmitri Stalov. You got my letter."

Chris was stunned.

"You?" Chris asked suspiciously. "You're Dmitri Stalov?"

"Yes, I am. And I would like to buy you a coffee."

Chris flinched at the thought.

"Why are you dressed like a..." Chris trailed off.

"Like a homeless man?" Dmitri finished the thought.

Chris climbed out of his car and plunked his arms on the roof. "Yes, like a homeless man."

"I dress this way because I am in the country illegally and nobody will give me the time of day. If you want to be ignored, just act like a homeless person. I am not truly homeless of course. I have a house nearby. Please, let's go get coffee."

Chris locked the car and walked around to Dmitri.

Dmitri held out his hand. "Thank you for coming all this way. Glad to see you figured out my riddle."

"I did, but can you just tell me why you think NASA is looking in the wrong place for the Martian laboratory?"

Dmitri held his finger up like he was going to say something profound.

"Coffee first!"

The two of them walked into a nearby coffee shop on the corner. The cashier saw Dmitri and smiled, yelling "Hi,

John Smith!"

Chris ducked his head toward Dmitri.

"John Smith?" he whispered.

"That's my unofficial American name," Dmitri admitted sheepishly.

"You're full of surprises," Chris said.

They ordered their coffees and Dmitri paid with money pulled from a thick wad of cash. The two brought their cups to the outside eating area and sat down.

Dmitri stirred his coffee slowly and took a sip. Too hot.

"So, Mister Chris, tell me why you are sending researchers to the bottom of the Tonga Trench in search of the cure for cancer."

Chris looked shocked. *Nobody* outside of Alexis's inner circle and the president herself knew that the coordinates led to the Tonga Trench. Dmitri noticed the surprised look on Chris's face.

"Ha, I see you are confused," Dmitri laughed. "I was once a very important man in the world. I still have friends in high places."

"I guess so," Chris admitted. "So who are you?"

"Like I said in the letter, I invented the CommKnock missiles. I did it twice. Once in my home country of Russia and then I did it again here."

"Wait," Chris smirked. "You invented the idea?"

"Yes, I hated the possibility that an accidental war would obliterate our species from the planet. So I came up with a foolish idea to make *friendlier* bombs and the people in leadership fell for it, thank God."

Chris looked confused.

"So what are you doing here? Why aren't you in some

think-tank in Washington... well, I mean the new Washington?"

Dmitri put his coffee on the table.

"I saved humanity from destroying itself. I don't think I could ever top that accomplishment, no?"

Chris laughed.

"So you just became a hermit?"

"No, I did not do *that*. I just disappeared."

"How long have you lived here?" Chris asked.

"I've been everywhere in your country. I have seen every sight. I love this country. I move every year or so."

"How do you afford that kind of lifestyle if you pretend to be homeless?"

Dmitri took a sip of coffee and laughed.

"Like I said, I still have friends in high places."

Chris looked into his coffee. It was almost white due to the huge amount of cream he put in it.

"If you think we are using the wrong reference point for longitude, then what is the *correct* reference point?"

"My dear friend Mister Chris. Your team was so close."

"How close?" Chris asked.

"You were off by thousands of miles," Dmitri replied.

"That's not very close," Chris laughed.

"I mean you were close with your idea, not the actual location," Dmitri answered. "You chose the top of the highest mountain."

"That's right," Chris confirmed.

"But Mount Everest is not the highest mountain."

Chris leaned back in his chair with a smile.

"Are you telling me that Mount Everest is not the highest mountain on Earth?" Chris asked with a devilish grin.

"That is a fact," Dmitri said. "It is not the *highest*. The top of Mount Everest is the highest point *above sea level*, but it is not the farthest point from the center of the Earth."

"Ha, that makes no sense," Chris said.

"Oh Mister Chris, the Earth is not a perfect sphere. It is fat at the equator, just like me!" Dmitri said with a huge belly laugh. "The Earth is wider at the equator. In fact, it is called the *equatorial bulge* by scientists."

"And?" Chris asked.

"And there is a mountain in Ecuador called Mount Chimborazo. Being so close to the equatorial bulge puts it nearly two whole kilometers farther from the center of the earth than the top of Mount Everest. You see, if you're looking for a landmark to set your starting longitude, that is where it should be."

"Mount Chimborazo, eh?" Chris confirmed.

He had the urge to pull out his smartphone and confirm this crazy idea. Dmitri noticed Chris was processing all of this new information.

"Go ahead, use your phone to confirm it."

Chris pulled out his smartphone and Googled Mount Chimborazo. Dmitri was spot on. The peak was much farther from the center of the Earth than the peak of Mount Everest.

Chris stared at Dmitri with a look of dumbfounded awe.

"Why me?" Chris asked. "Why are you telling me and not our cartographers?"

Dmitri took a long swig of coffee and plopped the empty cup down on the table.

"You don't remember me, do you?" Dmitri asked.

Chris squinted his eyes. "Should I?"

"During my first year of living 'off the grid', as they say, I was in Ohio. I was bored. So I started an amateur astronomy group. One night we invited all of the locals to come out and observe Halley's Comet. In the crowd was a little boy who had the wonder of science in his eyes. He asked so many great questions. I knew he would do great things. And I have watched his career grow."

"Wait..." Chris said incredulously. "That was *you* that night? The guy sitting on top of the ladder telling us all where to look to find Halley's Comet?"

"Yes, Mister Chris, that was me," Dmitri admitted. "You crossed paths with that awful president and you lost out big time. I am giving you this information to help you rise back to the top where you belong."

Dmitri stood up and shook Chris's hand.

"Mister Chris, have a safe flight back. Take the new information about Mount Chimborazo and use it wisely. I must go now."

"Will I hear from you later?" Chris asked.

Dmitri shook his head.

"No," he paused. "Well, only if I find you following the wrong path again. But I doubt that will happen."

Dmitri walked away. The bells on the door jangled briefly as he passed out of Chris's sight. The cashier looked up, then went back to cleaning his counter.

When Chris left Arizona that evening, he had a mix of emotions. Should he be impressed that he'd unknowingly crossed paths with such an influential historical figure when he was just a boy? Or should he be impressed that such a person would entrust information about Mount Chimborazo to him.

He arrived at DFW airport at midnight and immediately took the hour-long taxi ride back to western Fort Worth. The front gate to his hilltop neighborhood was broken and the driver went straight on through.

So much for security, Chris thought.

The taxi pulled up to his stucco clad house. Chris felt relief at being home again. He went in through the garage door and turned off the security alarm. The house had that smell that only comes from being away for a while. Before going to sleep, he went into his study and pulled the globe down from the top of his bookshelf. He reviewed some details that he'd scribbled down on the airplane ride.

Chris grabbed some Post-it notes out of his desk drawer and placed the corner of one right at the location of Mount Chimborazo, just below the equator in Ecuador. He carefully counted out 100 degrees of longitude to the East of the mountain. Then he placed the corner of another Post-it note roughly 17 degrees south of the equator. The corner of the Post-it note covered part of Angola — the last remaining part of Africa that was still struggling with both conflict and poachers.

That's not good, Chris thought.

CHAPTER 41

The large dining and banquet auditorium
Science & Technology Center
Sacramento, California

Adam became a millionaire in just one week. By the end of two weeks, he'd made over three million dollars. As his speaking engagements moved Westward, the nightly income started increasing. His bank account was piling up with dollars. In the mornings, he would appear on the local TV news shows — the result of such appearances would be to sell out any remaining tickets left for the nightly speeches.

Oliver, always one location ahead of him, would call after every speech and congratulate him on his newest tally.

And every night, Connie would call him and ask him to take a break. Tonight was no exception.

"Just a few more weeks," Adam told her on the phone.

"What if we came to visit you?" she would ask.

"I don't think that would be worth it for you. After I speak I just go to my hotel room and sleep. Then I start driving to the next location."

"Well, surely Oliver could cancel just one of them so you could spend time with the kids."

Adam bit his lip to think.

"I don't know. Oliver is putting in a ton of work to schedule each venue. And if I cancel, that's money out of his pocket, too."

Connie grimaced.

"Look, the kids are asking where their Dad is," Connie cried with frustration.

Adam's brow scrunched up with guilt.

"Just a few more weeks," he said, "and I'll be home for good."

CHAPTER 42

NASA Jennings Manned Spacecraft Center
Fort Worth, Texas

Chris Tankovitch sat at his desk, his fingers tapping nervously on the edge of his keyboard. He stared at a globe covered with Post-it notes. Using the point farthest from the center of the earth now seemed obvious. All he had to do was convince his boss.

"Here goes nothin'," he said as he stood up.

Chris walked down the hallway to Alexis's office. She was on the phone and saw him standing there. Chris heard the final part of her conversation.

"Okay, then it's a go. I'll be at the dock in two days. See you then," Alexis said and hung up.

"What's up?" Chris asked.

"I was able to change the mind of the ship's captain for

the Deep SEAK Explorer."

"The research boat with the deep-sea sub?"

"Exactly," Alexis said. "It went to the bottom of the Mariana Trench, so it should be good for the Tonga Trench, too."

Chris looked confused. "I thought you said their schedule was booked?"

"It was," Alexis said. "After we discussed the location in detail and I sweet-talked them, I guess they changed their mind."

Chris frowned with skepticism.

"And did I hear you say you were going there?"

"Oh, I plan to do more than that."

Chris looked confused.

"You're going out on the boat?"

"No, I'm going down in the sub," Alexis replied.

Chris looked stunned.

"That's a bad idea. You should let the professionals take care of this. The president will never allow that."

Alexis shrugged her shoulders.

"Already done. President approved. My support crew is already at the docks in Fiji."

"What?" Chris asked with incredulousness. "What if you get hurt?"

She ignored his question.

"Why are you here?" Alexis asked. "How did the lunch with your 'old friend' go?"

Alexis winked at him.

"It went well. We've known each other since I was a kid."

Alexis laughed.

"Really?" she asked.

"Yes, really," he answered. "Look, I have a question that pertains to your ocean voyage."

"Fire away."

"What if I told you that I think the longitude reference you're using is not correct?"

"So, you think your idea is better than our entire cartography division?" she asked with thick sarcasm.

"I just think it's worth revisiting."

Alexis walked up and put her hand on his shoulder.

"Let's talk about this when I get back. Right now I have a flight to catch. Now shoo!" she said, using her hand to make an imaginary broom pushing him away.

As she walked down the hallway, Alexis added one more thing. "You're in charge while I'm diving to the bottom of the Tonga Trench."

"I'm official?"

"Yes, you are the official deputy director. If anybody gives you flack, tell them they'll have to deal with me when I get back."

Chris returned to his office and plopped down in his chair. *I should've told her the details*, he thought.

He spun the globe and watched it come slowly to a halt. Then again and again. An idea popped into his head.

"What if I went on a little expedition too?" he asked himself.

Chris called around to get some rough numbers on airfare costs for about six of his most trusted engineers and scientists. Airfare to Angola was infinitely high because no flights went there – too politically unstable. However, he was able to get flights to nearby Zambia. They could probably get transportation from there to wherever they needed to go, but it would also require security. After more searching, he found that hiring two security/tracker guides would run over a thousand dollars a day.

Wow, this is adding up, he thought.

His final total was just over thirty thousand dollars.

Chris slumped in his chair, his fingers tapping nervously on his desk again.

He called his division budget manager to casually ask about discretionary funding. It rang and rang.

"Budget management, Fort Worth, this is Rick."

"Ricky!" Chris said with too much excitement. "Hey, I've got a question about some travel budget."

"How many people are going?"

"Six of us."

Chris could hear Rick typing on a keyboard.

"Where to?" Rick asked.

Chris paused, afraid to answer.

"Africa," he blurted out.

Chris heard the keyboard sound stop.

"Africa?" Rick asked. "Like, you're flying to the entire continent?"

"No, it would be Zambia."

"Friendly nation, I assume?"

"Yes, it's on the approved list."

More typing sounds.

"Well, I'll admit that's a strange request. International travel budget is tight these days. What's it for?"

"An expedition," Chris answered.

"I assumed it wasn't for your health. I mean what's the exact purpose."

Chris leaned back in his chair and swiveled back and for to think.

"Would my answer make a difference?"

"Look," Rick said. "I'm not sure what's going on here, but yes it makes a difference. If you're going for a conference, and I don't know why you'd go to Zambia for that, then you're approved for twenty thousand."

"That's not enough to cover our expected costs."

"Well, I'm sorry."

Chris spun his swivel chair around, thinking.

"Ricky, what if I told you it was to check on some research for global warming?"

"Hang on," Rick answered, typing even more.

"Well, then you'd be approved for *fifty* thousand dollars. Is that what it's really for?"

"Yes, it's about global warming," Chris said, grimacing.

"All right," Rick said with extreme skepticism. "I'll need to get approval from Alexis, though."

"She's on travel and I'm acting director until she gets back."

"Oh, then you can approve it, but you can't go."

"Why not?" Chris asked.

"New federal policy. You can't approve an overall travel budget that includes you. Do you want the charge number opened or not?"

"Yes, I'll take it," Chris replied.

"Done and...," Rick said, followed by a loud click on his keyboard. "Done."

"Thanks Ricky."

Chris hung up the phone. His elimination from the trip was very disappointing. He spent that evening calling up six colleagues and explaining his theory about the true location of the Martian laboratory in Africa. They were all excited, but none volunteered to lead.

As far as choosing a mission leader, Chris thought this would be a great opportunity for somebody who'd dropped the ball and might be looking for a little redemption in this big search for the cure for cancer. It was a somewhat dangerous mission, but he knew the perfect man for the job.

"Adam!" Chris said, after dialing up the cellphone of Adam Alston who'd just finished giving a speech in San Francisco.

"Hi, Chris," Adam said with some skepticism. "Long time, no talk."

"I agree. Look, I have a special favor to ask. I'm putting together a bit of a rogue mission to the interior of Africa to look for, how do I say this, the Martian laboratory."

"Ha," Adam laughed. "I think you've got the wrong place. I've heard it's in the Tonga Trench."

"Man, how does everybody seem to know that?" Chris asked. "Anyway, let's just say we have reason to believe that the previously published information is wrong."

"Really," Adam said with some curiosity in his voice.

"Yes, really."

"I'll be honest, Chris. My exciting days are over. I'm on a tight speaking schedule right now. I just finished giving a talk in San Francisco. I'm flattered by the offer, but..."

CHAPTER 43

Technology Innovation Center & Hotel
San Francisco, California

(9:45pm)

"...I'm just not interested right now. Thank you, though. Good night, Chris."

Adam hung up the phone and pulled his jacket tight around him. He was standing outside the lobby on a deck overlooking the San Francisco bay. He could clearly see the Bay Bridge to the east. He shivered from the cold weather. Adam was surprised at how much colder San Francisco was compared to the training facility that NASA had built in Watsonville the year before, just down the freeway and over the Santa Cruz mountains.

Adam went back into the big reception hall where he

had been sitting before Chris called. He sat down at the table in between a large stack of books and magazines. The book was his old Space Shuttle book — he'd renamed it "My Life On The Space Shuttle Before Mars" to help tie together his two accomplishments in life. The real reason for the new title was to finally get it off of Amazon's worst-seller list. Under the old name, "My Shuttle Life", it had been a dud for years. The magazine stack was a huge order of his special edition of Popular Mechanics where his face graced the cover. His manager, Oliver, had made sure to have a stack of both at every speaking event. Adam was charging an arm and a leg to sign them for audience members after the speeches. His self-deprecating humor would sometimes go too far when he'd joke about the book being worth less after he signed it, but with sales on eBay as proof, nothing could be further from the truth.

The previous evening he'd sold almost two hundred copies of the book. Tonight, being surrounded by wealthy tech titans from the Silicon Valley area, he'd already sold double that. Due to the location and audience demographic, his payday for tonight's speech would surpass the four-hundred thousand dollar mark. The numbers still boggled his mind.

Attendees stood in line in their tuxedo's and little black dresses, holding glasses of wine and talking about important subjects. What was the most durable interior choice for their new business jet? What color Ferrari was least likely to be pulled over by the police. And when was it time to trade up from that Ferrari to a McLaren? Decisions, decisions.

By midnight, Adam was pretty exhausted. His hand was cramped. He flexed his fist in between signings.

A woman with blonde hair, pulled back in a ponytail, was last in line. She held her shoes in her left hand, tired of standing in high heels.

"Hi, Captain Alston," she said brightly. "Your speech tonight was invigorating."

His tired eyes looked upward at her.

"Well, thank you. Thanks for coming out tonight. Now, who do I make this out to?"

The woman held the book open to the front page. "Wilhelmina."

Adam laughed at first, but then paused.

"Wilhelmina?" he asked with skepticism.

"Yes," she said with a smile. "It's an old family name."

"Okay..." Adam said and began to scribble. "To Wilhelmina, my wonderful friend here in the city by the bay."

"Thanks," she said as she winked.

Adam leaned over to pick up a new book. His tall stack had been whittled down to just five remaining copies. As he popped back up to the table, Wilhelmina was gone, but there was a room keycard on the desk in front of him with 614 written on it with a Sharpie.

Adam picked up the keycard, the corners of his eyes crinkled in contemplation.

Ten minutes later, an exhausted Adam found himself knocking on the door of a hotel room.

"Just a minute," a woman's voice from inside said.

The door opened and Wilhelmina was standing there with her hair no longer in a ponytail.

And nothing else.

Adam laughed nervously. "I'm afraid you accidentally

left this downstairs and I wanted to return it."

Wilhelmina smiled coyly back at him.

"Oh captain, my captain," she said. "That was no accident."

Adam gulped.

CHAPTER 44

Alston family home
Fort Worth, Texas

(Three hours later, 3:45am)

Connie's eyes jolted open. The sound of glass breaking triggered her heart rate into overdrive. She rolled out of bed, crept toward the armoire and swung open the doors. Connie reached through the dangling clothes and grabbed the old shotgun they kept around and assumed they'd never use.

Why wasn't the alarm triggered?, Connie thought.

She heard more glass breaking and some crunching sounds near the kids' bedrooms — some deep voices, too.

The Alston's had been paying monthly alarm fees for seven years and now that she needed the alarm, it failed.

Connie eased out of the bedroom and into the long central hallway. She heard some noises of struggling. A body came running toward her in the dark.

Connie held the shotgun up.

The approaching body walked by the glow of a nightlight. Connie let out a sigh of relief. It was Catie.

"Shhhh....," Connie whispered. "Go in my bedroom and hide in the closet."

Catie walked behind her Mom and disappeared into the bedroom.

Connie walked quickly but quietly down the hallway toward Cody's bedroom. She peered around the corner and saw two burglars trying to coax her son out from under his bed. They wore all black. One held a tire-iron and the other had a roll of duct tape.

"Come here you little brat!" they whispered loudly.

Connie's trembling hand reached toward the light switch and she flipped it on. The two kidnappers turned toward her with a look of shock on their faces.

"Get her!" yelled the one holding duct tape.

Connie's mama bear instincts kicked in. She pointed the shotgun and pulled the trigger. The blast filled the room with sparks and smoke as the man flew backwards, knocking over the duct-tape man. He, in turn, hopped up and tried to jump through the window.

BOOM!

Connie's second shot hit him in the back and he laid slumped over the window opening, his belly pierced by several pieces of window glass.

Connie stood trembling at the sight of the two dead men in her child's bedroom.

"Mommy?" came a voice from under the bed.

"Come on out, Cody. Watch out for the broken glass."

And blood, she thought.

A hand fell on her shoulder.

"Hey, lady," a strange voice said from behind her.

Connie whipped around to see a third man, standing right behind her. He raised his hand — it held a big wrench. She tried to get the shotgun around, but the barrel hit the doorway.

Swinging from out of the darkness beside the man, a baseball bat hit him in the back of his knees and he fell down. Connie finally got the gun pointed at him and she shot him in the belly. He flew back into the hallway. Out of the corner of her eye she saw her daughter Catie holding a baseball bat.

"Oh my sweetheart," she said, hugging her daughter. Catie was crying uncontrollably.

Cody came up beside her.

Connie grabbed her cellphone and they all ran to the master closet. She dialed 911.

"Nine one one — please state your emergency."

"We've had a break-in. Three big guys. I shot them."

Connie was trying to hug her kids and talk at the same time.

"Ma'am, are you injured?"

"I don't think so, but I don't know if there are any others, though."

"Okay, ma'am, we've already had reports of gunshots just about a minute ago and our officers are on their way."

"Thank you, thank you," Connie said through tears.

The police arrived quickly along with several ambulances. The neighborhood lit up like Christmas. The police sat down with Connie and she gave them the details. The police told her that the alarms didn't go off because the kidnappers didn't open any windows — no sensors were tripped.

"My husband said he was going to get the glass breakage sensors installed," Connie said.

"Those might've helped," said the officer. "But sometimes they're more trouble than they're worth."

Connie opened her cellphone and looked through the recent calls list. She skipped over her husband's phone number and found Chris Tankovitch's number. It was early in the morning, before sunrise, but she called him.

"Hello?" Chris asked in a groggy tone.

"Hey, it's me, Connie," she said. "Our house got broken into tonight."

"Oh no, Connie. Are you okay?"

"I'm okay, but Chris, it's been terrible. The kids saw a lot of bad stuff."

"I'm so sorry to hear that. I told Adam he needed to get you out of that neighborhood. Whether he wants to admit it or not, you're famous now and that requires extra costs."

"Well, we've always liked it here."

"Doesn't matter. You're rich and famous now. You need rich and famous neighbors. That's just how it works."

Connie sighed.

"Maybe," she admitted.

"Look, when you're done with the police there, bring the kids over here. I've got three spare bedrooms. You can stay at my house for as long as you want to. We've got lots of security here. I'll make you and the kids feel safe."

"Thank you, Chris," she said. "That means more than you can imagine."

CHAPTER 45

The restaurant bar
Technology Innovation Center & Hotel
San Francisco, California

(5:45am)

"Sorry if you wanted more than just an all-night chat," Adam admitted. "But I'm really a good man."

"I'm sorry to hear that," she said with a wink.

Wilhelmina drank the last sip of her beer which she'd been nursing from a coffee cup — the bartender ran out of clean mugs and glasses hours ago.

Out of the corner of Adam's eye, a flash caught his attention. When he turned, he saw a photographer snapping pictures of him and Wilhelmina at the bar. Adam stood up and walked over to the man.

"What are you doing, buddy?" Adam yelled.

"Hey, I just take pictures. My editor decides what to do

with them."

Adam knew this would look bad. He grabbed at the camera, but the photographer jerked it away and walked backwards.

"Whoa, there, Mr. Astronaut. Is that your wife there at the bar?"

Adam grew enraged and lunged at the photographer, missing him as the man took off running from the room. Adam gave chase. The photographer slammed open the front door and tore off into the shadows. Adam fell behind and eventually lost him after two blocks.

"Not good," Adam said, leaning over to catch his breath.

He started walking back toward the hotel and pulled out his cellphone to call his manager, Oliver.

"Adam, why are you calling me so early?" his beleaguered manager asked.

"I've got a serious problem," Adam admitted.

"What's up?" a sleepy Oliver asked.

"So, I spent all last night chatting with an audience attendee and —"

"Is she attractive?" Oliver interrupted.

"What? Um, yes she is very attractive."

"Go on...." Oliver said with a strangely curious tone.

"So we're in the hotel bar just chatting and some photographer takes our picture and runs away."

"That's not good," Oliver stated plainly.

"I know! What should I do?"

"Well, it's possible that it was a setup," Oliver suggested. "Tabloids do that sort of thing all the time."

"Really?" Adam asked with great enthusiasm.

"Sure, but it doesn't really matter. Your life is about to

take on a new chapter."

"In a good way?"

"No, in a crappy way," Oliver said. "What do you think? One of two things is going to happen. Either they'll come to you and ask for extortion money or they'll just print it in a tabloid."

"Both of those sound terrible," Adam admitted.

"Believe me, the extortion is much better."

Adam sighed.

"Look, just go tell your chat friend that you aren't allowed to talk anymore. Then pack up and drive to the next location. Act like nothing happened."

Adam hung up the phone and walked back into the hotel bar. Wilhelmina was gone, but she left a note on a napkin. It said:

"Adam, Sorry about that. I enjoyed the conversation. For what it's worth, you really aren't as good a man as you think you are."

He picked up the note and looked around the restaurant aimlessly, just in case she was still in the vicinity.

What used to take twenty four hours now took twenty four minutes. Before Adam could reach his hotel room, the famous tabloid website called CelebratoidNews had an image of him chatting with a mystery woman at the bar along with a headline blasting:

"SPACE MAN FINDS NEW PORT: Captain Adam Alston shares early-morning cup of joe with mysterious woman."

His phone started ringing with reporters on the other end wanting exclusive interviews. Oliver called and told him to ignore the internet for the day.

Adam checked out of the hotel and drove down the freeway toward NASA Ames in the Silicon Valley area. It wasn't far from the old NASA training facility that he and his fellow Mars crewmembers spent time at so long ago.

He arrived just before lunchtime.

There was one phone number that hadn't tried to call him yet: Connie.

Adam took out his cellphone and called her. It rang and went straight to voicemail. He called again. Voicemail. He left a message pleading for her to call him.

After lunch, Adam went to the auditorium and checked to make sure the lectern and microphone were both working. He sat down in the front row and tried to call Connie again. Finally, she answered.

"Hello?" a man's voice answered.

Adam was confused.

"Um, who is this?" Adam asked.

"Hi, Adam, this is Chris Tankovitch."

"And why are you answering my wife's phone?" Adam asked with extreme concern.

"Look Adam," Chris said calmly, "Connie saw the headlines and she's a bit upset to say the least."

"Nothing happened. I can explain it to her, just put her on the phone," the exasperated astronaut said.

"Adam, you need to take it down a notch. She's not ready to talk right now."

"Just put my wife on the phone!" Adam yelled.

Both sides went quiet. Adam began weeping.

"Adam?" Chris said calmly. "There was a break-in at your house last night. Everybody is okay, but they're staying at my house for now."

That was one crisis too much for Adam to handle.

"WHAT!" Adam exploded. "Put my damn wife on the phone right now. I have to talk with her about this. Are my kids okay?"

"Adam..." Chris said calmly.

"I said ARE MY KIDS OKAY!" Adam yelled, interrupting Chris again.

"Everybody is fine," Chris said. "She called me first because I am here. She doesn't want to talk with you right now. Look, I have a great idea. Take a break from the public speaking circuit and go on that African expedition I told you about. It'll give you and Connie time to calm down and you can think about what you've done."

"But I didn't do..."

"Adam. Just come back to Texas. I've got airline tickets with your name on them. You can meet up with my crew — they're heading to Zambia shortly. I'll email the info to you. Get yourself to Africa and help my team find that Martian laboratory. The key to the cure for cancer may be there. Besides, the drive home will give you time to ask if downing beers with Wilhelmina all night was worth it."

Adam hung up the phone and slumped in the auditorium chair. His phone beeped — the promised airline info had arrived via email. Adam looked at his phone and then dialed up Oliver.

"Oliver, I need to postpone the rest of my speeches. I have to go home."

"Go home?" Oliver asked with frustration.

"Yes, things are a wreck at home and I have to mend a very important fence."

"Look here, Adam. You've only got a week's worth of dates left and I've worked very hard to get them lined up."

"I know, but I have to leave right now."

"Dammit, Adam, if you cancel now, then you'll hear from my lawyer."

Adam was stunned at how quickly that had spiraled into lawyering up.

"Oliver, look, it doesn't have to be that way. Just postpone them."

Oliver hung up on Adam.

Adam checked out of his hotel and packed up the Porsche. For nostalgic reasons, he drove down Highway 17 over the Santa Cruz mountains, treating each turn like an unofficial race. He reached the Monterey Bay coast before mid-afternoon and ate a late lunch at the Denny's where he'd first met all of his fellow Mars astronauts long ago. This time he was all alone, so he ate at the bar. On his way into the restaurant, Adam picked up the local real-estate circular. He'd heard that Keller Murch's beach house had been put up for sale, but hadn't sold yet. While he ate his Grand Slam at the Denny's bar, Adam flipped through the circular and discovered Keller's house prominently displayed on the back cover in color.

Adam got in his Porsche and drove onto the beach-front road that led up to the secluded neighborhood where Keller's house resided. He parked his car and began walking along the beach, enjoying the cool mist from the breaking waves. When he finally reached the last and largest house, he saw the For Sale sign. He dialed the number and arranged to meet the realtor in thirty minutes.

Adam trudged through the sand back to his car and waited. The realtor showed up and Adam followed her through the huge access gate. He drove past mansion after mansion on the way to the last beach-front property. Keller's Ford Mustang was still parked in front. Sand had begun to pile up in little dunes on the windshield.

The realtor walked up the spiral front stairway.

"Follow me, Mr. Alston."

His emotions were still raw from the morning's tabloid nastiness, but he thought spending some money might make him feel better.

She unlocked the front door and they stepped into pure luxury. Slate floors and vaulted ceilings. Their voices echoed throughout the three-story beach house. The realtor took him on a tour of all of the rooms. When she got to the kitchen, she instinctively opened the refrigerator, looked in, and closed it. She then turned to talk with Adam.

"It's been on the market for a while now and the price has been reduced to two point five," the realtor said, casually looking at Adam for a reaction.

"I can give you two million. And I can wire it immediately."

"Well, it's just like any mortgage, Mr. Alston. We'll have to fill out forms and it'll take about a month to close on it."

Adam looked pained.

"Okay," he said. "It's a deal. Can I stay here today?"

"In the house? You want to stay here? That's a bit unusual."

"I just want to sit down and rest somewhere nice for a few hours. Please?"

"Well, okay. You're pretty famous, so I doubt you'll host

a rave here. Just lock the doors on the way out. If you need to get back in, the gate access code is 2MURCHMONEY."

"Of course it is," Adam laughed.

After the realtor left, Adam wandered around the home like visiting the scene of a crime. Each wall had pictures of Keller Murch and his friends and accomplishments. Over the extra-wide mantel was just one photograph — an image of Keller and fellow astronaut Molly Hemphill holding wine glasses together, obviously toasting some great event.

Sitting on top of a piano was a photo of Keller with his arm around an older man that looked just like him. It was signed "Keller, you're the best son in the world. Love, Dad."

Adam laid down on the big red sofa that sat in front of the panoramic windows overlooking the ocean. He closed his eyes to think about the day. He thought. He drifted. He looked at the windows and the ocean was replaced by a black backdrop with stars everywhere.

"Adam?" a familiar voice rang out peacefully.

He sat up, nearly floating off the red sofa. Yeva was standing out on the balcony. Adam walked through the door to the balcony to stand next to Yeva.

"Look at all those stars," she said.

"Yeva, I'm sorry about what happened."

She turned her head to look at him.

"It's okay, Adam. It's all okay."

She stared out at the stars again.

"What should I do?" Adam asked.

She smiled and then held his hand.

"You must do what is right."

The sound of his cellphone ringing jolted Adam out of his deep sleep. It was still daytime. The ocean still roared outside. The phone rang again. It was the realtor.

"Mr. Alston? You'll have to leave. Mr. Keller's former assistant is coming by the house to check on it."

"Okay, thanks. I had a good nap."

The realtor laughed. She had to. She'd just made an enormous commission from Adam.

"That's great," she said. "I'll be in touch with you about the paperwork."

Adam walked down the spiral stairs, looking back at the house which he was buying with his hard work. As his Porsche sped down the freeway toward Texas, one thought kept bugging him. Chris Tankovitch's last words were, "The drive home will give you time to ask if downing beers with Wilhelmina all night was worth it."

The only problem was that nobody knew her name except Adam.

CHAPTER 46

The Island Of Fiji

On the West side of Fiji is a large marina, home to both small boats and enormous yachts. Many belong to local fishermen, but an influx of tourists keep them all busy, providing food and entertainment in the form of deep sea fishing treks. Normally a destination for postcard beauty, today the entire island sat under an overcast sky with large waves slapping against the beach. The fishermen stayed in the marina.

Alexis Tankovitch and her assistant Regina walked along the wide boardwalk out amongst the boats. A large white boat sat far away at the very end. As they approached, the four-story boat bobbed up and down. Alexis could just see the name on the side — "Deep SEAK Explorer."

"Do you think the water is too choppy?" Regina asked, pulling her hair back under a ballcap.

Alexis turned toward her.

"Don't know. Maybe? The captain said to meet him at

three o'clock and they'd make a decision to go or stay in the harbor."

They reached the bottom of the gangplank that took them over to the boat. Alexis put one foot onto the heaving gangplank and grabbed the railing.

"Here we go!" she said with excitement.

The two of them walked up to the top, but stopped short of stepping onto the boat. Just a few feet away was a man with a dark complexion wearing a white polo shirt and a captains hat. He smiled wide when he saw them.

"Director Tankovitch, I presume?"

"Yes, that's me," she said with a laugh, "and this is my assistant Regina."

Regina waved.

"Captain Nadino?" asked Alexis.

"At your service," he answered, tipping his hat.

"Permission to board the ship?" Alexis asked.

"Yes, of course."

The captain motioned for them to follow him. He walked up a flight of stairs and across a hallway to a door with "Alexis Tankoffish" written incorrectly on a sign with tape holding it down. Alexis laughed.

"I'll have to get the sign fixed. Anyways, this will be your room, feel free to drop off your suitcase. Some of your team arrived a few days ago — they are down by the sub," the captain explained.

The two ladies walked into the room and put their suitcases into the cubbies in the walls – the cubbies were tilted to prevent the contents from falling out during rough seas.

The two women walked back out and closed the door

behind them. The captain smiled.

"Good, now let's go to the bridge."

The walk to the bridge took them up another flight of stairs and through several hallways. Their small talk focused around the technical aspects of the ship. Long gone were the diesel engines – this boat used marine gas turbines set deep in the hull of the ship. The huge quantities of air needed for the engines came in through a byzantine path of intakes all fronted with chevrons to sling any moisture out of the air. As a scientist, Alexis was fascinated.

Once on the bridge, things were lively. Seven sailors walked around, speaking with each other and checking computer terminals.

"Do you think we have a good chance to get out to sea tonight?" Alexis asked.

"Good question..." he trailed off.

The captain turned to his navigation specialist and spoke with him for a minute. He turned back around.

"There is a lull expected in the next hour and we can leave then. A huge storm is still over the dive site, so we'll have to play it by ear."

"That's good news," Alexis said with anticipation.

"My crew is just as excited about this as you are, Ms. Tankovitch. We'll try to get the sub there as soon as possible. Both of our sub crew are prepped and ready for the dive."

"Both?" Alexis asked.

"Yes, we have two trained engineers that always take the sub down."

"I thought it held more than two people?"

"It can hold three if need be."

"That's good to hear," she smirked. "I'd like to speak

with you about a special favor."

The captain laughed, anticipating what she was going to ask.

"No ma'am, we cannot put you at risk like that."

"Are the two engineers in danger?"

The smile left his face.

"Ms. Tankovitch, there is always danger when you go down to the bottom of the Tonga Trench. It is the second deepest place on the planet, just short of the Mariana Trench."

"Yes, but we're not going all the way down."

"True," the captain agreed. "But we're going *almost* all the way down."

Alexis looked determined. "Again, let me ask you — are the two engineers in danger?"

The captain stepped back.

"Not exceptional danger. They are highly trained and the sub has a proven safety history."

"Great, then I'll stay out of their way and not make a sound."

CHAPTER 47

Planning hangar
NASA Jennings Manned Spacecraft Center
Fort Worth, Texas

Several men hammered the lid shut on a crate in the old 1950's-era hangar. The side of the crate read *FRAGILE, SENSITIVE EQUIPMENT*. Chris Tankovitch walked along the side of the box, feeling the rough lid. A forklift ambled over and picked it up, setting it gently on a truck. Chris climbed up to the driver of the truck.

"Drive carefully. I need this to get on the plane at DFW airport in one piece."

"Sure thing, sir," the driver answered.

Chris hopped down and walked over to the corner of the hangar where a group of six people stood watching him.

"I wish I was going with you guys," he said with disappointment. "You'll like Adam Alston. He's a real American hero."

The men laughed.

"That's not what the tabloids say," said a tall man sporting a gray buzzcut.

Chris shrugged his shoulders.

"Don't believe everything you read, fellas," Chris said, shaking each of their hands.

"I appreciate you all freeing up your schedules on short notice. You're experts in your fields of archaeology, paleography and geology. This is a hush-hush mission and I need your help."

A chorus of "You got it, Chris" and "Happy to help" rang out.

"When you arrive at the airport in Zambia, get that crate and transfer it to a truck. It contains all of your equipment," Chris said.

"What then?" the buzzcut guy asked.

"We've arranged for some guides and some, well, protection along the way."

"Armed guards?"

"Well, you'll be in Angola and let's just say you may need some 'leaded' protection."

Chris's phone rang. He looked and saw it was from Adam.

"Hang on, fellas, it's from your soon-to-be leader."

Chris walked away from the group.

"Hello?" Chris answered the phone.

"Hi, Chris, this is Adam."

"Where are you?"

"I'm in New Mexico, but I should be there by nightfall. Or tomorrow."

"Well which is it?" Chris asked in a frustrated tone.

"Probably tomorrow," Adam answered.

Chris glanced over at his science exploration team. Then looked away from them again.

"Look Adam, the team is leaving in four hours, you need to be with them or you'll miss the transportation truck they're taking from Zambia into Angola."

"I'm driving as fast as I can," Adam answered.

"Okay, you'll have a special standby flight, good for when you get here."

"Chris, I have something to say to you."

"Look, Adam, Connie is not ready to talk to you."

"No, look, Chris, I want to thank you for helping them feel safe."

Chris was taken aback by the unexpected appreciation.

"I was available," Chris said coldly.

Adam paused.

"I want to talk with Connie and the kids. She won't answer her phone."

"That's not going to happen. You go to Africa and save the world again by finding another anti-gravity cube."

Adam sighed.

"Maybe I shouldn't go on your expedition."

Chris called Adam's bluff.

"That's fine. I'll just tell Connie about how you beat Keller Murch to death on Mars."

Adam was the lone car speeding east on the freeway through New Mexico. He instinctively let his foot rise off the gas pedal, coasting over to the side of the road. His Porsche came to a stop on the gravel, sending up a cloud of dust.

Adam mumbled something incoherent.

"What?" Chris asked.

"I thought you said you didn't get any of our video from

that excursion."

"Of course I did, Adam," Chris said with unusual satisfaction. "We saw the whole thing."

"We?" Adam asked in a sudden panic.

"Yes, we. We decided to sit on it until we figured out what to do."

Adam didn't know what to say.

"Just let me talk to my family," Adam begged from the side of a lonely highway.

"No. Just get your ass to Africa. When you get back, you can see about rebuilding your family."

"Chris?" Adam asked.

"Yes, Adam. Do you have anything more to add?"

"*Thank you*," Adam said with cold clarity.

CHAPTER 48

Fiji Harbor
Pacific Ocean

"Throw off the lines!" Captain Nadino yelled to his crew. One by one, the chains were released from the dock, sending the large research vessel towards the ocean.

The captain turned back toward his two NASA guests, Alexis Tankovitch and her assistant Regina.

"Do you get seasick?" he asked.

"Not usually," Alexis answered over the noise of chains retracting into the hull of the boat.

"You will on this trip. The seas are going to be rough."

"I'll manage."

"You'll have to," he laughed.

When they were safely out of the harbor and heading east toward the Tonga Trench, the captain invited his guests to follow him through the cavernous hallways toward the back of the boat. At the end of the long trek, he pushed open a white metal door. Below them was a large flat deck. It took up the back quarter of the ship. Sitting perched in a metal cage was the coveted submarine. It was more of a diving sphere with a submarine framework built around it. The sphere was eight feet in diameter and housed three seats and all of the sub controls.

The three of them walked down an external flight of metal stairs, all the while staring at this amazing machine in front of them.

Captain Nadino climbed up onto the platform and reached down to help Alexis climb up. She overcame her pride and took his hand. He hoisted her up.

"This is state-of-the-art technology in deep sea diving," the captain said with a proud smile on his face. "It can reach the deepest parts of the ocean: the Mariana Trench and the Tonga Trench. There is only about 400 feet difference between the two."

"Interesting..." Regina said, climbing up onto the platform.

The Captain gave a hand signal to an engineer working near the hatch then followed up with an inaudible command. The engineer nodded.

"Please, Alexis, climb up here, on top."

The engineer opened the entry hatch. It was a huge cone-shaped piece of metal that revealed the true thickness of the diving sphere wall — nearly six inches of steel. It had a window embedded in it. She stared over the rim of the hole and into the sphere innards.

The captain laughed. "Are you sure you want to climb in there and descend twenty-some thousand feet? Not even I am that brave."

Alexis looked into the sphere, lips pursed with determination. She rolled her head sideways to look at the captain.

"I can't think of *anything* more exciting."

CHAPTER 49

Alston family home
Fort Worth, Texas

The garage door rose up slowly, creaking every inch of the way. Adam had meant to oil the chain on the opener for years, but just never got around to it. He stepped out of his Porsche and gently closed the door. The sound of the engine pinging and cooling down faded into the background. Adam walked down to the mailbox and opened it. Nothing. There was a piece of paper taped to the inside of the mailbox with a note about forwarding all mail to Chris's house on Mount Olympus. It had Chris's mailing address. Adam ripped off the piece of paper and put it in his pocket.

He walked back into the garage and opened the door leading into the laundry room. The chirp of the tripped security alarm caught his attention. It had been a long time since he heard that familiar sound, but the old code silenced it quickly. Adam was glad the code hadn't been changed. As he rounded the corner into the hallway, it was obvious where the shotgun blasts had torn into the walls near his son's room. Adam stretched his hand over the holes to judge how big of a drywall patch would be required.

They must've been so scared, he thought and shook his head. *Damn, I failed at my one task as a father.*

Adam went into his bedroom and gathered some clothes for the trip to Africa. He grabbed a suitcase out of the main closet and stretched it open on the bed, filling it with clothing and other necessities. Adam opened the armoire and pulled something out, wrapping it in his old leather jacket before laying it all on top of his suitcase.

In the stillness of the quiet house, Adam stared at his luggage for a while and sighed. He walked through the rest of the house, touching mementos that reminded him of how his family used to be. He looked into the backyard — the swingset and the bicycles were gone.

A lightning storm was approaching from the west. The shadows of the backyard were illuminated by the occasional flashes from the storm. No rain yet, just lightning and loud booms.

After examining every last ounce of his former life, he grabbed his suitcase and leather jacket and dragged them into the garage, walking right past the security alarm without turning it back on. The rain drops were just starting.

He opened the hood of the Porsche and stuffed the suitcase into the front trunk. He put the leather jacket in the passenger footwell and then sat down in the bucket seat. Adam started the engine and backed out of his driveway. He gunned the engine and tore off out of his neighborhood, heading west toward the new NASA Jennings Fort Worth

Space Center. Conveniently, the NASA facility was only a few miles from Chris's new house up on Mount Olympus — a very conspicuous neighborhood.

First things first though — Adam needed an extra shot of courage for the next part of his trip. From all the movies he'd ever seen, a quick stop at a saloon was just what the doctor ordered. Unfortunately, there weren't any saloons nearby, so he stopped at a bar located between his house in Wanigas and the side of town that housed both NASA and Chris Tankovitch's new home. He sat in his car, contemplating the best plan of action.

I'll just wait out this storm with a drink or two, Adam thought. *Or ten.*

He stepped out of the Porsche and walked toward the bar, pulling his jacket tightly closed to keep out the driving rain. A sudden clap of thunder made him wince as he opened the door and disappeared into the dimly lit establishment.

CHAPTER 50

Two hundred miles east of Fiji
Pacific Ocean

Captain Nadino wobbled back and forth, just trying to stand upright in front of Alexis's cabin door on the research boat. He knocked on the door.

"Be right there!" Alexis yelled from inside the cabin.

The door opened, showing Alexis in her work mode. She had a pencil behind her ear, a laptop balanced on her left arm, and was typing with her right hand.

"You are working hard," the captain said. "I have an update for you — I would've called, but the cabin phones aren't working."

"Good news?"

"Not exactly," Captain Nadino said, leaning his head slightly. "There's a massive storm passing over the northern end of the Tonga Trench right now and we're going to hold back for at least 36 to 48 hours."

Alexis looked disappointed.

"We have a lot of people back at NASA waiting to find out what is hidden at that ancient location."

"I am even more disappointed than you are, believe me," he said. "But our mantra on the Deep SEAK Explorer is always safety first."

"But there are no waves once we go under the water," Alexis complained.

"That is true, but first we have to get the submarine into the water. We don't just kick it overboard. It is very dangerous to launch the sub in a swelling ocean. When that crane lifts it up and drops it over the edge, the last thing you want is for the sub to swing out of control. It could slam into the ship and be ruined."

Alexis nodded her head — she understood.

"Yes, better safe than sorry," she admitted. "So we can get going again in 36 hours?"

Captain Nadino nodded his head with a look of pain on his face.

"Maybe. More like 48 hours. Could be less. Depends on Mother Nature."

"Whatever," Alexis said. "This seems like a strong boat and boats are meant to float. I don't like waiting, but it's your call."

"Yes, indeed."

CHAPTER 51

Chris Tankovitch's exclusive neighborhood
Fort Worth, Texas

Adam Alston manhandled his Porsche through the fat rain drops falling down on Fort Worth this evening. The storm would not let up.

It was just after midnight. The rainfall made it impossible for Adam to read the street signs. He stopped the car and stared at the GPS screen. The little glowing star symbol was at the end of Gran Delito Drive. Unfortunately, the voice guidance was in French — a result of his drunken fingers fumbling through the touch-screen controls. All this technology and he still had to use it like a paper map. His eyes scanned outside the window looking for a road sign.

"Where the hell is it?" he asked with quiet resignation. "There's no sign for Gran Delito Drive."

Adam slammed his fists on the steering wheel. He stared over into the passenger footwell and then looked back out into the rain. Tears were streaming down his face. He wiped them away with a balled-up fist.

With his finger on the GPS touch-screen, he moved the map around until he figured out where he was in relation to the glowing star.

Adam ducked his head to look out through the rainy side window. Glistening in the occasional flash of lightning, he saw the sign for Gran Delito Drive.

"Bingo!"

Adam gunned the engine and turned onto the road he'd spent twenty minutes searching for. He slowed down as he approached the end of the street. All of the lights were out at the last house.

"There it is. Seven nine nine," he whispered.

Adam turned off the headlights and coasted into the driveway of the large single-story stucco home. He shut the engine off and reached into the passenger footwell. After some rummaging, he pulled out a flashlight and unwrapped his leather jacket to reveal a twelve-gauge shotgun.

Adam kicked open the car door and stepped out. He didn't bother to close the door — he didn't plan on returning.

Adam wandered over to the right side of the house in search of a gate to the back yard.

Wrong side.

He walked back across the waterlogged front yard again to the other side. The black wrought-iron gate was lit up by a floodlight, highlighting the torrents of rain. The storm grew even more intense. He walked up to the gate and opened it, disappearing into the shadows of the back yard.

Adam turned on his flashlight and stumbled slowly along the flat stone walkway that circled the house. Step by step he inched toward the back corner where he knew the master bedroom must be. The combination of rain and tears made it hard to see. Adam wiped his eyes again and shook his head. The five shots of whiskey were still raging in his veins.

He reached the window of a bedroom and slowly raised the flashlight. The beam fell through the glass and found the side of a bed. He lifted the light higher. The beam fell across the sleeping face of an old friend; the former NASA director, Chris Tankovitch. The balance of power between them had shifted significantly since they last met.

Adam lifted the shotgun and set the end of the barrel on the window sill, pointed straight at Chris. Adam was struggling now — shaking. The barrel of the gun was plinking on the window glass.

This is the right thing to do, Adam thought to himself.

He wondered what Yeva would think of him. He paused for a moment.

Adam stood there in the pouring rain with the flashlight in his left hand and the shotgun in his right hand. Both shook uncontrollably. The fluttering flashlight caused Chris to stir from his slumber. His eyes jolted open, illuminated by the flashlight beam.

Adam, in his inebriated stupor, was surprised and he panicked. His finger slid on the trigger.

Pull it, his alcohol-addled brain told him.

Just beyond Chris, another set of eyes rose up from the bed, staring out the window. Adam stood breathless as Connie stared out the window at him, her eyes squinting at the bright light. She tilted even more, leaning on her pillow, not realizing what the bright light was coming from.

"Oh my God," Adam whispered.

He dropped the flashlight and ran toward the front yard. The barrel of the gun banged on the fence as he ran through the gate opening, spinning him around.

He dropped the gun in the grass.

"Dammit," Adam yelled.

He saw lights turning on at the back of the house. He reached down to grab the shotgun and it fired, blasting a hole in the fence. Adam picked up the shotgun and sprinted to the Porsche. He threw the shotgun in the passenger seat and slammed the door shut. The car was filled with inches of water now, having been left open. He pushed the start button and nothing happened.

"What!?" Adam yelled. His drunk mind was so panicked right now. He looked out the window through the rain and saw the key fob sitting on the sidewalk near where he'd dropped the shotgun. Adam leaped out of the car and grabbed it, sliding and falling in the rain — his arm saving him from collapsing on his tailbone. He ran back to the car and jumped in.

The front porch light came on.

Adam gunned the engine, tearing through Chris's front yard and into the street. Adam floored it and the Porsche screamed away, disappearing into a wall of rain. At that moment, all of the power to the neighborhood went out, leaving Mount Olympus in total darkness.

Twenty minutes later, the front door of the Alston house slammed open. Adam came stumbling in, leaving a trail of muddy footprints. He kicked off his shoes and collapsed into a corner in the hallway, breathless and upset about the evening. His marriage, his life, everything was now a wreck.

He took off his wedding ring and flung it down the hallway.

"My precious," he said sarcastically. Adam laughed at his own joke for a moment, then sadness took over his face.

Sleep it off, he thought. *Sleep tonight off. Alcohol always makes people do stupid things, especially when they're upset. You should've known that.*

His eyes started to drift off, but they popped open again.

"Dammit, almost forgot," he said.

Adam went back out into the rain and drove his car into the open garage. He stared at the pond of water sitting in the footwell.

"What a mess."

Adam grabbed the shotgun and wiped all the rainwater off before it started to rust. He went back into the house and returned the shotgun to its hiding place in the armoire.

Crushed by exhaustion, Adam sat down on the edge of the bed, waterlogged clothes and all. He fell backward, spread-eagle onto the mattress and fell asleep instantly. He groaned a little bit and rolled over, falling off the bed and slamming into the ground and dresser. He snored himself into oblivion.

Adam reached the depth of sleep that remembers neither dream nor rest. He recalled shutting his eyes while sitting on the edge of the bed and then he remembered waking up to blinking lights. Flashing red and blue lights lit up the windows like flares. They competed with the sunbeams zooming through the windows.

The flashing lights weren't stopping. Adam hoisted himself up onto his elbows and felt his headache kick into action. He vomited into his dress shoes at the side of the bed. He stood up and stumbled into the kitchen. The flashing lights lit up the entire house thanks to the panoramic windows in the living room. Adam drank a huge glass of water. He was in no hurry to see what was waiting for him outside.

He tucked his shirt in and walked confidently to the front of the house. Adam opened the door and walked out.

Oh, he thought, with a look of confusion.

An ambulance was parked in front of his neighbor's house. Mr. Rodriguez and his family had lived next to the Alstons for ten years. Neither family had kids when they first moved in so many years ago. They'd been good neighbors and occasionally babysat for each other's kids. They had one daughter named Sophie who was somewhere around 9 years old, maybe 10 — Adam could never keep track. She often came over to play with Adam's two children.

Adam wondered if Mr. Rodriguez was having an emergency. He walked across the yard through his unmowed tall grass toward Mr. Rodriguez's house. A paramedic emerged from the front door and ambled to the ambulance to grab some medical supplies, then returned just as slowly.

Mr. Rodriguez walked out the front door and saw Adam.

"Adam!"

"What's going on?" Adam asked, trying his best to not act hung over.

"It's awful, man. Sophie, my little angel, she got so sick so quick," he paused. "She said her left side was hurting for a few days and she was getting hypoglycemic and all that."

"Is she diabetic?" Adam asked.

Mr. Rodriguez put his hand up over his mouth to hide his emotions. He was freaking out.

"No, we were at the doctor yesterday and they said she wasn't diabetic, but they were going to have a CT scan to see if it was something more serious."

"What's the ambulance for?"

"Overnight she was just going crazy with pain. Her left side hurt so bad, I mean she..." he paused as a stretcher came out with the fragile little body on it. Adam could see her long curly brown hair. She was clutching a teddy bear in her arms. The paramedics wheeled the stretcher down the driveway and hoisted it into the ambulance.

"Hi, Sophie!" Adam said instinctively, regretting his thoughtlessness immediately. She didn't respond.

The surrounding yards were filled with neighbors, all watching with wide eyes even though most had never met the Rodriguez family — neighbors twice-removed are complete strangers.

"Oh Jesus, there goes my baby," Mr. Rodriguez cried.

Mrs. Rodriguez came out of the house and over to her husband. They exchanged some quiet words and she stepped up into the ambulance to go with her daughter.

Mr. Rodriguez looked back at Adam.

"I'm driving down to the hospital in my truck. Pray for us."

"Will do. She's going to be fine," Adam said, instantly regretting his misjudgment of how serious the situation was.

The ambulance drove away with the lights on, but no siren. Mr. Rodriguez followed in his truck. The other neighbors returned to their boring lives.

Adam walked back into his house and only then realized

that he was missing a shoe. His clothes were covered with dried mud and his shirt was torn.

With the alcohol out of his system, Adam decided his best plan of action was to leave for Africa immediately to catch up with the expedition team there. He had to get away from here pronto.

After a long shower, Adam called the airline to arrange for his flight. He had a delay and used that time to clean up the muddy footprints and siphon out the footwells of his Porsche. He ran a heater and a fan in the cabin of his car for an hour before putting it all away. The seats were still wet, so he put plastic trash-bags on them before getting in.

Adam's Porsche was the smelliest one-month old Porsche that ever existed. The mildew odor was already overwhelming, so he drove toward the airport with the windows open.

After an hour of traffic, Adam arrived at the remote parking lot at DFW airport. He pulled his suitcase out of the trunk and dragged it over to the courtesy bus.

A man dressed in a business suit stood next to him. Adam noticed that the guy couldn't stop wiggling his knees.

"So...," the man said. "I'm going to Chicago. Where are you off to today?"

Adam smiled.

"If all goes well, I'll be in Angola in eighteen hours."

The man looked impressed.

"Whoa," he said. "That's one of those places where there's a hundred ways to die."

"Thank you for the kind words," Adam laughed. "Good luck to you, too."

CHAPTER 52

Chris Tankovitch's house
Fort Worth, Texas

A group of police stood huddled near the back of Chris Tankovitch's house. They talked about the evening's failed burglary. One of the officers held a plastic evidence-bag containing the flashlight that the burglar had dropped.

Inside the house sat a frightened Connie curled up in a ball on the leather La-Z-Boy chair. She heard the door open, turning her head to see Chris walk in.

"I'm glad we sent the kids to my mom's house last night," Connie said.

"Me too," Chris admitted. "That was a lucky break."

"Did the video cameras get anything?"

Chris calculated before answering.

"Unfortunately, no," Chris said. "The power kept going out and the camera recorder is set on a loop that records over itself. Normally I get a day or two before it loops, but every time the power went out last night, it started over. There's no sign it caught the burglar or his car."

"How did he get through the neighborhood gate?"

"Well, since the power was going out, the HOA decided to leave the gate open for the night. Otherwise, emergency vehicles couldn't get in."

Connie looked at Chris with disappointment.

"So we have no idea what the criminal looked like?"

"I'm afraid not," Chris said, shaking his head. "And the police said they don't run fingerprints unless somebody died."

Connie let out a sigh. "That's really frustrating."

"I know, but I'll put everything on battery backups so we won't have that problem again."

Chris walked over to Connie to give her a comforting hug, but she pulled away.

CHAPTER 53

Africa

(Twenty hours later)

"The terrain looks a lot different from this altitude!" Adam yelled over the sound of the small airplane engine.

"Absolutely," answered his guide named Jeffrey. "From this height you don't see all the poverty. This is one of the last remaining conflict zones on the whole continent."

The two men wore parachutes on their back and were staring out the windows of their propeller-driven Cessna 208 Caravan. It zoomed high above Zambia into the edge of Angola, south of the border near the Democratic Republic of the Congo.

"How far ahead is the rest of my group?" Adam asked loudly.

"They're about a day and a half into the drivable portion of the journey right now."

"Ohhhh," Adam replied. "Why can't we just catch up by car?"

"Not enough time, Mr. Adam."

"Okay, so why didn't the whole crew just parachute directly into the target location like we are?"

"Poachers," Jeffrey said very seriously.

"Poachers?"

"Yes, Mr. Adam. The region we are going is overgrown with jungle. There are many poachers there who will shoot at any aircraft."

Adam suddenly looked frightened.

"Are they going to shoot at us!?"

"Probably not. We're almost 100 miles from the target zone region."

Adam watched as they left a region of relative flatness with occasional trees and entered a hillier locale with dense green foliage.

"How soon?" Adam asked.

"In about a minute, we should be good to go. We'll be within a mile of your team and they are expecting us."

The airplane slowed down, the speed creeping below 100 knots — a speed low enough that it wouldn't break the skydiver's necks when they jumped out of the airplane and also slow enough that they wouldn't immediately hit the airplane's tail.

"Are you sure you're ready?" Jeffrey asked, skeptical of Adam's skills as a skydiver.

"Absolutely."

Jeffrey opened the door on the side of the airplane. Adam gasped at the sight of the huge hole that went floor to ceiling in the fuselage.

"Remember, Mr. Adam, release your chute at two thousand feet... and not any earlier. You don't want to remain in the air too long with poachers around."

Adam panicked.

"Wait! I thought you said—"

Jeffrey pushed Adam out of the airplane. He fell away with flailing arms and body tumbling. Jeffrey jumped out two seconds later.

Both men rocketed down toward the luscious green jungle. They could see the dirt road that their group was following. Once they landed, Adam and Jeffrey would follow that road until they found the group.

Adam looked at his wrist-mounted altimeter.

"Five thousand feet!" he called out.

He found a stable position, face down with arms and legs out. To his right he saw Jeffrey in the same position, but much higher than him.

"Four thousand!"

Adam's heart raced a mile a minute. The ground looked way too close.

"Three thousand feet! Ah screw it!" Adam said. The ground was coming up way too fast. He pulled his ripcord and his parachute dumped out of his backpack, caught the rushing airstream and inflated. As the air filled his canopy, he felt the strings pull at him violently, decelerating him from 120mph to much slower. Jeffrey careened down past him with his head turned as if to ask Adam why he released his chute so early.

When Jeffrey appeared to be a tiny dot, Adam saw his parachute open. Jeffrey would reach the ground a solid minute before he did. From this vantage point, Adam could see for miles. It was a glorious green landscape of nature — to the south he saw the drier golden-brown terrain.

Near the top of a nearby hill Adam saw a Jeep parked and two men sitting on the hood. He saw several flashes from the Jeep. A few seconds later, Adam heard a *pop pop pop* sound. One of his parachute cables snapped and a small portion of the canopy began flailing. Adam suddenly felt like he was falling faster.

He looked down below and Jeffrey's parachute had the same problem.

Adam looked back at the Jeep. It was now pulsing with flashes. Sounds of bullets zoomed past his ear. Another string snapped and he fell faster. Adam grabbed his steering handles and pulled, trying to zig-zag his flight path to get out of the way of the poacher's bullets. He looked down. Jeffrey was falling fast too and zig-zagging.

The flashes continued, but the zig-zagging helped prevent any more snapped lines or bullet holes in his body.

Adam looked down and saw Jeffrey plow into a treetop. His parachute's canopy collapsed. Adam steered in big wide circles to try to hit the same area. He was falling way too fast. He started circling tightly and his body was being flung out like a giant tetherball. He could see individual leaves now.

Crash!

Adam closed his eyes as he was thrown through the canopy before stopping. He dangled from the tree branches, suspended six feet up from the ground. After gathering his senses, he grabbed his knife out of his pants pocket and started slicing the canopy strings. He held onto a branch as he cut the last one and then fell to the ground with a thud.

Adam laid on the ground on his back — the wind

knocked out of him by the backpack of supplies that he'd been wearing on his front.

After thirty seconds, he sat up, panicked.

"Jeffrey!" Adam yelled.

There was no reply.

Adam had a rough guess of where Jeffrey had landed and he began running in that direction. Looking up through the tree branches he saw Jeffrey dangling. Adam climbed up into the tree and carefully inched his way out onto the branch, holding his knife in his teeth.

"Jeffrey?" Adam asked, his voice muted by his teeth clenched on the knife blade.

Still no response.

Adam began quickly cutting the parachute lines up high. When he got to the last few, he grabbed them with one hand and tried to lower Jeffrey down. It was too much weight and Jeffrey plummeted down through the maze of branches like a Plinko chip, landing on the jungle floor.

Adam nearly ran down from the tree and rolled Jeffrey onto his back. He cut away Jeffrey's front backpack straps and threw it to the side.

Jeffrey wasn't breathing. Adam felt for a pulse and found nothing.

Adam knew the situation was dire. Remembering his NASA first aid training, he put his hands together on Jeffrey's sternum and began pushing down rhythmically, performing CPR. However, Adam was shocked to hear cracking and tearing sounds as Jeffrey's ribs and sternum were breaking.

"Oh my God," Adam said in disgust. "That sound is just so —"

The crunching sound continued for one more push, but subsided as Adam continued CPR. He checked for a pulse and found nothing.

Just keep going, Adam thought.

Push.

Push.

Push....

Adam tried for a pulse.

"Come on, Jeffrey, come on!"

There it was. Jeffrey had a pulse. A weak one, but it was a pulse.

Jeffrey coughed and gasped for air, but was still unconscious. Adam removed his helmet and threw it into the jungle.

Adam knew that Jeffrey was in need of serious medical attention. The first step was to find the rest of his crew. They had satellite phones and could establish contact with some kind of medical help.

One thing was for sure — Adam couldn't drag Jeffrey or give him a piggyback ride.

"What would I have done in my Boy Scout days?" Adam asked out loud.

He wandered through the nearby overgrowth and found a few skinny, but strong tree limbs. He came back and used the parachute lines to build a flat A-frame structure. He dragged Jeffrey onto it and picked it up by the top point of the A.

"Here we go, Jeffrey," Adam said.

He began pulling the A-frame sled through the jungle and toward where he remembered the dirt road was. After a few minutes, he busted through some thick grass and onto the dirt road. The road itself had grass growing out of it — a sure sign that it saw very little traffic. Adam dragged the A-frame relentlessly, only taking breaks to drink from his water bottle.

The sound of an approaching engine made Adam freeze in his tracks. He squinted and thought he saw the front of a Jeep. Adam ran off into the foliage, pulling the A-frame with Jeffrey on it — Adam dove behind a small hill.

The Jeep approached, with men yelling in French. Adam surmised they were looking for him and Jeffrey. After a few seconds, the Jeep continued on, accelerating away.

When the sound was gone, Adam pulled Jeffrey out of the thick jungle and continued following the road.

Nightfall approached and Adam got nervous. What wild animals did this part of Africa have after sunset? Would he run into any more of the deadly two-legged kind?

As the final rays of sun disappeared, Adam realized that he should've seen his advance team by now. To be safe, he pulled over to the side of the road. As he cleared some tall reeds, he suddenly saw flickering light from a campfire. Adam lowered Jeffrey's A-frame down and creeped up toward the fire. Voices were conversing in French. Adam stepped on a twig , making a sound much louder than he'd thought was possible. The French conversations stopped. Now the only sound was the crackling of the fire.

From behind Adam, the sound of a gun being cocked got his full attention.

"Arrete toi la!" a man's voice yelled from behind him.

Adam instinctively raised his arms up.

"I'm unarmed," Adam said.

"Quelle?" the man asked in frustration.

Adam tried desperately to remember his high school French.

"Je ne parle pas francais," Adam blurted out.

"Oh," the man said. "Stop right there!"

CHAPTER 54

Approaching the Tonga Trench
Pacific Ocean

Alexis walked onto the bridge of the Deep SEAK Explorer ship. Captain Nadino stood at a large central desk examining a set of maps. He looked up and noticed Alexis.

"My dear NASA director!" he said with a warm happy smile.

"Hello, Captain. Is it time yet?"

"Well, I was just studying the weather charts. The worst of the storm has passed. We still have big waves, but we are going to head toward the target. We should be there by this time tomorrow."

"That is the best news I've heard in a long time."

"We aim to please," the Captain said, tipping his hat.

"I should think so. We're paying fifty thousand a day to rent this boat."

The captain was taken aback by her shortchanging the

amazing technology onboard the Deep SEAK Explorer.

"Alexis... if I may call you that," Captain Nadino said. "This is not a *boat* as you say. We don't have oars. We don't paddle our way across the oceans. This is a *ship*. And we have the latest in maritime technology including one of only three vessels on Earth that have ever touched the bottom of the Mariana *and* Tonga trenches."

Alexis's cheeks grew flushed.

"My apologies captain. Please do what you do best."

The captain smiled and looked towards his main pilot named Mr. Ricks.

"Mr. Ricks, set speed for twenty knots until the waves die down, then aim for thirty."

"Yes, captain," Mr. Ricks nodded.

Alexis grabbed for the nearest table as the ship accelerated.

CHAPTER 55

Africa

Adam stood frozen — a gun poked him in the back. The man who had told him to hold still was now forcing him to walk through the jungle toward the light of the campfire.

"Plongez," the man said.

"What?" Adam asked.

Wham!

Adam slammed his head into a low-hanging tree branch.

Several men in the distance laughed out loud.

"He told you to duck, you idiot," a stranger's voice explained.

Adam squinted his eyes to see who was talking.

He could make out three men sitting around a campfire, all wearing baseball hats with the NASA logo on them.

Adam was confused. He looked behind him and saw the man with the gun now smiling and lowering his gun.

"Are you guys," Adam paused. "Are you the team that

Chris Tankovitch sent?"

The man closest to him stood up and shook his hand.

"I'm Leroy McLaster, I'm one of the paleontologists that Chris asked to go on this crazy trip. There's three of us here plus a few guides."

Adam was relieved that he wasn't about to be killed by poachers.

"I'm Adam Alston."

In unison, all three men said, "The man from Mars!"

They all laughed loudly.

"Hey," Adam said. "I thought there were supposed to be six NASA guys?"

"The others got sick right after landing," Leroy answered. "I think they drank the water or something. So we told them to stay back in town. They were puking their guts out."

"Oh," Adam said, looking at the men standing around the campfire.

Leroy spoke up again. "You're a famous man, Mr. Alston."

"Just call me Adam, please."

"All right," Leroy agreed. "The guy with the red jacket is Roger Leuda. He's a geologist. The guy *without* a jacket is Roger Vickery. He's an archaeologist."

"Two Rogers, huh?"

"Yes, bit complicated, so we just call them Roger One and Roger Two."

"Roger that," Adam joked.

"Yup, we've never heard that before," one of the Rogers said coldly.

"Anyway," Adam said. "Nice to meet you all, but we have

a bit of an emergency."

The other two men stood up.

"My skydiving guide, Jeffrey, landed hard and I had to use CPR on him. I've been pulling him for about two miles."

"Where is he?"

"He's back on the edge of the road, hidden behind some shrubs. Your guy with the gun here only saw me. Can I get your help?"

The group of men stomped back through the jungle, ducking under the branch. They found Jeffrey, still unconscious on the A-frame, and dragged it over to their campsite. They set him down gently a few feet from the campfire.

"I'm going to get the medic," Leroy said. He walked toward a tent beside a large truck.

Adam knelt down next to Jeffrey to check his breathing.

"So you had to use CPR?" Roger One asked.

"Yes, first time I've ever had to do that."

"Did you hear all the crunching?"

"Yeah..." Adam paused. "They don't warn you about that in first aid class."

Roger One sat down and picked up a coffee cup.

"Well," he said between sips. "You did good work there, Adam. Jeffrey owes his life to you."

There's a first time for everything, Adam thought to himself.

Leroy walked back into the light of the fire, followed by a black man wearing a safari hat who carried a medical bag.

"This is Dr. Rolatu," Leroy said.

Adam shook the doctor's hand.

They both knelt down next to Jeffrey. The doctor opened

his bag and pulled out a stethoscope and began probing various locations on Jeffrey's chest and back, asking Adam to help gently roll him sideways.

"His lungs are clear — I don't hear any congestion or aspiration pneumonia. His pulse is normal, too."

Jeffrey opened his eyes wide, looking left and right.

"Jeffrey!" the doctor said with excitement. "We were worried about you."

"My chest hurts so bad," Jeffrey whispered.

The doctor reached into his bag and pulled out a tablet computer that had a box plugged into the bottom of it. Wires dangled out of it like cooked spaghetti.

"What's that?" Jeffrey and Adam asked at the same time.

"Gentlemen, this is a portable EKG. I'm going to monitor his heart for the next ten minutes. Jeffrey, I need you to relax and sit still."

"Sure thing, Doctor, but can I get a drink of water?"

Adam stood up and grabbed a canteen out of his backpack. He brought it back and gently poured some into Jeffrey's mouth.

"I think you'll be okay," Dr. Rolatu said. "Your chest is going to hurt like hell for several weeks. I've got some medication that will help."

The doctor hooked up the wires to various places on Jeffrey's chest and patted him on the shoulder.

"You've had a rough day. Please rest some more and don't move for another ten minutes."

Adam stood up and walked over to Leroy who was downing the last of his coffee.

"Adam, let me officially introduce you to Victor. He's our main guide."

The two men walked over to the large truck. Sitting in the front seat was a man wearing a tan jacket with pockets all over it — it was the man who'd poked the gun in his back and walked him through the jungle.

"Victor, this is Adam Alston," Leroy said.

Victor turned toward Adam with an emotionless face.

"We have already met," Victor said coldly with an accent sprinkled with tinges of French and African Bantu. He went back to looking at a map.

"Victor, I need to tell you something," Adam said. "While we were parachuting in, we saw poachers. They shot at us several times."

"Yes, we heard their gunshots. You are lucky. They were playing games with you."

"Playing games?" Adam said incredulously. "They ruined our parachutes and we almost died on impact."

"If they were really trying, you would have been dead before you hit the ground."

Adam grimaced. "Aren't you worried about the poachers?"

"No, they should not bother us tonight," Victor said with a confident tone.

"How do you know that?"

"Because I have already paid them a bribe. You see Mr. Adam, as your guide, it is my job to know how to deal with these — local — situations."

"Oh," Adam said curtly. "Well, what happens tomorrow?"

"We have about another eighty miles to go, but the trip will be difficult. Depending on how Dunongo goes, we will get to your target zone tomorrow night."

"What's Dunongo?" Adam asked.

"It is a place," Victor explained. "Now get some sleep. You have had a rough day. The doctor will take care of Jeffrey tonight. We will see how he is tomorrow. In Dunongo we can charter a driver to take him back to the city. For a fee, of course.

"Of course," Adam replied.

CHAPTER 56

Africa

(Daybreak)

The sun rose over the lush mountain ridge — rays of light hit Adam like lasers. He woke up, slightly confused at his location. He had a net draped over him.

Adam tried to get out of his cot. His body said no. He must've pulled a muscle in his back during the parachuting adventure.

He tried to sit up.

No joy. Too much pain.

He tried to roll over.

Nope. More pain.

Adam reached one hand over to grab the edge of the cot. He held his breath and pulled his body, rotating so that he faced sideways. He carefully lowered his legs over the edge, which caused him to lean up. Finally, he took a deep breath. After a minute or so of sit-down calisthenics, his back felt a little better. The other men were already cleaning up the campsite and loading everything into the big dark-green cargo truck. It looked like a holdover from World War II.

Adam went to check on Jeffrey, but he wasn't on the A-frame. He looked around. Jeffrey was sitting in the passenger seat of the truck, speaking with Victor. The two men saw Adam and summoned him over. Adam walked slowly, nursing his back.

"Mr. Adam," Victor said excitedly. "We will be leaving shortly. Please put your cot into the back of the truck and climb in."

Adam saw the NASA team cleaning up their cots and backpacks, then loading them into the truck. He followed their lead. In a few minutes, everybody was sitting in the back of the truck and staring aft — the rear doors had been removed.

"We're all ready to go," Leroy said, knocking on the window that separated the truck's cabin from the back portion where the NASA personnel were seated.

Victor started the engine, letting the diesel growl to life. He put it in gear and they drove over the bumpy campground terrain to the equally bumpy dirt road. Off they went toward even denser jungle.

Adam's back felt every bump and rut in the road. He grimaced every few seconds. The doctor saw him and handed him a white pill.

"It's for your back," the doctor assured him.

Adam washed it down with his canteen.

By the time it started to kick in, they were entering the

edge of a rural village that had mix of wooden buildings and huts. Each one had a stream of smoke rising from its chimney.

"Welcome to Dunongo," Victor said. He wheeled the truck over to a large plain building, constructed of bare wood.

Adam thought the town looked very innocuous.

A high-pitched buzzing sound came toward the truck from the front. The rear passengers couldn't tell what it was. Leroy and Adam stepped to the back door and tried to look out and around.

A large group of young men on old motorcycles came swarming around the truck, swirling in big circles. They wore a hodgepodge of T-shirts and jeans and shorts. Most ominous were the Ak-47's that each man had dangling from their backs. The men smiled as if they'd caught a fly in their web.

Leroy ducked back into the truck and walked to the front to speak with Victor through the small window.

"Victor, this looks bad."

"It is bad, Mr. Leroy. Welcome to Dunongo."

The chaos of buzzing continued non-stop. Leroy turned around and saw a Toyota pickup truck approaching. It pulled up next to their vehicle and a man wearing a white polo shirt and khaki pants got out, leaning on a cane. He looked in the back of the truck, observing the contents — both the people and the scientific equipment.

Adam waved to the man. In return, the man squinted his eyes, and walked to the driver's side of the car.

"Victor, Victor, Victor... I thought I'd never see you again."

"Hello, Mr. King," Victor said with respect. "We are just passing through."

The man picked up his cane and banged lightly against Victor's door. The chaotic buzzing of the motorcycles slowed down as the riders stopped to form a random sprinkling of thugs, staring at the back end of the truck, trying to see what valuable booty was hidden in back.

"You know, Victor," Mr. King said ominously. "One of my men is still in the hospital because of you."

Victor nodded.

"That is true, Mr. King, but he shot one of my helpers. I had no idea he was working for you... when I shot back."

Mr. King stared at Victor and did not blink. His dominance made Victor uncomfortable.

"Ah Victor, we all make mistakes. However, his medical bills continue to rise. His family needs some compensation."

"How much?" Victor asked, knowing that Mr.King wasn't concerned about his employee's wellbeing.

"I'd say one thousand would do."

Victor nodded in agreement.

"I can do that, Mr. King."

Victor reached into his pocket and pulled out his wallet.

Mr. King slammed his cane against the driver's side mirror, knocking it off.

"American dollars, Victor. Not Angolan Kwanza."

Victor sat up in his seat. He opened the door slightly.

"Please excuse me for a moment, Mr. King."

Victor squeezed out of his door and walked around to the back of the truck. He climbed in.

"Who is that?" Leroy asked in a whisper.

"Gentlemen, that is Mr. King. He runs this region."

"He's like a governor?" Adam asked innocently.

"Sort of, except he is elected using bullets."

Victor put his hand out in mid-air.

"To safely pass through Dunongo, you must fill my hand with one thousand American dollars."

The group all looked at each other. They pulled out their wallets and emptied all of their cash. Victor carefully counted it.

"Six hundred dollars. Not good."

Victor hopped down to the ground and walked back to Mr. King.

"Among all of us we have six hundred dollars. I can add in five hundred Angolan Kwanza or Congolese Francs — your choice."

Mr. King laughed and looked around at the two dozen men sitting idly on their motorcycles.

"That will do for today, Victor," Mr. King said with an ominous smile. "But I would like your spare tire."

"What for? It would do you no good?"

Mr. King leaned toward Victor.

"Good point."

Mr. King summoned the two nearest motorcycle riders to him. He pointed them to the spare tire mounted on the side of Victor's truck. The two thugs approached it, pulling machetes from their backpacks. They stabbed and hacked at the spare tire. It sent jets of air out in every direction, the noise faded quickly.

Victor closed his eyes, angry at the loss of his tire, but happy that the machetes weren't used to slice him or his clients to pieces.

Mr. King yelled out to the unseen passengers in the

back of the truck.

"Gentlemen, welcome to my wonderful town of Dunongo. May I ask where you are going?"

Victor tried to answer, but Mr. King covered his mouth.

"I'm talking to your friends," Mr. King said to Victor.

From inside the truck, a reluctant voice rang out.

"We're heading to the area known as Zhuvango Falls. It's upstream of Inga Falls by about forty miles."

Mr. King looked down to think.

"Forty miles, ha. You Americans and your crazy miles. I think you mean sixty kilometers."

"That's about right, sir," Leroy replied.

Mr. King walked to the back of the truck and looked inside.

"Zhuvango Falls eh? It has been years since we had visitors there. You must be going to see the firefly show?"

The Americans all nodded in unison, not having any idea what he was talking about.

"You're in for a treat, gentlemen. The fireflies there create a whole new night sky. A blanket of moving stars."

Mr. King stared at the scientific equipment and computer cases in the back of the truck.

"That's a lot of equipment to study fireflies."

"We're biologists," Adam said with his most convincing serious face.

Mr. King nodded up and down, acting as if he believed them. He knocked his cane on the floor of the truck.

"All right. All right. Gentlemen, have a safe trip."

Mr. King walked back to the Toyota pickup truck and sat down in the passenger seat. Victor stepped back into his own truck and slowly drove out of Dunongo, pausing to let the motorcycle riders get out of the way.

When Mr. King saw that the truck had left the edge of the village, he reached into the glove compartment and pulled out a large walkie-talkie with a long flexible antenna.

"Hey, Rowell, we have a group of men in a dark green truck heading toward your camp. Should be there by nightfall. Do what you want with them."

CHAPTER 57

Tonga Trench: Over the target
Pacific Ocean

Alexis and Captain Nadino leaned on the railing overlooking the launch deck. Below them was the high-tech submarine sitting in a cage, carefully mounted to the ship. A dozen men swarmed around it.

"We are over the target area, Alexis."

She smiled at the captain.

"Is this where we drop anchor?"

"Yes, if only we had a twenty-five thousand foot long anchor," the captain replied with a laugh. "We use lateral stabilizers to keep us in position. They work pretty good unless the waves get too high. Right now we've still got some chop to deal with, but it should calm down."

"Soon?" Alexis asked.

The captain pointed to the submarine.

"Very soon. Within hours. We will find your treasure."

CHAPTER 58

End of the road

Africa

The truck struggled to maneuver around the deep ruts in the road. The road itself was starting to vanish, intermingled with the dense jungle — unusual rainfall over the past few years had caused this region to become overgrown with foliage. They were literally at the end of the road.

Victor leaned back to speak to his passengers.

"Gentlemen, we have reached the end of the road. We might have to pack in our gear from here."

Victor maneuvered the truck off the road to a place in the shade of a tree. The ground around them showed signs of a previous campsite.

"Excellent," Victor said. "This will be a good place to camp for tonight. Tomorrow we will hike to the gorge and waterfall. Should be there before lunchtime."

"There's still plenty of light out," Adam said. "Shouldn't we hike in a little bit, to get a head start?"

"No, enjoy the sunlight. We will rest here," Victor answered.

The NASA crew unpacked their tents and other camping essentials. Two of Victor's men gathered dead wood for a fire and set about lighting one up. Victor's men were unusual because they didn't speak and Adam wasn't quite sure what they were there for aside from starting fires. Victor called them Lieutenant and Sergeant, but Adam doubted they had any military background.

Leroy noticed an old abandoned shipping container about thirty feet from the campfire.

"Hey Victor, what do you think that was for?" Leroy asked.

"Let us go have a look."

The two men trudged through the dense vegetation to the old shipping container. It was rusty, but it was obvious that it had been painted blue at one point in time. It had TRANSANG written on the side between rust spots.

Victor walked to the end and lifted the locking handle, pulling open a door. It groaned open as if it hadn't been moved in years. It was empty except for a few chunks of white solid objects. Victor reached down and picked one up. He felt it between his fingers.

"Ivory," Victor declared. "This must have been a campsite for poachers long ago. They probably stored their prizes in this container."

The two men roamed back to the campsite where a raging fire was boiling water for coffee.

"Leroy, why don't you go help Adam and Jeffrey set up their cots," Victor suggested.

Jeffrey really couldn't do anything. He was still in a lot of pain, even though Dr. Rolatu was giving him fentanyl. There's no way they could've left him in Dunongo.

Victor walked back to the fire where the NASA crew had gathered.

"Gentlemen, we still have some daylight left. Feel free to relax and get to sleep early. Tomorrow will be a long day."

The men poured cups of coffee and sat on their cots, enjoying the sunset.

Victor was speaking with one of his men and suddenly turned his head toward the dense wall of jungle behind the campsite — the dusk shadows had already made the edge of the jungle ominous. Adam noticed the sudden quietness from Victor and his men. When the NASA guys looked over, Victor was slowly pulling his pistol out of his holster. He leaned over and disappeared into the jungle.

The NASA guys looked around with confusion. They weren't armed.

"Should we do anything?" Leroy asked with a whisper.

Roger and Roger shrugged their shoulders.

"Just sit tight," Adam said.

From the jungle, they heard some voices talking. Then a commotion and then silence. Footsteps were coming back toward them through the jungle, but it was more than one person. A group of five men emerged from the trees with one holding a gun to Victor's head. Victor's face was bloody and bruised. The strange men all wore green hunting vests except for the man with the gun — he wore a red vest.

"Hello, my friends!" yelled the man holding the gun. "Please do not make any sudden moves. I don't want to kill *all* of you."

When the group of approaching men arrived at the campfire, they grabbed the NASA scientists and forced them to stand up, maneuvering them into a straight line — like a police lineup in the jungle. They stood Victor at the end of the line. Victor's two helpers were put on the opposite side of him.

The man with the gun wore his red vest over a khaki shirt and khaki pants with pockets everywhere. He pulled a cigar out of a pocket on his vest and leaned down to light it with the flames of the campfire. He took a puff and then stood back up. He saw that Jeffrey was still laying down, so he directed his green-vested men to attend to him.

When the thugs tried to pick up Jeffrey, he moaned loudly.

"What is wrong with him?" the man in the red vest asked.

"He is injured," Dr. Rolatu said.

"Well, he's no good to you," the red-vest man replied. He pointed his pistol at Jeffrey and fired several times.

Victor and the NASA crew all gasped in horror. Victor's helpers didn't flinch though — their eyes narrowed in controlled rage.

The red-vest man shrugged his shoulders and looked back up at the group.

"I hear you are going to Zhuvango Falls. You will like the fireflies. It's like a blanket of stars."

Victor clenched his teeth and said, "We've heard."

The men were still in shock over poor Jeffrey.

"Now I understand that one of you is quite famous."

The NASA crew instinctively looked at Adam.

The red-vest man laughed.

"My goodness, you made that too easy." He summoned his thugs to grab Adam and take him off to the shipping container. They walked across the dense grass. The thugs opened the door and shoved Adam into the cavernous metal box.

The red-vest man cupped his hands around his mouth and yelled toward Adam, "That is where we keep our prizes. You are our prize tonight!"

He laughed heartily.

Adam saw the dim sunlight peeking through the opening of the shipping container, but it soon vanished as the doors slammed shut. He heard the handle lock in place.

Adam stood in complete blackness. The sound of his own breath was echoing in the container.

Calm down, calm down, Adam thought.

He put his hands out in front of him and carefully walked over to the wall — he put his ear on the metal to hear what was happening.

The red-vest man was talking again. He was getting agitated and screaming in French. Victor was talking back in a mixture of French and English. The green-vested men got angrier. A burst of yelling and screaming scared Adam even more.

Boom! Boom! Boom!

Cracka! Cracka! Cracka!

Adam flinched as he heard rifle shots, followed by the sound of somebody screaming in pain.

Pop! Pop! Pop!

Suddenly, laser-like beams of sunlight appeared across the end of the shipping container, accompanied by the sound of bullets slamming into the steel walls. Sparks lit up that end of the container.

Boom! Boom! Boom!

More scared voices yelled in French and a mix of

English. Adam thought he heard the NASA guys screaming, too.

The yelling got louder and he heard footsteps. Somebody was hiding behind the container.

Bang! Bang! Bang!

Three more sunbeams pierced the container, this time halfway down – much closer to Adam. A bullet ricocheted inside the container, bouncing all around Adam. He instinctively covered his head.

"Dammit!" he yelled, jumping deeper into the container, covering his ears to protect them from the overwhelming roar of hammering-on-metal noise.

A new sound started up with fully-automatic machine gun fire, relentlessly hammering against the shipping container.

Ratt-tatt-tatt-tatt-tatt-tatt-tatt...

Sheets of sunlight tore through the shipping container, perforating it from front to back. Adam finally backed into the deepest wall in the container. He couldn't go anywhere else.

The gunshots pounded on the container, sparks flying everywhere.

Adam dropped to the ground to make himself as flat as possible.

He heard the thud of a body fall to the ground behind the container.

The gunshots stopped. All was quiet except for some French being spoken. Footsteps ran around the outside of the container, following the edge. Adam saw the moving shadow blocking off the hundreds of sunbeam holes.

Adam heard the sound of the door opening. He held

perfectly still. Suddenly, the container filled with a mixture of light — some from the sunset and some from the flickering campfire.

The silhouette of a man stood at the end of the container.

"Are you still alive?" a voice yelled.

"Yes," Adam said reluctantly.

"Come on out then. We have some bodies to bury."

Adam walked toward the front of the container, his shoes kicking bullets and scraps of metal from the deluge. His ears were ringing from the intense gunshot noise.

As he neared the door, he saw the smiling face of Victor.

"Follow me, please," Victor said.

The two men walked around the container to the spot where Adam heard the body fall. The red-vest man lay motionless in the grass with a rifle laying nearby.

"You grab one leg and I'll grab the other."

The man wiggled and slowly tried to reach for his rifle. Victor pulled his pistol out of his pouch and unloaded it into the red-vest man.

Adam stood aghast, mouth dropped open.

Victor looked nonplussed. He shrugged his shoulders.

"It is just business, Mr. Adam," Victor said nonchalantly. "Now help me with him."

They dragged the man through the grass and past the campfire to an area that was mostly dirt. Victor's helpers were digging holes. Nearby was a pile of dead green-vested thugs. The red-vest man was the last.

"What the hell happened?" Adam asked.

"These poachers were very dangerous men. They would have killed all of us — even you."

Victor's two helpers stood up and smiled at Adam. They each had AR-15 rifles dangling from their backs.

"You see," Victor said. "In my line of business, you hire the best. The Lieutenant and Sergeant here are trained in Krav-Maga and they are better marksmen than any you have ever come across. That is why I charge so much."

"So they're mercenaries?" Adam asked.

"No, these men will fight to the death," Victor answered. "Now, Mr. Adam, help me put this man into the grave."

Adam had a look of shock on his face.

"We're just going to bury them all here? Shouldn't we call the authorities?"

Victor shook his head. "You know that man who stopped us in Dunongo and took our money?"

"Yes."

"He *is* the authority around here. Come and help me," Victor said. "You act like you've never buried a body before!"

Adam didn't know what to make of that statement, but Victor laughed and laughed.

"But what about Jeffrey?" Adam asked.

Victor stopped laughing.

"Jeffrey was a good man. I've worked with him on a few occasions. We will dig a special grave for him and put a cross made from ironwood on top. When we get back to Zambia, I will inform his father."

Adam picked up a shovel.

"Let me dig Jeffrey's grave."

Victor nodded in agreement. "Okay. And tomorrow we will go find your hidden treasure. I hope it was worth the life of a good man like Jeffrey."

CHAPTER 59

Tonga Trench: The dive
Pacific Ocean

Alexis stood on top of the submarine that was about to take her down to the bottom of the Tonga Trench. Her balance was precarious. The main ship heaved in the ocean, making her hyper-reactive to any balance changes.

"Okay, Alexis, we're ready for you," rang a voice from inside the submarine. Alexis looked down into the entry hatch of the DSE2 vehicle. The two men already in the sub summoned for her. She knelt down and swung her legs into the hole, turned around and climbed down the short ladder.

Thank God I wore jeans today, she thought.

The inside of the submarine was tiny, barely enough

room for the three seats bolted into it. The submarine itself resembled a small classic sub shape, but most of that was just a thin shell to support the drive motors, batteries, electronics and cameras. The part that housed the human passengers was actually a sphere of stainless steel with six-inch thick walls — strong enough to hold back the enormous water pressure at deep ocean depths. The only hole in the sphere was the entry door. It was made from a high-strength acrylic window surrounded by a steel outer shell – it was their only window to the outside word, albeit the window was only five inches wide.

"Wow, this is a tight space," Alexis remarked.

Jim and Roberto, her companions, laughed. Jim was a slender man who wore a yellow baseball hat and a yellow T-shirt. He paid close attention to the knobs and computer screens. Roberto had a polo shirt and a ponytail — he handled all of the vehicle movement controls. Alexis thought they both seemed jovial.

"Now is your chance to turn back, Alexis," Jim stated, half smiling.

"No way."

"Like seriously," Jim said. "Are you claustrophobic at all?"

"No, I'm fine," Alexis laughed.

"Generally speaking," Roberto added, "we would never consider having a non-subject-matter expert dive with us, but we've made an exception here due to Captain Nadino's insistence."

"Thanks, fellas," she said.

"I'm sure the captain gave you the rundown on how this works, but let's repeat the safety lesson. You are inside a steel shell. We will be descending to just over twenty nine thousand feet today. Not quite to the deepest part of the Tonga trench, but still dangerously deep. Trust the shell. When in doubt, trust the shell. On the bottom of our submarine is a 500 pound steel weight. Once our dive is complete, we drop the weight and then buoyancy will float us back up to the surface."

"That seems very straightforward," Alexis said.

"Roberto here will handle all of the movement controls, cameras and grabber arms. My job, I'm Jim..." he reminded her.

"Yes, I know. Hi Jim."

"Well, my job is to handle the life-support systems as well as buoyancy systems. So, I'll be in control during the descent and ascent. Roberto will handle the maneuvering at depth."

"What does that mean?"

"Once we're on the bottom, we need to travel around," Roberto explained. "So I run the small propellers that help us move along the bottom of the trench."

A voice rang out from up above.

"Gentlemen... and lady, are you good to go?"

Jim and Roberto gave the thumbs-up signal.

"And...." the voice above waited.

Alexis gave a thumbs-up, too.

"Lock us in, guys!" Jim yelled.

The heavy hatch was tilted shut briefly, but then opened back up. The man up on top reached in with an envelope.

"Just got this from the captain," the technician said. His hand reached into the sphere past Alexis's face. She saw SECRET stamped on the manila envelope. Jim grabbed it and handed it to Roberto.

"What's in that envelope?" Alexis asked.

Jim gave a blank stare at Roberto, then turned back to Alexis.

"It's just some emergency backup plans."

Alexis was skeptical, but nodded her head.

"Wait," Jim said to the technician up top. "I'm going to do a FOD check on the hatch."

He stood up and ran his hand around the conically cut hole in the sphere shell to make sure there was no debris.

"We're good," he said.

The outside technician closed the hatch and Jim turned the locking lever.

Clunk.

"Well, Alexis, now for the fun part. They're going to throw us over the edge of the Deep SEAK Explorer!" Jim said, breaking into a laugh.

"Guys, I noticed that this sub is called DSE2," Alexis said. "Where is the DSE1?"

The two men frowned at each other, then turned to Alexis. "We'd rather not talk about the DSE1." At that moment, the sub lurched sideways.

Several technicians hooked a cradle of cables around the large DSE2 submersible. The crane operator gently moved the controls and the sub lifted up from its protective cage. The research ship heaved from the choppiness of the ocean. It was just a little bit more than the captain liked, but he was anxious to go find valuable treasure on the bottom of the ocean.

The sound of overly stretched cables permeated the

whole area as technicians got out of the way of the swinging submarine.

"Watch yourselves, people!" the team leader yelled. He was in constant communication with the crane operator. Four ropes emanated from the sub, each one being pulled taut by a technician on the boat. The crane swung the submarine over the edge of the large ship and dangled it over the Tonga Trench. The heaving of the seas made controlling it at this stage difficult. The men pulled hard on their ropes, but it was awkward at this point.

A huge swell hit the ship and the DSE2 banged into the side of the it.

A cacophony of "Whoa!" and "Watch it!" rang out from the guys pulling on the ropes.

The crane operator extended the boom faster than normal to get the sub away from the ship. At a point where it was thirty feet away from the hull, he lowered the DSE2 into the ocean and retracted the cable. The submarine was floating on its own, held upright by airbags temporarily attached to the outside hull.

Captain Nadino sat down in the control room on the ship and put on a headset.

"Gentlemen and lady," he said with formal tone. "How is the DSE2 performing?"

"We've run the bit checks and all looks good," Jim replied back through the intercom.

"Excellent," the captain said. "You are free to dive when ready."

Jim pushed a button and the airbags surrounding the submarine let go. The sub began to sink.

Jim and Roberto were busy marking off checklists while Alexis sat quietly not wanting to interrupt. She kept her eye on the depth meter. They were dropping fast. She estimated they would reach the bottom in about two hours.

Jim put down his checklist.

"Okay, for now we're done. Nothing to do but monitor the system gauges until we're at about a thousand feet above the bottom."

Roberto looked over at Alexis. "What exactly do you expect to find?"

"We have reason to believe there is a laboratory of some type here – built by the early Martian explorers about two hundred thousand years ago."

"That sounds very exciting," Roberto said. "I sure hope it was built to withstand the pressures. But it is very exciting."

"It really is exciting," Alexis nodded. "But the main goal is to find a very special bit of technology that we need to create a groundbreaking medicine."

"Is that the anti-gravity cube?" Jim asked.

Alexis nodded her head.

"Yes, we think that is the missing link to finally developing a cure for cancer. It's a bit of a stretch, but it's our last hope."

Minutes passed by.

Depth: 2500 feet below sea level

The silence became uncomfortable.

"Are you familiar with the first time anybody dove to these great depths?" Jim asked.

"I remember hearing about a similar dive in the

Mariana Trench back in the 1950's," Alexis recalled.

"Close," Jim corrected. "It was 1960, actually. The sub was called the Trieste."

"Okay, yeah, that rings a bell," Alexis replied.

"They went down to the bottom and stayed for around twenty minutes."

"What did they see?" Alexis asked.

"Not much. Their propellers churned up a lot of muck. On the way down, though, they heard a loud bang."

Alexis raised her eyebrows in worry.

"What was it?"

"It turned out to be a crack in their window," Jim answered.

"Why did they continue?" Alexis asked with extreme curiosity.

"They figured if they heard a loud bang and they didn't die immediately, then they were still good."

"That's a bit crazy if you ask me," Alexis laughed.

"Well, it was 1960. People were tougher then."

Roberto laughed at the idea.

"They were probably right, though," Jim said. "At these pressures, if there's a hull breach and water shoots in, it would cut anything it touched like a knife. If it's a serious breach, we'd probably die instantly."

"Well, that's a pleasant thought," Alexis said with a frown.

Depth:5000 feet

"At this rate, we'll be there in two hours or so?" Alexis asked.

"That's about right, we're falling as fast as we can," Jim

said.

Alexis shrugged her shoulders.

"It's all right," she said. "No pressure."

James and Roberto smiled at each other and broke out laughing.

"Oh, lots of pressure. *Tons* of pressure."

CHAPTER 60

Overlooking Zhuvango Falls
Africa

(Daybreak)

"There it is, gentlemen," Victor said. The expedition stood atop a sheer cliff overlooking a river, just downstream from a huge waterfall three hundred feet wide. Below them was a one hundred foot drop into the river. A jungle forest bloomed thick and high from the opposite river bank — wide vine-wrapped trees dominated the view.

"I don't see any Martian laboratory," Adam joked.

"Well," Leroy explained. "It's been two hundred thousand years. I'm sure it's around here somewhere — that's why we brought the ground-penetrating radar."

Adam leaned forward, looking down over the treacherous cliff. "Victor, how often do tourists visit here?"

Victor acted like he was counting on his fingers, then

looked at Adam.

"Never," he answered, leaning back and letting out a belly laugh. "It is too dangerous on so many levels. Many years ago, some biologists came to study the fireflies, but that was the only time that I know of."

"Do you have ropes for us to climb down this cliff?" Adam asked.

"We've got something better," Victor replied with a mischievous smile.

He walked back to the truck and picked up a long black metal case, lugging it back to the cliff edge. Victor opened the box which contained what appeared to be a shoulder-mounted missile launcher. He picked it up and placed it on his shoulder, aiming it at the trees across the river.

Adam stepped back. "Are you going to blow something up?"

"No," Victor answered. "But please cover your ears."

He aimed down at one of the lower trees. When he pulled the trigger, a large arrow shot out, propelled by a rocket. It squirreled its way across the river, dragging behind it a thin cable the entire way. Far across the river, the arrow slammed into a tree with explosive force, burying deep in the trunk. Much of the loose cable drooped across the long chasm. Victor walked backwards quickly from the cliff edge and laid the launcher down behind the truck. He grabbed the cable and wrapped it around the trailer hitch, using the ball as a pulley. He started walking away from the truck, pulling the cable tight.

"I need some help, guys, all this wire is heavy as hell."

Roger One and Roger Two helped him pull the wire. The drooping cable rose up out of the river and dangled in a loose curve from the cliff to the tree. When it was tight enough, they wrapped it around the trailer hitch multiple times and then used a C-clamp to keep it fastened.

"One more thing," Victor said, raising his index finger into the air.

He pulled another device out of the box. It was a little trolley with two pulleys on the top and a hook on the bottom. Dangling behind it was a long spool of rope. He set the trolley on the cross-river cable and walked back toward the truck, unwinding the trolley rope.

"Watch this, guys," Victor said with excitement. He grabbed one of their duffle bags and hung it from the trolley. Then he slowly fed the rope and the trolley zip-lined down the steel cable until it got to the opposite shore. He yanked on the rope three times quickly and the mechanism on the trolley unhooked the cargo. The duffle bag fell onto the black sand bank of the river.

"Very impressive," Leroy said.

Adam nodded. "Let's send the rest down there."

It took an hour to ship all of their supplies. This included large bags of shovels, food, tents. They put most of the scientific equipment into backpacks that they would wear — too risky to be damaged by the drop at the end of the cable.

"The only thing left is us," Leroy said.

"Don't we need to leave somebody here?" Adam asked. "You know, to pull us back when we're done?"

"Sergeant, you stay here and guard the truck," Victor decided. "If you run into trouble, shoot to kill and then contact me on the walkie-talkie."

"Oui, Victor," Sergeant said. He gathered up the rope and motioned for the first person to cross.

Victor volunteered. He hooked up a harness to the trolley and sat down in it. Sergeant released the rope and let the trolley cross the river. At the midpoint, Victor hung precariously above the water by at least forty feet. Sergeant fed more rope. When Victor reached the tree, he slipped out of the harness and landed on the soft black sand, feet first. Sergeant pulled the trolley back and repeated the process for Leroy, Roger One, Roger Two, Dr. Rolatu, Adam and Lieutenant.

The group looked upward at Sergeant who saluted to them. They saluted back. The men gathered up as much as they could carry and trudged toward the waterfall. From the top of the cliff, they'd scouted a small clearing just to the side of the waterfall, perfect for a campsite. The beautiful black sand stretched from the river's edge to the wall of jungle forest about ten feet away. It created a soft black sidewalk, taking them straight to the base of Zhuvango Falls. The roar of the water pounding into the pool at the bottom grew louder as they closed the distance.

The group wasted no time setting up tents and getting their scientific equipment ready to use, including the portable ground-penetrating radar. It consisted of what looked like a high-tech post-hole digger. Roger One, the geologist, tested it by standing it upright and pushing a button on the top. A beeping sound emanated from it and the LCD screen on the side displayed the density of the ground as a function of depth. It also estimated the material type. Roger walked along the campsite taking measurements, then further out in radial lines.

"Nothing so far!" Roger yelled back to the crew.

Adam stared at Zhuvango Falls. It was enormously wide

— much wider than the river.

"Gentlemen, let's go for a quick walk," Adam suggested.

He and the two Rogers walked along the black sand toward the rightmost edge of the waterfall. The roar was deafening as the water slammed down from a hundred feet above them. The thick mist being thrown off by the waterfall made it look like they were walking into a cloud. The three men put on ponchos and got out their powerful LED flashlights. Adam walked toward the roar of water. The ground turned from loose black sand to slick rock. Adam took careful footsteps — losing his grip here would be fatal. He kept a constant eye on the roiling pool of water to his left, where the full force of the waterfall was hammering away.

Adam looked up and saw a world of water falling at him. He took another step through the sheet of water and was now behind it.

Adam raised his arm and pushed the button on his flashlight. Directly in front of him was a sight that caused both confusion and bewilderment. His awestruck gaze moved upward and upward.

"What the hell is that?"

CHAPTER 61

20,000 feet below the Pacific
DSE2 Submarine
Tonga Trench

An unsettling *cracking* sound reverberated throughout the steel sphere that housed the three submariners. They threw panicked looks at each other. Alexis felt her stomach wrench up — a squirt of acid bubbled up into the back of her throat.

"Don't worry," Jim said, looking around frantically. "We're not dead, so it wasn't catastrophic."

"Are we still descending?" Alexis asked.

"Yes, of course," Jim confirmed.

"Why? We should stop and find out what's wrong!" Alexis yelled.

"Please remember that the same thing happened to the Trieste on its dive in 1960. We're still alive. Whatever made that noise is not a catastrophic failure," Jim said.

"That's not very comforting," she said nervously.

"Look at the window," Jim directed. "It's perfectly fine. Probably just a cracked battery cell on the outside."

Alexis quietly counted to ten, taking deep breaths.

Depth: 29,000 feet

"We're passing beyond the Mount Everest point," Jim remarked.

"What's that?" Alexis asked.

"We're now further below the surface of the ocean than Mount Everest is *above* the ocean."

"Interesting," Alexis said, still worried about the integrity of the hull.

"Almost there," Jim said with excitement. "We've got sonar detecting the seafloor. Looks like we won't break thirty thousand feet, though. Not as deep as the Mariana here, but not too shabby. Gotta start slowing the descent so we don't slam into the bottom."

Alexis was getting nervous now. This sphere was feeling very cramped.

Depth: 29,500 feet

"Okay, this is as deep as we're going," Jim said. "Just a few feet above the ground. Roberto, you're in charge now."

"Turning on lateral sonar," Roberto said as he flipped a switch on the console. The screen lit up with a sweeping green line rotating around the center of the screen.

"Do you see it?" Alexis asked with anticipation.

"No, nothing yet..." Roberto trailed off. "We should see some big solid green spots if there is anything other than the seafloor."

Alexis looked out the small window in the hatch and

saw a brownish green seafloor, devoid of any sign of life or even trash. Not even rocks. It was reminiscent of the Moon.

"Can you increase the diameter of the scan?" Alexis asked.

"Turning on the long-distance side-scanning sonar," Roberto confirmed. "Hey, lookie, lookie."

A large green blip showed up on the radar.

"Let's go for a ride," Roberto said. He maneuvered the joysticks so that the DSE2 began traveling toward the green blip. Like a skilled pilot he flew just a few feet above the seafloor as they navigated up a slight incline. When they flew just over the top of a slight ridge, splayed out in front of them was a huge boat anchor, heavily rusted.

"Well," Roberto admitted. "That's not exactly deep sea treasure."

Roberto flew the DSE2 upward a few feet to get a better range for the sonar scan. The crew stared at the sweeping green line on the screen. Nothing showed up except for the boat anchor.

"There must be something..." Alexis complained.

"This place is totally dead," Jim said. "There's nothing here. Did your cartographers correct for continental drift over all this time?"

"Yes, they ran a bunch of possible scenarios and this is supposed to be the most likely location of the laboratory," Alexis said, obviously very upset.

Roberto grabbed the joysticks which controlled the external propellers again. The ship dropped down and began moving laterally again, almost hugging the seafloor.

"I'll start taking us in wide sweeping paths. Maybe we'll see something."

Roberto carefully took the DSE2 on a slow pleasure cruise along the bottom of the Tonga Trench. Gliding above the mild moguls, the entire landscape around them was lit up by their external stack of LED lamps. After ten minutes, he brought the submersible to a halt.

"Alexis, I haven't seen anything."

"Are we done?" she asked.

Jim nodded his head. "I think so."

Alexis picked up the intercom microphone.

"DSE2 to Captain Nadino."

After a few seconds, a staticky reply came back. "I hear you, Alexis."

"We're all done here. Very disappointing. No joy on finding the Martian laboratory."

"I'm sorry to hear that," the captain said with surprisingly little disappointment. "Did you find *anything* interesting?"

"Just an old anchor. Not even a strange animal to make it worth our trip."

"I understand," the captain replied.

Alexis pushed the transmit button again. "Can you please send a message to Chris Tankovitch that the Tonga Trench dive did not find the target?"

"I will do that," the captain agreed.

"Over," Alexis said. She hung the intercom microphone back on the hook.

"Well, gentlemen, sorry to waste your time. Let's head back up."

The two men glanced at each other, both with a look of concern on their faces.

"Well," Roberto said. "There is plan B."

Alexis looked confused, leaning her head slightly.

"What plan B? Do you know something that my cartographers didn't?"

Jim laughed.

"No, ma'am, but there is something down here that may make it worth *our* time for this dive."

Roberto reached below his seat and pulled up the manila envelope with SECRET written on it.

"We're going to take a slight detour," Roberto said, removing a sheet of paper from the envelope.

"What are you talking about? Let's just go back up to the ship. We've got a long ascent ahead of us."

"Hold your horses," Jim replied.

"No, we are going back right now!" Alexis demanded.

Jim and Roberto smiled at each other as if they had some inside joke.

"Did you ever pause to think about why we suddenly had an opening in our schedule for this dangerous dive?" Jim asked.

"Patriotic duty?" Alexis answered. "The search for the cure for cancer?"

Both men laughed.

Roberto typed some coordinates into his navigation computer which put a new dot on the screen, roughly one mile away.

"Bingo," both men said simultaneously.

"Just bear with us on this one," Jim told her in a patronizing tone.

"Look you guys," Alexis said firmly. "I don't like this one bit. Every extra minute down here brings extra risk."

"So now you're suddenly averse to risk?" Jim asked with

sarcasm. "Our captain tried to prevent you from coming down here with us."

Alexis gritted her teeth.

"What if I pulled the ballast release right now?" Alexis asked.

"Well, then an externally actuated hook would release our 500 pound block of steel and we'd rise up to the surface."

Alexis slowly reached for the switch.

Jim stuck his hand over it.

"Please. Just give us a minute."

Roberto deftly steered the sub over the bland seafloor. From somewhere in the sphere, a clicking sound began. The clicks came faster and faster. Alexis looked around to find the source of the sound, but failed to locate it.

Roberto looked somewhat worried at the accelerated clicks.

Jim reached below his seat and pulled out a plastic bag filled with yellow cards marked with "RADwarn" on them. He gave one to Alexis.

"Hold onto this," he said.

The clicks were steady now. Alexis looked at her RADwarn card and the circle in the middle was green — she assumed that was a good sign.

"Can you see it?" Jim asked, eyes squinting at the display monitor. The green dot on the side-scanning sonar screen was very close to them now.

"There!" Roberto blurted out. "Look! It's right there."

Alexis looked at the monitor and saw a three foot long cylinder with big vanes emanating from it.

"So what the hell is that?" Alexis asked.

"That," Roberto said with a big grin, "is real treasure."

Jim nearly jumped out of his seat with excitement. He turned to face Alexis and blurted out:

"What do you know about Apollo 13?"

CHAPTER 62

Behind the waterfall
Zhuvango Falls
Africa

Adam huffed and puffed his way up to the top of a long dirt mound hidden behind the waterfall. As his eyes adjusted to the darkness, he began to make out details — he was standing in an enormous dry cave behind the waterfall, 300 feet wide by at least 200 feet deep. The ceilings were at least 75 feet above him. The air was damp and the walls were illuminated by the glow of sunlight filtering through the waterfall. At various locations around the wall of the cave were rock ledges that appeared to be covered in something that was moving.

"Hey guys," Adam called for his crewmates standing behind him. "What's up with those ledges?"

The two Rogers and Leroy climbed up the dirt mound and stood next to him. They squinted their eyes to get a sharper view.

"Bugs," Leroy declared.

"Just bugs?"

"Yup. A huge hive of them probably," Leroy stated. "I recommend not messing with them."

Leroy looked down at the earthen mound they were standing on. He stomped his feet to test the compactness of the soil.

"So did you think this was anything unusual?" Leroy asked, frowning with extreme sarcasm

Adam looked down and shined his flashlight along the ground to judge distance.

"It's a long dirt mound. About thirty feet long?"

"More like ten meters, yes," Leroy said.

Adam rolled his eyes at the correction.

"It is peculiar in shape and location," Leroy said definitively.

Roger, the geologist, walked down to the bottom of the mound, fifteen feet below. He picked up his portable ground-penetrating radar and unwrapped it from the poncho he'd used to keep the water off of it. Then he climbed back up, breathing heavily when he reached the top.

"Man that waterfall noise doesn't let up. It's deafening," Roger declared.

"Just get used to it," Leroy said.

Roger set the radar probe vertically over the dirt and pushed the button on top.

The LCD screen came back showing severe findings.

"Solid as a rock?" Adam asked.

"No, it's solid as steel," Leroy corrected. "Grab some shovels."

The four of them picked up their shovels and began

digging. The dirt was looser than they thought — it made quick work for removal.

Clink!

They stopped digging. An enormous grin enveloped their faces. All of them.

"Keep going!"

They dug furiously, uncovering a shiny surface as reflective as polished stainless steel. It was unscratched and mirror-like. After thirty minutes, they had uncovered one third of the roof of the building. They searched for the edges. All in all, it was covered by about eighteen inches of soil, loosely packed.

Victor found his way to the top of the dirt hill. "You've found something huge!"

"Yes, strangest metal I've ever seen," Roger admitted. "Covered by dirt for tens of thousands of years and no scratches or oxidation?"

Victor joined in the digging. After an hour, they had uncovered the entire roof and were starting on the front section. The shape resembled an enormous trailer with a completely flat roof. No seams or welds.

All of their shoveling was creating an enormous ring of dirt five feet away from the edge of the building.

"Adam, is this your Martian laboratory?" Victor asked breathlessly as he shoveled.

Adam paused shoveling and leaned on the handle.

"Without a doubt."

Victor let out a huge belly laugh. "Keep digging, my friend! Keep digging!"

CHAPTER 63

DSE2 submarine
The bottom of the Tonga Trench

"What do *I* know about Apollo 13?" Alexis repeated.

"Yes, that's exactly what I asked," Jim said.

Alexis rolled her eyes at the silly question.

"I know a lot about it," she declared. "After all, I'm the director of NASA. Apollo 13 was meant to land on the Moon, but had to abort due to an explosion from an oxygen tank. Instead, they flew around the Moon without landing, and returned to Earth with very little time to spare."

"Right. And what did they not do?" Jim quizzed her.

"They didn't land on the Moon," Alexis reiterated.

The non-stop clicking sound accelerated as they maneuvered right up next to the finned pipe laying on the seafloor. She looked at the RADwarn card in her hand. It was now a *lighter* shade of green.

"When they didn't land on the Moon," Jim explained. "They also didn't leave their scientific experiments that were meant to *stay* on the Moon."

"We all know they didn't eject the lunar module. It came back with them to Earth instead," Alexis said. "In fact, it was their lifeboat on the return journey."

"Exactly. And one of the Moon experiments they brought back was powered by an RTG," Jim said, like he was winning at Trivial Pursuit.

"I know what an RTG is," Alexis declared.

"It's a Radio-isotope Thermal Generator," Jim said in a patronizing tone. "A little electric power plant run by...?"

"Plutonium-238," she answered with authority.

"They not only brought it back in the Lunar Module, but it crashed into the ocean and the damn thing sank right down into the Tonga Trench of all places," Jim concluded.

"You're telling me that the pipe outside our window with fins is the Plutonium RTG from Apollo 13?"

"Do you hear the clicks?" Jim asked. "That's our Geiger counter."

"Oh my God," Alexis panicked. "You guys are playing with something more dangerous than you can imagine. Plutonium is the most poisonous element on Earth. We need to ascend right now!"

The clicking continued non-stop. Her badge was still light-green colored.

Jim swung his head side to side, slowly.

"We're not ascending without that RTG. It contains eight and a half amazing pounds of Plutonium. Do you have any idea how hard it is to make Plutonium? That is a prize worth more than *any* sunken treasure ship or Martian laboratory."

"How much?" Alexis asked with pure derision.

"At least one hundred million dollars. Maybe more."

"Is that the only reason you *found* an opening in your schedule for my dive?"

"Absolutely, it costs an enormous amount of money to conduct a mission like this. We were happy to have NASA pay for it. We just didn't expect a guest of your stature."

"What makes you think I'm just going to let this go unreported?" Alexis asked.

"Because," Jim paused. "The US Government is our customer. We have a salvage contract with the Department of Energy."

Click, click, click. The Geiger counter kept clicking.

Suddenly, a crackly voice came over the intercom.

"Okay, crew," said Captain Nadino. "We're watching your monitors. It's a thing of beauty all right. Now grab that RTG and come back up."

Roberto flexed his shoulders to loosen up — then he grabbed for the joysticks. Little movements of the external propellers made the DSE2 dance slowly toward the RTG. It was coated in a dusting of seafloor material. Parts of the fins looked burnt, as if it didn't quite make the journey unscathed during the Apollo 13 re-entry back in 1970.

The click rate increased. Alexis looked at her RADwarn badge — it was lighter green than just a minute ago.

Roberto maneuvered the grappling arms carefully. He unconsciously bit his lower lip to help with concentration. The mechanical fingers on the grappling arm nudged the RTG, sending a small cloud of silt floating up. He put one grappling arm under the left end of the RTG fins and the other arm under the right-side fins.

"Here goes nothing," Roberto said.

He pulled the secondary joysticks toward him and the arms raised up, lifting the pipe filled with plutonium. Two feet in front of their only access window were several pounds of plutonium, contained inside a shielded pipe.

"Phew," Roberto breathed. "Lifting just a bit more to stabilize it."

He pulled on the joysticks. The RTG rolled slightly back toward the big steel sphere that housed the explorers. Alexis could see the RTG cylinder through the window now.

To her horror, the RTG split in half along a previously unknown crack in the weld, made worse by decades of seawater corrosion.

A glowing red chunk of metal fell out, quickly surrounding itself with a globe of steaming bubbles that rose up in a column.

The Geiger counter went from a click, click, click, to a high-pitched whine.

The lights in the sub began to flicker.

Alexis looked down at her RADwarn card. It was bright red. Her skin felt tingly.

"Dammit!" she yelled. "Get us away from here! Go! Go!"

She looked at her RADwarn card again.

It was black.

She felt nauseous and vomited. Jim followed.

Roberto swung the joysticks away, but one of the propellers failed. The computer monitors glitched — the image flickered on for a few seconds before turning off completely.

The vertical-control propeller went full-blast sending them up a few feet, then reversing, slamming the sub into the seafloor. The crew heard pops and cracks coming from the hatch.

The propeller reversed again.

Over and over, the sub rose up and slammed back down to the floor right next to the roiling ball of bubbles from the plutonium. The ball of boiling seawater glowed an eerie shade of orange.

Alexis slammed her hand on the toggle switch to release the ballast so they could ascend quickly, but nothing happened.

Crack!

Each bounce on the seafloor caused more damage. The hatch started to fail, letting in laser beams of high-pressure seawater. One hit Jim on the shoulder, slicing his skin open — blood sprayed everywhere. He screamed in shock.

A rumble began, followed by a searing metal *crunching* sound. The three occupants stared at the hatch as the thick Lexan window began cracking and pushing inward toward them, as if it were being extruded inward. Instinctively they tried to back up, but there was nowhere to go.

Up on the ocean surface in the Deep SEAK Explorer, Captain Nadino watched the scene unfolding on monitors mounted on the walls of the research room. Several assistants looked to him for guidance.

"What can we do, Captain?"

He sat motionless, paralyzed with terror. His hand covered his mouth as he saw his worst nightmare unfolding nearly six miles below him. He heard their screams, followed by a final muffled *thump.*

The video went dead.

Captain Nadino's eyes were wide and glassed over. He

ran his palm over his entire face to remove the layer of sweat. Without saying a word, he stood up and opened the door to the hallway. He stumbled out, leaning on the wall, and made his way down the long corridor to the bridge. He ran up to the ship's pilot and pushed him out of the way.

The captain paused for a moment to take a look around at his crew — they stared at him like he was a madman. He turned back to the ship controls and slammed the throttle full forward. The huge research ship lurched.

"God help us all!" he yelled out.

CHAPTER 64

Behind the waterfall
Zhuvango Falls
Africa

Adam and his crew of shovelers now called this place the Martian Lab. After all, they figured, that's the only thing it could be. The construction was like nothing they'd ever seen. So far everything shone like polished metal, presumably stainless steel, but they didn't know for sure.

So far they had uncovered the entire roof and much of the front. After what felt like a wild goose chase, they were excited to have found the site where Martians landed on Earth. The structure had one peculiarity though — it didn't contain a single window or a door.

"So how the hell do we get in?" Adam asked.

"We'll dig through the night and keep searching I guess. There's gotta be a door," Leroy answered.

"There's always a door," Adam laughed.

They continued to dig until ten o'clock when all of the dirt on the top and sides was gone. It was as if a giant rectangular trailer found its way into a cave deep in the African jungle. *Buried in dirt.*

The group climbed down and stood in front of the structure, pondering the great question: how would they get in?

From the corner of Adam's eye, he saw a flash of light. He turned his head just in time to see it. All of the elevated ledges in the cave glowed brightly as the bugs started roiling. They flew around in a swarm, illuminating the entire cave with a pulsating storm of glows. Then all at once, they dove toward the trailer, flew right past the crew and out the side of the waterfall.

Adam ran after them, blasted through the waterfall, and kept running into the clearing next to their campsite. Above him, the fireflies enveloped the entire sky, creating a second star field, moving and undulating, covering up the Moon and Mars nearby. Adam stood there dumbfounded — he'd never seen such a dazzling display of lights before.

"Hey Adam!" Leroy yelled. "Come back in here!"

"I'll be there in a minute," Adam said. His grin stretched from ear to ear.

"No, you gotta come now."

Adam heard the urgency in Leroy's voice and jogged back into the cave.

"What is it?" Adam asked.

"Look up there!" Leroy pointed to the rock ledge.

On the wall just above the ledge were dark lines drawn

on the cave wall itself — they'd been obscured by the bugs earlier.

"Let's get up there right now," Adam said. "Before the fireflies come back."

The group ran over to the ledge and began to carefully scale the steep wall. They helped each other. Eventually, Adam was able to peek his head over the ledge. He had a flashlight clamped in his mouth.

"What do you see?" Leroy asked.

Adam spit the flashlight out on the ledge.

"It looks like a caveman drawing of the Martian Lab," Adam yelled. "They were probably just as confused by it as we are."

"That's it?" Leroy asked. "Gotta admit, I'm a little let down."

"No, it shows a ramp or something, just under the front. Back when the cave-dwellers were here, there was some kind of corridor *underneath* the main part."

Adam lifted his cellphone out of his jacket. It had no signal, but it worked as a camera. He took a picture of the ancient sketch on the cave wall. Then he let himself down from the edge of the ledge.

"Okay, I'm coming down," he said, carefully climbing down the steep wall.

They gathered around the front of the Lab.

"What should we do? Sleep?" Roger One asked.

"Are you kidding?" Leroy asked incredulously. "Let's keep digging!"

The men dug down underneath the front of the Lab. After digging down just a few feet under the building, the dirt became very loose and eventually fell into a large void beneath the Martian lab. Adam shined his flashlight through and saw a well-constructed hallway.

"Okay, let's clear as much dirt away from the ramp," Adam commanded. The crew dug furiously until they hit a metal ramp that went down to the subterranean hallway.

Each person turned on their flashlight and descended into the hallway. The ceiling was about nine feet above the floor — perfect for tall Martians, just like Adam had discovered on the mission to Mars the previous year.

The hallway itself was plain with a few round bumps on the walls that looked like they might be lights. Leroy tapped on them, but nothing happened.

"As interesting as this is, I still don't see any..." Leroy interrupted himself.

His flashlight illuminated a circular platform at the end of the hallway, roughly four feet in diameter.

"Elevator?" Leroy asked. "But where are the buttons?"

The men wandered over to it and stood on it. Adam stomped his foot down, sensing how solid it was.

"Maybe," Adam pondered, "but how do we make it go up into the lab?"

"Right there..." Leroy said, pointing his flashlight at the wall. Attached to the metal wall were a bunch of small protruding shapes. Some triangles, some squares, basic shapes. Beneath the collection of loose shapes was the outline of a square etched into the wall.

"Their elevator combination lock is a tangram?" Adam laughed.

"It's quite clever, actually," Leroy stated. "They didn't necessarily want to keep everybody out, just beings of lower intelligence than them."

Adam pulled at the shapes to see if he could remove them. They didn't budge in that regard, but he could easily slide them around the wall.

"I'm guessing cavemen at the time couldn't solve the puzzle," Adam admitted. "Well, gentlemen, let's go suit up."

The crew walked up the ramp and back to their campsite. The entire area was lit up with the morning sun peeking over the tree line. Victor had gone back to the zip line and Sergeant had pulled him across the river. Adam looked up at the cliff and saw the two men conversing.

The men at camp opened their backpacks and pulled out full-body Tyvec suits with respirators.

"Everybody ready?" Roger Two asked.

"Wait..." Leroy said. "Get your satellite phone out and Google how to solve the tangram puzzle."

Adam laughed. "I think I can figure it out."

Like visitors to an industrial accident site, the suited scientists and the astronaut walked back through the waterfall and down the ramp to the Martian lab elevator.

"Leroy, you're an archaeologist. How about you and I go first?" Adam asked. "Got your tablet?"

"Sure do," Leroy assured him.

The two men stepped onto the platform. Adam reached over and played with the tangram pieces. They slid along the wall very easily. As confident as Adam was, it took longer to solve than he predicted. Leroy sighed in boredom.

"I got this, okay?" Adam said in frustration.

More manipulations.

Almost a square.

Oops, that was close.

Finally, Adam had it down to one piece. He slid it into

place.

Booooooooom......

A slow rumble came and went. The lights in the hallway flickered to life. Adam saw the tangram pieces being dragged back apart by some invisible force. The roof above the elevator slid open and a rush of air blew down and out.

The platform rose.

Adam and Leroy looked at each other as they ascended. The two Rogers ran back up the ramp and stood in front of the lab.

Adam and Leroy rose up into blackness where the platform suddenly stopped.

"Okay, now what," Leroy asked.

"I don't know. Take a step forward," Adam whispered.

The two men took a step forward off the platform, their boots landing on a metallic surface. The laboratory lit up with intense brightness. The two explorers squinted their eyes. Shelves and tables outlined the walls. The furniture was huge and stainless steel like some giant industrial kitchen, but made for tall Martians.

Adam quickly swung around to make sure there wasn't a straggler alien ready to pounce.

Look left.

Look right.

They were alone. A loud humming sound started up and stayed constant. Then, to their amazement, the walls became transparent. They could see right through them out into the cave.

The two men walked toward the front wall of the lab, above the ramp area. They looked down and saw the two Rogers standing in front of and below them.

Adam picked up his walkie-talkie.

"Hey Rogers?" Adam asked.

"Are you being eaten alive?" Roger One asked.

"No, but I can see you guys right through the walls. Can you see us?" Adam asked.

"No, it still looks the same to us. Wait, are you serious?" Roger One asked. He held his fingers up in the V symbol and asked, "How many fingers am I holding up."

"Two," Adam replied.

The Rogers looked at each other. Roger Two held up his middle finger. "Now how many?" he asked.

"Nice," Adam said, chuckling.

Leroy took video of all the desks. There were stacks of things on the tables that looked like books at first, but when he opened them, they weren't filled with paper. Instead each one had pages made of shiny metal, thin as onion skins. Each one was covered in Martian writing. He looked up at Adam.

"I think we found the motherlode," Leroy said.

The two men flipped through more of the books.

"Oh my goodness, loooook..." Leroy said in a giddy tone. "Color photos of cavemen! They all have magnificent beards..."

"Do you see any images of the Martians?" Adam asked.

"No," Leroy answered, shaking his head. "Not yet."

Leroy took out his tablet and ran a special app developed by NASA that would take images of Martian text and translate it in real time. He pointed it at the book fronts and the following common term came back:

LOGBOOK

One of the curious aspects of the Martian language is that it didn't have lower case letters. This aided in the quick decryption back during the first Mars mission.

"They left behind so many logbooks," Leroy said.

"Left behind?" Adam questioned. "But where did the Martians themselves go? We know they didn't return to Mars."

"I don't know, but look at these logbook notes. They talk about all the local animals and plants — this is incredible stuff. This one has recipes — oh man, they were trying to develop reliable food sources. Look, they ate a wooly mammoth!"

"Just like the cavemen," Adam said. "Maybe the cavemen taught them how to hunt, you know, like the Indians taught the pilgrims?"

"Native Americans," Leroy corrected him.

In the middle of the room was an island table with a single sheet of metal paper on it, held down by a globe on a pedestal. The globe was white and had a button on top of it.

Leroy brought the translation tablet over to the island table and took a picture of the handwritten note. After a few moments, the translation came back:

"HALF OF OUR CREW HAS DIED BECAUSE OF GRAVITY SICKNESS. MANY FOOD OPTIONS HERE, BUT HUMANS ARE VERY VIOLENT AND UNINTELLIGENT. THAT IS A DANGEROUS COMBINATION. OUR COMMUNICATION SYSTEMS IRREVERSIBLY BROKEN DURING LANDING AND WE CANNOT CONTACT HOME PLANET. WE HAVE DECIDED TO RETREAT AND MOVE SECONDARY LABORATORY TO LARGE WHITE SATELLITE ORBITING THIS PLANET WHERE GRAVITY IS NOT AS DANGEROUS FOR US. WE WILL AWAIT THE NEXT CREW FROM HOME PLANET. RADIATION ON

WHITE SATELLITE IS STRONG, SO WE ARE MOVING SPECIAL MEDICINE SUPPLIES FROM THIS LABORATORY TO SATELLITE LABORATORY. IF YOUR SECOND EXPEDITION CREW FINDS THIS NOTE, PLEASE SEND HELP TO US ON SATELLITE SOON. LOCATION ON SATELLITE IS OUTLINED ON THIS WHITE SPHERE."

The two men moved their gaze from the tablet screen to the white sphere. Adam reached out and hovered his hand over the button.

"Shall I?" he asked.

"Do you think it's a booby trap?" Leroy asked, only half seriously. "Like, if you push that button and the Earth detonates?"

Adam thought for a moment and shrugged his shoulders.

"Probably not."

Adam pushed the button.

The sphere illuminated, showing a projection of the Moon. On one side was a red plus-sign. Adam touched it and the image zoomed in to display a giant hole in the surface of the Moon with a similar metallic laboratory sitting in the bottom of it.

"In his note, he mentions the medicine," Leroy said.

"I know," Adam agreed. "I bet they have an anti-gravity system up there."

"Anti-gravity on the Moon seems a bit redundant."

"Right," Adam agreed. "But they were obviously making it down here too, so they must have a *machine* to make it *anywhere*."

Leroy shook his head in frustration.

"I'm not sure how NASA is going to do it, but humanity needs that medicine pronto. Are you up for a trip to the Moon?"

"No way, my space travel days are over," Adam laughed.

Suddenly, sparks sprayed out from the front of the laboratory and the nearby rocks. Adam and Leroy looked up to see the two Rogers take off running, disappearing through the waterfall toward the camp.

"Uh oh," Adam said. "That can't be good."

The two explorers ran back to the platform and it sank down. They hustled up the ramp and out through the waterfall. They heard automatic machine gun fire coming from the top of the cliff near their truck.

Victor ran towards them along the black sand shore of the river.

"Take cover!" Victor yelled. "Get behind those rocks!"

Spurts of dirt were popping up all around Victor as he sprinted toward the NASA crew, jumping side to side to avoid the rain of bullets.

The men quickly dove behind the rocks. Sparks were flying everywhere as rifle shots rang out, tracers coming from the top of the cliff. A group of about a dozen men stood at the top of the cliff, all holding rifles — shooting at them.

Sergeant was hanging from the trolley and riding it down full speed with nobody to slow him down. As he neared the bottom, he let go and fell into the river. The poachers shot at him. Splashes of water popped up all around him. Sergeant got to the river's edge and ran in a zigzag pattern toward the NASA crew.

Victor and Lieutenant raised up their rifles and shot at the top of the cliff to give Sergeant cover, but a crescendo of tracers rained down on them. With no time to spare, Sergeant jumped behind a large boulder.

Victor looked at Leroy and asked, "Do you have your satellite phone?"

Leroy nodded furiously.

Victor pulled out his wallet, took a note from the billfold and handed it to Leroy. It had "US Embassy" written on it, followed by a phone number.

"Call this number. It's the embassy. *Then give me the phone.*"

Bang! Bang! Bang!

Victor fired back at the cliff.

The poachers shot right back.

More sparks flew from the rocks surrounding the crew.

Leroy called the number, occasionally flinching from the ricochets striking all around him. He handed the phone to Victor.

"Hello! I need to talk with Richard Alizon! I'm in a Foxtrot Uniform situation," Victor yelled into the phone.

After a few moments, Victor started up again.

"Richey! Just shut up and listen!" Victor yelled into the phone. "I'm with the NASA personnel and we're under attack by heavily armed poachers. They are up on the cliff over Zhuvango Falls. Do you copy me? You know all those favors you owe me? Well I need to cash them in immediately. Send help right now. Remember, the bad guys are on the top of Zhuvango Falls and we are at the bottom."

Victor paused to listen.

"How soon?" he yelled into the phone.

Victor waited again.

"Damn, okay. Send them ASAP! I don't know how long

we can hold them off!"

Victor hung up and gave the phone back to Leroy.

"We have to hold down here for at least twenty minutes. Help is on the way," Victor said.

"Twenty minutes!" Adam yelled incredulously.

"I'll try to hold them off," Victor said.

Every minute or so, one of the poachers would attempt to ride the zip line down. Victor would shoot at him and the poacher would scurry back to the cover of the cliff.

Victor, Sergeant and Lieutenant established lookouts trying to cover the area all around them in case poachers tried to sneak behind them.

For the next twenty minutes, shots came at them from the cliff and then the waterfall itself, the poachers having walked out into the river and dangerously close to the edge of the falls.

A low rumbling noise came from the southeast. An old C-130 aircraft came zooming over the trees and climbed upward quickly several hundred feet. The airplane leveled off and began flying a slow lazy circle around the poachers. The poachers began shooting at the airplane with the occasional tracer leaving their rifles.

Then a deafening *Bzzzzzzzzrt* sound emitted from the side of the C-130 as a rain of hell dropped down on the poachers. The airplane unloaded a shower of enormous bullets made from depleted uranium.

The heavy cloud of bullets slammed into the cliff where the poachers were hiding. The ground around them exploded with debris, forcing a landslide down into the river. The truck exploded — the carcass flipped up into the air and then rolled down the cliff into the river along with the dirt, crushing some of the poachers who'd survived the fall.

The C-130 flew in another circle and dropped a more explosive rain of tracers and bullets into the cliff and the surrounding area. After shooting into the river just below the cliff, the airplane flattened out, circled back and began firing at the top of the waterfall. A shower of red water came streaming over the waterfall.

And just as soon as it started, the C-130 rotated the wings flat and flew away over the trees. The sound of the engines faded into the jungle noises.

Victor slid down the rock he'd been leaning on and sat down, looking relieved.

"That AC-130 just saved our lives," Victor said.

Two minutes after the plane left, another low rumble sound rose up, but this had a regular *thump, thump, thump* sound.

A large Bell UH-1 helicopter, famously known as the Huey Hog, came into view over the trees. It dangled overhead with its lumbering flight movements and circled around a few times before settling down near the campsite. Several American soldiers jumped off the helicopter and ran toward the group.

"Which one of you is Agent Victor Nuvongo?" the lead soldier asked, still wearing his helmet and sunglasses.

Victor stepped forward.

"Okay sir," said the solder. "We've got two more helos inbound. We understand you found something of interest?"

"Yes, sir," Victor told the soldier. "You'll need to secure this site."

Over the next hour, a dozen solders arrived and secured the cave and the Martian laboratory, setting up posts at the extreme ends of the area, including up on the cliff.

Adam wandered over and sat down on a rock next to the NASA guys.

"Hey Leroy, I need to borrow your satellite phone."

"Okay, but go easy on it. Each call costs five bucks a minute," Leroy said, smiling.

Adam dialed Chris Tankovitch's phone number. It rang for what seemed like forever.

"Leroy?" Chris answered.

"No, this is Adam. I'm using Leroy's phone."

"Do you have good news for me?" Chris asked.

"Yes, I do have good news for a change. We found the Martian laboratory. And it's a treasure trove. You'll need to send lots of scientists."

"That is good news," Chris admitted. "But did you find an anti-gravity cube or anything related to the anti-cancer medication?"

"No, but we know where it is and I know where we have to go next."

"To Hell?" Chris asked.

"No, even worse. We're going back to the Moon."

CHAPTER 65

NASA Jennings Manned Spacecraft Center
Fort Worth, Texas

After ending the conversation with Adam, the phone on Chris's desk began ringing. The Caller ID said, "White House". Chris picked it up, fully expecting to get the calling service for the president. She never made the calls herself.

"Chris, this is President Bexar. I have some bad news."

His stomach sank.

"What is it, Madam President?"

"We just received a communications cable from our consulate office in Fiji. There was an accident on the submarine research ship. Three individuals were killed. One of them was Alexis."

Chris fell into his seat, his free hand palming the table for moral and physical support.

"Are they sure? I mean, maybe there is a miscommunication?" he suggested.

Silence.

"No, Chris. I'm afraid she's gone. I don't have any more information right now. I am very sorry about this. She was a great leader and a good person."

"I know," Chris replied.

He was numb. Within the span of just two minutes, he'd received some of the greatest news of his life and then the worst news of his life. Alexis may have no longer been his star, but he always missed being near her light, and now the glimmer was gone forever.

"Chris, I need you to be strong," the president said. "I'm making you the official administrative director of NASA again. I know you'll know how to handle this. You did a great job before, no matter what anybody said."

"Thank you," he said.

The phone slid out of his hand and onto the floor.

"I'll do my best," he whispered.

Chris laid his head on top of the desk.

PART THREE

"There are nights when the wolves are silent and only the Moon howls."

— George Carlin

CHAPTER 66

Conference room
NASA Jennings Manned Spacecraft Center
Fort Worth, Texas

"Ladies and gentlemen, it's been two weeks since we found the hidden Martian laboratory," Chris said, closing the door to the conference room. "And here is a list of rockets we have available that can get us to the Moon."

Chris turned on the projector and showed a blank screen.

The engineers looked around the room, confused. A mumbling erupted from the group.

"Nothing!" Chris shouted, slamming his fist on the table. "We don't have anything that can take us to the Moon and the cure for cancer is just sitting up there, waiting for us to go get it. How can we fix this?"

"What about Whittenberg Space Launch Systems?" a voice on the telecon asked. "I know they're out of business, but don't they have any legacy vehicle sections we can cobble together?"

Chris shook his head. "No. I spoke with Mr. Whittenberg. He said he was sorry, but none of his ships could get to the Moon. He said that if he pooled all his resources together, then maybe he could have something for us in two years."

"Two years!?" the red-headed engineer said incredulously. "Half the population could be dead by then, sir."

"I know," Chris agreed, pointing his pen at the engineer. "We have to get a better solution."

A fairly large engineer sat quietly in the back of the room, swiveling his chair left and right.

"Mr. Tankovitch..." he said.

"*Doctor* Tankovitch," Chris corrected him.

"Sorry, um, but you always told us to call you Mister?"

"Well, things have changed."

"Okay," the engineer shrugged. "Nobody has mentioned that we still have access to some of the Apollo rockets. They cancelled the Apollo program before they were all used."

Chris laughed.

"True, but those are half a century old. They've been rusting away in museums for decades —"

"All except one," the engineer interrupted.

Chris turned his head, surprised.

"Which one?"

"We have a full Saturn V Apollo Moon rocket that was recently refurbished by the Smithsonian. No joke. Right down to every last nut and bolt."

"How recent?" Chris asked.

"Back in 2007. I helped with it. I work in the airframe

division."

Chris walked up to the dry-erase board.

"Hypothetically speaking, of course, but let me write down some details. So we have an airframer here. Do we have any propulsion engineers here?"

Chris looked around the room. One of the people on the telecon screen raised his hand and spoke a warbled, "Me."

"Great," Chris said. "Let's start with the airframe guy. Again, hypothetically speaking, how long would it take you to check out the airframe and make sure it's good to go?"

Another engineer on the side of the room laughed and asked, "You can't be serious about all this, can you?"

Chris stared at him. "That's why I said hypothetically."

He turned back to the airframe engineer. "So, how long would it take you to check out the airframe?"

The engineer looked up and bounced his fingers on his chin as he thought out loud.

"Well, I know all of the fasteners were methodically checked and any corroded parts were replaced. We'd need to run pressure tests and some other basic system safety tests. If I had a big enough crew, maybe a couple of months?"

Chris wrote "Airframe — 2 months" on the board.

"Now what about the propulsion?"

The engineer on the screen was busy writing and punching numbers into his calculator. He looked up.

"Those F-1 engines produced one and a half million pounds of thrust... each. If we found some of the old-timers and brought them out of retirement, maybe, we could refurbish them and the J-2 engines, but wow, I'd be afraid to put my seal of approval on engines that were over a half century old."

Chris looked frustrated.

"Look, if I absolved you of all responsibility, how long would it take?"

"Like airframe says, if I can find enough old-timers, we could have the engines rebuilt and test fired in a couple of months."

Chris began writing on the board, "Propulsion — 2 months"

The propulsion guy kept talking.

"But keep in mind that technology has advanced since that rocket was built and we might be able to make it a lot better."

"How's that?" Chris asked.

"Well I'm sure the flight controls guys would concur, but the flight computers are really old in the Saturn V. Your cellphone has more processing power."

The engineers let out a nervous laugh.

"That's no joke — it's true," he said. "The F-1 engines are on complex gimble-mounts and refurbishing that part of the system could be very troublesome. I'd recommend adding a ring of smaller rocket engines around the outside and have those on tiltable actuators. Use *those* for steering."

Chris nodded his head to show his consideration.

"And how long would that take?" Chris asked.

"Well, if we worked 24/7 and you gave us immunity from all responsibility, then maybe four months?"

"But that would greatly improve the flight control reliability?" Chris asked, looking for confirmation.

"I think so," the engineer on the video monitor answered.

"What about the rest of the flight controls and

instrumentation?"

Another engineer at the table leaned forward in his chair.

"We could convert it to a modern glass cockpit and replace the thrusters in about a month if we can work 24/7, but we'll need you to bring in engineers from all the NASA locations."

"And old-timers?" Chris asked.

"Old-timers would be preferred," the engineer confirmed.

"I call this hypothetical," Chris admitted. "But I honestly don't see any other realistic options. And it sounds like we *might kinda maybe* have a working Saturn V rocket ready in... four months if everything went perfectly?"

"No!" yelled the familiar red-headed engineer in the back of the room. "That means you'll have the *rocket* in four months. The old launchpad will need to be refitted for the Saturn V."

Chris pointed his pen at the guy.

"Shouldn't it already be ready for the Saturn V?"

"Well, we're talking about Launchpad 39A and it's been modified for the space shuttle and it was also used for Whittenberg Space Launch Systems. It's been a long time since Apollo."

"Might the parts still be around?" Chris asked.

"I'm sure they're in storage somewhere."

"Great, I want *you* to build a team and get Launchpad 39A ready to launch a Saturn V in four months."

The red-headed engineer's eyes bulged.

"Um, okay?" he said with little confidence.

The airframe engineer stood up and said, "Doctor

Tankovitch, there is one slight problem with this plan."

"What's that?" Chris asked.

"When the Smithsonian was done refurbishing it, they put the Saturn V into a climate controlled building."

"That doesn't sound like a problem to me," Chris said. "In fact, that sounds like an ideal situation!"

"Yes, but that building is in Houston."

CHAPTER 67

Alston family home
Fort Worth, Texas

Adam sat in his comfortable La-Z-Boy chair, staring at his phone. On the screen was Connie's cellphone number. He pushed Talk. The phone rang and rang. It went straight to voicemail. Adam started to leave his fourth message of the week.

"Hey Honey, this is Adam. I'm back from the business trip to Africa, but I'm sure Chris told you about that already. Look, I'd really like to see you and the kids. Can you give me a call?"

Adam hung up the phone and sighed.

A loud knock came from the front door. Adam walked over and looked through the peep hole. A college-aged kid stood there, wearing a dress shirt and tie. Adam opened the door.

"Hi, I'm Ricky, the one who called about the Porsche on

Craigslist?"

"Oh yeah, yeah. Let me go open the garage door. Hang on."

"Wait a second," Ricky said, his eyes swelling with surprise. "Aren't you Adam Alston, the Mars astronaut?"

Adam nodded.

"True. You got me," Adam laughed. "But the Porsche is in the garage."

Adam closed the front door and walked into the kitchen to grab the key fob. He removed the house key as he walked through the laundry room and into the garage. He pushed the button on the wall that opens the garage door. Sunlight burst in, shining on that beautiful red Porsche. Ricky was standing in the driveway.

"Wow!" Ricky said, his eyes wide as saucers.

"There it is," Adam said, opening the car door. "Now like the ad says, it got some rain in it, so it smells a bit moldy."

The kid walked up and excitedly sat down in the seat. His smile turned to a frowny gag.

"Wow, that's a strong smell," Ricky admitted. "Did you find it in a lake?"

Adam laughed.

"Nope, just rain. But that's why you're getting the bargain of the century."

"It's a bargain that's making me puke, though."

Adam laughed. "Yeah, but where else are you going to find a new Porsche for five grand?" he asked.

"You've got a good point."

Adam nodded.

"Besides the awful smell, why are you selling it?"

Adam stared blankly out the front of the garage. "My wife and I are sort of separated, so I guess it was time to move on."

"Okay, well I'll take it."

"Don't you want to test drive it?" Adam asked.

"Does it run?"

"It runs perfectly," Adam admitted.

"Then I'll drive it away."

Adam reached into his pocket and pulled out the title and signed it.

"Here's the title. Let's go to the DMV and take care of the details," Adam said.

Adam got in the passenger seat. Ricky started the engine and backed the Porsche into the street. The air conditioning came on and the most powerful mold smell hit Adam. He opened his mouth and gagged, half laughing at the putrid experience.

"Windows!" they both said in unison and lowered the windows.

At the Department of Motor Vehicles, it took two hours to process the paperwork and get a new title for Ricky. Even though the kid's new car smelled like a swamp, he had a permanent grin on his face. On the way home, Adam asked Ricky to drop him off at a used car dealership. Adam stepped out of the Porsche and slammed the door. He leaned down to speak through the window.

"Well, Ricky, I hope you have a lifetime of fun with this car. Add an air freshener and it'll be fine."

"And a gallon of bleach."

Ricky squealed the tires, fishtailing as he pulled away.

Adam watched the car disappear up the road and onto the freeway. He turned around and walked onto the used car lot. He'd barely made it past the parking lot entrance when the salesman came out.

"How can I help you today?" the salesman asked.

"I'd like an old pickup truck. An old Ford F-150 if you've got one."

"This is Texas, sir," the salesman laughed. "The only question is which color you'd like that F-150."

CHAPTER 68

Former NASA Johnson Manned Spacecraft Center
Houston, Texas

When towns are abandoned quickly, it's only a matter of hours before looters swoop in, break windows, and steal everything that isn't bolted down. In the case of a nuclear disaster, however, that timeline is greatly shifted — often taking years or decades for the looters to risk the poisonous air and ground.

Much of Houston sat frozen in time, locked to the day when the bomb hit downtown. The suburb of Clear Lake, where the old NASA facility resided, was spared most of the blast damage, but radioactive dust and debris did settle onto the ground and external structures. It was dangerous for any animals to spend much time there.

Don't tell the dogs that, though. Formerly domestic pets, they now lived in packs and roamed the suburbs. Howling all night long, they moved quickly through the abandoned backyards. New running paths were worn through the overgrown grass. At first it was a mix of breeds, from golden retrievers to pitbulls to various mutts of every kind. However, after many months of animal lawlessness, only the pitbulls remained. Hundreds of marauding gangs of the strongest pitbulls. It was truly survival of the fittest.

A pack of them slept comfortably outside the long metal structure that housed a 363-foot long rocket on the old NASA Johnson Space Center property. The building had enormous blue lettering on the side that spelled out ROCKET PARK. For several months, the Saturn V rocket sat comfortably in the darkness of the building, still protected from the elements.

Today, however, was rocket moving day.

Just east of the NASA facility was Galveston Bay, long famous for rising during hurricanes and flooding the nearby neighborhoods. Today the waves lapped quietly against the concrete barriers.

Several long barges floated effortlessly towards the concrete walls that protected NASA Parkway from the water. The first barge bumped up against the concrete and a huge metal deck unfolded to form a ramp.

One by one, large flatbed salvage trucks gunned their diesel engines and drove off the barges onto the road, making wide turns to stay on the pavement. The barges popped up a few inches as each truck left. These trucks had massive tires and the beds were at least 100 feet long and 15 feet wide, built for carrying oil industry equipment.

The truck drivers themselves wore full hazmat suits complete with high-efficiency respirators to keep out dust contaminated with atomic waste. They hoped to spend as little time as possible here today. Accompanying each driver was an assistant who had the job of both navigation and protection — they were armed with Tasers and a pistol.

The fleet of trucks drove west from the bay down NASA Parkway until they reached the old NASA Johnson Space Flight Center. From the main road, they could see the big ROCKET PARK building. They tore through the gates and pulled up in a long line in front of the building, holding off about one hundred yards away.

"What's with all the dogs?" asked the lead truck driver. "I've never seen so many."

"They don't look very friendly," his assistant responded.

One by one, groups of dogs came wandering over to the truck to investigate the new visitors. The dogs barked and clawed at each other.

"Well," said the driver. "Call in the choppers."

The assistant pulled out the walkie-talkie and said, "All right everybody, we're at the target. Bring in the can openers."

In a few minutes, four large Skycrane helicopters approached the building, each one dangling several cables. At the bottom of each cable was a man carrying a massive backpack with a portable cutting torch. One by one they flew over the roof of the building and dropped their man off, then flew away so their downwash didn't knock those men off the roof.

The group of men scrambled around the roof, carefully walking up to the edges and leaning over so they could reach the fastener bolts that held the roof onto the massive steel uprights. They used the cutting torches to slice through the massive bolt-heads and gussets that had protected this structure from dozens of hurricanes over the years. One by one they worked their way down the long roof, eventually cutting through all the fasteners on three sides. When they were done, they gathered toward the middle of the roof and signaled for the choppers to return.

The Skycranes approached. Each man grabbed one of the dangling cables and walked it to the primary attachment points. When all done, four Skyrcrane helicopters were cabled to the roof of the ROCKET PARK building. It looked like a ballet of helicopter piloting.

One of the smaller salvage trucks drove up right next to the building. A roof man attached a rope to the lightning rod and let the rest of the rope dangle down toward the salvage truck.

"Come on, guys, let's get off of here."

With the thundering Skycranes overhead, the men rappelled down the side of the building and landed on the bed of the truck.

Surrounding the truck were hundreds of pitbulls. The dogs stared at the men like they hadn't eaten in weeks. They barked and snapped at the men. The dogs bit at each other and angrily tried to jump onto the salvage bed, but its seven-foot height was just beyond their reach. The dogs were stirring themselves into a fury and biting at the fiberglass truck-body panels, ripping them off.

Several dogs figured out that if they got a running start they could make the leap. Suddenly, the men were facing several raging dogs on the bed of the truck.

Each of the men grabbed their cutting torches and dialed up the oxygen knobs causing huge bright flames. They pointed the flames at the dogs to keep them at bay.

The truck driver leaned out the window and yelled, "Hang on, guys!"

He gunned the engine, lurching the truck forward. It knocked the dogs off balance and caused them to fall over the side. They landed among the throng of other dogs.

The truck drove over to where the group of long salvage trucks were waiting and pulled up next to each one, letting one of the cutting-torch men step off onto a truck. Their jobs were about to get even trickier.

The Skycranes throttled up and raised their collective pitch levers. The vehicles ascended slowly and the cables suddenly went taut. With a ripping and sheering sound, one edge of the roof lifted up, releasing a cloud of dust and old bird nests. The roof continued to tilt up, like the lid on a massive treasure chest. The Skycranes powered up even more as they were reaching their lifting capacity.

Suddenly within their view was the precious Saturn V rocket that had been painstakingly refurbished by the Smithsonian. It gleaned in black and white, having been broken up into the three main elements for display purposes and carefully set atop metal supports.

The helicopters continued lifting until the roof was vertical. Then they drifted slightly away from the main shell of the building and released their cables. The huge roof structure began falling under its own weight, outside the building. It came crashing down on the northside of the building, releasing a storm of dust and debris.

The helicopters flew off to a rendezvous point about 500 yards away to allow the trucks do their work.

Four of the trucks circled the building, each one backing up to the middle of one of the four sides of the structure. The cutting-torch men, now safely out of reach now of the pitbulls, walked the length of their trucks until they reached the rearmost sections, closest to the building. They each picked up what looked like a harpoon device; a large rifle with a claw and a cable. They aimed them as high as they could and fired.

The claws shot up and over the top of the bare walls, drooping down and grasping some of the main steel structure of the walls, stringing a cable back toward the bed of the truck. The men grabbed the ends of the cables and, leaving twenty yards of slack, they wrapped them around a hook on the truck.

"Everybody ready?" the lead driver asked.

The four cutting-torch men said "Yes" simultaneously.

The trucks gunned their engines and slowly drove away from each of their respective walls. A series of popping noises erupted. In slow motion, the large steel walls began to fall outward. An ocean of dogs began running away from the structure.

The trucks continued to pull. The walls fell and slammed into the ground, sending out a storm of debris and folding clouds of dust. The men on the trucks turned away and knelt down to keep from being knocked off the truckbeds and into the deadly throng of dogs.

"All right, now for the hard part," the lead helicopter pilot said. He returned to the rocket and hovered over the top portion where the pristine command module was located.

One of the salvage trucks rolled over the fallen wall, its

massive tires easily climbing over the structure. It pulled up next to the front of the Saturn V rocket. A cutting-torch man jumped from the back of the truck onto the support frame structure that held up the forward command module.

The Skycrane dropped down a bit, giving the man access to the cables. The cutting-torch man hooked the cables onto the four corners of the long support structure.

"Lift up!" said the cutting-torch man over his walkie-talkie.

The Skycrane throttled up and the command module rose up from its moorings. The helicopter pilot deftly maneuvered the expensive cargo up and over to the truckbed where he set it down gently. The cutting-torch man released the cables.

"Cables are released!" he yelled over the walkie-talkie.

The truck driver gunned his engine and slowly drove away, heading back toward the barges waiting in Galveston Bay.

"I'm low on fuel," the lead pilot announced. "Need to head back to the barges."

Next up was the second section of the Saturn V. This portion was far too heavy for any helicopter to lift completely, so they planned to do a two-step movement. They would lift the front section onto the truck, then lift the back section up onto the truck.

This maneuver required a truckbed that was slightly lower. Two cutting-torch men stood on the back of the truck, holding pistols in case any dogs made the leap.

The longest salvage truck drove up next to the massive rocket section. A Skycrane flew up and hovered over the front of the rocket booster section. Two cutting-torch men clambered over the structure, attaching cables.

They gave the signal.

The Skycrane lifted up. A loud metal popping sound was heard as the front of the rocket section tilted up. The two men held on for dear life, one on each side of the rocket. The helicopter drifted towards the truck and the entire rocket structure began to turn. The Skycrane lowered the front end of the rocket onto the truck.

The cable slipped a little and the rocket dropped the last few inches. The man on the passenger side of the rocket support structure fell off, hitting the edge of the truck and falling to the ground.

A group of dogs grabbed him and dragged him beneath the truckbed. Screams could be heard even over the roar of the helicopter.

The assistant to the truck driver opened his door and climbed out onto the truckbed. He laid down on his belly and looked under the truck. He saw a flurry of pitbulls biting at the cutting-torch man.

The assistant pulled out his pistol and aimed.

A dog jumped up and knocked the pistol from his hand. It fell onto the ground next to the injured cutting-torch man.

"Dammit!" the assistant yelled. He pulled out his Taser and aimed it at the lead dog, firing it immediately. The dog yelped and hollered, then ran away. The other dogs backed off.

The man on the ground reached for the pistol and began firing it into the air over the heads of the dogs. The remaining dogs ran away.

The assistant reached down as far as he could.

"Give me your hand!"

The cutting-torch man stood up, obviously in pain, and grabbed the assistant's hand. He pulled him up and the injured man laid out flat on the truckbed, looking up at the midsection of a Saturn V rocket.

"Let's finish this and get out of here!" the assistant yelled. The secondary cutting-torch man nodded.

The Skycrane now hovered over the back to the rocket section. The remaining cutting-torch man and the assistant driver climbed up onto the support structure and attached the cables. The helicopter throttled up and the back end of the rocket lifted up. It rotated through the air until it was aligned over the bed of the truck. The helicopter set it down onto the salvage truck.

"Go! Go!" the assistant yelled.

The truck rumbled away, crushing the laid-down wall sections.

Last up was the longest and heaviest bit — the first stage of the Saturn V. Fortunately, this huge section was already sitting on a flatbed, complete with wheels. This was the only way NASA had been able to transport the final section of the rocket to this building. So they left it on the flatbed trailer.

The tractor portion of a salvage truck backed up to the end of the heavy rocket section. The driver kept a careful eye on the trailer hitch and his fifth-wheel plate, hoping to make a perfect latch.

The driver gunned the engine and his truck backed up. The fifth-wheel slid under the pin located on the front of the trailer bed. The flatbed trailer rose a few inches, then fell into the truck mount with a loud *thud*. The truck rocked forward a bit.

"Bingo!" the driver yelled.

He put the truck in first gear and gunned the engine. The old massive tires on the first stage flatbed began to roll for the first time in years. They rolled with the loud sound of squealing rubber. The truck plodded forward, grinding under the heavy load of the largest rocket in history.

This truck, the last one, drove out toward the bay where the other salvage trucks had already gotten onto their barges. When the truck arrived, the driver made a wide turn to leave the main road. The big truck wheels rolled onto the last barge, causing it to tilt a bit toward shore. When the driver slammed on the brakes, the momentum carried the barge away from shore. The barge pilot retracted the ramp, leaving a throng of dogs that had followed them the entire way.

For the first time in over half a century, NASA had a Moon rocket again.

CHAPTER 69

Press room
New White House
Reston, Virgina

"Hello, everybody," the president said, smiling at the quickly assembled crowd of journalists. "Please have a seat."

The president motioned for everybody to sit down. She turned behind her to see Chris Tankovitch standing there. She gave him the OK sign. He nodded and looked over at a cube-shaped object sitting on a table next to him — it was covered in a blue sheet.

"We have some exciting news to share involving our space agency."

She paused to look at her notes.

"Before we go into that, I need to touch on a subject that has been a tragedy for both NASA and our nation. Several weeks ago we lost our administrative director of NASA in a freak scuba diving accident off the coast of Fiji. She was an incredibly smart engineer and tireless advocate for our space program. Alexis Tankovitch took over during a very challenging time for our nation. We continue to rebuild, but I do ask all of you to keep her in your prayers. Fortunately, we have another Tankovitch who has graciously agreed to be the interim director of NASA. Many of you may question this decision, but I assure you that nobody else has the experience that we currently need."

She took a drink of water.

"And that brings me to today's announcement. Three weeks ago, we sent an expeditionary team to Africa. We were led to this location by interpreting the information that our Mars crew discovered on the walls of the Martian temple. If you recall, the temple was a dedication of sorts to their own expeditionary team that was sent to Earth to find alternative food sources — or perhaps to find viable land as their own planet faltered."

She turned around and motioned for the cartography team to come forward. A gaggle of engineers stepped up, laughing nervously as they got in line.

"These ladies and gentlemen," the president said, pointing to the line of people, "worked tirelessly to uncover the true latitude and longitude coordinates of the Martian lab. I understand it involved some pretty complex math."

The cartographers all looked at each other with a look of concern — they didn't consider it complex. However, they all nodded their heads.

"Without them, our expeditionary team would not have been able to find the Martian lab. And speaking of our expeditionary team...." she trailed off.

The cartographers moved to the side of the stage as a group of four men walked up and reformed a line behind the president.

"Behind me are the four fearless explorers who led us to the discovery of our lifetime."

She read straight from her notes, "Leroy McClaster, Roger Leuda, Roger Vickery and the most famous astronaut of all time — the man from Mars himself, Adam Alston."

The reporters in the audience gave them a round of applause.

"I understand that there were some other support individuals."

Adam raised his finger up to catch her attention.

"Yes, Captain Alston?" she said. "A few words?"

He humbly walked up to the microphone.

"I'd just like to add Victor Nuvongo, Jeffrey LaGuerre, Dr. Willem Rulatu, and the Luodzo brothers, Sergeant and Lieutenant. Unfortunately, Jeffrey lost his life during the expedition — he was a good man. The other names that I mentioned were our experienced guides, but could not be here today."

Adam walked back to his line. The president turned to face the press corps again.

"Yes, let's give a hand for Victor and the Luodzo brothers. And our prayers for Jeffrey's family."

Everybody applauded.

"Gentlemen, please have a seat."

The cartography team and the expedition team sat down on rows of chairs at the side of the stage.

"Now for the news you've been waiting for. We found an abandoned Martian laboratory near what would be considered the edge of the African jungle. It was left there about two hundred thousand years ago. It was hermetically sealed and contained a treasure trove of documents. Take a look at this."

The president turned to show a projected image on the screen. Various photographs taken from the inside of the Martian lab showed the enormous number of books and other information found there.

"Now, ladies and gentlemen, I can't even begin to tell you how valuable the information stored in those books is. Starting this afternoon, we are publishing PDF scans of all those books, along with their translations. Our experts were able to perform a translation because, if you recall, the Martian language was deciphered shortly after the Martian temple was discovered on the Red Planet. They are mostly logbooks, but to our amazement they also contain photographs taken by the Martians during their visit to Earth two hundred thousand years ago. Personally, I've found these photos simply stunning — you can call me a Martianatic!"

She chuckled at her own joke.

"And yes, there are photos of prehistoric humans interacting with the Martians. You can see in... this one, right here, there is a huge height difference."

On the screen behind her, a photo showed a prehistoric human standing next to a Martian. The difference in height was about four feet. The alien wore what looked like a long-sleeved red shirt and actually seemed to be smiling, showing huge teeth – not sharp scary teeth, but more like giant regular human teeth. The Martians had surprisingly thick hair on their arms and head, but their faces were cleanly shaved. They had an olive-tinted skin color. In fact, they looked like large-scale humans.

A murmur went through the crowd as the president continued.

"We did not find any bodies of the Martians. Instead, we discovered that as much as they may have enjoyed their time on the surface of Earth, the high amount of gravity was making them ill.... so they retreated, somewhere with lower gravity."

A hush went through the crowd of reporters.

"They retreated — to the Moon."

Behind her, Chris Tankovitch reached over to a table and removed a blue sheet that was covering the cube-shaped object. Inside was a small pedestal with a white sphere on it. It was all incased within a clear acrylic box.

The president continued. "I'd like to introduce our new interim NASA director, Dr. Chris Tankovitch."

Only half of the crowd applauded as Chris carried the clear box up and set it on the lectern.

"Thank you, Madam President. Thank you, members of the press corps. I'd like to discuss where we're at and where we're going."

Chris carefully lifted the clear box from the lectern and set it down on the floor. He reached into his pocket and removed a white glove, put it on his right hand, and pushed the button on top of the white sphere.

"This white sphere was found in the Martian laboratory. However, as you can see, it's a globe of our Moon, complete with all the usual craters. If you can look right here," Chris pointed at a location and then looked back at the screen on the wall. An image of his enlarged finger on the globe was projected onto the screen.

"That hole you see right there with the red circle around it, that is where we believe we'll find the remains of a secondary Martian laboratory – one that may contain the missing information for us to produce the anti-cancer medication. Now, I'd like to show you a close up of that area in the red circle."

Chris turned around and the image on the screen was replaced with a high-definition image of what looked like a sinkhole in the Moon.

"This hole that you see is what we call a *lunar pit*."

A reporter yelled out, "What's a lunar pit?"

Chris looked at the reporter and smiled.

"That's a *great* question. It's almost like you and I practiced this beforehand."

The room let out a big laugh.

Chris removed his glove as he explained.

"The Moon is permeated with ancient lava tubes below the surface. Some of them were close to the surface and on rare occasions, they caved in. Perhaps a meteorite hit them and knocked the roof in. This image you see here was taken by NASA's Lunar Reconnaissance Orbiter, or LRO. As with all things in the heavens, this lunar pit has a name. We believe the Martian laboratory is in the lunar pit called Mare Tranquillitatis."

"Where is that?" a reporter asked from the back of the room.

"The Moon — I thought we covered this," Chris answered sarcastically.

"No, I mean where *on* the Moon."

"It's about 200 miles, or 322 kilometers, northeast of

the Apollo 11 landing site."

The reporter nodded his head and sat down.

Chris took a drink of water.

"As you can imagine, this sudden change in our agency's plans is huge. We've shifted gears from going to Mars to going back to the Moon. Rest assured, we have a plan. In the past few days, NASA has extracted the last remaining viable Saturn V rocket from Houston and it is in transit to Florida where it will be updated."

A rumble went through the crowd.

A reporter from the *New York Times* jumped up to say, "But that technology is ancient!"

"Well, I like to use the term *proven technology* instead of ancient."

The audience laughed.

"Those rockets took us to the Moon safely many times and, yes, I understand the Apollo 13 mission was the exception, but I should point out that even with that mishap, the Saturn rocket got our astronauts safely back to Earth."

"Who knows how to work on those?" the reporter asked again.

"Good question," Chris said. "We are currently scouring the nation looking for legacy employees who worked on the rockets during the Apollo program. So far we've contacted four hundred and many of them were happy to come back on board. Our time frame is four months."

A chorus of "What?" and "Impossible!" rang out from the press corps.

Chris pointed out at the crowd with his index finger.

"That short timeline is necessary. Each of you knows someone or several someone's who have been affected by cancer from the fallout. We have strong evidence to believe that the cure for cancer is sitting in that lunar pit. Time is of the essence."

"How will you pay for it?" yelled another reporter.

"We've moved all of the remaining Mars exploration budget over to the Lunar Mission budget. We also found some questionable contractual issues with the old Murch Motors contracts and we've performed a clawback on those payments — in fact, his former flight test engineer, Tommy Richtover, is under indictment. If all goes well, this mission is already funded. Believe me, getting to the Moon is much cheaper than Mars. Especially at this point with our space infrastructure in a mess."

"Okay, okay" a New York times reporter complained, "But who will go on this mission?"

Chris smiled.

"Well, we've already chosen a Mission Commander named Sally Monta and a Command Module Pilot named Tucker Rosedale. They've been selected out of the existing astronaut pool. I promise you they have been carefully vetted and are highly skilled. We were able to find the old Apollo simulators and have hauled those out to our training facility in Watsonville, California — if you remember, that's where we built the Mars spacecraft simulation facilities."

"Surely, you're updating the equipment?"

"Absolutely," Chris said. "We're updating all the steam gauges with modern glass cockpit displays. We'll be updating all of the thrusters. The vehicle itself is going through a lot of hull pressure checks. The F-1 engines are being disassembled and rebuilt. Most importantly, we're adding an external ring of small rocket engines for better steering control during launch."

"Can you elaborate?" a voice rang out from the back of the room.

"Sure," Chris said. "As you can imagine, flight controls have made huge advances in the last half century, so we've added a ring of smaller rocket engines surrounding the main set of five engines. These smaller engines can tilt inward and outward and will be used for more fine control of the rocket."

"What about the third?"

"The third what?" Chris asked, genuinely confused.

"The Apollo missions always had three astronauts, but you only mentioned two?"

"Yes, we are currently searching for a qualified third crew member. He or she will be the Mission Pilot."

Chris looked over at Adam Alston who was sitting on the side of the stage. Adams eyes bulged wide open. He shook his head from side to side. He mouthed the message "No way."

Chris turned back toward the audience.

"Thank you for the questions. As President Bexar said, all of our findings from the Martian laboratory will be published on the NASA website for you to look at — starting today. And we'll issue regular updates on the Lunar Mission. Once again, time is of the essence."

Chris put the acrylic box back on the Martian globe. Two armed guards came and picked it up, transporting it through the curtains off stage.

Chris started walking toward Adam, but Adam got up and walked away. Just when Chris was getting upset, his cellphone beeped. The screen displayed: "This is your old friend in Arizona. Call me immediately."

Chris chuckled. He never expected to hear from Dmitri Stalov ever again. Chris wandered backstage and found a vacant room to sit in. He called the number back.

It rang and rang.

"Hello, Chris, I'm glad you got my message. I am panicking."

"Dmitri, I thought you shunned technology like cellphones," Chris said with a laugh.

"I do," Dmitri answered. "I'm using the clerk's cellphone here at the coffee shop. I just saw your press conference and had to call you immediately. You have to abandon your new ring of external rockets."

"Whoa, whoa, why?"

"Do you know that my home country, the Soviet Union, tried a huge engine-cluster idea like that on their Moon rocket?"

"You mean the M1 rocket?"

"Close, it was called the N1. We built four of them to beat *you guys* to the Moon."

"And?"

"And we had a huge cluster of thirty engines on the first stage alone. My estimates are that your current ring plan will add 25 engines to the Saturn V. Is that true?" Dmitri asked.

"That's actually right on. How did you —"

"I'm a bit of a Saturn V aficionado," Dmitri interrupted.

"Well, how did that work out for you?" Chris asked.

"On the N1? It caused the largest non-nuclear explosion ever created by mankind."

"I assume that was not the expected result," Chris asked.

"Of course not!" Dmitri hissed loudly into the phone,

clearly upset.

"Don't worry, Dmitri. We're going to throw together an engine-control computer to manage all of them."

There was silence from Dmitri.

"Are you still there, Dmitri?"

"We had an engine-control system called the KORD — it's Russian, don't worry, but it was meant to manage the engine throttling and positioning. Very advanced. We found out that a mixture of aerodynamics and just the expected failure rate on the engines caused massive problems on all four of our N1 rocket flights."

"How far did they get?"

"We never got past the first stage. Those huge liquid-fueled engine clusters kept failing in unimaginable ways."

"You have my attention..." Chris said.

Dmitri sighed.

"Look, Chris, I just updated the Wikipedia page on the N1. Read it. Learn from their mistakes. Go with the standard Saturn V engine layout. It got you to the Moon many times."

Chris sensed that Dmitri was done.

"Dmitri, thank you for calling."

"No problem. Please stop causing me panic attacks. Trust your gut. The Saturn V is the most amazing machine ever built by mankind."

Dmitri hung up.

Chris bit his lip to think about the conversation. He dialed up his counterparts down in Fort Worth. When they answered, Chris said, "Hey guys, I need you to read about the N1 rocket that the Russians tried to launch to the Moon. Pay close attention to the huge engine-cluster problems."

Ten minutes later, a text arrived from Fort Worth:

"Looks like managing the big liquid-fueled engine-clusters was a serious problem. Caused constant failures."

Chris sent a return text: "Okay, let's kill that plan. Go with the standard setup. Get those F-1 engines rebuilt and cleaned up ASAP."

CHAPTER 70

Tankovitch house
Mount Olympus neighborhood
Fort Worth, Texas

Connie watched the entire press conference from the living room of Chris Tankovitch's house. Up on stage she saw Chris and Adam interacting. It had been a long time since she'd seen them in the same room together.

Cody and Catie sat on either side of her, watching the TV. They jumped up and down and clapped when their Dad stood up to speak.

"I miss Daddy," Catie cried. "When's he coming home?"

"I don't know," Connie said. "He's been very busy."

She held their hands.

"Let's go for a ride."

She loaded the kids into the minivan, and drove east toward their old house. She exited at the Wanigas exit and drove through the winding spaghetti streets of their neighborhood. She pulled into the driveway and opened the garage door.

Connie stepped inside the house and disabled the alarm system. Then she paused, somewhat reluctant to go back into the house with so many memories. The place had that smell you get only when returning from a long trip.

This was the first time she'd been back since the attempted kidnapping. She was, in fact, returning to the scene of the crime. When she got to the living room, she halted at the image above the fireplace. It was their family portrait taken just before the Mars mission.

Connie walked up to the portrait and saw a Post-it note tucked into the frame that simply said, "I miss you all so much. Call me sometime. Love, Adam."

She took the note.

"Kids, let's get out of here."

CHAPTER 71

Jose T's Mexican Food Restaurant
Fort Worth, Texas

"I'd like a Mexican Coke," Chris told the waiter. The man wrote down his order and walked away.

"What's special about a Mexican Coke?" Adam asked.

"It's bottled in Mexico, but made with real cane sugar instead of corn syrup. It tastes great."

"Yeah, I don't really drink soda anymore. My stomach can't handle the acid."

Chris ignored Adam's complaint and looked around. They were eating in an outside dining area, complete with palm trees, fans, and traditional Mexican music.

"So how can I get you on that rocket to the Moon?"

Adam rolled his eyes.

"Chris, my flying days are over. Besides, why would you want me on that mission after how poorly the Mars mission went?"

"Look Adam, Sally and Tucker are first-class astronauts.

You'd be along for the ride. Besides, you are the most famous astronaut in the world right now. Our nation needs a boost of morale and having you on the mission will garner a lot of attention."

Adam didn't reply immediately. Instead, he picked up his glass of water and sipped. He set it down, swirling the ice around.

"Let's get down to brass tacks here, Chris. Forget about this Lunar Mission. I want to see my family and Connie won't answer her phone. I have to assume you are feeding her a line of garbage about me."

"You did it to yourself by talking all night with Wilhelmina."

Adam gave Chris the death stare.

"You know her name was never made public..." Adam trailed off.

"Oh," Chris said, obviously realizing he'd been caught. "My mistake. Too bad that fact won't make it any better."

Their food arrived and the two men ate in silence. The tension was at maximum. Adam used his knife extra hard on the plate to make irritating screeching sounds. Each man occasionally checked his cellphone. Chris drank his entire bottle of Mexican Coke. Adam noticed Chris was dripping sweat.

When they finished, Chris said "I've got the bill." He left some cash on the table and stood up.

"Adam, I want to show you something. Come with me."

The two men exited the restaurant and headed out to Chris Tankovitch's car — he'd recently upgraded to a Cadillac CTS, befitting the director of NASA. They nearly fell down into the bucket seats and then headed down Main street.

They drove in silence for ten minutes and pulled into the parking lot of the Clark Children's Hospital.

"Why are we here?" Adam asked.

"I want to show you the cost of *not* going to the Moon."

"Chris, I think the Lunar Mission is absolutely critical. However, it's not critical that I be on that rocket."

"Just follow me," Chris said, heading toward the hospital entrance.

The two men walked into the front lobby and headed toward the pediatric oncology building. Formerly just a floor, it had expanded to an entire building after the explosion of cancer cases from the bomb fallout around the country. They spoke with the nurse at the front desk.

"Oh you're Adam Alston!" she yelled. "Hey everybody, Adam Alston is here!"

Chris leaned in, "Captain Alston is here to visit some of the kids getting treatment."

Adam looked up at Chris incredulously. The nurse walked from around the counter and grabbed a few sets of face-shields and gloves. She put them on Adam and Chris.

"These kids are going to get a kick out of seeing the Mars man," she said with incredible enthusiasm.

They walked into the first room in the hallway. A little girl laid on the bed. Her hair was very thin – Adam couldn't quite guess her age, perhaps eight or nine. She looked up and smiled at Adam.

"Captain Alston! My Dad took me to one of your speeches last month — it was before I got really sick."

"Oh, hi there...," Adam looked at the dry-erase board to see her name, "Mindy. Thank you for coming to the speech. How are you?"

Mindy looked confused.

"I'm really sick," the girl said, looking upset.

The nurse piped up.

"Mindy has brain cancer. It's being treated with chemo right now. She's one of the lucky ones here because it's working."

Adam panicked. He'd never met a child with such a cruel illness before. He gave her a hug and wished her well. The nurse, Chris, and Adam walked out of the room and across the hallway to a room where a little boy was asleep.

The nurse whispered, "This little boy is Mark, he has lung cancer that is not responding. He starts a new medicine today."

Adam looked astonished.

"Lung cancer? But he can't be older than five or six."

"I know, but he's from the Houston area, so who knows what he's been exposed to."

"Wow," Adam said with a sigh. "Excuse me, nurse, but I have to talk with Chris about something."

"Sure thing," she said. "You can go down to the end of the hallway – there's a conference room there."

The two men walked down the hallway.

"Chris, this is awful."

"I know, Adam. You need to be on that rocket."

"No, you need to put somebody more experienced on that rocket."

"Adam, you went to Mars. Nobody has more experience."

"Yes, but everybody on my mission died!"

"Well, we know that Keller and Molly died."

Adam stopped just outside the conference room.

"What are you trying to say?" Adam asked in an angry tone.

"We never found Yeva's body, Adam."

Adam poked Chris in the chest with his pointer finger.

"It happened just like I've told people."

Chris shook his head.

"Look, Adam, howabout—"

"Mister Adam!" yelled a little girl's voice from across the hallway.

Both men turned to look. Adam's eyes opened wide.

"Sophie!" he said, running over into her room. He looked back at Chris and said, "She's my neighbor."

Chris smiled, ignoring the heated conversation they were just having.

Just then, Sophie's dad walked in.

"Hi, Adam!" he said, shaking Adam's hand.

"Hello, Mr. Rodriguez," he paused, "Why is she here today?"

Mr. Rodriguez grabbed Adam's hand and led him out into the hallway. He began whispering.

"Her situation has gotten worse. It's pancreatic cancer. They said she has three or four months left."

"Oh my God, I'm so sorry. We've known her since she was a baby."

Mr. Rodriguez started tearing up.

"I know, I know, it's ripping us to pieces."

Adam gave him a spontaneous hug. Then the two men walked back into the room.

Sophie sat up in bed, tubes running into her arms.

"Hey Mr. Adam, Dr. Tankovitch here says that you're going to the Moon to find the cure for my cancer."

Adam looked like a deer in the headlights.

"Oh he did, did he? Well, um, we're certainly working on it," Adam stuttered.

"The doctors say there is a monster in my belly and the medicine isn't working like it should."

"I know, Sophie, I'm hoping that the Moon mission finds something important for you," Adam replied.

"I know you'll do your best," she said.

Adam smiled. He hugged her again and shook Mr. Rodriguez's hand. Chris and Adam left the room and went into the conference room again. They shut the door.

Adam immediately went into attack mode.

"How dare you put me on the spot like that!" Adam demanded.

"The world needs you."

"I'll make you a deal. If I go on this mission, you'll tell Connie everything about Wilhelmina. How it was a setup."

"Agreed," Chris said.

Adam looked dumbfounded at the quickness of Chris's answer.

"Wait, that was too easy. What if I don't make it back?" Adam asked.

"Then I tell her nothing and I adopt your children."

"What!" Adam yelled. "No, no, no. Regardless of what happens, you tell her the truth."

Chris laughed.

"Look Adam, I don't think you have any leverage here."

"How can you say that?" Adam demanded.

"Because if you don't go on this mission, then I'll just tell the police about you trying to kill me while I slept in my own bed."

Adams jaw slacked open.

"Yes, Adam, I saw your face that night. I told Connie that the security cameras didn't work, but they did."

CHAPTER 72

Indiana Science Center Ballroom
Indianapolis, Indiana

The past forty eight hours had been a roller coaster for Captain Adam Alston. He publicly announced that he would be the third crew member on the Lunar Mission. He did three television interviews and two telephone interviews. Finally, he'd driven to Indianapolis to give one last speech to a crowd of one thousand people. He was going to make one million dollars from this single speech. His old agent, Oliver, had arranged it as a parting gift for both of them.

The speech was nearly identical to all of his previous speeches. In this one, though, he added a part about doing his part to help solve the cancer crisis that was clawing its way across the world.

Adam had an ulterior motive for this speech and it had to do with proximity.

The next morning he drove up to the small town of Elkhart, the hometown of Keller Murch. Adam maneuvered his pickup truck down an old brick-paved street looking for 354 Bricknell Street.

"350.... 352.... Bingo," Adam said. He pulled over to the curb next to a small ranch house. The grass was cut and the hedges were squared up. The owner definitely cared about the place.

Adam stepped out of his truck. He reached into his pockets and pulled out a key fob that contained a single key. It looked like a house key. He took a deep breath and walked up the three stairs to the tiny front yard and then onto the porch. Adam pulled open the storm door and knocked a few times.

He looked to the left to see if he could see in through the windows. As he glared through one of the windows, the door flung open.

"May I help you?" said a man wearing a white bathrobe. He had shoulder-length gray hair.

Adam stood back up. "Oh, hi... are you Elbert Murch?"

"Well that depends on what you're here for," the man replied in a gravelly voice.

"I'm an old coworker of your son."

The man pulled his glasses from a pocket and put them on, squinting at Adam.

"You're Adam Alston, aren't you. Oh my, come on in, come on in..." Mr. Murch said and walked back inside the house. Adam followed him.

"Please, have a seat. Can I get you a drink? Coke or some other pop?"

"No, thanks."

"Okay. Beer?"

Adam laughed as Mr. Murch disappeared into the kitchen.

"No thanks, I ate breakfast just a little while ago."

"Well, then, suit yourself!

Adam looked at the walls – filled with photos of Keller and only Keller. One picture showed him in a Cub Scout uniform holding his Pinewood Derby car proudly. Next to that was Keller holding a certificate that said, "Junior Achievement Champion." It seemed like Keller spent his childhood earning impressive awards, with the final one showing Keller holding a check with his Dad – it was in the amount of $8million from when he sold the computer game company he'd started with a coworker he'd met at Wendy's.

Mr. Murch came back in and plunked down into a recliner. He popped open a beer and took a big swig.

"Keller was quite the achiever," Adam said.

"Yes, he was. He really was. Got it from his Mom, definitely not me," Mr. Murch laughed. "So what brings you here today? I thought you lived in Texas."

Adam looked away from all the photos.

"Two things, really," Adam said. "I wanted to come and tell you that..." he trailed off.

"It's okay," Mr. Murch said. "I'm dealing with things okay now. It's been hard, but I'm dealing with him being gone."

"Well, I was on Mars with your son when he died."

"I've heard the stories, Mr. Alston. I appreciate you coming here, but you really didn't need to. His motor company is taking care of me."

"That's one of the things I wanted to tell you about.

413

Some of the contracts that his business folks made have been clawed back by NASA."

The old man looked confused.

"Clawed back?"

"That means that the money the company was paid gets pulled back to NASA. It's clawed back out of the Murch Motor bank accounts."

"No, Keller set it up so I'd be taken care of if anything bad happened. He told me that many times."

"Well, something did happen. The company has been liquidated. I just found out last week."

A tear slid down the old man's cheek.

"You know, Adam, I worked in the RV factory here for thirty eight years and I got nothing to show for it except for this house and the property tax bill that comes with it. Keller was a good boy. He built a company that made money and he said he would take care of me."

"I know he probably told you that, Mr. Murch," Adam said remorsefully. "I have something that might help."

Adam reached into his pocket and pulled out the door key to Keller Murch's beach house which he now owned. He dangled the key between them and Mr. Murch picked it up.

"What's it to?"

"It's to your son's beach house in California. I bought it and now I'm giving it to you."

Mr. Murch furrowed his brow. He looked very confused.

"Why are you giving me this? I'm a simple man, Mr. Alston. I can't afford a house in California. I can barely afford this house here in Indiana."

"No, Mr. Murch, I'm giving it to you. You can do whatever you want with it. You can sell it and the proceeds will be your retirement."

Mr. Murch squinted his eyes, piercing Adam to his soul. He kept his eyes on Adam as he took a long swig of beer. Neither man spoke for an eternity.

"Mr. Alston, I've only known a man to give away a prize like this once in my life. And he done it because he felt crazy guilty about something. Is there something you want to tell me? Is there something you gotta get off your mind?"

Adam tried to hide his emotions.

"No, of course not. I just... Keller gave up his life for me and I want to give you this as a gift."

"Is that right," Mr. Murch asked sarcastically. He stood up and walked to the front door. He opened it and summoned Adam to leave.

"But..." Adam trailed off. He knew nothing could save this conversation.

Adam stood up and walked out the door. Mr. Murch grabbed his hand and shoved the key back into it.

"Mr. Alston, I won't pretend to know what happened up there on Mars. I know it was bad. I have a suspicion that you aren't telling me the whole truth. But to be honest, I don't want to know the whole truth. He was my boy. I loved him like nothing else in the world. And now he's gone. My boy was supposed to outlive me. He was supposed to bury me. You left his body up on Mars, so I don't even get the chance to bury him. Take your *gift* and leave."

"But Mr. Murch—"

"Listen to me, Mr. Alston. Fixing your guilt is your own problem. Not mine."

Keller Murch's father raised his fist and wiped a tear from his own cheek. Adam put the key back into his pocket

and walked over to his truck. He got in and drove away —
destination Fort Worth.

Mr. Murch limped back into his front room and shut
the door. He walked over to the pictures. He picked up one
that showed him and his wife standing behind a young Keller
at Disneyworld.

He smiled gently, then walked into the garage.

CHAPTER 73

Downtown Water Gardens Park
Fort Worth, TX

Two days had passed since the surprise phone call. Adam sat on a concrete bench, his foot tapping up and down nervously. His right hand clutched a red rose.

He looked at the area around him, a downtown park so strange and foreign looking that it resembled a Minecraft level. Every square foot was covered by concrete, with angular block steps leading to raised garden beds. At one end there was a monstrously large funnel-shaped waterfall with families walking down the steps to visit the pool at the bottom. It was a place so unique that it had been used as a movie set in the past.

Adam stared at the huge funnel-shaped waterfall and listened to the roar. In the past, he'd brought his family here many times.

He felt a tap on his shoulder. Adam turned around and saw Connie with the two kids in tow.

"Daddy! Daddy!" they screamed, jumping up and down.

Adam leaned down and picked both of them up. He playfully staggered backwards.

"Oh my, you two have gotten so big!"

He smiled at Connie and flexed his hand out to give her the rose. She took it loosely and smelled it.

Adam looked around.

"Where's Chris?"

Connie tilted her head in confusion.

"Why would he care where I was?"

Adam shook his head side to side.

"I don't know, I just..."

"Oh, I see what you're doing," Connie said. "Trying to shift what you did back on me."

Adam sat stone-faced.

"It's not that, Connie, I just figured you two had grown close...."

"What?" she said incredulously. "He was just a family friend who helped us out when we had an emergency."

"I know, I know—"

"Now what about you in the tabloids?" Connie asked accusingly.

"Look, that woman was just one of the crowd that night who asked for an autograph. We got to talking and that's it."

Connie pursed her lips in disbelief, but secretly she wanted to believe him. Before she could say anything, Adam continued.

"I'm leaving for training tomorrow. Then it's off to the Moon in a few months. I know you don't believe me now, but what the tabloids said wasn't true. I still love you more than there are fire-ants in our yard."

Connie laughed, but quickly hid it.

"Why don't you just say no to Chris and stay here with us?"

"He said the country needs a hero right now and I might be that person."

Adam set the kids down. They took off to climb on the concrete block landscaping.

Connie reached up and grabbed his hand.

"You don't need to go to the Moon. Stay here and be *our* hero."

Adam's heart sank.

"I *have* to go. Look, this mission is my last chance at redemption. I led a mission where all three of my crewmates died. People call me hero, but I'm no hero at all. The only thing I accomplished was *not* dying on the way back."

"That's all that matters to us," Connie said.

"I can't really explain it, but I don't have a choice."

"Well, we won't be at the launch."

"I'm sorry to hear that," Adam said.

Connie sighed.

"Come on, kids. We have to let your Daddy get back to his training."

The kids gathered around to give their Dad a goodbye hug. He hugged them tighter than ever.

"Can't you take us with you?" Cody asked, with a tear running down his cheek. "We just got you back from Mars."

"I wish I could, buddy. I'd like to hide you two in my backpack, but NASA said no."

"NASA is not nice," Catie cried.

"I'll file a complaint," Adam said, giving her an extra hug.

"Be safe, Daddy!" Cody yelled.

"I'll try," Adam said. He watched his family walk off to their minivan and drive away, melting into the rush-hour traffic.

CHAPTER 74

NASA West Coast Training Facility
Watsonville, California

Much had changed at the training facility since Adam, Keller, Molly, and Yeva trained for their mission to the Red Planet. Gone were the Mars spacecraft simulators — in their place were the crates housing the mothballed Apollo simulators.

Dozens of engineers worked around the clock to not only re-assemble the simulators, but to replace many of the electronics with LCD-panel cockpits and modern flight control computers. An identical process was being carried out on the legacy Apollo rocket taken from Houston, but it was happening on the opposite side of the country in Florida.

The entire California facility had been built here at the Watsonville Airport because Keller Murch said so. He held the patents on the high-tech Murch rocket motors that were responsible for getting the Mars spacecraft to the Red Planet so quickly. He wielded his patents like weapons and NASA eventually caved to building this place not far from Keller's beach house on the Monterey Bay. For Keller, it had been the perfect setup.

Until he died on Mars and then Adam bought his house. Keller's father didn't want the house, so Adam kept it. As a kind gesture towards his new crew, Adam invited his two crewmates, Sally and Tucker, to live at the beach house. For those two, it was a new experience living so high on the hog. Sally brought her husband and Tucker brought his wife.

Today, though, the crew sat up on stage in an elementary school. Since the simulators were not quite yet ready, the crew was doing some public relations work with the local community in Watsonville. With the nearby industry dedicated mostly to agriculture, many of the school children were those of migrant workers – eager to learn and avoid the backbreaking work of the fields that battered the bodies of their parents.

Adam, Sally and Tucker sat on stools up on the stage. They each had a microphone. The principal was sitting in the front row. She looked behind her and then back toward the stage.

"The kids should be arriving here soon."

The doors in the back of the auditorium opened and young school-aged children flooded in. They filled the front rows and worked their way back. The commotion and noise echoed throughout the room. When the room was full, the principal turned on a wireless microphone.

"All right, everybody," the principal said. "Everybody quiet down. Put a bubble in it!"

The commotion quieted down to silence. It was impressive control by the principal.

"Thank you. We have three very special guests from

NASA today. They are working at the training facility over at the airport, but have taken time out of their busy day to come talk with you. Let's give them a round of applause."

An enthusiastic roar of applause rose up and then quieted down.

"They have instructed me to tell you that their names are Adam, Sally, and Tucker. They're going to talk with you about their upcoming mission to the Moon and then you can ask questions, okay?"

Adam reached down to the floor and picked up a huge display model of the Saturn V rocket.

"Can any of you guess where the three of us will be sitting when this rocket launches?"

"At the bottom!" yelled a student in the front row.

"Not exactly," Adam laughed. "We'd probably get our toes burnt if we did that."

"At the top!" yelled half the audience.

"That's right," Adam said.

He pointed to cone shape at the very top, known as the Command Module.

"We'll be at the very top. We're essentially sitting on top of the biggest rocket ever successfully flown. If you laid it down on its side, it would be longer than a football field."

A chorus of *Whoa's!* rang out from the crowd.

"And on the bottom are five engines. Each one is twelve feet wide and each one pushes with over one and a half million pounds of thrust."

Another chorus of *Whoa's!*

Adam handed the model to Sally and she continued the presentation.

"After we take off, this first stage at the bottom will push us until we're moving at six thousand miles per hour. But then it runs out of fuel, so we get rid of it."

She pulled the first stage off the bottom.

"It falls down into the ocean. Then the second stage rockets turn on and keep pushing us, even faster until we reach fifteen thousand miles per hour. But eventually that one runs out of fuel too, so we have to get rid of that second stage, too."

Sally removed the second stage.

"Now the third-stage does a bit more. It pushes us all the way into orbit around the Earth, going roughly twenty five thousand miles per hour. It stops for a while and then it pushes again, sending us out of Earth orbit and on a trajectory to the Moon. Then we get rid of that stage, too."

Sally removed it and handed the rest of the rocket to Tucker.

"Hi, kids," Tucker said, running his hand through his crew cut. "The rest of what you see keeps flying toward the Moon. Hidden inside the section that we're dragging behind us is the Lunar Module. That's another spacecraft – it's the one that will actually land on the Moon."

"What about the funnel-shaped one at the front?" asked a little girl in front.

"That cone on the nose is where we spend most of the trip and it never lands on the Moon. In fact, it has a long piece on the back that acts like a supply closet and it has a rocket motor, too. That part is called the Service Module. That whole package, the Command Module and the Service Module will orbit the Moon, but not land on the Moon. It doubles as our return ship back to Earth."

A collective "Oh..." rang out from the crowd.

"Between the Earth and the Moon, we have to do a crazy maneuver. We'll spin the front of the ship around, the part that has us inside of it, and we'll dock it with the Lunar Module that we've been dragging behind us. Once we get into the Moon's orbit, Sally and Adam will climb into the Lunar Module and push away."

Tucker demonstrated the Lunar Module breaking free from the Command Module.

"I'll stay in the Command Module and orbit the Moon. The Lunar Module will go land on the Moon. When they're done, the top half of the Lunar Module will light a rocket motor and leap off the Moon. It will re-dock with my part of the ship orbiting the Moon. We'll kick off the Lunar Module and then the three of us will return to the Earth in the Command Module, dragging the Service Module behind us."

"Will you be scared?" asked a boy in the middle of the crowd.

Adam looked at the other two astronauts. He leaned toward the microphone.

"We'll probably be too busy to be scared, but sure, we might have butterflies in our stomachs."

The next thirty minutes consisted of the common questions. How do you pee in space? How do you sleep in space?

"Uncomfortably," was the usual answer.

The principal stood up. "Let's give them all a round of applause." The astronauts were surprised at how loud elementary kids could be.

The Lunar crew spent ten minutes signing autographs and then headed back to the training facility.

Within weeks, the simulators were up and running. Each morning, the three astronauts would jog for three miles along the beaches of Santa Cruz, seeing the occasional whale off in the distance and soaking up the morning breeze.

After breakfast, a large SUV would appear at the beach house and pick up the three astronauts. They would travel to the Watsonville training facility and spend the first half of the morning reviewing operating manuals for the legacy systems on the Saturn V. After lunch, they would be in the simulators until well after dinnertime. It was a madhouse operation as they would occasionally have to pause as systems were installed or replaced.

Adam was worried about one thing in particular. This mission had two goals. Primarily, they were to mix up as much Blue Hope medicine as possible in the low gravity of the Moon. Their secondary mission was to investigate the Martian laboratory.

Adam's strong point was math and engineering. He'd never been a PhD level at chemistry, knowing just enough to get through the engineering curriculum. He was worried about the mixing of the chemicals to make Blue Hope.

Fortunately, his worries were about to be eliminated.

CHAPTER 75

NASA West Coast Training Facility
Watsonville, California

The three astronauts shuffled into a small conference room, accompanied by Chris Tankovitch — he'd come out to check up on the training schedule. On the table was an electronic box the size of a microwave. It was made from stainless steel and had a touch-screen. On the top of the machine were three small pipes protruding upward.

A man wearing a pin-striped suit and greased hair stood behind the device. He shook the hand of each astronaut and invited them to sit down.

"Good morning, everybody," he said, smiling broadly at them. Unlike the astronauts, he continued standing.

"My name is Matthew Kohler. I'm a chemist at the Teraxo Chemical Corporation. We produce a lot of generic antibiotics and some limited-run pharmaceuticals. You've probably never heard of us, but you've definitely used our products if you've ever bought generic amoxicillin or doxycycline. We were contracted by NASA to build the machine you'll be using on the Moon to produce the anti-TRK1 enzyme inhibitor."

The astronauts gave worried grins, showing slight confusion. The chemist saw this and interrupted himself. "That's the technical name for Blue Hope, the anti-cancer drug."

The astronauts nodded their heads.

"I'm here," he continued, "to show you how to use this machine. It will be installed in the Lunar Module. We've tried to make it as simple as possible for you. It involves three chemicals, the first is tetraoxy..." he trailed off as he looked at the eyes of his audience glaze over.

"Yes, well, to simplify, we've labeled them Bottles A, B and C. That's all there is. You just mix these three chemicals together in a very low-gravity environment and after an hour, our prediction models show that it will start to give off a turquoise glow. That means the mix is complete."

"How do we install the bottles?" Adam asked.

"Good question," said the chemist, pointing at Adam. "Why don't you come up here with me?"

Adam pushed his chair back and walked around the table.

"Okay, Adam, now imagine you are in the cramped Lunar Module and you're about to put the chemicals in this machine."

"What do we call the machine?"

The chemist laughed to himself.

"It's technically called the ELGRAMIX which stands for

Enhanced Low Gravity Mixer, but in the lab we've been calling it the *Hope-A-Matic.*"

Everybody in the room laughed.

"Stand right behind it," the chemist instructed.

Adam moved into position behind it. The chemist gave him a three-liter sized bottle with a lot of writing on it, but the most prominent mark was a big letter "A".

"Turn it upside down and just poke it onto that pipe."

"So it's like an office water bottle?" Adam asked.

"Exactly."

The chemist handed Adam two more bottles, marked B and C. Adam repeated the process of bottle A and poked the bottles down onto the pipes that stuck out of the roof of the machine.

"Now all you do is push the Start button."

"Really?" Adam asked.

"We've been working 24/7 for a month to make this user interface simple."

"Even a caveman could do it," Adam suggested.

"You bet," the chemist grinned.

Adam reached over and pushed the Start button.

Air was injected into each of the bottles, causing the contents to be pumped into the little pipe. Three of the walls of the machine were made of glass and lit up from the inside. The NASA crew saw the liquids going into a complicated mixer.

"Keep in mind," the chemist said. "If you were in the Moon's gravitational field right now, in about an hour, this liquid would start glowing turquoise."

"Which means it's done?" asked Sally.

"Yes, that's right."

"That seems almost too easy," Tucker said.

"Well," the chemist trailed off. "There is one catch."

"Hah! There's always a catch," Chris said, breaking his mute appearance in the room.

The chemist reached under the table and brought up a very fancy stainless steel cooler roughly two feet long on each side. It had a top half and a bottom half with large clamps on each side.

"We worked with a company that makes cryogenic insulation systems to build this. This cooler is very simple, yet very effective. It is pressure sealed and the Blue Hope ingredients must be kept in here during the trip to the Moon."

"How does it stay cool for that long?" Sally asked.

"We looked at a lot of ways to tie it into the existing Saturn V electrical system, but we couldn't find a lightweight reliable solution on such a short time frame. So the cooler uses a grid of dry ice cubes. The clamshell top of the cooler is sealed with high-pressure tape. That, in addition to the clamps, keeps anything inside from getting outside."

Sally looked very concerned.

"Won't that emit carbon dioxide?"

"No, not a significant amount," the chemist explained. "The shell has a two-inch vacuum between the inside and the outside walls. If you don't open it, the dry ice will stay there for two weeks — more than enough time for you to get to the Moon. Once you mix the chemicals, you won't need any special temperatures other than room temperature. At that point, just throw the cooler out onto the Moon's surface ASAP. You don't want a source of CO_2 contaminating your life-support systems."

"I produce CO2," Tucker laughed. "Will you throw me out on the Moon, too?"

"Of course not," Sally said sarcastically. "You'll be orbiting the Moon in the Command Service Module."

Adam turned toward the chemist. "What if the cubes melt on the way there and the bottles get warm?"

The chemist frowned.

"They won't melt much — they'll sublimate"

Adam rolled his eyes. "You know what I mean."

"I know, it's just semantics, but the conversion from dry ice to CO2 gas during your short trip will be very low. I suppose if you opened it up and left it open, the cubes would sublimate completely in about a day or so. And the Blue Hope chemicals would be ruined, depending on how warm they got."

Tucker nodded his head up and down.

"I think we've got it. Land on the Moon, break open the cooler, install the bottles, run the Hope-A-Matic and then get rid of the cooler."

The chemist could see the worry in the astronauts' eyes about the cooler.

"Look, don't worry about the cooler. It's a fool-proof system. It's clamped together and can withstand a lot of pressure. NASA has spent over three million dollars on this cooler alone. You worry about flying the rocket."

The chemist leaned in, as if sharing a secret. "Rumor has it that NASA has already licensed the cooler design to BigIceCoolers — you know, they make the expensive coolers for campers?"

The crew smirked at such an odd disclosure.

"I have one last question," Adam said. "Can we leave the

Hope-A-Matic running in the Lunar Module while we explore the surface?"

"Yes," the chemist confirmed. "Once the liquids are pulled into the machine, the unit becomes a self-enclosed system, complete with temperature regulation."

Chris stood up and the three astronauts followed.

"Thank you, Matthew," Chris said, shaking the chemist's hand.

"My pleasure. I'm on my way to Florida to install this very unit in the Saturn V."

They exited the room and walked down the hallway, back toward the training hanger. Midway down the long beige corridor, Chris got a phone call and pointed at the astronauts to wait for him.

Chris had an animated conversation with somebody, but the astronauts weren't close enough to eavesdrop. When he hung up, Chris turned to the crew.

"Do you want to go see something amazing?"

CHAPTER 76

Redstone Rocket Engine Test Center
Huntsville, Alabama

A private jet landed on the runway in Huntsville and taxied over to a waiting limousine. Three astronauts and Chris Tankovitch walked down the stairway and onto the tarmac, quickly ducking into the limo. The long black vehicle drove away and left the airport property. Ten minutes later they found themselves cruising through the front gates of the legendary rocket test center.

They kept driving until they came to a large earthen bunker. In the middle was a beefy concrete installation with an F-1 rocket motor mounted in a huge metal skeleton structure — the rocket pointed downward. On the roof of the structure were two giant spheres, one filled with kerosene and the other filled with liquid oxygen. These were the two components necessary to fuel the F-1 engines.

The three astronauts exited the limo and walked down into a building with thick concrete walls and thick greenish windows.

They stepped into a control room. One entire wall was lined with computer monitors. Another wall was lined with old-fashioned so-called "steam gauges" that had black printing on a white background and a physical pointer that moved back and forth.

Several men were sitting at computer workstation tables. A handful of small green-tinted windows lined the leftmost wall — a direct view of the F-1 engine test stand, albeit they were at least three hundred feet away.

Chris spoke to the room manager who was running around checking the steam gauges. The manager wore a white button-down shirt with a black tie. He was at least 70 years old, but ran around like his younger brethren.

Chris came back to the astronauts.

"All right, crew. The man you see running around is Norman Rogers. He used to work at Rocketdyne and helped with the design of the F-1 engines. He's one of the experts that we've called back out of retirement."

Norman was full of energy, almost hopping with hyperactivity. He walked over to the astronauts.

"Hello, y'all. Thank you for coming here. If all goes well, you'll see the test of the fifth and final F-1 engine."

"We're ready!" yelled a man from behind Norman.

"Excuse me, we're about to test," Norman said. "Oh, you'll need these..."

Norman handed out earplugs to the astronauts.

"But we're inside a bunker," Adam said.

Norman laughed.

"Believe me, you'll want them."

They inserted the earplugs and walked over to the green

blast-proof windows.

The engineers behind the group began calling out sequences.

"Area is clear."

A minute passed.

"Water on!"

Water started spraying into the pit below the engine.

"Pumps starting!"

"Ignition in five, four, three, two, one!"

The astronauts were not ready for the sound.— the BOOM that rocked the building and *never stopped*. It nauseated the astronauts. At first the underside of the test stand looked like it was on fire. Then they saw the rocket plume suck all of the nearby smoke into the exhaust cave beneath the test stand. Massive jets of smoke and steam came roaring out of an exit pipe far to the side of the test stand.

The engine roar became a *cracka-cracka-cracka,* pounding on the chests of the viewers. It was almost hard to breathe from the pressure waves hitting them. Two monitors fell off the wall in the control room. The people living in nearby Huntsville took notice as their windows rattled.

One minute in and the crew found it hard to concentrate.

An engineer ran up and grabbed Norman, frantically pointing at a flashing red light on the wall. Norman jogged over and quickly took off his glasses to look at the warning readout flickering red. Then he ran back to the window. In the distance, Norman could see a small flame shooting out of a pipe up above the engine.

Norman sprinted across the room and pushed a large red button on the wall. The roaring came to a quick stop as the engine stopped. He ran back to the window. Norman turned around to face his engineering staff.

"Turn on fire suppression in area three!"

The safety engineer pushed a button on his console. Norman turned back to the window. He looked out and saw a mist enveloping the top half of the engine.

"Wowee, wow, that was close!" Norman said with a frown.

"How bad is it?" Chris asked.

Norman nervously straightened his tie.

"Five more seconds and we would've been dodging supersonic flying bits of rocket engine. Fortunately, we saw this problem a few times back in the 1960's. We'll have it fixed by the end of the day."

The crew laughed incredulously. Chris turned to them and said, "And that is why you hire old-timers."

CHAPTER 77

Alston family home
Fort Worth, Texas

Connie and the kids sat on their couch, transfixed by the images on TV. The Saturn V stood atop Launchpad 39A, with plumes of gasses escaping from the connection hoses. In two minutes, NASA would be launching a rocket to the Moon for the first time in a generation.

Connie decided to avoid the paparazzi and watch it from the comfort of her old home. She'd hired a contractor to come in several weeks ago and get rid of any evidence of the break-in. Their old home resembled how she remembered it in the happier days. She even had a new swingset installed.

As the countdown reached the final few seconds, Connie squeezed her children's hands.

"T minus ten seconds," the announcer said in his mechanical voice.

Ten.

Nine.

Eight.

Seven.

Six.

Five.

Four.

Three.

Two...

CHAPTER 78

Launchpad 39A
Kennedy Space Center
Cape Canaveral, Florida

One... Liftoff.

The pipes below the towering Saturn V gushed with cooling water spray. The engines ignited. An eruption at the bottom of this towering beast gave birth to seven and a half million pounds of thrust, pushing it toward the heavens.

The supersonic exhaust gasses turned the water instantly to steam, surrounding the Launchpad with clouds. The large steel gantries holding the rocket sprung away. The lockdowns around the base of the rocket let go. Every car alarm within ten miles burst to life — an applause of sorts for America's return to space exploration.

Up, up it went, clearing the top of the tower in just a matter of seconds. The astronauts rattled in their seats, despite being heavily strapped down. Adam looked over at Sally — she was focused on the G meter.

"One point five G's," Sally yelled.

After just one minute, Sally happily reported, "We're officially supersonic!"

Two minutes passed by and the acceleration decreased a bit.

"Center engine cutoff," Sally said. However, the acceleration still continued for another half of a minute.

"Four G's," Sally reported, grunting under the stress of being pushed into her seat with 600 pounds of force.

The astronauts performed their anti-g exercises, breathing in and grunting.

A brief moment of silence took them by surprise as the first stage separated.

"Altitude two hundred thousand feet, speed six thousand miles per hour!"

Kaboom!

The J-2 engines of the second stage came to life, pushing them even faster. The second stage pushed hard.

Six minutes roared by in an instant.

"Passing through altitude one hundred miles. Just under sixteen thousand miles per hour," Sally reported.

Stage two broke away and drifted behind the rocket. The third stage kicked in, pushing the Saturn V into Earth orbit, travelling nearly seventeen thousand miles per hour.

The third-stage motor shut down, but it did not eject. It would have a secondary use in a couple of hours.

"Gentlemen, we have arrived at our parking orbit," Sally proclaimed.

Adam laughed. "Hard to believe that just twelve

minutes ago, we were sitting on top of one of the biggest conventional bombs ever made. Now we're orbiting Earth."

In the meantime, the astronauts ran system checks. The medics back in Fort Worth Mission Control checked the medical readings on the astronauts. Aside from elevated heart rates, they were doing well.

Two hours later, the astronauts fired the rocket on the third stage yet again, letting it run for nearly six minutes. The entire assembly accelerated out to twenty five thousand miles per hour and left Earth Orbit.

"We're on our way to the Moon," Sally said.

For the first time since launch, the astronauts unbuckled themselves and floated about their tiny Command Module. For now, it was the only space they had to move around in. But that would change very quickly.

After running several system-integrity tests, they separated from the third stage, floating slightly ahead of it. The Command Module still had the large cylindrical Service Module attached to the back. That assembly did a 180-degree flip so that the nose of the Command Module was pointing at the top of the third stage.

Tucked in the top of the spent third stage was the Lunar Module — the spacecraft that was meant to take them safely to the Moon.

Adam grabbed onto the handholds and footholds to steady himself. He looked out the small window on the Command Module while maneuvering the joystick. The Command-Service Module assembly floated toward the top of the Lunar Module. He kept his targets lined up and moved forward.

Slowly.

Slowly.

Clunk!

"Hard dock it!"

Adam pulled a lever that locked the two spacecraft together, sharing a common access hatch between them.

"We can breathe a sigh of relief," Tucker said. "The hard part of the launch is all over."

A staticky voice came over the Command Module speakers.

"Crew, this is Fort Worth Mission Control, congratulations on your translunar injection. Can you spare a minute for a phone call?"

"Fort Worth, this is the crew of the Sky Turtle. We are available for a phone call."

The crew of three laughed to themselves.

Sally put the microphone on mute.

"I hate the name Sky Turtle," Sally said to the rest of the crew.

Adam grinned, "I know, I know – it's my fault. They named it for my benefit because of the two Mars ships being named Little Turtle and Big Turtle. The good news is that the Command/Service module is named Sky Turtle, but the Lunar Module is called Moon Turtle."

"Don't remind me," Sally said, rolling her eyes in disbelief.

"Hello?" a loud female voice boomed over the speakers.

"We hear you loud and clear, Madam President. This is the crew of the Sky Turtle."

"To the crew of the Sky Turtle on your way to our only natural satellite, I want to thank you for taking on this challenge. I wish you Godspeed in reaching your destination and I hope the precious chemical cargo you are taking there comes back as something that can change humankind."

Adam turned to his fellow astronauts and whispered, "No pressure, right?"

"Thank you for the good tidings, Madam President," Adam said.

Two hours later, Fort Worth Mission Control disturbed the silence on Sky Turtle.

"Crew of the Sky Turtle, we have some information for you."

"Roger that, Fort Worth, go ahead," Adam replied.

"Sky Turtle, you'll be passing through geosynchronous orbit and we're tracking a few pieces of debris. They're pretty small, but we wanted to make you aware."

Adam looked at Sally – they both had the same concern.

"We copy you, Fort Worth, but is there anything we can do? Perhaps a maneuver to avoid the area?"

"Hold on, Sky Turtle."

A minute of silence passed.

"No," said the speaker. "Just keep on your trajectory."

The crew continued unpacking items that had been strapped down for lift-off purposes. This included the foam-wrapped tablet computers that each person used during the mission.

Adam noticed that his tablet was updating. They had a wifi connection to the Command Module which had a deep-space antenna pointed back at Earth. Adam turned on the tablet and saw a curious message about NASA installing MarTranVoc.

"Hmmm," he wondered.

Then he smiled.

"Hey," Adam laughed. "Do you want to learn how to speak Martian?"

CHAPTER 79

Rural farmland
Ohio

David Milan bought the farm. Literally. After his mother passed away, her will was read in front of David and his three siblings. David was left out completely. However, his older brother didn't want to be a farmer and defied their mothers wishes, selling the farm to David. He couldn't have been happier, but he never spoke to his brother again.

David surprised everybody by farming the land professionally and making a profit. He enjoyed every aspect of it, including modernizing the equipment with GPS and using targeted fertilizer spreading. He tried to share how happy farming made him, but his string of girlfriends never believed him. *Nobody* believed him, but it was true. Farming made him happy.

During harvest season, he drove the combine back and forth across the fields, working his way from the house to the row furthest away on the land. The last row abutted his apple orchard – a real treat after such a long day of work.

Today he would finish the harvest. This particular day was overcast with a continual threat of rain. As he drove the tractor past the orchard, he stood up and stuck his foot in the steering wheel and leaned out. It is precisely this type of behavior that leads to so many farm deaths. But David had done this many times before. He reached far out and grabbed an apple right from the tree and took a big bite.

What he saw next caused him to choke on his bite of apple. Underneath the tree was a white object, roughly shaped like a person. David hopped back in his seat and slammed on the brakes. He climbed down to the ground and walked across the remaining three humps of dirt and into the orchard. He ducked under some apple-laden branches.

There it was. No mistaking it. A white suit, covered in a light dusting of dirt and old leaves. It had been there a while. David clenched his jaw — a mixture of fear and curiosity. He was all alone, spooked by the creaking of the trees swaying in the light breeze — the smell of the diesel exhaust wafting down from the idling tractor.

How did I ever miss this?, David thought.

He approached the white suit carefully. It was definitely a space suit. The face visor was pulled down and cracked. David couldn't see who, or what, was in the suit. He reached over and gently wiped the dirt from the chest, revealing a badge with some writing.

It said: "Yeva Turoskova."

CHAPTER 80

Sky Turtle
Twenty two thousand miles from Earth

"Fenoda," said the tablet in a mechanical voice. The astronauts chuckled like children.

"I don't get it," Tucker said. "How could we possibly know how the Martian voices sounded?"

Adam wrinkled his forehead in thought.

"In the Martian temple on Mars, we found a listing of their alphabet symbols right next to corresponding rumble strips. A series of serrated edges — it was really just a mechanical representation of sound. The Martians were trying to pass on the sound of their voices, too."

"Here, let me try," Sally said.

She tapped her fingers on the tablet, pecking at the touchscreen.

"Now... translate," Sally commanded, pushing the

translate button.

A mechanical male voice said, "Fenoda. Mayato poodroo Sally."

"Can you guess what I said?" she asked coyly.

"Hello, Sally has diarrhea?" Adam joked.

Sally hit him on the back.

"No, goofball, I said, 'Hello, my name is Sally.'"

Tucker grabbed his tablet and typed feverishly. He pushed the translate button.

"Ralto kvera nomia doo ral. Ralto kvera grelsh doo croot."

Adam shook his head back and forth. "I don't have a clue, Tucker."

Tucker snickered to himself.

"I just *Rickrolled* you two!"

Adam sighed.

"Let's see what else these can do. Let's see, the tablets can obviously speak what we type in, but oh look!" Adam exclaimed. "They can listen to me speak and then translate automatically. I guess we don't need to type."

"Let me try that," Tucker said.

He held his tablet up to his face and pushed the Listen button.

"Hello, my name is Tucker. I come in peace."

When Tucker lifted up his finger, the tablet blurted out: "Fenoda. Mayato poodroo Tucker. May merno payache."

Tucker chuckled with a subtle smile.

Ka-thunk! A noise rattled the entire capsule, echoing inside the Command Module.

All laughter stopped immediately.

The astronauts' ears hurt for a millisecond as the brief

sound caught them by surprise. It was like metal piercing metal.

The astronauts hurriedly checked out each other's flight suits to look for blood. Adam looked out the window and saw a dusting of shiny metal bits floating away.

"You okay?" Sally asked, panicked.

"Yeah," Adam and Tucker replied simultaneously.

A subtle whistling sound rose up. It was constant.

"Do you guys hear that?" Sally asked.

They didn't speak, heads twisting all around to locate the source of the sound.

Adam noticed a red light pop up on an instrument panel. A pleasant mechanical female voice blurted out from the flight computer.

"Warning. Command Module is losing pressure."

CHAPTER 81

Sky Turtle
Twenty three thousand miles from Earth

"Sky Turtle, this is Fort Worth," roared the speakers, "We're getting warnings down here that there is a pressure problem in the Command Module."

"Roger that, Fort Worth," Adam said nervously. "We heard a loud sound. Two, actually. The crew is okay, no injuries. But yes, the pressure gauges show a slight pressure drop."

Sally and Tucker frantically tried to find the source of the whistling sounds, looking behind every cabinet and bulkhead.

"Sky Turtle, do you suspect a debris impact?"

"Uh, that's a good hypothesis, Fort Worth. We're trying to find the source of the leak right now. I doubt it's a very big hole or we'd be dead already."

Adam reached into the emergency repair kit and pulled out a thick sheet of rubber with adhesive on one side. He took scissors and cut out a small three-inch patch and handed it to Sally. She continued to search for the leak.

"It's somewhere behind the control console," Sally said. "Let me try to reach."

She stretched her arm back there, but with so many bulkheads, she couldn't find it.

"The hole must be tiny," she admitted.

The speakers roared again.

"Sky Turtle, have you found the hole and patched it yet?"

"Negative, Fort Worth, it's too small to find the exact location," Adam explained.

"Well, you're going to have to fix it. Even a slow leak will do you in over six days."

"If we only had some smoke," Tucker laughed. "It would tell us where the leak is."

"Well, there is no source of smoke in this Command Module," Sally replied. "Fire is the last thing you'd want."

Adam stared at the cooler. "Not exactly."

Tucker and Sally looked confused.

"Howsabout we borrow a small chunk of that dry ice and plop it into a big drop of water," Adam said. "Instant fog. Like Halloween special effects."

"Adam, protecting the crew from poor decisions like that is partially why I'm on this mission," Sally said disapprovingly.

Adam stared at her, a look of surprise on his face.

"Oh come on," Adam begged. "We can reseal the cooler. Seriously, it would be no big deal. Two minutes tops."

The awkward silence between the crew only highlighted the whistling sound coming from the leak.

"Two minutes?" Sally asked.

Adam nodded. "Tops."

"Fort Worth, we are going to attempt something to find the leak. We'll let you know in a couple of minutes."

Adam reached over to the cooler. One by one, he undid the clunky latches on each side. He removed the top half of the cooler and saw the layers of cubes embedded in the bottom. They were more jumbled than he remembered them in the training. He donned a glove and grabbed one of the small ice cubes. Adam floated over near the back of the console.

"Tucker," Adam said, "bring me a bag of water and a pen, and Sally, you hold the flashlight up under the bottom of the console."

Tucker handed him a bag and a pen. Adam slowly squeezed the water bag, producing a spherical, yet wobbly, ball of water. It was slightly animated. He stuck the pen into it so he could control its position somewhat. Then with a gentle push, Adam touched the dry ice cube to the ball of water. It instantly got sucked into the middle of the sphere, which immediately roiled with bubbles, producing a cloud of CO_2 water vapor. The cloud, lacking any buoyancy from gravity, hugged the boiling water-ball. However, wafts of the fog floated slowly behind the console and then turned sharply past the third bulkhead.

Sally shined the flashlight in that area. Sure enough, she saw a small hole the size of a BB.

"Okay, I'm going to reach in with the rubber patch," Adam said, his voice straining. "Tell me when I'm close."

Sally watched as Adam's hand got close to the hole.

"Right there," Sally confirmed.

Adam pushed the sticky rubber patch down onto the wall and the whistling stopped.

Adam let out a big sigh of relief.

"Please, no more excitement," Sally said.

Before Adam pulled his arm out from behind the console, he asked Sally for the flashlight.

"What's up?"

"Well, a piece of debris came into the Command Module, but we don't know where it ended up."

Adam took the flashlight and tried to estimate the trajectory of the debris.

"So if that hole was the starting place," Adam deduced. "Then where did it go?"

His eyes bloomed open.

"Ohhh no...," Adam trailed off.

"What? What is it?" Sally asked, full of concern.

"The good news is that it didn't puncture the other side of the Command Module. The bad news is that it put a big hole right in the cooler."

CHAPTER 82

Twenty four thousand miles from Earth
Sky Turtle

"Fort Worth, we found the hole and we patched it."

"Roger that, Sky Turtle, we see that your pressure is rising back to normal. However, we notice that your CO_2 is elevated."

Adam looked at Sally with a guilty expression on his face.

"Yeah, to find the leak we had to use some *drama department* science," Adam admitted. "We used a small bit of dry ice and water to make smoke. You know, to lead us to the hole."

"Roger that, Sky Turtle. You may need to replace the CO_2 scrubber earlier than usual. Keep an eye on it."

"Will do," Adam said. "We do have another slight problem."

"What's the problem, Sky Turtle?"

"The debris was a tiny bolt. The little piece of space garbage poked a hole in our ship, but didn't exit the other side. Unfortunately, it embedded in the Blue Hope cooler and it pierced the outside and the inside lining."

"What's the status," Fort Worth asked. "Are the chemicals okay?"

"The chemicals are fine, but we've got the holes patched with duct tape," Adam reported.

"Duct tape?"

"Yes, it was the best solution at hand."

"Sky Turtle crew, why hadn't you already transferred the cooler to the Lunar Module yet?"

Adam shrugged his shoulders.

"Well, Fort Worth, we were evaluating our tablets when the incident happened."

"Okay, but watch those CO_2 levels. If they continue to stay elevated, then you've got a serious problem."

Adam raised an eyebrow of concern. "You mean like an *Apollo 13* problem?"

A few seconds of silence followed.

"Negative, Sky Turtle. Apollo 13 made it back alive."

CHAPTER 83

Sky Turtle
Approaching lunar orbit
(72 hours later)

Adam stared nervously at the stack of used CO_2 scrubbers. After three days, the crew had gone through double the expected number of these precious air filtration devices. These cylindrical filters contained a packing of beads that would pull CO_2 out of the cabin's air. With the cooler slowly leaking, the CO_2 had been elevated for the entire trip.

These closed-loop breathing systems are not the most forgiving, he thought.

However, no time to focus on the negative for now. The Moon view filled up all of the windows, its off-white glint bouncing through the corners of the small command module windows.

"Firing Service Module rocket to slow us down," Adam

said.

The entire flying contraption was backwards now, with the rocket engine facing the Moon. Adam started the ignition sequence. The electronic flight controls lit the rocket and fired it, slowing down the entire spacecraft. It continued to descend and slow down until it reached a circular parking orbit roughly 70 miles above the surface of the Moon.

At this altitude and speed, they could orbit the Moon indefinitely.

"Fort Worth," Adam spoke to Mission Control. "We are parked in orbit around the Moon."

"Congratulations, Sky Turtle. Proceed to your Lunar Module setup."

Sally and Adam gathered a few items and crawled through the hole into the Lunar Module. The leaky cooler had been put into the Lunar Module the previous day to reduce its impact on the Command Module systems — however, the damage had been done. It was still affecting the CO_2 scrubbers in both spacecraft. The astronauts couldn't wait to dump it on the Moon.

When the crew was done setting up the Lunar Module, Tucker returned to his position in the Command Module where he would orbit the Moon until the others returned. He reached through the hatch and shook Sally's hand and then Adam's hand.

"Good luck, you two. I'd be lying if I said I wasn't jealous," Tucker admitted. When Tucker pulled his hand back from Adam, he noticed a small square of folded paper pressed into his palm. Tucker looked mildly confused, silently waving it at Adam. Adam said nothing. He just winked.

"See you in a few hours," Tucker said. "Godspeed."

They both closed the hatches on their respective spaceships. Sally and Adam took their positions in front of the triangular windows in the Lunar Module. Adam was the pilot and stood on the right. Sally stood on the left and would be the navigator.

"Undocking in five, four, three, two one."

Clunk.

The Lunar Module floated away from the Command Module, rotating slightly. The two astronauts could now see the Command Module through the windows.

"That's quite a sight..." Sally said, shaking her head at the wonder.

"Engaging autopilot," Adam said. "Next stop, the Mare Tranquillitatis lunar pit."

The Lunar Module continued its slow descent toward the Moon. As they neared the surface, the autopilot engaged the descent rocket and the directional thrusters kicked in, giving guidance — hopefully leading them toward a safe landing next to the rim of the lunar pit. The astronauts looked out over the Sea of Tranquility, marveling at the bright coloration of the terrain.

"Do you see hints of orange color over on that ridge?" Adam asked.

"Sure do," Sally replied. "I bet the Apollo 11 guys saw that, too."

Lower and lower they went. The details of the terrain were amazing, especially the small craters. Many of them had little mountains in their center — a result of the violent impact of the meteoroids that strike the Moon.

"There it is!" Adam yelled.

Just past a medium-sized crater was a large hole in the ground, roughly 300 feet in diameter. The Moon Turtle approached the lunar pit at a slow speed. It passed above it briefly to give both the crew and the downward video cameras a good view.

After all, the world was watching.

The Lunar Module now hovered over the giant hole in the Moon. At the bottom was a structure very similar to the Martian laboratory found on Earth, except it had an extension, making it a giant T shape.

Spooky, Adam whispered to himself.

He was nearly hypnotized at the view.

"Watch your fuel," Sally said.

Adam broke his hypnotic stare.

"We're good," he replied.

The Lunar Module would not land inside the pit — the terrain was unknown, making it unsafe by default. If it was too rocky, then the Lunar Module might fall over. Being inside the pit would also greatly limit communication. Instead, they would land ten meters or so from the edge of the pit and cables would uncoil and droop down over the cliff edge. The astronauts had a handheld cable-climber device that would lower them down and pull them back up.

The Lunar Module descended slowly. The four landing pads gently touched the Moon surface. Before the rockets could shut down, though, the ground began to crumble. The astronauts felt the entire ship tilt.

"What the hell?" Adam yelled.

He throttled up the engine again and the Lunar Module lifted up just as the ground gave way, falling into a huge chasm.

The debris caused a small avalanche to slide down the side of the lunar pit, but it fell in a surreal slow manner.

Alarms blared in the Lunar Module. Lights flashed.

"I got it! I got it!" Adam cried.

The Lunar Module veered violently back out over the gaping lunar pit.

"We've only got fifteen seconds of fuel!" Sally exclaimed.

"I know! I'm trying to get us back to the rim!"

"Just set it down! Straight down!" Sally yelled.

Adam knew she was right. They didn't have enough fuel. He reduced the rocket power and the Lunar Module descended into the pit.

"Four seconds!" Adam reported.

They kept dropping. They were two hundred feet below the opening to the lunar pit. It was enormous.

The rockets puttered out. The butterflies in Adam's stomach were doing somersaults. Just as they were feeling the minute acceleration of the Lunar Module, it suddenly stopped.

Whomp!

The Lunar Module, named Moon Turtle, sat on the bottom of the lunar pit at a slight angle.

"We're not dead," Adam said, leaning his head forward and breathing heavy. "Oh thank God, we're not dead."

One by one, Adam disabled the alarms. The last one was a warning about another CO_2 scrubber. Adam pulled out the spent CO_2 filtration device. The beads were bright red – a sign that they were used up. He shoved a new one in.

"This is not good news," Adam declared.

The excessive use of CO_2 scrubbers was weighing

heavily on Adam. He did some simple calculations in his head. It didn't bode well for the return trip. Adam thought he saw Sally grimace as she did the math too, but she didn't say anything.

"We'll cross that bridge when we come to it," Sally finally told him.

Sally was looking out the window, trying to gauge their location relative to the rim of the pit.

"We're pretty deep down here, Adam. We'll only have direct line-of-sight communication with Tucker every two hours. Maybe two or three minutes at a time?"

"I know," Adam agreed, nodding his head. "The situation is not ideal."

Sunlight illuminated the craggy walls of the pit and more than half of the lunar pit floor. Thirty meters away was the expectedly tall Martian Laboratory complex. The two astronauts stared at it through the windows of the Lunar Module.

Adam turned around and looked at the cooler that was causing them so much trouble.

"Let's get this show on the road," he said.

Before starting the chemical mixing, Adam used an old logbook as a wedge to level out the Hope-A-Matic machine.

He opened the cooler and removed the three very cold bottles. One by one, he plunked them down on the intake pipes for the Hope-A-Matic. Adam pushed the start button and the process began. The liquids were sucked into the blinking box and the sound of electric motors permeated the Lunar Module.

Adam looked over at Sally. "While we're brewing some of this blue juice, what do you say we go explore a Martian laboratory?"

The two astronauts began the process of maneuvering into the their Lunar Exploration suits.

"Wow, this is so much easier here than on Earth. I can almost jump into the suit," Sally said.

After gathering their equipment, the two astronauts moved toward the door.

"Once we open this door," Adam said nervously, "that will activate the auto-launch countdown. The ascent stage will return to Tucker and the Command Module whether we're in it or not — and Earth gets its Blue Hope. We'll only have two hours to explore here."

"I remember," Sally said. "If we can't do any meaningful exploration in two hours, then we're doing something wrong."

Adam laughed. "Time to go?"

"Time for you to be the first person to set foot on the Moon in nearly a half century," Sally laughed.

Adam thought for a moment.

"When is Tucker flying over?"

Sally looked at the monitor on the flight computer.

"In ten minutes," she answered.

"Let's wait," Adam declared. "Once we're in line-of-sight with Tucker overhead, we can transmit video from the outside cameras and show the world what we're doing.

How arrogant, Sally thought.

Adam added one-click to the auto-launch computer, delaying the auto-launch system by ten minutes.

They waited in silence. Eventually, a crackly sound invaded the cabin.

"Can you hear me?" the voice of Tucker asked over their

communication radio.

"Loud and clear, Sky Turtle. For what it's worth, the Moon Turtle has landed."

"Thank God. Our last video feed showed you disappearing into the pit."

"We don't have a lot of time," Adam said. "Can you transmit our video? We're about to exit the Lunar Module."

"You're live right now. Say hello to six billion people."

Adam laughed. He unlatched the door. The sound of air escaping only lasted for a second. Through the hatch they could see an incredibly bright white powdery surface with some black striations — they were staring directly at the Moon.

Adam grabbed the contents of the cooler and threw them out onto the Moon along with the spent CO_2 scrubbers. They bounced for a long time.

Good riddance, he thought to himself.

"Go on," Sally commanded. "Your turn."

Adam looked out at the Moon and then back at Sally.

"No," Adam said. "Ladies first this time."

Sally raised her eyebrows in surprise, but she didn't second-guess his decision. Adam moved away and Sally backed out through the door and down the ladder. Step by step, she walked down the tiny external ladder. She got to the bottom and did a little hop away and planted both feet on the Moon.

She looked up and saw the Command Module still in view. It was just a bright speck cruising across the black sky.

"That's one small leap for a *woman*," Sally said with a mile-wide grin. "And one giant leap for humanity."

Adam nodded at how wonderful her words were.

Moments later, he followed her out and hopped down onto the ground next to her.

"Would you look at that? We're standing on the Moon. Woohoo..." Adam said jokingly. "I think we'll make a good team."

Five seconds later, the Command Module, far above them, slipped beyond the rim of the crater. The video feed went blank, but not before the world saw Sally Monta become the first woman to walk on the Moon.

CHAPTER 84

Mission Control
NASA Jennings Manned Spacecraft Center
Fort Worth, Texas

The door flew open and two men walked in wearing dark blue suits. They showed their FBI badges to the security guards, then moved quickly towards Chris Tankovitch.

"Director Tankovitch, we need a minute of your time."

Chris looked at them, with his forehead scrunched, wondering what they were doing here at this crisis moment.

"Well, I'm right in the middle of an emergency."

"I know," the lead FBI man said without emotion. He leaned slightly toward Chris and said, "This will just take a minute."

Chris removed his headphones.

"What is it, guys?"

"Sir, a farmer in Ohio found Yeva Turoskova's body. It's been transferred to Wright Patterson Air Force Base. They're running an emergency autopsy right now."

Chris took in a long slow breath. He was very concerned.

"You know that he's up there right now with another astronaut on the Moon?"

"We understand sir. It's just unfortunate timing."

The other man leaned forward with a grin. "Or *fortunate* timing, depending on your concerns."

"I don't even know what that means," Chris said. "Just let me know what the autopsy finds."

One of the FBI men handed Chris a business card.

"Will do, sir."

In lockstep, the two men walked toward the far end of the room and disappeared through the door.

CHAPTER 85

Martian Laboratory — Exterior
Lunar Pit

Unsurprisingly, the Martian lab wasn't the only thing that caught their eye. The lunar pit was more than just a hole in the ground. Since it formed from a giant lava tube, it was more of a very long cave with a large opening directly overhead.

Adam shone his flashlight down both ends of the cave and it seemed to go on forever.

"This cave is massive," Adam noted. "I wish we had days here to explore."

"The primary mission," Sally said, " is to mix up a few gallons of Blue Hope and return home. This exploration is just icing on the cake. Hopefully we find something useful in the lab."

"Like an anti-gravity cube," Adam said.

"Exactly," Sally replied.

This Martian lab shared many similarities with the one at Zhuvango Falls. They were both made of a shiny metal, but this one had a few dents, probably from the meteoroids that struck it over the past two hundred thousand years.

The two astronauts continued hiking toward the lab. There was a lot of debris outside the building. The long portion of the T-shaped lab had a ramp underneath that they assumed led to the entrance platform.

"They sure do have a thing for basement entrances," Adam said.

"I'm sure they had a good reason."

As they approached the ramp, they noticed a large pile of bleached white bones. Very large bones, in fact. Scary large bones with some appearing to be from an animal fifty feet long. The bones had hack marks on them, as if they'd been processed manually. At the end of the longest set of bones was a small crater where the bones had been decimated into fragments.

"That's not very comforting," Sally said nervously.

When they arrived at the ramp, Adam froze.

"Boot prints," Adam said, shining his flashlight down. "Everywhere. I mean, *everywhere.*"

The two astronauts looked in awe at the tracks of large boot prints that led from the ramp off in various directions, most of them to the pile of bright white bones.

"Old boot prints, I'm sure," Sally surmised.

"Agreed. Boot prints on the Moon would last forever unless something disturbed them."

Adam shined his flashlight down the ramp. It was generally clean underneath the lab. More boot prints, of course. The two astronauts walked down the ramp side by side. At the end of the underground hallway, there was a familiar circular platform just like in the lab at Zhuvango Falls. As they neared the platform, the lights on the walls turned on, illuminating this below-ground room.

Adam and Sally stepped onto the lift. Adam turned to the wall right next to him and saw the familiar tangram shapes.

"I got this," Sally declared, reaching around Adam.

She maneuvered the geometric pieces around until they formed a square. She slid the shape mass up until it fell within the square outline etched on the wall. They felt a vibration in the floor. A transparent cylindrical shell rotated out from behind them, encapsulating them in some type of airlock. They heard the sound of gas being pumped in. Their suits went slightly limp as the pressure outside their suit equalized the pressure inside.

"Oxygen levels at twenty percent," Adam said.

The platform began moving upward.

The two astronauts saw the lights below disappear as they rose into the main portion of the Martian laboratory. When the platform eventually stopped, they were surrounded by complete darkness.

The airlock shell rotated around, stowing behind them.

Adam took a step forward into the blackness.

CHAPTER 86

Sky Turtle — Orbiting the Moon

"Tucker, this is Fort Worth Mission Control. You should be able to see them in another 90 minutes."

"Understood, Fort Worth," Tucker replied. "Hey, have you done the math on our CO_2 scrubber situation?"

The silence lasted too long.

"We have, Tucker. It's not good. You've used up more than half of the CO_2 filters and all of the spares. All you have left are the ones in the Lunar Module. Right now, there's isn't enough to support the return trip for all three of you."

"Damn," Tucker said, shaking his head. "Isn't there some miracle contraption we could build?"

"We're working on it, but the prognosis isn't good. You'll have just enough to get *two* of the crew back to Earth."

"Just two?" Tucker asked in a somber tone.

"Yes, Tucker. Only two — and that's if you're lucky."

CHAPTER 87

Martian Laboratory — Interior
Lunar Pit

The laboratory lit up like a mid-summer day. The lights were blindingly bright. Both astronauts squinted their eyes like they'd just exited a movie theater. It would take a full minute for them to be able to see again. The walls were not transparent like the lab on Earth. Instead, it had what appeared to be traditional windows, albeit not glass – they were made from a variant of the metal used on the other walls.

Adam walked over to one of the windows and knocked on it. "Sounds metallic, right?"

He looked down at the data display on his wrist.

"Sally, would you believe the oxygen is at 22 percent and the temperatures are at 20 degrees Celsius?"

"Downright balmy," she laughed.

"Should we take our helmets off?" Adam suggested.

"I think that would be another bad idea, Adam," Sally answered. "Let's keep them on for now."

Compared to the cluttered interior of the lab on Earth, this facility seemed almost barren. They stood at what would be the bottom of the long T-shape. They could see down the long corridor. Lights were blinking on in the distance and instantly becoming brilliant white.

Adam turned to the wall right behind him at the end of the corridor. It had a tall door with a star symbol at the top. Midway up were ten keys with strange symbols on them. Having spent a lot of time playing with the TranslationTablet, Adam recognized them as the ten basic numbers used by the Martians. He tapped Sally on her arm, then pointed out the number keys on the door.

"Look at this huge door," Adam said in awe. "It's got a combination lock. There's the keypad."

"Ten unique numbers, huh?" Sally laughed with a mischievous smile. "Zero through nine. What are the chances they'd use a base-10 number system like us?"

Adam held his gloves up in front of Sally and wiggled his fingers.

"It's no coincidence," Adam grinned. "They started counting on their fingers just like us. After all, that's the only reason we use a base-*ten* counting system. If we had a left and right flipper instead of fingers, we'd have a base-*two* binary counting system. And we'd be seals."

Adam laughed at his own nerdy observation.

Sally pressed her glove against the door and visually scanned it from the floor to the star symbol at the top. "Something important must be behind that door."

"Let's get walking down to where the T junction comes

together."

The corridor was wide with hooks and shelves lining both sides. Various satchels and kits hung from the hooks.

"Do you find it unnerving that none of these things has even a sprinkle of dust on them?" Adam asked.

"Maybe the Martians were clean freaks."

"Maybe the Martians *are* clean freaks," Adam replied.

Sally rolled her eyes.

The two astronauts walked steadily, but slowly, down the corridor. When they arrived at the T-junction, they stood in a large room with the branches of the T going off to the left and the right. The floor and ceiling had the same matte silver tiles. At this end of the corridor they heard a loud humming sound.

On their left was what looked like an office area. A stainless steel desk of sorts – really just a desktop, cantilevered from the wall (sticking out of the wall with no visible support).

To the right was an area with four circles on the floor. Hovering above each circle was a chair of some sort. They looked like very robust wheelchairs without the wheels. However, each of the chairs was levitating!

Adam and Sally were drawn to the chairs like moths to a flame. They pushed on the chairs and they moved slightly, but never drifted away from the circular platforms.

"See, I wasn't lying about the anti-gravity cube," Adam said with vindication.

Sally stood back and grabbed the camera from her suit pocket. She began taking pictures.

"This is fascinating," she said with amazement.

Adam waved his hand underneath the chairs to show

Sally the "no strings attached" implication.

"We'll come back to these in a minute," Adam said. "But let's look around some more."

They returned to the T junction area.

"And then there are *those* things," Adam said, pointing to the three huge orange doors. They looked just like garage doors and were numbered left to right using the Martian symbols for 1, 2 and 3.

"Door number one?" Sally asked. She reached up to push a big green button next to the door frame.

Adam grabbed her arm. "We didn't find any Martians on Earth. Presumably they are *here*. And they haven't given us a welcome party."

"Adam, they're two hundred thousand years old," Sally explained. "They're dead."

Sally finished reaching and pushed the green button. The orange door rose up with a clatter – it sounded like a hydraulic lift kicking into action on the other side of the door. Fog poured out from under the door, just like you'd expect from opening a freezer. The room behind the door remained a dark secret until the door reached maximum height.

The lights flashed on, lighting every nook and cranny. This time, all white walls. In the middle of the room was a long platform roughly four feet wide. On top of it, frozen in glorious fashion were two large tigers, each roughly seven feet long. They had impossibly long fangs.

"Whoa," Sally said. "Saber-toothed tigers?"

"Whoa is right," Adam said with awe.

The two astronauts wandered around opposite sides of the display. A skin of ice, roughly one inch thick, coated both specimens.

"Looks like...," Adam ducked down to look at the bottoms. "One male and one female."

"For breeding?" Sally asked.

"Maybe. Perhaps they were looking for a food source," Adam said.

"But you'd think they'd go for big herbivores," Sally suggested. "That's what humans did."

"Yeah, that would make more sense. But farmland was getting scarce for them as their population exploded. Maybe they couldn't spare the land for grazers?"

"Why don't you ask the Martian standing right behind you?" Sally asked.

Adam spun around and saw nothing, but he did hear Sally laughing.

"Okay...," he said. "You got me."

"Let's get back to exploring," she said, lifting up her camera.

Sally and Adam both took pictures of the saber-toothed tigers. They were too busy to see the drops of melted ice falling from the corners of the frozen specimens.

Adam lowered his camera.

"We gotta try door number two," Adam said.

Sally left the room, walking backwards, still taking pictures. Just beyond the door frame, she pushed the green button and the door dropped down, closing off the room again.

They found themselves standing next to the big green button for door number two.

"Here goes nothing," Sally said.

She pushed the button. Fog rolled out from the growing

gap. When the door reached maximum height, the lights came on.

"What is that?" Sally asked in wonderment.

"That is the biggest snake I've ever seen," Adam said.

A snake was coiled up into a pile, twelve feet tall, nearly touching the ceiling. At its thickest, the snake's body was about two feet in diameter. It had a thick coating of ice similar to that of the saber-toothed tiger.

"Probably a Titanaboa," Adam declared casually.

Sally looked at him with skepticism.

"How would you know that?"

Adam sported a devilish smirk.

"I'm wicked smart," Adam joked. "But really, my kids love dinosaurs and strange animals. They watched a movie on the mighty Titanaboa — they told me all about it."

"Nice," Sally said.

"Except Titanaboa lived in South America," Adam said with a puzzled look on his face. "Not sure how the Martians would've gotten this. I presume their specimens came from Africa?"

"If those floating chairs are just an inkling of their transportation technology, they could've traveled far distances from their laboratory at Zhuvango Falls."

"Good point," Adam replied.

"They have two tigers, but only one snake. I wonder why?" Adam asked.

"They might've had two at some time in the past," Sally explained. "That long scary skeleton outside looks like it might've been the other Titanaboa at one time."

"Good observation," Adam said, nodding his head.

Once again, the cameras came out. The two astronauts

buzzed around the massive snake, taking picture after picture.

"I think you know what we have to do next?" Sally asked.

Adam looked at his wrist-mounted suit display. "We only have thirty minutes, so we better go fast."

The two of them backed out and shut door number two.

Adam pointed to the green button on door number three and said, "After you..."

Sally leaned in and pushed the green button to open door number three.

Nothing happened.

She scrunched her forehead in confusion. She pushed the button again.

Nothing.

She pushed it five more times. Five more nothings.

Adam examined the door edges to see if there was an obvious problem.

"I see hydraulic hoses, but we don't really have time to take it apart to fix it," Adam said with disappointment.

The two of them moved over to the office area and examined the desk. It had a few more logbooks on it. Adam opened one, but it proved hard to leaf through the pages with his gloves. He saw a few more color photos of early humans on Earth and what looked like photos of the Martians trapping both the tigers and the Titanaboas.

On the desk was a plain metallic box, roughly one foot wide and one foot tall. For some reason, the corners were painted blue. The front of the box had buttons on it and a dispenser.

"Is that their coffeemaker?" Adam joked.

"Hah, I somehow doubt it," Sally said.

In the middle of the office area was one of the Martian levitating chairs. Sally climbed onto it. The large chair made her look like a child in a big rocking chair. The armrest had a joystick on it. She pushed it forward and the chair moved toward Adam.

"Watch out!" she laughed with fake alarm.

A crackle came through their communication headsets.

"Are you having a party down there on the Moon?" the familiar voice of Tucker said.

Sally smiled. "We're inside the laboratory."

"Are you playing chess with any Martians?" Tucker joked.

"No sign of them," Sally replied. "They have some amazing technology, though."

"We have to discuss something and quick," Tucker said, suddenly serious. "We don't have enough CO2 scrubbers for the return voyage."

"So what's the Plan B?" Adam asked. "Has Fort Worth given you any quickly assembled solutions?"

"Guys, this isn't as simple as fitting a square peg in a round hole. Did you already get rid of the cooler and the dry ice?"

"Yes. It's now litter on the Moon," Adam confirmed.

"Good. Fort Worth told me they think there's enough CO2 scrubbers to support two people on the return trip."

Sally laughed incredulously.

"Wait a minute — just two?" she asked.

"What if we promise to breathe really slowly?" Adam asked, trying to insert levity into a desperate situation.

Humor failed.

"Adam. Sally. We've got to make a very serious decision when you two get back up here."

"Roger that, Tucker," Adam replied.

"My readouts up here in the Sky Turtle are showing me that the Ascent Module is leaving the Moon with or without you in twelve minutes. Better hustle. I'm about to lose visual con—," Tucker's voice cracked up as he left their line-of-sight for communications.

Sally stared at Adam, but didn't say anything.

"Let's get going," Adam said.

Sally picked up the alien logbooks and stuffed them into collection pouches that were sewn into the leg of her suit pants.

They walked to the T-junction area and turned down the long corridor, heading toward the door with the big star symbol on it. They eventually reached the end and stood on the circular platform.

"Ready?" Sally said.

"Yes."

Adam reached over to the wall and pushed the lower of two buttons there, very similar to the lab on Earth.

The cylindrical shell wrapped around them and the platform lowered back down. In less than thirty seconds, the two astronauts were standing in the hallway under the laboratory. They climbed up the ramp and started off toward the Lunar Module. Adam pulled a bag out of a pocket on his pants and began collecting Moon rocks. If all went well, they would leave the Moon with a fresh mixture of cancer-killing Blue Hope and a big bag of Moon rocks. Quite a valuable stash for just one trip.

Sally grabbed the bag of Moon rocks from Adam and

climbed up the ladder, opening the hatch. She maneuvered through the door and looked at the Hope-A-Matic. Sitting in the bottom of the machine was a large volume of glowing turquoise liquid.

"Hey Adam, I'd say the Blue Hope is all done cooking. What do you think?"

Sally did not hear a reply.

"Adam?" she asked.

Sally turned around and saw him standing on the Moon surface near the bottom of the ladder. He had a humble smirk on his face.

"I'm going to make the decision easy for everybody," Adam explained.

"Wait, no, no, no," Sally admonished Adam. "We're both going back up to the Sky Turtle to make a decision like rational professionals."

"And then what?" Adam asked. "Rock paper scissors to find out which one of us gets shoved out the hatch?"

Sally sighed. She was crushingly relieved and felt terrible about it.

"Besides," Adam said. "We don't know if the ascent-stage rocket has enough fuel to get us both out of this lunar pit. We didn't plan to land several hundred feet below the target landing zone. There's no reason to risk neither us nor the Blue Hope getting back up to Tucker."

"Well...." she trailed off.

"Just do me a favor," Adam said. "I wrote a letter to my wife and I gave it to Tucker right before we disconnected from the Command Module. Please make sure she gets it."

"I..." Sally felt an uneasy lump in her throat and didn't know what to say.

"I'll make sure she gets it," Sally said. "I promise."

"Good," Adam replied. He climbed up the ladder and reached his glove through the door.

Sally reached out and shook his outstretched glove.

"Sally, it's been an honor to work with you."

"Likewise," she replied.

"Give my regards to Tucker," Adam said solemnly.

Adam closed the door. He turned around and hopped down, landing on both feet, just a bit wobbly. He turned and waved to her. Then he began walking back toward the Martian laboratory. It was a lonely walk. Each step was confirmation that he'd never see his family again. The ramp came sooner than he expected and he descended down below the Martian laboratory. With a slight reluctance, he stepped onto the circular lift platform.

Adam sighed and stood there for a moment. He reached over and organized the tangram pieces. The cylindrical airlock shell enveloped him and it took him up to the laboratory. It was still lit up, but it was much lonelier now without a friend nearby.

Adam wanted a front-row seat to watch the ascent-stage of the Lunar Module carry Sally up, up, and away. He trudged down the corridor and turned toward the office area. With nothing to lose, Adam closed his eyes and took off his helmet, setting it down next to the metallic box on the counter. He took a deep breath and paused, waiting to die from some horrible foreign bacteria.

"Not a bad smell," he said, shrugging his shoulders. With the oxygen, temperature and pressures similar to Earth, he was able to breathe just fine. Adam climbed onto the floating oversized chair in the office and used the joystick to maneuver himself closer to the window. He stared out at the Lunar Module.

"Adam?" said a crackly version of Sally's voice over the headset.

"Yes, Sally."

"Thank you."

"De nada," he said, laughing as he realized his last words ever spoken to another human would be a simple phrase learned by watching Dora The Explorer with his kids.

Minutes passed. Adam saw a huge flash from under the Lunar Module. No boom. No grinding roar. Just silence. It felt like the audio track was missing.

The top half of the Lunar Module rocketed upwards, leaving the descent-stage down on the Moon. Up, up, and away it went, wobbling the entire way, but it did keep going.

"Good," whispered Adam. "Keep going."

The ascending ship came within a few feet of the rim of the lunar pit. Adam craned his neck to keep following it.

Eventually, it was out of view and Adam realized his fate even more so. He was going to become a permanent fixture like the tigers and the snake.

Maybe I can freeze myself and they'll get me on the next mission, he wondered. *I mean, they will come back, right?*

As Adam pondered his frozen future, his peripheral vision saw something move. He kept his head perfectly still, but rotated his eyes.

Door number three began to open all by itself, but it stopped after only six inches of movement. Fog rolled out from under the partially opened door.

CHAPTER 88

Sky Turtle — Command Module
Orbiting The Moon

"Sky Turtle, this is Fort Worth Mission Control. The Lunar Module should be ascending now. Please begin your rendezvous checklists."

"Roger that, Fort Worth," said the lone astronaut circling the Moon in the Command Module. He floated over to the window and looked down at the Moon to get one more glimpse at the Martian laboratory in the lunar pit. Unfortunately, he was too far beyond it on this orbit. His headphone speakers lit up with a tinny voice.

"....Tucker, I'm ascending with the precious cargo..."

"Hello, crew of the Moon Turtle," Tucker replied.

Tucker pulled his SLR camera from the Velcro that held it against the wall. He pointed it out the window, adjusting the zoom to maximum power. A small object was ascending from the lunar pit and Tucker saw it tilt and start to accelerate toward him.

"I see you guys," he said. "Launch looks good."

He took several pictures, adjusted the zoom, and took many more.

"Heya... Tucker?" Sally asked.

"Yes, Sally, I hear you loud and clear. We should be able to try re-docking on the next pass around."

The radio was silent for a few seconds.

"Adam isn't with me," Sally said. "He stayed."

Tucker closed his eyes in anguish.

"Oh no...," he whispered.

"He saved us from having to make a terrible choice."

Tucker reached into his pocket and pulled out the folded paper that Adam had given him before the two spacecraft separated. It was folded in such a way that only an external note was visible:

"Only read this if I don't come back."

CHAPTER 89

Martian Laboratory — Interior
Lunar Pit

"I don't believe I'm seeing this," Adam whispered to himself.

Yes, the door had partially opened.

Yes, fog was pouring out.

Yes, he was probably about to die.

Adam still hadn't started breathing again. He would've jumped out the window if he could. He looked around to find something heavy and deadly to pick up.

His hand reached into his space suit pocket and pulled out an ultra-lightweight wrench made of an aluminum alloy — space flight required lightweight tools. What he wouldn't give for a frying pan right now. Adam stood up slowly, keenly aware of every snap and crackle his middle-aged knees were making. He took a step toward door three.

The door closed.

Then it opened again.

With each tender step, Adam got closer. When he'd finally made it to door number one, he stepped in a massive puddle pooling out from under the door.

That's not good, Adam thought.

From his vantage point, he could see that door three was only opening a few inches each time. It seemed to be jammed and whoever, or whatever, was in there was having a tough time. Adam got within a few feet of the door and stopped, leaning up against the wall next to the opening. He looked down and found another puddle emanating from door two this time.

Fog continued to pour out of door three each time it opened and closed. Adam could hear the low mumble of what sounded like somebody talking, but it wasn't speaking English by any measure.

Adam's pulse raced to 170 — the same as when he sprinted on the treadmill, except now he was standing perfectly still.

Then he saw it.

The terror of all terrors.

A hand poked out through the opening. A hand like his, only larger and with a pinky as long as the other fingers. Opposable thumb. It was human-like, but huge.

This can't be good, he thought.

Adam examined his own glove to compare. Just the long pinky was different. An arm reached out from under the door and searched the nearby wall, nearly touching Adam's foot — he jerked away. The hand on the arm reached up and pushed the green open button, but nothing happened.

Wow, that's a really long arm, Adam thought.

His mind was racing and he suddenly remembered the

basic messages from the TranslationTablet.

Adam leaned his head toward the alien arm.

"Fenoda," Adam said loudly.

The hand stopped pressing the green button and yanked back under the door.

There was absolute quiet except for the humming sounds coming from the laboratory inner workings. Adam took one step closer, his foot crunching on some pebbly dust on the floor that wasn't there before.

"Fenoda?" asked a terrifyingly deep voice from behind door three.

Adam gulped. He pulled the TranslationTablet out of his suit pocket and launched the translator application with furious speed. He typed the following: "HELLO. MY NAME IS ADAM. I COME IN PEACE."

He pushed the Translate button and the "busy" icon showed for a few seconds. Finally, it displayed the phonetic translation in Martianese. Adam pushed the SPEAK button and it announced with a mechanical female voice: "Fenoda. Mayato poodroo Adam. May merno payache."

"Ah, nuts," Adam complained. He clambered for the options menu and changed the voice to male. He pushed the SPEAK button again and a strong male voice rang from the tablet: "Fenoda. Mayato pootoo Adam. May merno payache."

Silence. Adam held his wrench in the other hand, ready to strike. Adam expected the Mars man to speak, so he pushed the AUTO-LISTEN button on the TranslationTablet. A reluctant voice from under the door broke the silence.

"Fenoda Adam. Mayata poodroo Heshayta. Diesh may rexeta morfo gru maycash esh Heartho?"

The app beeped. After a few seconds the screen

displayed: "Hello, Adam. My name is Heshayta. Have you been sent to rescue me and take me back to Heartho?"

Oh no. He thinks I'm here from Mars to rescue him, Adam thought. He held the tablet up close to him and spoke slowly into the microphone. "No. I am from the nearby blue planet. Nobody is alive on your home planet."

The app captured his words, translated them and spoke them to the Mars man.

Thirty seconds of silence followed before the Mars man replied. The TranslationTablet heard the alien and spoke his message, translated to English.

"How do you know my language?" Heshayta asked.

Adam spoke into his tablet. "That is a long story. I have actually visited your home planet."

Another long delay until Heshayta replied.

"How long have I been here?"

Adam wasn't sure how to represent time to the man, but he tried his best. "About 200,000 blue planet years."

Silence.

"Can I see you?" Heshayta asked.

Adam reluctantly walked away from the wall, toward the middle of the room and knelt down. He saw the face of what looked like a very tall human, laying down. He had brown hair, pulled back in a bun. Brown eyes. Long arms. Very large teeth. Not sharp scary teeth, but big flat teeth, like he'd stolen dentures from a horse.

They stared at each other, observing how weird they looked to each other. Adam gawked rudely at the Mars man's teeth which he found almost amusing.

"You are so short," Heshayta said.

Adam laughed at the curtness. "Yes, gravity is stronger

on my blue planet than on your home planet. Generation after generation grew shorter until we balanced out."

"Are any of my crew still alive on blue planet?"

Adam frowned.

"No, but my people are descendants of them."

"Am I the last of my kind?" Heshayta asked despondently.

"Yes, I am afraid so," Adam said, nodding his head up and down.

"Why are you afraid?" Heshayta asked.

"Sorry, that is a figure of speech we have here," Adam said, chuckling at the simple miscommunication.

"You said *we*? How many of you are here in this facility?"

"Just me. My crew had to leave me here."

The Mars man with the big teeth sighed.

"I was in a similar situation. I lost contact with my crew on the blue planet. I had to go into hibernation. I woke up about ten thousand blue planet years ago and went to search for my crew again, but returned emptyhanded. In my anger, I did some irreparable damage to this laboratory which may explain this door problem."

"Ten thousand years ago?" Adam said with curiosity. "Did you interact with any of the creatures down on the blue planet?"

"Only once. I came upon a group of hunters that were starving and I felt sorry for them, so I showed them how seeds and farming work. The savages attacked me afterwards, so I came back here. I went back into hibernation sleep. Your arrival woke me up."

"Really. That's, interesting, Heshayta. Are you alone

here?"

"Yes, it is just me. That is why I kept the door locked after you arrived. I didn't know who you were and you made a lot of noise."

"We are both stuck here," Adam sighed. He sat down on the floor, crossed his legs and scooted away from the growing puddles emerging from doors one and two.

"Do you have a family?" Heshayta asked.

"Yes, I did have a family, but I seem to have run them off," Adam admitted.

"Do you have children," the Mars man asked.

"Yes, I have two small children."

"With children, you always have something to look forward to," Heshayta said.

"That is true for most people except me. I'm going to die here. So what about you?" Adam asked. "Family?"

"Yes... I did," he said solemnly. "Most assuredly, they grew up without me there to teach them. I hope they lived long lives and died of old age. I did most of my grieving when I awoke ten thousand years ago. No amount of time gets rid of the pain. Adam, how long are you staying here?"

"Until I die. My crew had to abandon me here," Adam said. "Speaking of that, would it be possible to freeze myself like you did? I assume another rocket will be sent here in a few years."

Heshayta stared down the long corridor.

"You don't need to do that," Heshayta declared. "There is a way out. We have one escape capsule."

"Really?" Adam asked, suddenly hopeful. "We searched and didn't see anything."

He noticed Heshayta staring down the corridor with

intense focus.

"The escape capsule is in this room with me, behind this door. If you help me open this door, I will share the combination with you."

Adam raised an eyebrow. "Are you going to kill me?" he asked with skepticism.

"No, I will not kill a man with a family," Heshayta replied. "Are *you* going to kill me?"

"No, of course not," Adam replied. He thought for a long time, ready to ask the obvious question, but afraid to. Finally, he caved.

"Why are you helping me instead of escaping yourself?"

"Adam, I have nobody left. Nobody to console me. Nobody to grow old with. I would be treated as a strange beast on your planet. Prodded. Probed. Studied. The escape capsule holds no escape for me. But it does for you."

"I understand," Adam said. "Thank you."

Adam stood up, carefully avoiding the water.

"Heshayta, there seems to be a water leak from the other two doors."

"It is not a problem," Heshayta said unconvincingly. "Condensation from experiments we were doing for possible new food sources. We had many failures. You probably saw them outside the laboratory."

"I did see that," Adam answered. He grabbed his lightweight adjustable wrench and continued.

"I have a wrench. Let me undo the hose that's causing the problem," Adam said. "Perhaps we can swap it out with a hose from one of the other doors."

Right along the door jamb, Adam found what looked like a hydraulic hose. It had leaking fluid. He tried to tighten the coupling with his wrench.

To his amazement, the nuts were very similar to standards on Earth — at least in shape. The Martian fasteners had nine faces instead of the traditional six-sided nuts on Earth. Adam's wrench couldn't get a grip on the nut.

"My wrench won't fit," Adam said.

"Let me give you one of mine," Heshayta said.

The Mars man stood up behind the door and walked around, grabbing metallic-sounding things. Then he plunked down on the ground next to the bottom of the door and pushed a toolbox out through the gap toward Adam. Then he grabbed a wrench from inside the box and handed it to Adam.

Adam took the wrench and used it to tighten the hydraulic line coupler. Instead, it cracked, spraying hydraulic fluid everywhere. The door began to fall.

"Dammit!" Adam yelled. He kicked the toolbox into the opening to block the door from closing all the way and crushing the Mars man's arm.

They were both silent, not knowing what to say.

"Sorry, Heshayta. I made things worse."

"It is okay. Please come down here," the Mars man said.

Adam knelt down on the ground.

"Yes?"

"This door problem does not look good. I must admit something. There is another escape capsule here. It is at the end of the long corridor." Heshayta pointed one of his long fingers down the corridor.

"The door with a star on it?"

"Yes, that is the one," Heshayta confirmed.

"We couldn't get in that door," Adam explained. "Do

you know the combination."

"Yes, it is the first *four* prime numbers."

"I can do that. Thank God you Martians used base-10 numbers."

The alien showed both hands to Adam and wiggled all ten of his alien fingers.

"Yes," Adam laughed. "I get it."

"When you enter the escape capsule, you will be asked if you want to return to your planet or my planet. I assume you will want your own planet."

Adam was almost giddy. Ten minutes ago he'd been planning how to freeze himself until humanity returned to the Moon. Now he had a free ticket, possibly, to not die on the Moon. He tried not to act too happy.

"Adam, I will go back into hibernation and perhaps, someday, you can return here and truly set me free. Perhaps when that time comes, you will have a spaceship for me to return to my home planet."

"Perhaps," Adam said. "I will do what I can."

Adam felt tears welling up. This alien man who'd lost his family and his civilization was giving him hope to go on living. It was the complete opposite of how he'd felt long ago on Mars when Keller Murch had left him to die.

"Heshayta, I have one question that I must ask. Your society created a medicine that is believed to be a miracle medicine. Do you have any of that here?"

Heshayta smiled and nodded. "You speak of Nilasu. It stops sicknesses that are based on uncontrolled cell growth."

Adam nodded. "Yes, that's it. Do you have any here?"

"Yes, Adam. When we traveled in space, the radiation from the Sun caused many of those types of sicknesses, so we carried a machine with us that mixed the medicine when we needed it."

Adam's eyes opened wide. He turned to look at the box-shaped machine sitting on the desk.

"Is that metal box on the desk the Nilasu mixer?"

"Yes," Heshayta answered. "The box with the blue corners."

"Does it only work on this Moon?" Adam asked.

Heshayta squinted his eyes at Adam, thinking.

"It works anywhere," Heshayta answered.

Adam stood up and walked away from Heshayta, but then stopped. He turned and looked at the broken door, with the desperate hand still sticking underneath.

Adam walked back and knelt down.

"We have a custom on Earth. I'd like to shake your hand," Adam said. "To thank you for saving my life."

"That is a strange custom. Why not wiggle our fingers together?" the alien laughed.

"Good point," Adam said. He reached out his hand.

The Mars man slowly grasped Adams hand and shook it up and down. The first handshake across two alien species.

"Thank you," Adam said. "I will make sure that we return some day and allow you to return to your home planet with dignity."

The Mars man said nothing, but didn't let go. In fact, his grip tightened to the point of causing Adam some pain.

"Thank you, but now it is time to release," Adam instructed him.

The Mars man didn't react, but kept crushing Adam's hand. Heshayta bared his teeth and started saying "Kel Mataar!" over and over again.

494

The TranslationTablet, still in Adams other hand began yelling out in a mechanical voice, "So hungry!" over and over again.

Another set of alien hands suddenly reached out from under the door and grabbed Adam's feet, knocking him down. The new hands tried to pull him through the crack in the door.

"What the hell?" Adam screamed as the hands kept slamming him against the door.

Wham, wham, wham!

He could feel the tendons in his hand snapping.

Adam looked around for his wrench – it was out of reach. All he could find was the TranslatorTablet. He grabbed it and slammed it against the new alien hands that held his feet.

A scream came from under the door and let go of Adam's lower half. He swung his body around so he could push with his feet against the door. He pushed with all his strength, but the alien with the big meaty hands wasn't letting go.

"Let me go, Heshayta!" Adam yelled.

A loud boom came from door number two. It dented outward as a terrifying screeching sound emanated from inside. The awful thing behind door number two wanted out. It dented again.

Adam didn't know what was worse: an alien trying to extrude him through a tiny opening or the Titanaboa about to escape and eat him.

Door number two ripped away from the opening and the longest, scariest beast sprung out of it, uncoiling down the long corridor toward the escape capsule door. The snake shook its head and then turned around to see Adam struggling with the Mars man.

From behind him, Adam heard a loud grinding hiss and the Titanaboa came at him full speed. Adam jerked to the side and the snake slammed into door three, partially crushing it in. The Mars man let go of Adam's grip and he fell to the side. The snake's tail slammed into door one and knocked it open. A loud growl emanated from that room.

"That can't be good..." Adam started to say.

The snake turned toward him. Adam stood up and ran quickly to the desk. He reached both arms around the Nilasu mixer box and lifted it up. It was laughably lightweight. He threw his helmet on top and ran, sprinting down the corridor and jumping over the tail of the Titanaboa.

The Titanaboa's tail whipped through the air and slammed through one of the windows, shattering it. Air gushed out.

Adam's ears popped as the air pressure fell. He put the helmet on as he sprinted the rest of the way toward the door with the star on it. He lurched at the combination keycode panel.

"First four prime numbers!" he yelled, remembering the unlock code. Adam pushed the numbers 1, 2, 3 and 5.

The door did not open.

Adam turned around to see the Titanaboa come slithering toward him — the undulating body knocking everything off the walls. It screeched again.

What a horrible sound! Adam thought.

"Oh wait, wait, wait..."

The snake was almost on him!

"Think!" Adam yelled to himself.

The Titanaboa was opening its huge gaping jaw, about to eat its first meal in two hundred millennia. It suddenly stopped and screeched in anger. It turned its huge head backward to look at its tail. Two saber-tooth tigers were chomping down on the Titanaboa's tail and tearing it to shreds.

The snake screeched in pain, trying to shake its tail loose from the tiger. It flung one of them off and out the laboratory window. Even with the remaining saber-tooth tiger biting its tail, the Titanaboa turned back to look at Adam.

"Uh oh...," Adam said, turning back to the combination keypad.

Memories of middle-school math came rushing back to Adam.

"Oh how could I be so dumb! ONE is not a prime number! It's TWO, THREE, FIVE, SEVEN!" Adam yelled, slamming the buttons one at a time.

The door opened and Adam fell into the escape capsule. The snake screeched behind him.

In front of Adam was a small closet-sized room with one tall seat and a window in front of it. He set down the Nilasu machine and climbed up onto the seat. Adam looked like a kid strapping into a La-Z-Boy chair. He looked behind him and saw the Titanaboa, having killed the remaining saber-toothed tiger, coming back down the hallway.

Adam searched the edge of the door opening and saw a green button, similar to those that raised and lowered the cryogenic chamber doors. He pushed it and the door slammed shut. He heard a winding-up sound that got louder and louder — no doubt the computer systems coming on line.

Bang!

The snake rammed its head into the outside of the escape capsule door. The capsule shook.

Adam turned to face forward. The dashboard had a pulsating red button. Adam hovered his hand over it, hesitated for a second, and then slammed down on it.

With a loud *boom*, the capsule shot straight upward. Adam was slammed down into his seat by the G-forces. Through the windshield, he could see his ship clear the top of the laboratory and soon after that the rim of the lunar pit.

His escape capsule kept on rising. Looking through the window on the bottom of the capsule, he saw steam and debris escaping from the broken laboratory window. He could only imagine what hell was breaking loose down there right now.

The capsule trajectory began to arc as it entered a circular orbit around the Moon. The rocket engines turned off. All was silent except for the familiar sound of cooling fans on the electrical equipment. Adam looked out the window to see if he could see any signs of the Sky Turtle, but he realized that they would've already started on the return journey back to Earth.

The dashboard in the escape capsule lit up with two phrases. Next to each one was a button. This was just as the Mars man had told him. If what he was told were true, one of them would take him to Earth and one would take him to Mars. Unfortunately, he had destroyed the TranslationTablet while trying to escape.

Button one or button two?

If only he had a way to communicate with NASA from

this alien ship!

"Dammit!" Adam yelled.

The escape capsule continued on a steady orbit around the Moon, awaiting Adam's choice. The Earth was fading behind him.

Button one or button two?

Panic rose up from his belly and Adam vomited into his helmet.

Button one or button two?

Adam closed his eyes to think. The smell of vomit was overwhelming him. His thoughts were racing.

If I'd designed this system, I would've put my home planet as the primary and the foreign planet as the secondary... so Earth must be number two.

He hovered his hand over the second button.

Wait! If this was like any modern airplane GPS system, the first button would take me to the nearest safe landing location.... so that means the first button. I think.

Adam moved his hand over to the first button.

"Here goes nothing!" Adam yelled with a grimace.

Adam slammed his hand down onto the first button.

Nothing happened.

"Aw great, now I've —"

Adam choked as his entire body slammed into the seat by sudden and incredible acceleration. The rocket motors went full throttle and the Moon began to visibly slip by faster and faster below him, starting to blur from the vibration. The Earth faded from view behind him as the capsule reached escape velocity and left the Moon's orbit.

"Shazboooooooooooooooot!"

CHAPTER 90

Sky Turtle — Command Module
Approaching Earth
(72 hours later)

"Fort Worth, this is our last status update before beginning the re-entry process. Looks like we've got a good angle. Can you confirm our position data?" Tucker asked.

After a brief silence, a staticky voice came over the speakers. It was Chris Tankovitch from the Mission Control Center.

"Greetings crew, hope you all had a good night's sleep."

"Would've been better if Captain Alston were with us."

"Yes, we are all grieving his loss," Chris said. "And speaking of which, we've arranged for a private line between you guys and Captain Alston's wife, Connie. She's on the phone. Hang on, we'll patch you through."

Several click sounds were heard.

"Hello?" Connie asked.

"Mrs. Alston? This is the crew on the Sky Turtle."

"Chris Tankovitch told me that you had a private message for me?"

Sally looked at Tucker with sadness. She nodded her head as a signal for Tucker to start the message.

"Yes, ma'am," Tucker confirmed. "Before your husband sacrificed himself, he left me a note. It was only meant to be read by you, but seeing as how we're about to crash into the earth at twenty five times the speed of sound, we decided we would read it to you over the communications line — just in case we don't make it back."

"I understand," Connie said.

Tucker unfolded the paper and began reading out loud.

"Dear Connie, I know my decision is hard to understand, but it was the only option to save the crew and return a significant amount of Blue Hope back to Earth. Sally and Tucker have a long life ahead of them. I've only made a few good decisions in life. The best one was marrying you and starting a family. I know you won't believe me when I say this, but be careful around Chris Tankovitch."

Tucker's brow scrunched up in concern. He looked at Sally to show his surprise. Tucker continued reading.

"For some reason which I never determined, he continuously wanted me to go on dangerous missions. And I have no doubt that he set me up with the tabloids. I was foolish, for sure, and almost fell into the trap, but I promise that I was never unfaithful to you. Tell the kids that I love them. Tell them that I will miss them forever. Tell them to think of me whenever they look at the Moon. I love you all — more than there are fire-ants in the yard. Love, Adam."

Connie dabbed a tissue against her cheek.

"Thank you, Tucker."

"I'll give you the note personally when we return."

"I look forward to that," Connie said, crying. She hung up the phone.

"Sky Turtle crew, this is Chris Tankovitch again. I hope you had a good message for Mrs. Alston."

Tucker shrugged his shoulders.

"It was the best," Tucker lied.

A moment of silence fell between mission control and the crew.

"The president is preparing a memorial service for Captain Alston after you get back," Chris said.

"Thanks for the info," Tucker replied.

"About your re-entry question, you're looking good. We are estimating initial entry in about thirty minutes. Looking forward to having you back. It's been a long week."

The crew on the lunar module smiled.

"We agree!" both astronauts yelled.

"I have some information that you may find interesting. Cosmonaut Yeva Turoskova's body was located several days ago and an autopsy was performed. Everything Adam Alston told us... was true. She had acute appendicitis and Adam performed a makeshift surgery to remove the appendix. Unfortunately, she later developed sepsis."

"Wow," Tucker said. "So Adam performed the first emergency surgery in space?"

"That seems to be the case," Chris nodded. "Last, but not least I have our chief medical officer standing next to me. He'd like to ask a few questions."

"Better be quick," Tucker said. "We're getting ready to

hit the Earth atmosphere going Mach twenty five."

The crew heard some mumbling over the speakers and then a voice.

"Hello, crew. This is Dr. Exler. I'll be in charge of distributing the Blue Hope medicine once it arrives. How much were you able to produce on the Moon?"

Tucker looked at his notes and then replied, "We made all of it. It's all glowing blue. So nine liters?" He paused. "During our trip, Captain Alston asked that he be allowed to pick one of the first recipients."

"Absolutely," said Dr. Exler. "We can discuss that further after you land. We believe nine liters will help about twenty thousand patients and, perhaps with a sample to work with, our chemists might find an alternative way to synthesize it here on Earth. We plan to distribute it to about nine regions and from there, doctors will send it to the most needy."

"Amazing," Tucker replied. "Are all of those in the US?"

"Oh no," Dr. Exler said. "We'll be distributing worldwide."

Chris came back on the line. "You want an updated ETA?"

"Yes, of course."

"We have you dropping down in the eastern Pacific in about 20 minutes."

"Thank you, Fort Worth. Over," Tucker replied.

"Proceed with re-entry procedures," Chris said. "See you at Mach zero."

The crew buckled in and everything was tied down.

"Are you ready to go home?" Sally asked.

"My mind is already there," Tucker said. "I wish Captain

Alston was with us."

"I know. He sacrificed a lot for this blue medicine."

A robotic voice came from the navigation computer. "Retro rockets firing." The crew felt the sudden deceleration, but it only lasted for a few seconds. That was all it took to initiate the slow down. Gravity would start pulling them downward and they would slam into the atmosphere at nearly seventeen thousand miles per hour.

"Sparks," Tucker said, pointing to the window.

Sparks and streaks shot past the windows. The friction from the capsule scraping through the atmosphere was causing the bottom to burn away — a planned method for getting rid of the intense heat expected during re-entry.

The capsule was now buffeting with a slight oscillation from side to side. The sparks vanished as the blackness out the window turned into a turquoise glow. As with the previous Apollo crews, they were just along for the ride now.

Far beyond the window they could see the Pacific Ocean, parts of it hidden by majestic white clouds.

The buffeting stopped, but the deceleration was intense. The air was slowing them down quickly. A loud clanking sound came from the roof as three parachutes ejected upward. The deceleration, almost unbearable before, intensified even more. The astronauts performed their anti-g maneuvers of grunting and flexing their muscles to prevent blood from pooling at the bottom of their bodies.

The crests of the beautiful Pacific waves came into view. The capsule dropped softly into the water as the inflatable ring around it popped out to keep it from sinking. The parachutes collapsed downwind of the capsule, floating in the water.

Sally and Tucker yelled in excitement. They'd made it. They were home. They'd gone to the Moon and made it back with the most precious cargo mankind had ever created.

The two astronauts opened the hatch and looked outside. First Sally and then Tucker.

Clear blue skies with a few puffy clouds.

Within just fifteen minutes, they heard the *wop, wop, wop* of a helicopter approaching. It hovered over the capsule and a few Navy seamen dropped down into the water with a large package. The package suddenly ballooned into an inflatable raft.

Sally and Tucker climbed out of the capsule and into the raft. All they carried with them was the container of Blue Hope. One by one, the astronauts and then the sailors were hoisted up into the helicopter. After securing the vital cargo, the helicopter flew away, leaving the capsule there all alone. A ship would come by eventually to pick up the capsule. It bobbed up and down, alone in the ocean, having just transported a miracle across space and time.

CHAPTER 91

10:22pm
Six hours after the Sky Turtle returned to Earth
Fort Worth, Texas

An ambulance raced down Interstate-30 at high speed, leaning toward, but never quite kissing the other cars. The streetlights illuminated the driver's face in pulses, sending darkness across his sweaty brow again and again. In the back of the vehicle sat two men dressed in white doctor's coats — each had an arm wrapped tightly around one of the side railings to keep from falling. The older of the two men used his other arm to clutch a cooler with lots of medical jargon written on the outside. They rocked back and forth as the van took the curves too fast. Both were holding back vomit. Had it not been for a raging storm, they would've taken the Life Flight helicopter instead.

The driver pressed a cellphone to his head. The voice on the other end whispered, "She's breathing very shallow now."

The driver turned on the siren and roof lights.

The ambulance exited the freeway at the Clark Children's Hospital exit. With one hand on the wheel and one smashing the cellphone to his ear, the driver ignored stop signs and skidded around corners, flooring it and running red lights. He turned hard into the emergency entrance to the hospital, skidding to a halt. The back doors swung open. The two doctors hopped out with the cooler and ran through the ER doors.

The ambulance driver followed them, holding the cellphone to his ear. The voice on the phone said, "She's leaving us."

The doctors sprinted down the hallway, slammed open a door and sprinted up the stairs, skipping three steps at a time. On the second floor, a door flew open, ejecting the two doctors. They ran next to each other. One opened the cooler while the other pulled out a syringe.

The driver was still in the stairwell, out of breath. He yelled into the phone, "We're in the building. Keep her going," he panted, leaning over. "Please."

"We're almost there, Sophie!" yelled the two doctors as they sprinted down the hallway past surprised patients and staff.

The doctors grabbed onto the door jamb, skidding into the patient's room. It was filled with family members, all surrounding Sophie Rodriguez, the little girl in the final stages of pancreatic cancer. The attending hospice nurse laid her phone down on the desk; she had been feeding updates to the ambulance driver.

Sophie's family crowded even closer, everybody holding on to her. The cries were inconsolable, waiting for their precious daughter to go to heaven.

Now the family was confused by all the commotion.

The winded doctor holding the syringe searched the crowd. He found an older man in a white lab coat and asked, "Are you Dr. Defranco?"

"Yes, I'm her oncologist," Dr. William Defranco said.

"Here. Inject this right into the primary tumor site."

Dr. Defranco was handed the syringe — he shook his head and said, "I'm afraid you're too late."

"Please just do it now!" yelled the winded doctor. "This syringe contains the Blue Hope serum created on the Moon mission. This is her only chance. For the love of God, use this medicine!"

"Well, let me disinfect the area..."

"No!" yelled the winded doctor. "There's no time! Just inject the medication right now!"

Dr. Defranco opened the girl's gown just enough to see the surgery marks above the pancreas where they'd tried to remove the main tumor. He took the syringe and pushed it deep into the scarred area toward the pancreas and injected the entire thing. The glowing blue liquid disappeared through the needle and into her abdomen. Sophie didn't move thanks to the morphine drip.

"Now what?" Dr. Defranco asked.

"We wait."

The doctors stared at the minute hand on the clock. The family stared at the second hand.

How cruel, thought Sophie's mom. *To give us this shred of hope as the last few moments of life faded away.*

Their daughter laid there being devoured by cancer.

The skin near Sophie's injection site became very red. Dr. Defranco put his hand on it and felt intense heat. A chemical process was happening beneath the skin, one which had never happened on Earth before. Dr. Defranco's brow furled, a combination of confusion and wonderment.

Sophie's whispered breathing became noticeably deeper. She grew agitated and moved her arms. Her pulse and oxygen levels started climbing back to normal. A smile came over Dr. Defranco's face. He was witnessing a miracle that would eventually to put him out of a job and he couldn't have been happier.

Sophie's vital signs climbed toward normal levels on the computer readout. Ten excruciating minutes passed by. Her eyes slowly fluttered open like a butterfly testing its new wings. She was confused by the dozen visitors crowded into her room. She moved her lips, speaking too quietly for anybody to hear. Her parents leaned in close to listen.

"Mama?" the groggy girl asked. "Papa?"

"Si mi hija. We are here," her papa said, his eyes filled with tears. He squeezed her hand.

"Am I okay?" she asked with a raspy whisper.

Papa wiped away his tears with his fist, knocking his glasses off, barely catching them with his other hand. His face quivered back and forth, not knowing whether to smile or cry out.

"The monster...," he trailed off. "It's gone, sweetheart. It's all gone. Now I get to see you grow up."

CHAPTER 92

Zhuvango Falls
Africa

Mist hung over the jungle like a blanket, with air so humid it constantly felt on the verge of raining. Birds perched high up in the trees out of reach of most predators. A cacophony of squawking between them filled the tree canopy with an orchestra of nature's music. It had been this way here for millions of years.

The beautiful chaos stopped. Great swathes of birds leapt from their branches, cawing and chirping noisily as they flew in random directions at first and then ultimately *away* from this spot. Some flew down to the black sand along the river that emanated from the roaring waterfall nearby.

A rumbling noise from high up in the sky pierced through the squawking, coming and going depending on the breeze. It rose to a grinding roar and then faded back. A strong breeze blew through the leafy canopy and the roar never went away after that. A bright spot in the sky competed with the sun disc, except the spot got brighter and brighter. The roar was now deafening to the local fauna, sending a stampede of animals across the jungle floor, away from the river's edge.

As the bright spot got larger and lower, it revealed a cylindrical shape on top of it. Once it reached tree height above the stream, it paused and hovered for a moment. The engine plume from the rocket hit the surface water like a constant explosion, sending spray and steam in every direction.

The craft glided sideways as three landing pads unfolded from the sides. It descended until the round landing feet pushed into the soft black sand. The rocket quieted down and the flame disappeared. The feet continued to sink as the capsule began leaning to one side. It kept leaning more and more, finally falling over with a loud hollow clunk sound.

With the roar gone, the jungle noises resumed their natural volume.

The muffled sound of a metallic latch emanated from a round door on the side of the toppled capsule. The disc-shaped door fell open and bounced a few times against its hinge. Two gloves flew out of the hole and landed in the stream where they bobbed like two tiny rafts. A moment later, a helmet fell out, hit the sand, and rolled into the stream, too.

A middle-aged man crawled out of the hole and fell to the sand, landing on his back. He rolled over onto his belly and grabbed the sand with both hands, squeezing it until it flowed through his fingers. Tears of happiness streamed down his cheeks, like a man who'd just escaped a death sentence.

"Water..." he said with a horribly parched voice. "Waaatttter..."

The man slowly spun on his belly and slid his way toward the stream, making small movements. He looked up and saw a figure walking toward him from behind a waterfall in the distance — it was a man wearing khaki shorts and hiking boots.

At first the khaki-shorts man walked normally, but he began jogging as he got a better view of the strange vehicle on the river shore. His running footsteps kicked up black sand behind him.

The khaki-shorts man didn't know what to make of what he saw — an astronaut who was face-down in the sand, in the middle of nowhere? He arrived at the scene and poked the strange astronaut with a stick.

Nothing.

Oh man, he's dead, the khaki-shorts man thought.

He poked him again.

The strange man rolled onto his back, startling the khaki-shorts man.

"Captain Alston! Is that you?" the khaki-shorts man asked with surprise. "You're supposed to be dead. Like, really dead."

"I guess I'm not so easy to kill," Adam joked. "Now help this old man up."

"Sure thing, sir," the khaki-shorts man said, leaning down to help up the astronaut. "I'm part of the residual support crew left here at the waterfall. I'm a geologist. There's five of us on site."

Adam grabbed the water canteen dangling from the shoulder of the khaki-shorts man. He removed the lid and drank like he hadn't had a drop in days.

"Whoa, okay, sure, drink all you want."

"I'm glad you're still here," Adam said, wiping the water overspill from his face. "And boy did I have a rough ride home."

"I'll bet you did," the man said, noticing the foreign markings on the side of the rocket capsule.

Adam reached back into the rocket opening and pulled out a box-shaped device that had blue corners. He laughed at how light the object was, seemingly weightless, yet so important to humanity. Adam limped over to the geologist and leaned on him for support.

"What is that box for?" the khaki-shorts man asked.

Adam raised one eyebrow.

"That, my friend, is...," he paused for a moment. "Salvation."

The two men hobbled back toward the waterfall — that glorious spot where the early Martians chose to hide their first laboratory. With each step, the water lapped at their heels, washing away their foot prints.

"By chance, do you have your satellite phone with you?" Adam asked.

The khaki-shorts man reached into his pocket and pulled out his laughably large satellite phone.

"May I?" Adam asked, gesturing to borrow it.

"Sure. Just go easy, it's like five dollars a minute."

"I'm sure NASA will pay," Adam said.

While they walked, Adam dialed in a phone number and pushed the Call button. It rang and rang.

"Hello?" asked a sleepy woman at the other end of the call.

"Hey honey, it's me," Adam said with a huge grin.

"Adam? — ADAM! Oh my God, you're alive!" screamed the voice on the other end. Adam had to hold the phone away from his ear. He heard her say, "Kids! Kids! Come here, your Daddy is okay!"

Connie talked a mile a minute.

"Where are you?" she cried. "I have so much to tell you. I got the note. I got the note you gave to Tucker. I asked Chris about it and he told me everything about Wil... Wilma, whatever her name was. All I can say is, Chris has serious problems."

"I'm glad that's cleared up," Adam said with a sigh. "I still have a lot of explaining to do myself. Hey, I've had a long time to think about things and I was wondering if I could invite you to go on a date. Maybe, we can start all over again."

"Uh huh, I think I'd like that," she said. "Maybe we can go to the park. Take the kids for a bike ride?"

Adam laughed.

"Sounds like the best day ever."

ABOUT THE AUTHOR

John Dreese is an author who lives in Texas. He enjoys stories about adventure, technology and people. If you enjoyed this story, please consider leaving a review on Amazon.com.